MW00960338

Chapter One

"Ok, that's definitely enough of this garbage for one sitting," Jethro "JT" Clarke said in a grumbly voice, closing his iPad with a satisfying slap of its magnetic cover. He stared blindly into his half-empty coffee cup, swirling the brew while digesting the updated war coverage of the day. He couldn't help but notice the wrinkles and scars on his sixty-five year old hands as the morning sun's warm glow highlighted each imperfection with uncanny precision as it's sharp beams made their way through the kitchen's east window. "You sure ain't a spring chicken anymore but at least you're too old to be recalled," he muttered to himself with a slight chuckle and a groan as he stood. "But Luke isn't," he thought to himself solemnly, knowing that if this war expands a draft could very well could be initiated.

The rehashed media storylines of the now two week old war with Iran that earlier blared from JT's iPad lacked any new substance, each segment only serving to reinforce the necessary political narrative while simultaneously infecting the minds of millions every second of the day. JT completely understood the value of targeted propaganda, but even to him this is getting out of hand. The media, blatantly in lockstep with the current administration is desperately trying their best by using this conflict to prop up the failing president. To date, the scheme has enormously backfired, his already historically low polling numbers having shrunk steadily since the president ordered the retaliatory attack. Yes, Iran nearly sank a U.S. warship, killing hundreds of its sailors when a rogue Iranian naval commander somehow managed to successfully launch a hypersonic missile. Then, within a day, every Iranian warship that was afloat was sent to the bottom of the ocean. The general public now believes vengeance has been clearly served, and more and more people think he is just looking for his own 9/11 moment.

In an attempt to keep viewership until the lucrative commercial breaks, the networks are employing the use of constantly rolling video clips in the background. A seemingly unending flow of Tomahawk cruise missiles are shown being launched from warships in the Arabian Ocean along with B1 Bone and B2 Spirit bombers dumping load after load of munitions on yet more isolated and unimportant Iranian mountain tops. The tactics are performing flawlessly, keeping viewers glued to their screens while fattening the wallets of the networks and advertisers alike.

Being former Air Force, JT knew just how dangerous things had gotten. A disturbing idea presented itself: if Iran had the significant military capability that the Western media and intelligence agencies painted for the world to see, why hadn't they marshaled a counter-offensive yet? Just the thought of what a desperate Iran could unleash when they emerge from their bunkers caused a cold nervous sweat to form on JT's wrinkled forehead and the hair on his arms to stand up. Something inside of him screamed, "this one isn't going to be fought just "somewhere over there" much longer."

JT is well aware that Iran possesses the ability to conduct military operations globally through the use of proxies and sleeper cells. He also knew of their significant cyber capabilities and the fact that their military had perfected the tactic of using freighter ships as strategic missile launch platforms a decade ago. If his trained mind is anywhere close to being on track, it could only be a matter of days until this escalates. Persia simply won't go down without a fight.

As a news junkie himself, JT has likewise found himself endlessly stuck to the screen since this thing kicked off. Now, because of that he is two weeks behind the eight ball on nearly everything around the ranch.

Draining his third cup of coffee, JT stood, stretching his arms over his head and twisting his body. The audible cracks emanating from his back only reminded him of his impending list of overdue chores. He contemplated which project he should tackle today, hoping that keeping busy would deflect his mind from the current doom and gloom situation. Looking out the kitchen window, JT saw the early morning October sun now illuminating the large pile of cut up oak in the east pasture with a brilliant beam of light that found its way through tree line. He took this as a sign that he should finally split and stack the firewood to bolster his supply for the upcoming winter. JT knew he should have gotten to it sooner because if the winter drags on, this batch won't be totally cured.

"All right dogs, Ive got some aggression to burn off and that wood ain't gonna split itself," JT said to his three canine companions. After tidying up his morning mess, he was soon walking outside with his furry buddies, Pepper, Duke and Harley.

Heading to the shop, the unseasonably mild temperature and the earthy fall scents in the air instantly felt refreshing as he stepped out the south door. The warm sun on JT's head already helped to relieve the tension and uneasiness in his gut as he fired up his old Polaris ATV. As JT waited for the engine to warm, he switched out the pair of leads from the solar charge controller to a different battery pack. He also swapped out the battery pack powering his small inverter, which kept his old but trusty beer fridge running ice-cold.

"Priorities," he said to himself with a smile before setting a two gallon can of gas on the ATV for his homemade wood splitter.

After riding the old Polaris the short distance to the small mountain of oak, JT twisted the gas cap off of the engine on the wood splitter and was met with the putrid smell of turpentine. "Dammit," he muttered to himself, vividly remembering he'd forgotten to treat the fuel last fall. He hadn't even given the machine a second thought since then. Getting back on the ATV, JT cursed himself under his breath, knowing his own negligence is causing even more work to do.

Back at the shop, he began gathering tools and his can of "shit gas" knowing he'd have to drain the tank and clean the carburetor. "Well son of a bitch, that thing has to be around here somewhere, the next time I go to Fleet Farm I swear I'm buying a six pack of ten millimeter sockets," JT mused to himself, searching around his cluttered workbench for the illusive socket. This was becoming a typical start to his days, it may not always be a wayward tool that's been lost, postponing the beginning of the "work" day, sometimes it's just his favorite coffee cup being misplaced, but it's always something it seemed.

"Ah, there you are you little bugger," JT said with satisfaction, seeing the socket magically appearing stuck on the end of a three inch extension. Naturally, it was laying exactly where he left it, on the workbench under the front driveshaft of his old truck. Now he could finally get to work.

Loading his tool bag, along with a fresh can of carburetor cleaner and the can of old gas on the Polaris, JT paused saying, "Oops, almost forgot something." The whitetail rut had just begun in

Wisconsin, and he had taken several deer in the past while working the woodpile. JT needed to bring his crossbow.

JT rode back out to the east pasture, enjoying the annoyance he caused his dogs by crossing over their "invisible" fence boundary. The hounds barked, creating quite a ruckus for a few minutes before eventually giving up and finding shade where they'd contently watch the old man work from the cool, still green green grass.

Examining the carburetor on the engine of the wood splitter, it seemed that there was enough space to remove the bowl, float, and needle valve without physically taking the carburetor off. The process should be straightforward and relatively quick. After using nearly half a can of carburetor cleaner and several rags, JT managed to put the carburetor back together in under an hour.

"Damned ethanol," he muttered, draining the tank as the stinky old gas ran into his can. It's been a habit of JT's to save old gas where it ends up in the can labeled "shit gas". The old fuel while being useless for an engine, still has its purpose. It's ideal for lighting the burn barrel or the fire pit as it doesn't "blow up" when a match is tossed on it.

With the oil level checked and fresh gas in the tank, JT switched the choke lever to the start position. After a few pulls on the rope, the little predator engine roared to life. JT pushed the choke to the run position, and the engine idled smoothly, emitting a comforting thump that brought a broad smile to his face. Once he picked up his tools, double-checking to make sure the mischievous ten millimeter socket was in the bag, JT was finally ready to begin working.

With the machine purring like a kitten, JT was able to work uninterrupted, his mind finally freed from his troubling thoughts of impending doom. As he watched the towering pile of logs gradually shrink and the stack of freshly split wood grow, JT took a swig from his canteen and decided that after a brief lunch break, he would take a look at the old truck and pick up a spare gallon of gear lube in town. Then, he could return to the satisfying work of working his way through the wood pile.

The old truck, a chocolate brown 1972 Chevy K10, has been sitting for a day with the transfer case and differentials draining, its front driveshaft also having been removed to replace a worn universal joint. Having the truck out of service for an extended period of time is unacceptable to JT and thinking of this, he gave himself one more hour of splitting wood before he'd shut the machine down and get the old truck road worthy. The wood pile can wait.

As he struggled to split an especially obstinate section of ancient oak, its knotted wood stubbornly resisting the hydraulic pressure, JT decided to give the log one last forceful shove, opening the throttle as wide as it would go. Finally, with a resounding crack, the oak succumbed to the splitter's relentless power, exploding in a cloud of superfine termite dust that smothered JT's nose and eyes. Taking his glasses off and safely resting them on the seat of the Polaris, JT removed an ever-present blue shop rag from his pocket and began wiping the sweat and dust from his face. Suddenly feeling a sneeze building up, JT squinted and looked towards the bright southern sky when, abruptly and for just a fraction of an instant, the sky blazed with an intense, brilliant light.

"What-da-fuck-was-that," JT exclaimed loudly, slowly drawing out the words. Rubbing his eyes and blinking them ferociously as his vision slightly dimmed, JT was stunned, unaware of what he'd just witnessed.

Looking at the rag in his hand, it didn't appear to be overly dirty other than the grime he'd just wiped from his nose and eyes. Bringing the rag to his nose, he cautiously smelled it, the scent of carburetor cleaner clearly evident. "Man, I gotta be more careful, that crap can kill ya," he said to himself, stuffing the rag back into the pocket of his BDU trousers. Blowing the event off as nothing more than him getting a good dose of carb cleaner up his nose, JT, satisfied for now that he wasn't seeing things put his glasses back on returning to the wood splitter.

After guessing it had to be close to noon JT, who never wore a wristwatch because they always got snagged on something, reached around the hot engine and turned the ignition off, shutting down the wood splitter.

Settling atop the Polaris, JT slid the machine into gear and started slowly moving towards the shop, crossbow safely cradled on his lap. Taking in the panoramic view of the ranch, he couldn't help but marvel at the maple trees as their stunning leaves, painted gorgeous shades of orange, red and yellow, glimmered spectacularly in the fall sun. Meanwhile, the beds of flowers that Kate had meticulously tended to throughout the year were still blooming gloriously, casting vibrant hues amidst the autumn landscape. As he reminisced, he couldn't stop smiling as he recalled moments when his wife had relentlessly brought home more trees and flowers to plant. Today, utterly satisfied with the beauty that their labor had created, JT acknowledged it was all worthwhile.

As JT approached the shop, a strange premonition suddenly fell over him, sending a shiver down his spine as moisture began to build on the backs of his hands. It wasn't that he felt feverish or lightheaded, but more like when one expects a wrench to slip off a bolt an instant before it actually happens but all the body has time for is to brace for the impact of your knuckles painfully crashing into an engine block.

With his heart racing, JT withdrew the crumpled rag from his pocket and turned it over apprehensively, hoping to find a logical explanation for the ominous feeling that was starting to hijack his thoughts. Taking another tentative breath of the cloth and confirming once again the presence of carburetor cleaner, JT tossed it into the trash can. Foolishly hopeful that this action would quell the mounting anxiety, JT's uneasiness refused to subside.

Sitting down on a dilapidated lawn chair that groaned even under his relatively light weight, JT realized he hadn't seen the dogs around since leaving the wood pile. Suddenly, a gut-wrenching feeling seized him. His eyes had missed the absence of the dogs at first, but his brain caught up eventually. He should have realized that Harley, in particular, would have been around. Harley always ran excitedly, chasing after the ATV carrying his favorite stick. JT searched around with his eyes but could not spot him or the other two anywhere.

After installing the invisible fence several years ago he wasn't too worried that they had ran off, well, except Duke. Still being a pup, he'd chance a run through the mild zap the electronic perimeter gave him for the opportunity to chase a rabbit. Whistling, then calling for the dogs, they didn't come to either command and now feeling even more troubled, JT got up to go find them.

JT checked the music stage first, the dogs favorite spot to play hide and seek. He and his son Luke had built the stage years ago, it's twelve foot deep by twenty two food wide deck structure sat a few feet off the ground and is tucked into a small grove of mixed trees. Kneeling down, he peeked under the edges of the stage but the dogs weren't there. He moved on, carefully looking around the barn and outbuildings and still couldn't find them. Just as he was about ready to give up searching around on foot for them, JT's ears perked up hearing a faint whimper from somewhere under the front deck of the house. Looking through the narrow gap between the steps, a wave of relief came over him as JT saw all three of the dogs, huddled together in a ball all the way back in a dark corner.

"Well, what spooked you guys so bad?" JT asked the dogs softly, trying to coax them out with words. For whatever reason the three mutts weren't in the least bit interested in leaving their hide so JT, hoping a few treats will bring them out, headed inside the house for their favorite snacks.

Entering the house, JT was met with a deafening silence. No humming of the refrigerator or freezer motors running could be heard. The old battery operated clock on the kitchen wall read 12:35, while the electronic clock on the kitchen stove was dark, as was the light fixture over the kitchen island and the Wi-Fi extender plugged into one of its outlets. Flipping the light switch in the closet where the treats are kept, it too was dark, not that he needed the light in the first place. "Great, the power is out again. Whatever," JT mumbled to himself in disgust, unscrewing the top off the treat canister.

Finally coaxing the dogs out with the treats, the three animals were not themselves, timidity following JT around with their tails tucked between their legs. Wondering to himself what on earth could have spooked them this bad, he thought maybe it was that pack of coyotes that have been running around lately, laying their scent by peeing all over the place. Possibly they came back while he was splitting wood and didn't hear the tussle over the sound of the machine. However, after thoroughly checking the dogs over, JT didn't notice any blood or any evidence at all of them being in a fight.

As he walked back into the house, JT's attention was drawn to the electric hand-style clock over the piano. To his surprise, it read a couple minutes before eleven o'clock. "Wow, the power's been out for an hour and a half and I didn't even know it," he said, chuckling to himself.

Imagining the phone lines of the co-op were already saturated with calls, JT didn't bother calling in the outage especially being an hour and a half into it. Gathering his wallet and cell phone from the shelf by his chair in the kitchen, he headed outside for the short five mile trip south to the auto parts store in Somerset. "Yet another trip to town, it's a good thing gas is cheap," he mumbled sarcastically, pissed about the outrageous cost of gasoline.

Hopping in the car and checking under his seat making sure his Glock is where he left it, JT hit the starter of the little Chevy Sonic only to be met with silence. No bright red and yellow dash lights flashing, no gauges functioning and no engine running. "What the hell is wrong now?" JT said out loud, unsuccessfully trying the ignition again.

Turning back towards the shop, JT grabbed his electronic multimeter from the shelf and made his way to test the battery of his car that he had installed just two weeks ago. After selecting the DC voltage setting on the meter, JT saw that the display was completely black, much like his car's dashboard. The threatening sensation he had experienced earlier came back, and he could feel his gut twisting in painful knots once again. Slowly, almost tentatively, JT took his iPhone out from his front shirt pocket, gazing at the dead screen as he hit the home button repeatedly in a desperate attempt to awaken it from its slumber.

With what was going on around him beginning to make more sense by the second, like the power being out, the phone dead, the car dead, even the timid behavior of the dogs, his mind instantly went back the wood pile, and the millisecond the sky intensified. "Ho-ly Shit. That wasn't carb cleaner, that was a damned nuke detonating in space, that's what that flash was. The dogs probably heard or sensed the blast and smelled the ionization of the atmosphere, I bet that's why they were scared to death hiding under the deck!" JT exclaimed to himself out loud as the dots finally connected.

As an avid reader, JT had come across several post-apocalyptic novels about EMPs. Their stories about the effects of an electromagnetic pulse were so profound and believable that even though he knew the odds of such an event occurring were slim, he began seriously preparing for it. When he surveyed the damage around him, JT knew instantly that his fears had come true. "All the boxes are checked," he said to himself. "What else could do all this?" His thoughts turned immediately to the Minneapolis/Saint Paul metroplex only fifty miles away with its hundreds of thousands of people living in and around the urban center. "That place is going to be a total nightmare in a couple of days," he said darkly.

Leaving the shop, JT began walking around aimlessly, trying to wrap his head around what just happened, if it even happened. Opening the door to his Jeep and turning its key, just like the little Chevy, it too was dead as a door nail, basically sealing the deal in his mind.

Looking at the old Chevy pickup, JT wondered if it would run as he walked over to it. Besides having a lifelong infatuation with the body style, much of his justification for buying the thing in the first place was for just this type of situation. Opening the door of the truck, JT found himself nervous and apprehensive to give it a try. Reaching in and turning the key, the red generator and oil lamps on the vintage dashboard lit up, then, letting out the breath he didn't know he was holding, he hopped up onto the wide bench seat.

Pumping the gas pedal a few times and pulling the choke lever out and with sweat building in the palms of his hands JT ever so slowly turned the key to "start", the engine while turning over fine, didn't catch, worrying him. Pumping the throttle three more times and again hitting the starter, this time the old 350 rumbled to life with a light wisp of blue smoke leaving the twin tailpipes. Grinning ear-to-ear as the engine settled into its gentle lope at idle from the performance camshaft he'd installed just a few months ago, JT relaxed somewhat listening to the fifty year old engine running.

For now though, this would have to wait. The differentials and transfer case are empty, the oil pans still under the truck collecting whatever is left in them and the front driveshaft is laying on an oil soaked piece of cardboard on his workbench. Having a solid two hours worth of work to do before he could drive it, JT didn't have that much time. He needed to get his wife from work, then snatch up his mother who lived a short distance from where Kates office is.

As he readied himself to collect his wife and mother, JT's thoughts wandered back to the previous weekend's visit from his son Luke and his girlfriend Amy. They had even brought along Pete and Brian, two old friends, for an enjoyable day of shooting and discussing the current state of affairs. After dialing in their equipment, they passed cans of cold beer, and a plan was haphazardly created for those four to bug out to the ranch should the war escalate and anarchy rule the land soon.

Chapter Two

Pete and Brian were exhausted after a productive morning of walleye fishing on the Mississippi-St. Croix rivers convergent rock ledge, each having reached their limits by 9:30. They had decided to take one of the many comp days they had banked for fall fishing, as time off was unavailable to them during their busy season at a local chain restaurant where they both manage. In college, Pete convinced Brian to move in and share a house, and the two have been friends ever since.

One person unfortunately unable to accompany them was Luke, their mutual friend since they opened an upscale brewpub in New Richmond ten years ago. Pete and Brian were the establishment's managers, and Luke was the brewmaster. The place was successful initially, but ultimately succumbed to small-town operating costs after several years. From that shared experience, Luke, Pete and Brian bonded like brothers, supporting each others' personal and professional feats.

This morning's fishing adventure in the cool fall air burned up some calories and Brian was hungry.

"Let's pull into Treasure Island for the breakfast buffet," Brian said.

Pete hesitated. "I'm not a fan of leaving my boat unattended for very long," he said.

But Brian was persuasive. "C'mon, I'll buy," he said with a grin.

Since they were already on the Minnesota side of the river, the short detour to the casino wouldn't take long.

Sitting on the banks of the Mississippi River, Treasure Island Casino boasts a picturesque location just a stone's throw away from the Prairie Island nuclear power plant. As they were driving past the imposing structure of the nuclear plant, Brian couldn't shake the eerie feeling of unease that washed over him. He felt his skin crawl as a sense of fear and dread began to take hold.

"Don't even slow down here Pete, that place looks like death if you ask me," Brian said.

"It is pretty creepy, you sure you don't wanna pop in and take a few selfies in front of the reactor," Pete asked, laughing.

"Screw you Pete, just drive," Brian replied. Brian wasn't sure why, but that place always gave him the creeps.

Pulling into the huge blacktop parking lot of the casino, Pete found a nice spot close to the security gate with only one car nearby. Walking in, it was nearly 10 AM and Brian was wringing his hands in anticipation of the massive spread of food that was sure to be laid out.

"Ok, I've pissed away enough of my hard earned cash," Pete said, getting up from blackjack table in the dark and smoky casino. Brian had already spent his mad money on breakfast and a Bloody Mary for the both of them, then he happily amused himself by watching just how fast Pete could lose a C note.

While walking out of the casino, Pete saw a green Toyota driving away from where his truck was parked. Convinced that his fishing gear had just been stolen from the bed of the truck by some random criminals, he took off running towards the exit, hoping to catch a glimpse of the car's license plate for the inevitable police report he would be making.

"Pete, it's all in here," Brian said, leaning on the fender of the truck catching his breath.

"You've gotta be shitting me, I ran all the way to that gate for nothing," Pete replied, gasping for air.

"Not everyone is a thief Pete," Brian said.

Catching his own breath and letting a sigh of relief, Pete looked at his phone, it was 10:56. "We'll have plenty of time to run up to the hunting land and check the trail cameras, there's a big boy running around chasing does," Pete said excitedly, hoping to make the most of their day off.

"It's early for rut, ain't it?" Brian asked, getting in the passenger side.

"Not when your that big, he'll get all the does to himself," Pete answered. After making sure for himself all the gear was still there, Pete began walking to the rear of the boat, checking the drain plug as a thunderous explosion erupted just beyond the tree line.

"Holy shit!" Pete exclaimed, jumping at the sound and running to the gate for a better look. Brian jumped back out of the truck at the exposition and mouth agape, stared at the small red hot mushroom cloud clearly visible rising over the trees. An instant later, they felt the shock wave, their ears popping when the pressure variation hit them.

"What the hell was that Pete, that came from the nuke plant," Brian said frantically. "Get in the truck, we gotta get out of here."

Hopping into the truck, Pete started the engine and slammed it into gear, sharply flooring the gas pedal as they exited the parking lot and careened down the county road that leads to highway 61. The boat trailer wildly fishtailed behind them as they took the turn onto 61. Suddenly, the truck stalled, lurching to a halt on the road. "What in the holy hell is happening?!" Brian shouted in frustration and panic as Pete frantically tried to restart the vehicle.

"Fuck!" Pete yelled excitedly, slamming his hand on the wheel, "it's like the battery just went dead."

"Aw shit, you hear that, someone's shooting over there now?!" Brian yelled frantically, listening as shots methodically rang out one after another.

"This ain't good buddy, let's get our gear and get out of here." Pete said.

"I sure hope the boys and Amy were in a decent place this morning," JT said to himself, still working on his preparations to get Kate and his mom. He knew Luke was going to be bidding a job forty miles north from where he and Amy live down by Wilson. Amy should have been home working and if he remembers right, Pete and Brian were going to be on the river early down by Red Wing, fishing fall walleyes on the St. Croix. If Pete and Brian did well early enough, they may have made it home before the lights went out.

Standing next to his truck, some very troubling thoughts began infiltrating JT's mind. "How in the hell could Iran be able to launch missiles our way," JT asked himself aloud. "No way," he reasoned, "that just couldn't happen, not from the mainland anyway. They allegedly don't have anything even close to having the range of hitting the United States," he replied to himself just as a vision of freighter boats entered his head.

"Enough of that," he said to himself, going to the shop where his handheld ham radio was stored. JT kept that along with other electronic gear zipped up in anti static bags inside a couple of old microwave ovens.

"Well, at least this thing works," he said after switching it on, tuning it to 52.525 on the 6 meter band. From the ranch, he can easily pick up the repeater station eleven miles away with the fifteen inch antenna. In his brief monitoring of it in the past, he knew they have a battery back up system and he hoped the system wasn't fried

The sound of chatter on the small radio was instant and JT listened intently as the transmissions became increasingly troublesome. The voice on the other end warned that multiple power substations had been destroyed by suicide bombers and gunfire, and reports suggested that two or three electromagnetic pulse (EMP) devices may have been launched and detonated from the Gulf of Mexico.

"That explains that, the Iranians finally came out of their bunkers and flipped the off switch," JT said to himself, his heart skipping a beat hearing the news. Then, JT sitting down on the bench seat of the picnic table began a lively conversation with himself. "How accurate is this information, where did the person on the other end get it from, is it even real, rumors maybe or simply just propaganda." At the moment though, JT had to assume it was accurate, all the markers have been met and he'd read about Iran perfecting missile launches from freighter ships a long time ago. A deathly cold sweat began to bead up on his forehead as the realization set it.

"Well, this is it then," he thought, turning the radio off. "I gotta get Kate from work and pick up mom, then hope that Luke, Amy and the boys are all right and can make it here," he said, speaking his thoughts.

Going to the shop, JT turned the key on the smaller of his two Polaris 4 wheelers, relieved when the cooling fan of the 300 turned on. Pushing the starter button, he held his breath when it turned over and started right up. "Good, this one runs too so I have a spare if the 425 breaks down."

"Man, how I love old machines, they are a pain in the ass at times, but there are zero millivolt computer parts in them," he muttered aloud while checking the fuel level in the machine. Just because, he walked to the Jeep and after opening the hood, disconnected both battery cables. He touched the pair together for a few seconds attempting to drain the engine control system of residual electricity, then reinstalled the cables to the posts. He tried starting the Jeep again but was met with the same result, nothing. JT wasn't too surprised, but it was worth a try.

Before leaving, JT went back to the house and after letting the dogs outside, he went to the file cabinet for the SHTF folder. It's been a while since he's had this out, but he did find it in the the back of the top drawer. The folder contains list of things to do first if or when some disaster ever happened and he knew for sure there are a few items on that list that he should knock out before leaving.

JT was intentionally taking his time, doing his best to not get himself emotionally wound up. He knew he had to remain calm no matter what and knocking out a couple of mindless tasks will help keep him that way. Going to get Kate and his mom wouldn't take long, two or three hours if all went well, so he bypassed the number one item on the list which is to gather up the battery cart and the smaller of the two 12VDC to 120VAC power inverters then plug in the kitchen refrigerator. He wasn't even remotely worried about the upright freezer, it's good for damned near a week if no one is hanging on the open door staring blankly at the contents.

He did however check the generator in the shop, number two on the list to see if it runs and makes power. Giving the starter rope a couple of pulls, the unit fired to life. Plugging a drill motor into one of the 120 volt outlets on the generator, the electric motor ran, confirming that the generator functions. "Good deal, that ground rod must have done the trick," he thought to himself.

Not having a faraday cage for the generator, JT instead drove a copper grounding rod four feet deep into the ground next to the shop. Running a single 8 gauge wire secured to the rod to where the generator was stored on a rubber wheeled cart, he used a large alligator type clip soldered to the wire, grounding the unit by clamping it to the frame.

Although not incredibly powerful, generating 6250 watts and twenty amps from its 10 hp Tecumseh engine, the generator boasts enough amperage to kickstart the well pump and supply JT's main concern - water. The device is robust enough to power his entire home but for the water heater, though he has only relied on it mostly when trees bring down the power lines or blow a fuse link during storms. Its primary mission, however, remains the provision of power to the well pump.

Then going into the bathroom he began item three on the list, capturing whatever water was still under pressure. Putting the plug in the bathtub and turning the faucet on, the tub filled to about a quarter full before the pressure tank ran dry. "No sense in wasting that pressure," he reasoned, knowing it would have bled off before he returned.

Satisfied with his work for the moment, JT decided to head back outside. He climbed onto the 4-wheeler and attached the smaller of his two trailers - a homemade 4'x6' unit meant for hauling miscellaneous items and equipment around the ranch.

In the side of the barn where the horse hay is stored is the removable rear bench seat from the Jeep and a single rear seat from a van Kate used to have. Having been bolted onto this trailer plenty of times in the past when he'd take the grandkids for rides on the logging trails, in no time JT had them secured them to the deck. "This will work," he said to himself out loud, putting a keeper pin in the ball hitch.

With those tasks complete, JT was nearly ready to head out. Mentally, he felt more centered now that he had given himself some time to calm down and reflect before heading out cross country.

Glancing at the battery operated clock on the kitchen wall, the hands read just after two in the afternoon. This meant there are about five hours of daylight left for him to complete his mission. While being inside, he grabbed his AR 15 and two spare magazines. Checking his gear, JT activated the light on the Burris fast fire holographic sight mounted on the rifle. Somehow, much to his delight it magically still functioned. Slinging the rifle over his back and calling the dogs back inside, he closed the door. He then snatched his Glock from under the seat of the little Chevy and hopping on the ATV, he hit the road.

After JT turned out of his long driveway onto the quiet township road he stopped, taking a moment to smooth over the tracks the ATV had left in the soft gravel with his boots. For early October the weather was quite pleasant, for now anyway, and he was grateful for that. If an EMP would have happened a month later, he very likely would be making this journey on snow covered roads, if he could even make the trip at all pulling a trailer. With his mind occupied by all the "what if's" that kept flooding his brain, the miles seemed to pass rather quickly and about the only thing JT did take notice of was the total lack of traffic. He'd passed a few random vehicles stalled out on the road, their former occupants having at least enough common sense to pull them to the skinny shoulders.

Having previously mapped out a route to Kate's work by riding primarily only township roads, JT knew that no matter what he'd have to cross two main state roads, highways 35 and 64. At 35, he'd have to physically cross and 64 would be an overpass. The last three quarters of a mile though would take him on a heavily used two lane bypass road leading into New Richmond.

Soon, JT arrived at the first highway and began crossing it slowly. To the south, he could see for almost two miles, the view to the north was obstructed by a hilltop. But, even this partial view looking south astonished JT when he noticed the large number of stalled vehicles dotting the road. People loitered alongside their cars and from the details that he could just manage to pick out, they appeared to be glued to their smartphone screens. JT wondered how many of these individuals had unraveled what had occurred that morning just three hours ago. Not much he reckoned. All these people just stood around their vehicles being confused and apparently hoping for help to arrive.

As JT approached New Richmond, he knew he had only two more miles to reach the bypass road. Getting closer, the road made a sharp left turn to the east. The fields on either side were planted with tall corn ready for harvest that obstructed his view of what lay beyond the turn. As he turned the corner, however, JT was suddenly confronted by a dozen or so men. They blocked the road, forcing JT to come to an abrupt halt. These men, all of them dressed in bright orange prison jumpsuits, fanned out before him.

"Boy, did I screw this up," JT said frantically, realizing he'd totally spaced out the pre-release/rehabilitation facility that was just up ahead. In an instant, the group began moving on JT, and without even thinking he hit the gas, aiming for the ditch and it's tall grass on his left side, trying to go around them.

Suddenly the man closest to JT jumped in front of him, a stick the size of a baseball bat cocked towards his head. Involuntarily ducking, JT kept the throttle open as the sickening sound of breaking bones and the accompanying wail of pain rose above the roar of the engine as the brush guard of the Polaris caught the man just above the knees.

At the sight of the man falling three others tried jumping into the moving trailer, two of them missed, crashing to the ground. The third man was partially successful, landing halfway inside with his legs dangling off the right edge as he struggled to climb in. Looking back and seeing the man desperately clinging to the van seat, JT took the ATV deeper into the ditch, trying to shake the man's grip.

Racing up the opposite bank of the wide ditch, JT then turned back towards the road, gaining speed as he did so. Keeping the throttle wide open, the tires of the ATV spun rocks and dirt into the air as they searched for traction. JT quickly reached the shoulder of the road, causing the ATV and trailer to lift off the ground as they launched onto the blacktop surface forcing the trailer to bounce wildly upon landing. Quickly looking back, JT watched his would-be passenger crash headlong onto the pavement before tumbling down the road in a tangled jumble of arms and legs.

Keeping his speed up for a couple hundred yards and putting distance between him and the group, JT finally slowed, gathering his wits through the rush of adrenaline. But now, the pre release facility that held around a hundred detainees was just ahead of him about a quarter mile.

"I'm screwed, there's no choice but to pass the jail to get to where I'm going," he said to himself, his hands shaking. Taking in the scene, JT noticed the fields on either side are all fenced with four strands of barbed wire, meaning there's no leaving the road. The group behind him didn't have any guns that he knew of, thinking for sure they'd have used them if they did. Using that logic, JT figured if they didn't have any most likely no one else would either. Unslinging his AR, JT held it in his left hand taking off steadily down the road, not too fast, not too slow.

Finally reaching the facility several more prisoners were outside, standing around the grounds to his left. However passing them with the rifle clearly visible pointing their way, none were making any moves his direction.

With his adrenaline still pumping, JT felt relieved that he hadn't suffered a heart attack and started to reflect on what had just happened. "At least you didn't have to shoot anyone," he told himself. The thought rattled him, not so much because of the situation he had just faced, but because of how quickly things fell apart at the pre-release facility. "If this is just the beginning, we're in for a world of shit," he mused to himself.

Surveying the road ahead, in a half mile JT will have to turn left heading east onto the bypass highway for the last leg after crossing the overpass of the four lane highway.

After making a turn south on County Road K, JT was soon riding on the overpass. Looking east and west as he went over the highway, the four lanes were littered with stalled cars in both directions with plenty of people visible and more than a couple of orange jumpsuits mixed in.

Getting to the intersection of K and the bypass, the bypass normally a busy stretch of highway leading into the west side of New Richmond was apparently packed with traffic around eleven this morning. Seeing at least a dozen stalled cars along the half mile section, many with people standing or walking around them, JT began weighing his options.

"To hell with it, at least they aren't in oranges jumpsuits," JT said aloud, making the turn onto the bypass. Rolling by the people, JT smiled, waving at them as he kept moving through the stalled cars and people. Striking him as being odd, only a couple people attempted to wave him down while most of them were looking at phones in their hands. "Why are these people still here, don't they know what just happened?" he asked himself. "Short answer, no. They obviously don't have a clue," he said, answering himself.

Shortly after crossing the bridge over the Willow River, JT turned right onto county road A. Noticing only a few cars stalled, JT easily maneuvered around them while seeing Kate's workplace to the left, off of West 8th street.

Arriving at her complex, JT rode around the east side of the building, taking cover between a dense row of lilac trees and the building. After shutting the machine down and pocketing the key, the steady hum of the generators coming from the hospital next door was a welcome sound. "That's good, at least for now," he said, knowing the building codes for hospitals are very strict and those jenny's must have been hardened at some point. Sadly, also knowing that when the fuel tanks run dry it's game over for whoever is still left inside.

Not wanting to leave his rifle unattended, JT kept it slung it over his shoulder, walking the short distance along the lilacs to Kate's office window. Knocking on the glass and getting her attention, within a few minutes she was outside and asking questions a mile a minute.

JT told her what he thought, what has already happened on his way here and what was next for them.

Riding to the parking lot where her car was parked they unlocked the doors with the key and tried to start it. The Malibu is unsurprisingly in the same shape as his car and the Jeep, dead. Quickly opening the hood of the car, JT disconnected the battery putting it in the trailer, knowing that decent batteries would soon become a valuable commodity.

Going to the the trunk, they retrieved Kate's Walther P22 which Kate put in her purse then grabbed her small go bag. After getting what they needed from her car and locking it up, they were off to his moms place with Kate riding on the ATV behind JT.

Riding rather slowly east along 8th street, it proved to be an uneventfully short ride to his moms. They did manage some sideways looks from a few people milling about in their yards, bring a smile to JT's face. Four blocks east on 8th street, three blocks north on Dakota Ave, a half a block east on 5th street and they were there.

While they rode along, JT recalled taking his mom for a pacemaker battery swap a couple of years ago. He had asked the doctor if the device was hardened enough to withstand occurrences like solar flares or any kind of external interference. The pacemaker doctor had confirmed it was hardened and they had a pleasant albeit brief conversation regarding EMPs. The doctor had read the book One Second After several years earlier and knew exactly what JT was referring to. At the time, that conversation left JT feeling more comfortable with his mom's chances in case such an event occurred. As they arrived at his mom's driveway, JT felt even more relieved.

"Momma" was sitting in her chair, looking through a large-print reader's digest as Kate and JT walked in. Skipping the customary pleasantries, she shot out "my damned chair is broken and I can't get out of it." She had purchased the electric-powered unit years before due to hip problems, but now she was literally stuck there. Kate and JT helped her out and they tried explaining to her what they thought was going on.

"Mom, we're gonna have to go for a ride out to the house. The power is out and it won't be coming back on anytime soon," explained JT, helping his elderly mother pack her things. To JT's surprise, his Mom didn't even notice that the power was out. She was old school and rarely turned any lights on until it got dark. After gathering some of her clothing and all of her medications into bags, they settled her in the trailer for the trip back home.

Because there's no way in hell they are going to travel past that corrections facility again meant they will need to come up with a new route. The only option JT could think of is heading southwest out of town on county road A for a couple miles to a township road, 95th street, that turns north crossing the Willow River, then to where it ends at the four lane highway. This route will add a few miles, but there was nothing else he could do. JT was hoping to avoid having to cross that busy highway, but now he would be left with no choice and all he could hope for is that it would be better than his ride in earlier.

Riding along this stretch was very quiet, peaceful actually. The small country road wound its way along the slow moving Willow River, the oak and maple trees lining the sides completely covering the road with a canopy of brilliant fall colors. Passing a few of the meticulously maintained century farms the area is famous for, JT noticed people here and there milling around, making him wonder how those dairy farmers were going to milk their cows this evening.

As his mind wandered off JT soon found himself on the sharp S curves, signaling that they are coming dangerously close now the busy four lane highway. Remembering the last time JT took a blind corner, he slowed slightly, moving the rifle from his back, slinging it over his head in front of him with muzzle pointing down, the side of the fore grip against the left side of the gas tank.

Rounding the last curve and slowing for the intersection, JT stopped short after seeing several cars stalled in the intersection partially blocking his pathway with four men standing in front of them. The four grubby-looking men wearing high-visibility shirts, like those worn by construction workers immediately took notice of JT and his ATV, shuffling their feet on the concrete roadway as they moved as one towards him. JT had expected to see people, but he was not prepared for this rough-looking group approaching him.

Clearly visible on the lead man was a rifle of some type, but from this distance, JT couldn't identify it. Slowly reaching for the Glock tucked in his waistband, JT set the .45 on the seat between his legs while slowly inching the ATV forward. JT had taken notice of the gap in the cars that looked wide enough to pull the trailer through.

"Honey I'm scared, what do you think they want?" Kate asked from the front seat, where she faced backward.

"We're about to find out, give mom your pistol," JT said quietly.

"How much you want for that wheeler?" the man with the rifle asked, it's barrel now half way pointed at JT.

"Sorry there mister, but it ain't for sale," JT said as calmly as he could, noticing the other three man fan out on either side of the leader.

"Look here, everything's for sale, everyone's got a price. Now, you can decide what that is or I'll decide for ya," the man said, clearly agitated by JT's comment.

"Hey fellas, calm down, I'm certain there will be help coming soon, I mean hell, it's been what, five or six hours already so for sure someone is getting something moving to help all these folk out here," JT said, slowly reaching the grip on his Glock.

"Bullshit. There ain't been shit moving nowhere and there ain't gonna be. I'm done fucking around here, now get off that machine or I swear I'll blow you off it," the man said, the crazy in his voice clearly evident.

"This is surreal, what is wrong with people," JT thought anxiously, his silence now severely aggravating the man with the rifle.

Raising the butt of the weapon to his shoulder while taking a few steps closer, the man began yelling completely unintelligibly. Spit flew from his mouth with each syllable as he brought the rifle to bear, flinching as he pulled the trigger. JT had to act and right now, he had already lost the race of the draw. With a two handed grip on his pistol JT quickly raised it, firing as soon as the barrel cleared the handle bars. His shot struck the man next to leader in the foot, sending him to the ground with a shriek of pain as a loud crack came from behind JT.

Now having the lead man in his sights, JT's trigger finger began to build pressure as he saw the barrel of the rifle slowly lower. The man holding the rifle seemed stunned, standing there like he was dumbfounded or had suddenly forgotten what he was doing. The man turned his head, looking at the man wailing on the ground next to him with half of his foot missing.

Taking a step towards the stricken man, the leaders left hand went to his chest. As he stared at his blood soaked palm in disbelief, he buckled at the waist, coughing out a mouthful of blood. Then, with a loud clang, the rifle fell from his grip as his knees hit the cement pavement. One of the other two men snapped out of his shock from the sudden violence and lunged for the rifle, but JT already had his pistol to bear on him. Again feeling the pressure on his trigger finger build, the .45 caliber handgun in JT's hands barked, rocking his wrists back with the recoil.

This was like a movie playing in slow motion, momentarily stopping frame by frame. JT clearly seeing the man's chest expand when the 230 grain hollow point hit him. Then the ringing of the spent shell bouncing off the concrete that seemed to vibrate JT's ear drums. The man being thrust backwards as his arms flew forward to his chest with the impact and the thump his head made after crashing to the ground. All of it, so surreal that it just couldn't be happening.

Being brought back into the moment by the wailing of the footless man, JT got off the machine and slowly began walking to the man who had the rifle. Laying on the ground, the man was trying to say something to the last man still standing over the mournful screaming coming from along side of him. The man he was trying to talk to seemed paralyzed, staring at JT with his hands halfway up expecting to see the the muzzle flash from the .45 aiming at him.

Shaking his head JT began to speak. "This didn't have to happen, you could have just moved out of the way and let us pass, now look at you," JT yelled, startling the standing man who was now shaking. Keeping the pistol trained on the lone man, JT bent over and quickly picked up the weapon, a Remington 870 shotgun.

Standing over the man who originally had the shotgun, JT could see he was barely breathing. Noticing the blotch of blood on the man's vest bubbling with each breath and the frothy pink mess that was leaking out of his mouth meant that his moms shot must caught him in a lung.

Moving the pistol to his left hand, JT raised his rifle with his right, flipping the safety off as he aimed it at the still standing and shaking man.

Turning his attention back to the lung shot man, he yelled to him. "What is wrong with you, why do you think you can just take whatever you want from people." Getting more pissed off by the second JT lowered the pistol until it's muzzle was right in front of the man's left eyeball, again feeling his finger slowly building pressure on the trigger. "Why," he yelled again while keeping his own eye and rifle on the man standing. Opening his bloody mouth to speak, the man on the ground either passed out or died before JT finished squeezing the trigger.

Turning his attention to the last man standing, JT spoke. "Tell you what. I'm going to ride across this intersection and stop. Then I'll count to ten. You grab your footless buddy there and if you are still in range of that shotgun when I finish counting, I'm going shoot you both with it. What happens after that is up to you."

Walking backwards to the Polaris with his rifle still on the man, JT mounted the machine, made his rifle safe then laid the shotgun across his lap. Kate and his mom were still sitting, his mom holding the small Walther in her old hands, looking at it.

"Up up and away," she said.

"What's that ma?" JT asked.

"Up up and away," she repeated. "That's what Kate told me to do with the safety switch, push it up, up and away." Poor Kate, she was shivering so badly she was nearly a blur, covering her ears as tightly as she could with her gloved hands.

Checking often over his shoulder while crossing the wide four lane highway, JT wasn't too surprised seeing the lone man trotting away to the west leaving his injured friend. Stopping on the other side, JT didn't bother to count as he raised the shotgun. Anticipating the recoil, JT flinched when the rifle didn't fire. Turning the weapon over in his hands, he saw the trigger bar safety was still engaged.

"Holy shit," he said, drawing out the words. "The only reason I'm still alive is because that guy was probably too jacked up on meth to remember the safety."

Laying the shotgun in the trailer, and giving his mom a quick, sheepish smile, they left. Within thirty uneventful minutes they were approaching home. Noticing no fresh tracks in the gravel, JT slowly began moving down the driveway of the ranch. Thankfully with no more issues, but with no sign of Luke, Amy or the boys.

Chapter Three

Running late getting rolling this morning, Luke found himself having to load tools and supplies into his old truck, a twin to his dads, from the big Chevy Duramax diesel that is sitting with a pair of dead batteries.

"I could have got those in Saturday if the old man wasn't so paranoid," he said, smiling to himself.

"If you'd have bid this last week you could be fishing with Pete and Brian this morning," the voice in his head replied.

"Yeah yeah yeah, I know," he replied to the voice. The potential job is forty miles north of their place, in between Lake Wapogasset and Highway 8. After transferring his tools, the ride ended up taking him an hour and fifteen minutes using the side roads he preferred to drive.

"This is going to be a good job," Luke said to himself, finishing the last of his calculations. The six hours he spent measuring out this job will be well worth it, if he gets the bid that is. The potential customer is converting a pole barn into rental house, an expansive project. The framing is done, and once the electrical and plumbing is completed this could be an exceptional job, hanging, taping and painting the 4000 square feet of sheet rock in the middle of the woods.

Checking his phone for the time, the device was dead. The cigarette lighter in the old Chevy doesn't work, so he couldn't plug the phone in to charge it's already low battery on the drive up. "It's gotta be damn near five," Luke said, firing the truck up as he looked around for the sun through the thick trees. The beauty of the woods, the time of the year and this location made him decide right then to not pad his bid.

Taking in the sights of this gorgeous fall day, he again stayed on the backroads, not wanting to take the busy highway 63 home where he'd have to push the old truck just to keep up with all the traffic headed back south from the north woods.

After making a sharp curve on on a gravel road, Luke found himself having to swerve hard, the old truck fishtailing and throwing gravel as he cranked the wheel, barely missing a Ford Focus parked right in the road.

"Hey asshole, park off the road to get to your hunting spot," he yelled out his open window, wondering how anyone could be so stupid. This route was taking Luke through the heart of some blue ribbon whitetail hunting lands and he needed to remind himself to keep an eye on the road from time to time instead of gawking out the side windows looking for deer.

Driving through the small village of Star Prairie, Luke noticed people waving excitedly to him from the sidewalks, but there were no moving cars on the streets. "It's pretty dead even for Monday," he noted as he pulled into a rural gas station on Highway 65, just south of the village. As he approached the gas islands, he noticed that the business' marquee sign was dark, with no lights on inside. Starting his journey only an hour before, Luke suddenly realized he hadn't seen any moving cars. Parking next to a pump, he looked around and saw a few guys sitting around a pair of pickup trucks off the east side of the building, eyeing his approach with suspicion. When he entered the dark gas station, he found the cashier holding his hands up and apologizing, "Sorry man, no gas. The power has been out since early this morning. Cash only for stuff inside."

Warily, Luke asked, "No shit?"

"No shit, and your truck is the first vehicle I've seen moving since eleven," the cashier replied.

Looking back outside, the group gathered around the trucks were moving towards Luke's truck. Taking off at a quick walk, Luke was intercepted by the lead guy of the group.

"Where ya headed," the man asked almost cheerfully.

"Home," Luke said flatly.

"What direction is home? Me and my buddies need a ride, we was up north hunting and both our trucks are dead there in the parking lot," the man said, pointing to a pair of Ram pickup's loaded with gear.

"Sorry pal, I got a full load the way it is, I'm not anyones taxi," Luke said calmly, walking to his truck.

"Hey, don't be an asshole, all we want is a ride," the man yelled, the agitation clearly building in his voice.

"It is what it is," Luke said, checking the Glock in his waistband.

"No it ain't," another of the group yelled pulling a pistol, shooting towards Luke and missing wildly. Ducking behind the car opposite of his truck for cover, Luke pulled his Glock from his waistband firing two quick rounds at the man, at least one hitting him as he fell screaming in pain from the nine millimeter round.

"What the hell," Luke yelled, now running towards his truck. Another of the group had ran back and pulled a long gun from one of their pickups, leveling the gun as Luke slammed on the gas pulling away, all the while sending rounds towards the group. With a thunderous boom the shotgun went off and Luke heard the loud "slap" of the twelve gauge slug hitting his door frame as his left leg began to burn. The sound of pistol rounds popping caused his truck to instantly begin pulling hard left, one of those rounds hitting his left front tire.

Keeping the gas to the floor, Luke kept firing his pistol left handed out his window until the slide was locked back, the magazine empty of its seventeen rounds. Tossing the empty handgun on to his seat, Luke reached down, checking his left calf. Seeing his hand covered in blood, he knew he had to get off the road and do something about his leg.

Swerving around the few cars on highway 65, Luke began connecting the dots. No power at the gas station, the morons wanting his truck bad enough to shoot him for it, cars parked all along the highway. "Shit, this is it. The old man was right," he said, pulling slightly off the side of the road after turning on to 210th avenue.

"You fucking deserved to get shot dipshit," the man holding the shotgun said, holding his own bleeding arm. "What in the fuck were you even thinking, taking a shot with a fucking derringer, you couldn't hit the broadside of a barn standing inside it," he said, pissed off.

"We could have tackled that guy and just took his truck, but no, you had to fuck that up," another man said to the dying man on the ground, the twenty five caliber double barreled derringer still in his hand.

"I, I, I'm sorry guys," the gut shot man said, the blood pouring out of the hole the 9 millimeter hollow point made in his belly. "I just wanted to get ho…" not finishing his words before dying.

"Now what," one of the men asked.

"Now what - what, what do you fucking think, we start walking," the man with the shotgun said in reply, looking at the trough left from a bullet in his forearm.

"What about Bill, we can't just fucking leave him here to rot," the man answered.

"Carry him then, I don't give a fuck, I'm outta here," the man with the shotgun said.

From under his seat, Luke pulled out an old wife beater T shirt, gently wrapping it over the shop rag he'd covered the wound with, holding it in place around the piece of steel in his calf. Then reaching into his go bag for a fresh magazine, he reloaded the Glock, laying it on the seat next to him. The sun was now just below the tree line as he made the decision to head to the much closer ranch instead of going home to Amy, saying to himself "She'll be fine, she's got Clover."

The sound of the tire shredding off the aluminum wheel made Luke wince, as he was praying the wheel wouldn't wear down before he made it to the ranch. Taking the radio from his bag and removing it from its anti static bag, Luke keyed the mic after setting it to MURS frequency they use when they go four wheeling, hoping the old man would have his radio on too, calling out "old man," repeating the call every half mile.

Kate brushed past JT to the door with tears running down her face not saying a word as she went inside the house. Silently, together, they quickly got JT's mom settled in the small downstairs bedroom.

"You ok there honey?" JT asked.

Not answering, Kate looked at him with blank, blue eyes wet with tears. Not knowing what to say, JT just gave her a hug that she didn't return, but didn't refuse as she headed to the bedroom.

Being fairly certain that she was in a mild state of shock from what just happened, he decided for his own good and her's to give her what ever space she needs. They have had several conversations about this kind of thing happening, but they always ended up being fairly short chats. Kate has a very kind heart, and she pretty much checks out when he'd get into his version of what societal breakdown would look like and its timeline. From the looks of today's events, JT figured he was pretty close in his predictions.

Heading outside, it was nearly dark JT as went to the shop to get his slick-line antenna for the handheld radio. After a couple tries of throwing the pull rope for the long antenna, he finally got it draped high enough over a limb of the tall maple tree by the smoker. JT powered up the radio after swapping antenna leads, listening in for a while hoping he could catch some intel before tackling a couple tasks that needs done. Turning the volume up, the chatter on the little radio was instant.

A person about 50 miles away in Minneapolis was going on about the looting taking place. Apparently he had a bird's eye view of what was happening as he was giving a play by play report of the action.

"There's another shot, and another," he said, then "they're just throwing shit through windows and walking out with armloads of stuff."

Listening a little longer, another voice broke in saying that people are burning cars in the parking ramp at the Mall of America, with one hell of a fire burning now. He also said there are quite a lot of other smaller fires he could see and plenty of what he assumed was gunfire.

JT is not a HAM guy, about all he can do is turn the thing on. He and his son Luke had each bought themselves a Baofeng UV5R a few years back, using them primarily in the MURS mode when they would go four wheeling up north. Luke grew up with technology, so programming the radios identically and adding the relevant frequencies came easy for him. He had explained how to scroll through and select the different frequencies, and man, was that helpful right about now. JT, hearing enough to confirm his fears, swapped antennas again, tuned the radio back to the frequency used for four wheeling then clipped it to his pocket.

Going back in the house, JT saw his mom in the kitchen feeling around inside a drawer.

"Whatcha up to ma?" he asked.

"Looking for matches, I want to light the oil lamp in the dining room," she replied. Finding a book, they got the lamp lit, carrying it to the island in the kitchen. He told her what I'd heard on the radio and she just shook her head.

The conversation got around to Kate, who was in their room curled up with Harley, her pup and she just said "that's a hell of a thing to see."

"Yeah," JT replied. "I think she's in shock after I shot that guy."

Looking at JT, she said, "it wasn't just you who shot him," as she reached into the pocket of her apron and pulled out the Walther, laying the .22 on the island.

"Thanks mom, that dude was about ready to shoot me," he said.

"I know he was, I guess all those years shooting penny's out of trees with my brothers paid off," she said, frowning as she did. "Do you still have that old revolver I gave you years ago?" she asked.

"I do, do you want me to get it for you," he replied.

"Yep, this one feels like plastic, I don't like it," she said.

JT's mom was surprisingly "with it" today. Her asking about the old .38 was very much out of her current character, making JT both happy and confused. Her dementia has been rapidly advancing to a point where one of her kids physically checked up on her every day. It didn't matter really what caused todays spark in her brain though, JT would take this any day.

Still having work to be done before it became completely dark, JT headed outside, again. In the barn JT kept old clothing bins on a shelf, using them for watering the horse whenever the paddock was shut down to regrow grass where the permanent Richey waterer is.

Grabbing a couple bins and sliding them under the fence by the barn, he then retrieved a 50 foot garden hose from the other shed, connecting it to the 275 gallon cube used to collect rainwater off the barn roof. After attaching the hose and turning the valve on, both bins quickly filled with water. Next, he filled a pair of five gallon buckets to use for toilet flushing, and a smaller pail to water the chickens with.

The barn is not huge, but the roof section on the south side is 40 feet by 40 feet, all tin. He had ran a gutter the full length of the barn, putting a down spout above the cube. During a good storm, the roof can fill the cube in half an hour.

When setting the whole thing up, JT had made a rude filter out of nylon window screen, keeping leave's and box elder seeds out, also covering its sides and top with black burlap, stopping algae from growing inside. Finishing those tasks, he walked toward the shop to put one of the battery packs on the cart for the inverter.

The sky was nearly pitch-black by now, with no clouds and no moon. Gazing up at the stars overhead, JT marveled at their clarity and wonder. Even though he was fifty miles away from the Minneapolis/St. Paul metro, which was typically plagued by light pollution, tonight was different. Above the twin cities, the southwestern sky was completely dark, unlike the bright, illuminated sky he was used to seeing.

Standing there still staring into the inky black night sky, JT thought he'd heard static on the radio. Pulling the radio from his pocket the screen was lit up, the MURS frequency they use was displayed as active. JT's heart began pounding so loudly that he could hear the blood rushing through his ears. Standing there staring at the screen, the little radio crackled again, this time JT faintly hearing the words "old man?"

That was the call sign the boys pinned on him a few years ago, so he knew it was one of them, most likely Luke. Keying the microphone, he said the call sign "Luke?" with a question mark in his voice.

"Five minutes out," came the faint reply, as a huge wave of relief came over JT, one kid down, and three to go.

"That sounds like a damned bulldozer," JT said to himself after hearing one hell of a racket coming from the township road. With the sound diminishing, JT could tell it had turned down his long driveway, seeming to quiet down a bit. Being too dark to see clearly, the headlights sure looked like Luke's truck and sure enough, coming closer he could see the 1972 Chevy 4x4, a twin to his own and it's leaning hard to the drivers side.

Pulling the truck around the corner of the yard by the plum tree, Luke stopped, throwing the shifter into park as he shut the engine down. Walking to meet him, JT surveyed the damage to the truck as best he could in the dark. The left front tire was nearly gone, the only part of the tire left on the rim was one bead but other than what looked like a hole in his drivers door frame, it looked ok.

"What the fuck Luke, what happened here?" JT yelled surveying the damage.

"Give me a hand here will ya, I got hit with something, it's stuck in my leg," Luke said wearily. Opening his door and looking in, there was blood all over the floor of the cab near the door.

"Holy shit!" JT shouted excitedly, seeing Luke's leg.

Luke had shop rags wrapped around his left calf, the blood leaking out of it in steady drips. Luke slowly slid out, maneuvering himself to get his right leg on the ground first, then gingerly tried to put weight on his left, buckling in pain with his foot touching the ground.

Wrapping his left arm over his dads shoulder, he limped to the house and once inside, he took a seat in the rocking chair in front of the wood stove. Lifting his bad leg on to the small coffee table, he leaned back while JT got a couple clean towels for the table.

Unwrapping the rag that was around his calf, JT was met with a piece of steel stuck right in the middle of Luke's calf muscle. Protruding out about an inch or so, the piece of steel looked to be at least two inches wide at the skin and around an eighth of an inch thick. He had no idea how deep it was stuck in there.

Coming out of her room during the ruckus that roused her, JT's mom helped Luke get comfortable. After he was settled in, she then went to the island lighting two more oil lamps while JT went to the "secret room" as Kate calls it, getting the med kit. Taking the large red bin back to the kitchen, JT extracted a bottle of saline solution, filling a plastic irrigation syringe. Luke's gramma brought over a large aluminum cake pan, placing it under his calf to catch as much of the blood and saline as they could. Using the syringe, JT rinsed the area around the piece of steel before clamping two hemostats on it. That last maneuver causing Luke to wince, but he sat there.

"You want beer before this next part?" JT asked. "Yeah sure," Luke replied. Feigning getting up, JT reached down, quickly grabbing the instruments and yanking the shard of steel from his leg in one swift move.

"What the fuck, dad!" Luke yelled, letting our a yelp, the comment and its volume causing his gramma to jump back.

After JT extracted the triangular piece of steel from Luke's calf, the wound started to bleed profusely. JT advised Luke that he wanted to let the wound flow for a few seconds to flush out any debris inside, adding, "it's supposed to hurt less if it's a surprise."

Luke retorted with a hint of sarcasm, "I wouldn't want to know what not a surprise feels like." Noticing the steady flow of blood, JT was relieved that it wasn't an arterial bleed, but probably just a severed vein or two.

Using the same syringe, JT thoroughly irrigated the cut and then applied pressure with a large gauze pad, but realized that this alone wouldn't stop the bleeding.

"Pressure alone isn't going to work, Luke," JT said, as he retrieved a packet of butterfly sutures. He started with two medium-sized strips but had to replace them with fresh ones as they came loose from blood soaking under them. Eventually, he managed to close the wound and inspected his work. Satisfied with the makeshift stitches, JT simply said "looks good, Luke."

Luke looked at his dad and said "thanks old man, how about that beer now?"

With a beer in hand, Luke recounted about how he'd gotten in a tussle at a small country gas station with a group of people who wanted his truck. Luke had stopped for some gas and water when he noticed the place was dark inside.

The handful of people that were milling around outside the place were starting to move to his truck while he was going to go inside the station, he was curious as to why the place was dark. But seeing the group moving, he went back outside as quickly as he entered the place. Luke said that a couple of them had pistols of some kind, and one guy had a shotgun, a big long duck gun it looked like.

They asked where he was headed, saying they were looking for a ride, and when Luke said he's not a taxi, they got pissed. One of the guys with a pistol took a shot at him, but missed wildly. Luke pulled his 9 millimeter Glock from his waistband, putting a round into the guy, causing the other ones in the group to run for cover. Luke kept putting rounds back towards the hiding men, keeping them pinned as he ran the thirty feet to his truck.

Starting the old truck, he slammed it in gear and hit the gas as he emptied the Glock out the window at the group. He said he felt his leg get hit when the big assed shotgun went off, and then felt the truck start to pull hard left. He never let off the gas until he was a good mile away. Luke stopped long enough to wrap his leg with an old shop rag and a shirt he had, changed the mag in the Glock and being much closer to the ranch than their home, he headed that way.

"I'm glad you had your kit and radio with you, that could have turned out bad," JT said.

"Me too, those idiots had no plans on taking no for an answer," Luke said.

"I hear ya there, we ran into the same kind of shit earlier," JT said, recalling the ride home from getting Kate and Luke's gramma. "Those rednecks we're about to shoot me off the Polaris," JT said.

"At least you had your rifle," Luke said.

"Yeah, it didn't do me much good though, I shot two of them with my pistol, shit man, you would not believe the mess those .45 hollow points make," JT said.

"Damn, I bet," Luke said, shaking his head.

"I hit the first guy in the foot. The thing blew half his shoe and foot off," JT recounted.

After cleaning up the bloody mess in the kitchen, they talked some more, comparing thoughts about the type of people they had both encountered and how those folks had acted just a few hours after the lights went out.

Kate soon emerged from the bedroom, Harley following close behind. First taking a good sniff of Luke's leg, Harley gave his hand a lick, bumping it with his head in hopes of getting some petting. Kate seemed better, at least saying hello to Luke. Upon noticing his leg, she asked what happened. Luke gave her the abbreviated version, which managed to delight JT.

JT had to ask Luke the obvious question, "do you know where Amy is?"

"This apparently happened around eleven this morning, so she was at home I hope, given that she typically has video conferencing with clients from nine to noon," Luke said.

"Where were you at when it went down," JT asked.

"I was up almost to 8 , north of Wapo bidding a job, but honestly I didn't even know the power was out until I got to the gas station," Luke answered. He'd literally been in the dark all day.

"I'm wiped out pops, mind if I grab a beer and crash on the couch?" Luke asked.

"Not a problem, I'll get you a couple, then I've got a few things to get done. After that, I'm gonna go for a walk," JT said.

"A walk? Where too?" Luke asked suspiciously.

"Donno really. If this is from an EMP, then by Wednesday or Thursday people are gonna be bailing out of the twin cities looking for water and food," JT said, continuing with "I may walk down towards the high bridge, try to put my mind in those peoples heads."

Needing to cool the refrigerator first, JT headed to the shop, getting the cart with a pair of 12 volt batteries wired in parallel. Then, opening the microwave slash faraday cage, he took out the small 1500 watt inverter and bringing them in the house he plugged the fridge into it. These batteries will only last a few hours so tomorrow he will have swap them out for a fresh pair while these recharge from the solar panels. Maybe. He had no idea if that system even works now, and wouldn't know until the sun hits it. At least the fridge will stay cool for a while, there's a boatload of food in there he didn't want to waste.

Yawning, JT thought about the day, how long it's been, and how much longer it still will be. JT's Mom was tired, now in bed and Kate is still in shock, back in bed with Harley. Luke had leaked out quite a bit of blood and was now fast asleep on the couch, a light camouflage blanket covering him and Duke at his feet, while on the other hand, JT was wound tighter than a snare drum. With everyone settled in, JT rounded up Pepper, putting a leash on her for a walk about. Tonight he wanted her nose and her ears. Slinging his rifle, they headed out into the darkness.

Tomorrow, they'd get Amy if Luke was up to it. Then, if Pete and Brian weren't here by nightfall, they would go to check the route they should be on from Hudson.

Chapter Four

Stunned, Pete and Brian stood by the stalled truck. Both of them were well aware of the nuclear power plant just down the road from where they stood. While they didn't have a clue what just happened, they knew that nothing good comes from an explosion at a working nuclear power plant. The both of them being avid hunters were also well aware of what gunshots sound like and they had just heard too many of them off to their southeast.

Just because, Pete reached into his truck, trying the ignition again - nothing. The brand new Chevy Silverado 4x4 didn't even make a sound. In the console was his phone and picking it up Pete realized that it was dead too.

"Hey, Brian didn't we just talk about shit like this Saturday with Luke and the old man?" What did he say about an EMP?" Pete asked.

"Well that wasn't a damned EMP Pete, it was an explosion at a fucking nuke plant, and we gotta get the hell out of here and fast," Brian answered excitedly.

Grabbing what they could stuff into the backpacks that every guy in their 30's seems to carry with them these days, anything of value they did find they made room for. Pete had an unopened carton of Marlboro Lites, a couple bottles of water, three butane lighters and a smaller size LED flashlight.

Brian already had a surprising amount of useful stuff with him. In his backpack were two MRE's or meal, ready to eat, that Luke gave him Saturday. Also his Glock 43 and with two magazines, a 50 round box of ball ammo, a small tarp and his hunting knife.

Pete also made a habit of keeping an old H&R 12 gauge single shot shotgun that he and Luke had shortened in his truck and he had an almost full box of 6 shot shells for it and a few random slug rounds that were stashed in the armrests.

After gathering their gear, Pete reluctantly tried locking the doors of his brand new truck, only to find out the locks refused to function. "Fuck it," Pete muttered, throwing his keys on the seat and slamming the door closed. Taking one last look at his boat, it saddened Pete having to leave their morning catch in the cooler and all the fishing equipment, and he was reluctant to leave.

Pete and Brian weren't far from home, if they were driving that is but they were 30 miles away and all they had was their feet to carry them. It was just after eleven when they left, at least that's what they figured, and there was no way they would make the walk before dark set in and the cold air descended on them. Doing the math, they figured on making it home in about fifteen hours if they went non-stop, which is exactly what they decided to do.

Their walk took them up county road 18 until they came to county road 54, or what's called Ravenna Trail that took them to Hastings Minnesota where they crossed the bridge into Wisconsin - the route well known to both of them. The day was pleasant for walking and both men took notice of the silence. Besides from their chattering back and forth, the only noises they heard were the light breeze rustling the autumn leaves and the sounds of birds chirping.

It had been around 4 or 5 hours since they'd left the truck and while they had encountered several people, not a one of them appeared threatening to them. Most everyone they came across walking the road was standing by, or sitting in their vehicle with a cell phone in hand, oblivious to their surroundings.

It made the boys wonder just what in the hell were these people expecting? By now Pete and Brian had basically come to grips with what had happened, and it was exactly how the old man had figured it would pan out. No one was coming to the rescue, not for a very long time anyway.

Pete and Brian are not "small" men. Both of them are beasts, not obese and out of shape, just big, strong, bearded and intimidating looking men. Pete carrying that 12 gauge over his shoulder was probably the main reason not many people talked to them as they walked by.

While the exact opposite is true of both of the boys, their physical presence made their journey almost uneventful. Almost, because there is always someone that is severely lacking in common sense. Pete and Brian would soon encounter that specimen where county road MM meets county road F, just south of Hudson, where a pair of local boys decided to set up a "tax stand", relieving people of their possessions at gun point for the privilege of passing by.

After walking for ten or eleven hours now, the darkness had set in with a vengeance. With no light pollution for a night light and with cloud cover rolling in, Pete and Brain could barely make out the road in front of them.

Walking and talking about the day, not even trying to be quiet, they suddenly were illuminated by a headlight. The light was not a crazy bright light, maybe a headlight from an ATV or motorcycle. It was just dim enough that Pete was comfortable with moving the shotgun to hang alongside his right leg where it would be invisible to whoever lit them up.

Pete, always the social butterfly broke the ice saying "sup," with Brian moving into a spot that blocked the light from fully illuminating Pete and the shotgun.

"That's far enough there boys," came the reply to Pete's question.

"What can we do for ya?" Pete asked calmly.

"Well that depends on whatcha got on ya I suppose, yer gonna have to pay if you want past," the man said, his comment drawing a chuckle from a second man that the boys hadn't seen. Brian wasn't liking this advantage of hiding behind the light the other men had.

Reaching into a cargo pocket in his pants for his flashlight Brian whispered to Pete, "I'm gonna light them up, you bring that shotgun up when I do."

"Yup," Pete quietly replied, squeezing the stock of the old shotgun.

Pulling the light out from his pocket, Brian aimed it in the general direction of the voices while hitting the on switch, anxiously yelling "show me your hands, show me your fucking hands." The powerful LED light, while temporarily blinding the two men, also turned the location of the light into a target and the crack of a bullet flying between Pete and Brian was the next thing they heard.

Unconsciously raising the shotgun Pete pulled the trigger, firing blindly towards the men, it's thunderous report quickly followed by a scream as loud as the shotgun. Watching Brian take off towards the second man, Pete was quickly reloading his shotgun as another crack of the gun rang out, Brian feeling the burning sensation in his thigh with the report of the gun. Slowing only slightly at the shot, Brian continued moving forward. His massive right fist propelled by the momentum of his two hundred and fifty pound frame flew forward, smashing into the man's face with a sickening crunch. As the man crumbled to the ground, his head bounced off the blacktop with a loud, dull thud.

"Holy Fuck," Pete screamed, seeing the mess in front of him as his stomach began revolting at the scene. Sitting hunched over in a huge puddle of blood was a man, clearly bleeding out while holding his leg from the knee down in his lap. Being only 15 feet apart at the shot, the 1 1/4 ounce load of number six bird shot was still in the wad as it struck the man, the mass of the load severing the limb.

"I'm hit," Brian said, leaning on the 4 wheeler, looking at his blood soaked pants leg.

Being brought back into the moment, Pete yelled "ah shit, where are ya hit, you ok?"

"In my leg, I'm ok I think," Brian said, holding his hands over the wound. "Grab the light," Brian asked.

Glancing back where the beam of the flashlight illuminated the ditch Pete walked to it, picking it up doing a quick scan of the scene. Seeing the man Brian knocked out now starting to move around,

Pete, slamming his huge boot into him yelled "go to sleep," while bending over and picking up the pistol that was used to shoot Brian, a Ruger Mark 3 .22 caliber.

Dropping his pants, Brian watched the trickle of blood running down his leg. Using the light, Pete bent over, taking a closer look at the wound checking to see if the bullet had went through. Brian, now obviously in pain, but still being Brian, grabbed his shorts and feigned pulling them down. "Hey, as long as your down there....", Brian said with a chuckle.

Pete lost it, laughing loudly at Brian's joke, but the humor didn't last long as Pete stood, again seeing the man who's jaw Brian had smashed starting to come back around, looking for his gun.

"I fucking told you to go to sleep," Pete yelled, walking to him. Using the flashlight as club, Pete repeatedly beat the man, sending him back into unconsciousness. "Some people just don't learn," Pete said, walking back to Brian.

Producing a couple full sized bandaids from his backpack and some toilet paper, Brian quickly made up an impromptu bandage, patching up his leg. Checking out the 4 wheeler, Pete hit the starter button on the Honda Foreman, it's engine coming to life.

"We got wheels," he yelled to Brian. Shining the flashlight into the gas tank showed it was nearly full, bringing Pete and Brian's spirits up.

Brian, not totally convinced the man who shot him was sufficiently subdued, grabbed the Ruger pistol, smashing the man two times in the skull for good measure. Checking the mans pockets, Brian came up with a spare magazine for the gun, a pack of Marlboro Reds and a lighter.

"You're riding bitch," Pete said while lighting a smoke and surveying the mess around them as Brian got on the rear rack of the machine.

"What the hell just happened, Pete?" Brian asked, his voice shaky and his leg throbbing as they rode the Honda ATV along the dark, deserted county roads.

"I don't know," Pete replied curtly, his grip on the handlebars tight. "But those two came out on the short end of the stick this time."

They rode in silence for a while, Brian scanning the darkness with the shotgun on his lap while Pete concentrated on navigating the the dark side roads. Both men were still in shock, coming to grips with what had just happened. Pete dug deep inside himself, knowing full well that he simply could not dwell on it right now and switched his mindset into gear, formulating a plan to get home. He knew they needed to cross Interstate 94 to get to the house, and now with having wheels, they would need to use one of the overpasses to do it. Pete stayed on the less populated east side roads, hoping to be able to navigate the dangerous minefield of stalled vehicles certain to be on the overpass at exit 4.

Pete was right, the overpass was jammed with stalled vehicles of all types. A tractor trailer combination had stalled right in the middle of making a left turn, the fifty three foot long trailer blocking the entire road. Fortunately for them, the driver had left just enough room during his turn for their ATV to squeeze along side the guard rail and front bumper of the big rig. Once they had passed the crowded truck stop on the northeast corner of the intersection, Pete, who had kept the headlights off until now turned them on and kicked the ATV into high gear, weaving back and forth through the maze of cars as they sped out of the busy area. Seeing little activity once they were beyond the truck stop, Pete turned off the headlights and slowed down. He guided the ATV along a confusing series of country lanes--a left on McCutchen, a right on Dailey, a left on Green Mill... and finally they hit Trout Brook Road, their home stretch.

The road was pitch-black, with only the silhouettes of a few houses visible in the distance. They rode slowly, Brian twitchy and alert, but there was no sign of further human contact. Soon they were pulling into their driveway, and Pete deftly opened the garage door, parking the ATV inside.

Chapter Five

Pepper was anxious and still not herself from what she had witnessed earlier as JT leashed her. It was clear that whatever she had heard, smelled or seen had utterly terrified her and the two other dogs. Walking quietly in the dark towards the invisible fence boundary, she sat down, refusing to budge. JT slung his rifle around to his back and with a smile he bent down to scoop up his dog, who was not exactly small with her fifty pounds and his back creaked with her weight. After taking a few long steps over the boundary, he set her down. Pepper looked back to her invisible boundary, then at JT, then back again. He could almost read her mind as she thought, "So all I have to do to escape is jump?"

JT didn't really need to bring Pepper along, but the deafening silence seemed to magnify the tinnitus in his left ear and he wanted her with him, knowing she would alert well before he would ever hear anything. Over the years, they had developed a deep understanding of each other's body language. Though Pepper disliked gunshots and they didn't hunt together, they spent every minute of the day together, making it easy for JT to understand her alerts and cues.

Without realizing it, JT found himself standing in a daze in the middle of the blacktop road at the end of his long driveway. He knew he was exhausted from the events of the day, but it was rare for him to completely zone out. Gathering his thoughts, he began piecing together ideas in his head.

JT isn't too concerned for now about how his immediate neighbors are going to react to the recent events, as most of them are lifelong country folks who are more than accustomed to hunting and growing their own garden as a hobby. His primary worry, however, lies with the people living in the eastern portions of the Minneapolis-St. Paul metropolitan area. Reports on the radio suggest that some people in the cities have realized that law and order as they knew it is now nonexistent, and this realization has JT's senses on high alert.

JT gazed to the west under the moonless star-filled sky, but there was nothing remarkable in sight. The Rice Lake hill was visible in the distance, with the road he stood on continuing west before bending north, descending towards Rice Lake Flats. There, dozens of remote homes snaked along the flats with only two points of egress - one of which was the very road JT happened to be standing on.

To the east there is the county road then a few miles south on it is the cut off, a shortcut of sorts that ultimately ends up at four lane Wisconsin highway 64, which then leads directly bridge over the St Croix River in Stillwater Minnesota.

Three bridges span the St. Croix River to interconnect the neighboring states within a six-mile south-to-north run. Southmost, the breathtaking new highway 64 bridge towers over the riverbank adjacent to the monumental Allen King Power Plant's coal-fired main stack, another key area landmark. Further north along the mighty river lay the "old" bridge, an aged lift-style bridge that historically traversed across the river into the busy downtown Stillwater. Its more recent reincarnation restricted access to solely pedestrians. Then, a few miles north, the end of the trio, hailing from 1910, rose the mammoth rail bridge known as the High Bridge.

With caution etched in his mind, JT and Pepper steered towards that very direction.

Despite being only three and a half miles away from the ranch as the bird flew, the High Bridge, the site of potential trouble, demanded a five-mile journey through winding township roads. JT planned to grab the path of least resistance, as there was no need to settle for an off-road trek.

Under this now nearly moonless night with no sign of neighboring light pollution, visibility was compromised in the darkness. JT's first notable landmark was the Apple River Flowage, then one mile southwards towards the cut-off road. Unsure of the exact time, he was painfully aware that it had taken at least an hour to navigate this leg of his journey on foot.

The cut-off road, also known as 192nd Avenue, stretched two miles westwards, before curving south and turning into 37th street, the very route leading to the High Bridge. Homes were scarce along 192nd Avenue, shrouded in darkness with no lights visible from any of them. Before long, a distant barking pierced through the dead of night and pulled JT's focus to a seemingly agitated dog in the distance. JT tugged gently on Pepper's leash, bringing her close. In response, she emitted a barely perceptible growl, apparently enough to silence the barking dog in the distance and bring peace back to the quiet night.

JT and Pepper advanced along the notorious 37th street; little could be heard except for the occasional chirping crickets amidst the enveloping blanket of silence. Soon enough, the two reached the makeshift gate that served as the first and only layer of defense for the High Bridge, standing to prevent anyone except authorized personnel from crossing onto the deteriorating railroad tracks. Quietly yet resolutely, JT proceeded to circumnavigate the gate and lead Pepper into the gray void of the bridge beyond.

"I was hoping to see a string of rail cars out there," he said softly to Pepper, staring at the bridge. JT was slightly disappointed by the lack of obstacles looking westward, wishing to face up to more challenging journey for those who will ultimately be crossing the bridge. Anticipation still resides within him, however - for the thousands of refugees that will be forced to abandon city life, the bridge will serve as a relatively safe route to the perceived salvation through the vast, eye-catching woodlands of western Wisconsin.

To get closer to the psyche of those poor souls who will be forced to leave their homes, it was imperative that he clears his mind and contemplate their journey. They will be on foot, or riding bicycles carrying what little, if any, possessions they have left on their backs. They will be hungry and thirsty, and by then, no doubt they will be willing to do whatever it takes to survive.

A deafening silence had washed over him until the muffled echo of a far off gun shot broke the quiet, the shot probably nothing more than an unfortunate deer caught out in the open by a hunter's flashlight. Peering out to the west, nothing could be seen against the black void. Was he ready? Expected or not, the uncertainties that lie ahead were near impossible to predict.

In the past JT has read extensively about this type of event and up until now it's been nothing more than an artistic blend of fiction and speculation. There was one particular book he read titled "One Second After". The author William Forstchen, was very detailed in his writings which really woke JT up to just how possible this type of event could be and it's inevitable ramifications. Possible, but in his mind it didn't seem plausible, it would be an instant death sentence to whoever perpetrated it because surely US satellites and radar systems would detect any launch from Russia, China, North Korea, any of the nuclear armed countries that have ICBM capabilities.

In the event of a launch from one of those suspected militaries, air defenses like the Aegis and the Aegis ashore would be activated and launch their SM2, 3 and 6 missiles at the targets. Fort Greeley, Alaska and Vandenberg Air Force Base in California would launch their ground based mid-course (GMD) interceptors that are housed in underground silos. Most people wouldn't even know the intercept had happened. But that was then, and the US isn't at war with a nuclear superpower. We are at war with Iran.

Feeling completely impotent as he considered the enormity of what has obviously happened, JT began doing the math. His best guess is that it's been around sixteen hours since he saw the flash, that means that in about 56 hours the water supply in the metro will be down to zero and the grocery stores will be out of food, if not sooner. He couldn't even imagine what that place will look like in three days.

Apparently those thoughts were enough to bring his mind around to where it needed to be as he said to Pepper, "let's head towards home girl, it's getting late." Walking the dark tracks to the east, the pair crossed 38th street then, turning left on 45th street, began heading north. All the while they walked, he thought about different ways to divert foot traffic from going north. There's no truly effective way to block the road to people walking, shoot, even doing so would only convince a hungry or thirsty person there is food and water on the other side.

Stopping abruptly in the road JT looked around, momentarily confused. "Sheesh, I'm really struggling to keep focused here, I just lost track of where we are," he softly said to Pepper as he gathered his bearings. Soon, after walking by the west side of Tommy's gravel pit, they were back on 192nd Ave turning east to the county road.

After taking the different route so as to not retrace their way in, now they had no other option but walking the county road again. Of the four houses on this stretch, all but one of them are well off the road, and knowing those people vaguely, JT wasn't expecting any problems, especially at this early hour. Before long pepper and JT were standing on the "bridge" for lack of better words of the spillway from the small hydroelectric dam on the Apple River. The dam, sitting 200 yards to the east of where he stood is a fairly secure area with the entire property being fenced right up to the blacktop with 6 foot tall fencing, topped with three strands of barbed wire.

With the nighttime darkness beginning to fade ever so slowly, JT took in everything he was seeing. "Here, right here is where the road can be blocked between the fences," he said. "This ain't defendable, not here, but if it came to it, one shooter up on that slope can turn a decent crowd back," he said to himself.

"There," he thought. "you've finally got your brain back in gear."

Content with this "plan", JT was already feeling better about the situation. Any crazies who would attempt to get into his neck of the woods would now have a tough time doing so. Two natural barriers, the massive St Croix River to the west a half mile and the Apple River, a much smaller river but quite fast one a couple of a miles to the south will force people to take the only easy way to get there, and now he knows he has a shot at blocking it.

At the top of the grade on the north side of the flowage JT stopped, relaxing for a bit to caught his breath while Pepper explored the early morning sounds and scents. Looking east down 205th Avenue through the waning darkness, JT wondered how many, if any people were walking along the highway a scant two miles away. "What did all those people do last night?" JT asked himself, watching the darkness give way to the coming daylight on the eastern horizon.

"Let's go Bubs," JT said to Pepper, who needed no encouragement to get moving. "How you doing anyway girly, you liking your walk with dad?" he asked the old girl, scratching her ears. Pepper is getting older, JT knowing quite well that she's still in great shape, was happy she was with him. Rounding the curve near 208th avenue, Pepper stopped, her ears erect and her eyes looking south, telling JT with a low growl that something is coming.

"What is that smell?" Luke asked himself, waking up in the darkness to the sounds of pans rattling and feet shuffling on the wooden kitchen floor. He had been sleeping on the couch, rolled up in the old man's poncho liner, or Wooby as he calls it, the sounds and smells emanating from the kitchen being more than enough to roust him from sleep. Rolling to the left, Luke immediately regretted even moving his bandaged leg. Looking down at his injury, he saw the wrapping was blood soaked and pressing on the bandage it was mildly painful to the touch. He did manage to get up and while it hurt, he was able to limp his way to the smell of bacon. In the kitchen he found his granny standing over the gas stove, pushing slices of bacon around in a jet black cast iron skittle with a old wooden spatula.

"Would you like some eggs?" she asked, seeing Luke. That was her common question when she asked if someone wanted breakfast.

Eggs, could be anything, pancakes, waffles, an omelet, bacon or sausage or hash brown potato's. As she looked at his leg with a few small rivulets of blood leaking out of the bandage, she told him to sit down so she could have a look at it. "Oh, I'm good for now gramma and I'd love something to eat. Have you seen anything of my dad yet this morning?" he asked, saying that he didn't hear him come in since he left last night.

"No, I haven't, where did he run off to?" she asked. Luke was well aware his gramma has dementia but it's beginning to become more noticeable almost by the day. Just then Luke felt something on his leg, it was Harley the dog, ever so stealthily licking the tasty blood leaking from the bandage. Luke didn't even move, he just let the dog go about his business.

Chuckling to himself after telling Harley "don't get any ideas about eating me for breakfast," Luke heard a snap and a loud "WHOOSH" sound come from where his gramma was at the stove. Jumping at the sound, Luke turned, noticing his gramma standing in front of the stove with a befuddled look on her face as the smell of burnt hair began to waft through the room.

The little fireball of propane gas that erupted from the gas stove had quickly dissipated but not until it rearranged her hair cut. Luke got up quickly and asked her if she was ok, which she was for the most part and said "next time I think I'll light the match before I turn the gas on," then she started to laugh a contagious kind of laugh and soon Luke was caught up in it, laughing as well. He had no idea why he was laughing, gramma could have been burnt severely, hell, the house could have blown up if the gas was on much longer. But it wasn't and his gramma is fine, maybe a little pink on the cheeks and definitely shorter hair, but she's fine.

Hobbling over to the stove, Luke helped his gramma finish the scrambled eggs. It wasn't long before Kate came out of her bedroom in a robe asking "what's so funny and what is that awful smell?" She was met with even more laughter as Luke re-enacted the scene for her. Kate didn't quite see the humor in all this as she looked at her mother in laws hair and face. Dipping a paper towel in the water bucket, Kate said "you hold this on your cheeks for a while momma."

Gramma already had the old percolator coffee pot set out, about to fill it from a two gallon jug when Luke quickly snatched the coffee pot from her setting it on the stove saying "I got this one granny, you go eat while I make this coffee."

Asking Luke if he had a clue where his dad may have went last night, Kate said she was worried because neither him or Pepper came home. Luke just shrugged his shoulders saying, almost too nonchalantly, "shit who knows, he was going to go to the High Bridge, but he could be anywhere out there. I'm not too worried about him yet, it's still early."

And it was early, the pitch black of night had just turned into the dark blue of morning when Luke was awoken up by the smell his granny's cooking. "Kate, where does dad keep his red medical bin at?" he asked, saying he wanted to clean and re-dress his wound before getting into anything else.

"It's in his secret closet, the one with all the rest of his crap, hang on, I'll get it for you," she said.

That secret closet as she called it is the old man's prepper stash. Against one wall of the big walk in closet are stacks of sealable plastic bins, big ones. The bottom bins in each stack contained two forty pound bags of high quality jasmine rice in them. Shelving on the opposite wall being neatly stacked full with cans of Spam, canned hams, canned chicken and canned beef. Other bins were packed with sealed pasta, boxes of stuffing, all kinds of random food items and beans, beans and more beans. Neatly stacked from floor to ceiling on shelving were bottles and bottles of dishwashing soap and laundry detergent. Next to those were boxes of batteries of all different sizes, bottles of bleach and vinegar, boxes and boxes of matches, rubbing alcohol and peroxide. The top shelf that circles the room was packed with toilet paper.

The medical bin was only slightly smaller than the rest, on the top of another stack of bins, and solid red in color, the only red bin in the room. Grabbing that one, taking it out to where Luke was just beginning to unwrap his leg, Kate then went to a drawer under the sink getting an already open container of hydrogen peroxide, setting that by Luke.

Once the wound was unwrapped and cleaned Luke began replacing the steri-strips one at a time. The wound wasn't huge, maybe two inches long at best, but it was deep and had obviously severed a couple of small veins. Being tempted to open the wound and irrigate it with the peroxide, he quickly passed on it, remembering the old man doing that same thing last night with saline. At the time, the old man was fairly convinced there was nothing inside his leg shouldn't be there.

Finishing with the strips, Luke left the wound uncovered, slipping on a clean pair of sweatpants that Kate had given him. His logic being that he'd rather be able to keep an eye on it in case of infection and did not want to deplete the supply of bandage wraps any sooner than necessary. He was already certain that those supplies would all be gone soon.

Pulling the garage door closed on the darkness around them, Pete felt his way along the walls to the door leading inside the house as Brian pulled the flashlight out of his pocket, cupping his hand over the lens as he turned it on.

"Thanks," Pete said, opening the door into the kitchen, heading strait to the bathroom. Pulling out a chair from the table, Brian nervously dropped his pants to his knees to check his wound. Putting his right leg up on the chair, he inspected his makeshift bandage that was now partially soaked through with blood. Brian pressed his fingers around along his thigh, and though it was surely tender, it was not terribly painful.

Still wanting to change that bandage and wash the wound, Brian pulled his pants up, absentmindedly walking into the bathroom headfirst into the stench that was escaping Pete's bowels.

"Holy shit man, what in the fuck is wrong with you?" Brian screamed, gagging.

"Hey man, you're the one who walked in on me, don't hate the player, hate the game," Pete said, chuckling. Brian, grabbing the first aid kit from its spot went back into the kitchen, still holding his breath from the assault his senses just endured.

"That fucker is rotten, I swear," Brian muttered under his breath. Going to the sink and opening the faucet, he was met with nothing. No water flowed.

"Well shit," Brian said, turning the faucet off. Seeing a half full case of Walmart water on the counter, taking one of those Brian took a good pull on the plastic bottle then soaked the gauze pad he had with what was left. Peeling back his bandage, Brian was surprised to see just a little purple looking hole under the blood. Wiping it clean with the pad, then opening an alcohol wipe he cleaned the wound again.

With the wound not bleeding at the moment, he took one more piece of gauze and after putting some antibiotic cream on the hole he taped it in place. "Good enough for now," he said to himself.

Pete, finishing his business by announcing "I'm glad I went first, there was only one flush in the tank, I think the water is out."

"Yeah, it is. What do you wanna do?" Brian asked.

"Well, I'm wiped out, but I think we should get the hell out of here as soon as we can and head to the ranch," Pete relied.

"Yeah, this town is going to be a damned madhouse in no time," Brian said.

"How's the leg?" Pete asked, looking Brian up and down.

"It's good enough," Brian replied then saying they should see if Pete's small aluminum trailer will fit the hitch on that Honda.

Looking at the Honda, they could see a ball hitch already on it and they hoped it was the same 1 7/8" size of the trailer, which it was. Knowing the trailer will make life much easier for the two, they pulled it into the garage by hand connecting it to the Honda. The loading was going fast, all the food they could find in the house then all the frozen meat from the big top load freezer was the first thing in. The meat in freezer alone filling two big coolers.

After the food came what other guns they had which was their deer rifles and the Mossberg 12 gauge.

Next in was a full five gallon can of gas. Pete, having one more smaller can, drained it topping off the Honda. Then came sleeping bags, a large Coleman gas camp stove, the case of water from the house, a bag of wrenches and screwdrivers, some other assorted tools, a couple of fishing poles and a tackle box.

Taking a quick look around, they decided they were done loading, even if they'd have found something else they'd have to leave it behind, the little trailer was full, and getting heavy. Looking at the battery operated clock in the kitchen it read 4:10, which was perfect Pete figured. They had a little less than a 20 mile ride to the ranch and were planning on taking only township roads to get there. They would have to ride up county road I for a couple miles though, but there weren't many houses along that stretch of road.

Brian decided to use a cooler in the trailer as a seat while Pete did the driving. The boys knew every back road in a three county area and were taking their time, driving with no lights, blacked out. Just before they left though, Brian took a side cutter from the tool kit and cut the ground wire for the tail light that came on as soon as the key was turned. It may not be that big of a deal, the four wheeler was already noisy but being that it's still dark he figured any one outside might hear them, but now they'd have a hell of time seeing them.

Taking it easy, Pete decided only going maybe 20 mile per hour or so at the most would give him the chance to avoid any stalled cars they will encounter. The large Honda seemed to pull the load fine, but Pete was concerned about if it could stop the load should he need to hit the brakes hard.

Just like their ride to the house, this one was proving to be uneventful, the early hour of the day wasn't hurting them. Soon enough the boys were slowly coming up the north side of the flowage hill on county road I, the engine of the Honda working much harder now making the climb up the steep grade.

Knowing this short section of road is notoriously famous for deer crashing into cars, Pete carefully scanned the road, was fully prepared with his shotgun ready to smoke one if he saw it.

Hearing the rumbling sound of the engine coming closer, JT edged Pepper just off the road into the grassy mouth of a field driveway. Both of them got low in the tall grass as JT shouldered his rifle, muzzle to the ground in front of him. Seeing the silhouette of a blacked out ATV coming into view, a knot began growing deep in JT's stomach. He felt certain there likely isn't going to be anyone running around on an ATV at this time of the day with good intentions.

Eventually making its way almost to where JT and Pepper were laying low, JT watched as the driver appeared to be very intently looking at the shoulders of the road. JT, wondering if maybe the driver is wearing night vision optics and saw him. Sliding lower into the grass, he pulled Pepper tight to his side. Suddenly, the driver slowed abruptly, a flash of fire exploding from the front of the machine from a gunshot.

Jumping at the shot, JT tried holding on to Pepper with his left hand and getting his feet under him while at the same time bringing the rifle up to fire. Being unable to make out the form on the 4 wheeler in the dark he had no idea where to aim, the sights useless as he pulled the trigger.

The thunder of the short rifle stunned Pete and Brian, causing Brian to yell "don't shoot, don't shoot." With a voice inside JT's head telling him not to shoot again, he stopped and quickly retrieved the flash light from his pocket lighting up the ATV. His rifle still aiming at the ATV, JT couldn't believe his eyes.

"Pete, holy shit, are you ok, are you hit?" JT yelled.

"Who the hell's out there?" Brian yelled, his Glock in hand and his ears ringing from the gunshots.

"It's the old man," JT replied, letting Peppers leash drop as she took off in search of the fresh blood she smelled.

"I'm good pops, but you scared the living shit out of me," Pete replied.

"Damn Pete, I thought you'd taken a shot at me," JT said.

"Oh hell no pops, I didn't even know you were there, I shot at a deer," Pete said.

"Damn, it's good to see you guys, sorry about sending a round your way, I didn't know it was you guy's," JT said excitedly.

"You got my fucking attention, that rifle sounds like a damned cannon," Brian said, getting out of the trailer with a limp. In the light of JT's flashlight, he saw the blood on Brian's leg. He knew that it wasn't his bullet though, the damage would have been far more severe.

"Brian your bleeding, did shrapnel from my shot get you?" JT asked, getting frantic, thinking he'd injured one of the boys.

"Well, I got shot, but not by you," Brian said, his words a relief to JT.

"Let's get the hell out of here boys, this ruckus will definitely rouse the neighbors," JT said, hopping in the back of the trailer with Brian. Keeping an eye out for the deer Pete shot at, sure enough, 30 yards up the road Pepper appeared, licking the blood leaking out of the big doe.

The addition of the deer was about all the trailer could handle and JT had to move forward to keep weight on the rear end of the 4 wheeler for the rest of the ride to the ranch. Fortunately for Pepper, Pete kept the speed down and she was able to trot along behind, keeping an eye on "her" deer.

Approaching the driveway, JT told Pete to shut it down for a bit, telling them that Luke had made it to the ranch last night and no doubt he'd heard the gunshots even from inside the house.

"I'd bet we are already in his crosshairs," Pete said.

Removing the Baefeng from his pocket and turning it on, JT caught the tail end of a transmission saying "....old man." Keying the mic, JT said "Luke, old man inbound, on-site with Pete and Brian, don't shoot when you hear the machine."

"I won't," came the reply, "but you really shouldn't be wearing that red shirt old man," Luke's voice said through the radio.

"Yep, that little shit already had us in his scope," Pete said.

Expecting the old man, Luke had been walking around outside before sunup, just taking a listen when he heard the sound of an engine carried by the wind, quickly followed by two gunshots.

Hobbling in the house Luke had grabbed the old man's varmint rifle, a stainless Savage Model 12 chambered in .223 Remington with a 6-24 power Vortex scope mounted on top. Slinging the rifle over his shoulder, he had gingerly climbed one step at a time up the twelve foot ladder the old man kept planted between the house and the shop, getting up to the ridge of the roof for the view it offered.

After the radio call, Luke slung the heavy Savage back over his shoulder, sliding down the 12 pitch of the roof where he'd taken his position by the chimney, to the 4 pitch roof where he walked to the edge, climbing back down the 12' ladder repeating the same process he used to get up.

By the time he was on the ground, the ATV was pulling around the curve in the driveway by the plum tree, maneuvering around Luke's pickup. With the door to the house opening, Harley and Duke blew by Kate as she let them out, the two dogs flying out to greet the group.

All three of JT's dogs love people, sometimes a little too much, but today was different. Blowing by Pete and Brian, Duke, full of youthful vigor dove full bore into the deer, grabbing the dead creature by the neck in his powerful jaws as he tried to drag it out of the trailer. Harley on the other hand, while definitely interested, was simply content to raise his hackles and growl menacingly at the thing from a distance. Pepper didn't give a hoot about any of it, in her mind her job was done and now she just wanted a nap.

Brian had extricated himself from the trailer and limped the few steps over to Luke, shaking his hand. "What's with the gimpy leg, the fuck you do now?" Luke asked as a greeting.

"You first, you don't look any better off than me," Brian replied.

"Ah, I got stabbed in the calf with a piece of shrapnel," Luke said,

"Huh, how?" Brian asked.

"Long story," Luke replied.

"Well, I got fucking shot," Brian replied.

"Huh, how?" Luke asked.

"Long story," Brian said.

"Ok stop, you guys are making me dizzy, is there any coffee yet Luke?" JT asked.

"Should be," he replied.

"But first, let's get this deer hung in the barn and dressed quick before Duke goes insane," JT said.

"I got this, go get some coffee pops," Pete said grabbing the doe by the ear.

"Save the lungs and liver for the dogs Pete, that will make a nice meal for them," JT said.

"Uh huh," Pete replied over his shoulder, pulling the deer by it's ears into the barn.

Talking seriously now, Luke said "Brian, let me have a look at that wound, it's obvious that it's painful,"

"Probably wouldn't hurt, I did clean it up good after we got home though." The boys both limped to the picnic table where Brian dropped his pants to reveal his thigh. Brian chuckled out loud at the thought of him having dropped his drawers twice now so other dudes can look at his leg.

"The fuck you laughing at?" Luke asked.

"Oh nothing," Brian, laughing again as he remembered telling Pete "as long as your down there."

"I'm gonna get my kit, hang on a second," Luke said, hobbling to his busted up truck where he began fishing around under the box topper for his med kit. Luke's med kit was a raggedy old olive drab canvas tool bag carrying a tourniquet, some Israeli bandages, blow out bandages, sterile gauze pads, alcohol wipes and plenty of other random items.

Bringing the kit to the table, Luke removed the makeshift bandage Brian had applied earlier, looking at the wound. Brian explained that it was a .22 round he was hit with, leaving the neat little hole that was beginning to close. Luke, pulling on a pair of blue medical gloves began to examine the area, trying to see if the bullet stayed under the skin, not penetrating the muscle tissue. By the looks of the bruising, Luke could see the path the slug took. Asking Brian how he was standing when he was hit, Brian said that he thinks he was directly facing the guy, but it was plenty dark so he really wasn't sure.

Brian's entry wound was on the edge of the leg, and although small in size the hole was oblique in shape. Then, with Luke pressing on a spot about four inches behind the entry spot, Brian let out a shriek.

"Hang on a sec, I'm gonna push around a little behind the entry hole and see if I can feel the bullet, I think it's close to the skin." Luke said. Taking the glove off his right hand to enhance his sense of feel, Luke, being a little less than gentle pressed the area with two fingers where the bruising was more prominent.

Brian clearly wasn't a fan of this part because when Luke rocked his fingers back and forth over the projectile Brian yelled "ok, ok, that's enough, I think you found it!"

"Brian, I'm not worried so much about the bullet as I am about the possibility of fragments of fabric from your pants being in there. It only takes a tiny piece of thread to cause a massive infection and as fast as that entry is healing up I think we should get that bullet out and irrigate the shit out of it," Luke said solemnly. That news caused Brian's palms to sweat at the thought and he asked if maybe he should take a four wheeler into Somerset. Maybe if things aren't too bad yet the small urgent care clinic by the town hall might be operational. Luke shrugged and said "I donno, but take them pants off so I can look and see if the hole is cut at all."

As fate may have it, as soon as Brian had his pants off standing by the picnic table in his boxers, Pete came out of the barn carrying an old feed bag. "Oh for fucks sakes Brian, was Luke an easier mark than me?" he said while laughing uproariously.

"Fuck you Pete," was all Brian could muster in reply. Changing his tone to a more serious one Pete asked how the leg felt. "Pretty much the same really, not bad, not good. Luke is trying to see if there are threads missing from the hole in my pants, he's worried about some of it being in my leg," Brian lamented, clearly worried about the risk of infection.

"Well what's the verdict doc?" Pete asked Luke.

"Man, I ain't sure, this looks pretty clean where the bullet went in, hard to tell though with all the blood in the fabric," Luke replied.

"What are you guys thinking," Pete asked.

"I'm thinking about riding a four wheeler to town and see if the clinic is running," Brian said.

Luke stopped him saying "Brian, this ain't bad, we can keep an eye on both of our legs for a day or two. The old man has antibiotics if they get infected, but right now we really don't have the time to fuck with this shit. I'm the only one that has slept in the last 24 hours now and that was just for a few hours."

Brian, now being a little concerned about getting an infection asked "well, what then? In two days there's no way the clinic will still be open."

"Hold on, let's talk to the old man before we get ahead of ourselves here," Luke replied.

"Coffee, it's almost as good as beer," JT said to himself, filling his cup for the second time. The hot steam nearly burning his nostrils as he inhaled the dark aroma while walking outside in the cool morning air. The boys were standing by the smoker, he could see Brian still in his boxers after Luke's examination of the bullet wound to his thigh. It's been a very, very long day, and JT's humor was no where to be found so he didn't attempt making a joke, instead he asked Brian the obvious question, "how's the leg?"

"Ah, it's good, thanks for asking," Brian answered, gently rubbing the fresh bandage Luke had applied.

"Luke, we gotta get Amy, she has to be besides herself by now," JT said, his brow furrowed with concern, ending any thoughts of Brian going to the clinic.

"For sure. I'm a little worried about her too out there by herself. But she's got her dog Clover for company and protection, and the place is pretty secluded. I'm actually more worried about her worrying about me to be honest," Luke said, trailing off.

"Take my truck Luke, it runs. It will take me a little while to get it ready though, I have to fill the transfer case and differentials. The u-joint can wait, I'll just slap the driveshaft back in," JT said, looking at his old pickup.

"Pete, you're gonna have to go with him. Get your gear ready while I get the truck up to speed, you can catch a nap on the way," JT said, looking at the completely exhausted Pete.

"I wouldn't have it any other way, I can sleep when I'm dead," Pete replied with a forced laugh as he headed back in the barn to finish up the deer.

"If you take all the back roads you shouldn't see much in the way of walker's. I'd imagine most folks stranded out on the big roads are gonna stay on the those roads waiting for help," JT said with urgency in his voice.

"Cool, thanks old man, how much gas is in the old girl?" Luke asked, slapping the fender of the old truck.

"It's full, 20 gallons, but grab a 5 gallon can from the shed and toss it in the back just in case, wanna pull a trailer? How many bins do you guys have packed," JT asked.

"Plenty. I'm gonna need a rifle though, all I had with is the Glock, mind if I take your AR with?" Luke asked.

"Not a problem," JT answered as he walked towards the shop. As part of their contingency plans, the ranch was to be their Alamo. Luke and Amy had bins of clothes, long term foods, ammunition, tools..all kinds of necessary items packed and ready to load out at the drop of a hat if they needed to ever bug out.

JT is so very grateful they had the little gathering last weekend because Pete and Brian, while not having everything packed had at least heard Luke and Amy talk about all the items they had ready. Later, after they had gotten home the pair had taken a visual inventory and now knew what they had and how they could move it. That little bit of planning had helped when they packed up their stuff just a few hours ago.

Luke, looking around at his choices, decided he would pull the bigger of the trailers, a 7 by 14 footer his dad picked up a few years ago to haul hay for the horses. There isn't much difference between pulling a big one or small one except now Luke has the option to bring more stuff back if he has the time, energy and space.

Finishing his deer dressing, Pete went to the water bin by the horse feeder, diligently scanning the woods to the south while rinsing the blood off of his hands. "How can that guy be so alert?" JT asked himself, watching Pete wash up.

Brian got his pants back on just in time as Kate stepped out of the south door still in her robe. "Momma is cooking everything in the upright freezer, should I stop her?" she asked.

"Oh hell no, let her have at it. The old man said he doesn't have the battery power to keep the fridge and the upright freezer both going, so let her empty it out, what's she cooking?" Luke asked.

"Well, it smells like sausage I think," Kate said. At those words, Pete and Brian's heads popped up in anticipation. Momma, indeed having a hay day in front of the stove was cooking up everything in sight. Being born during the Great Depression, momma simply isn't wired to waste anything, not even a crumb of food - everything will get used.

After filling the the transfer case and differentials and popping the front driveshaft back in the old truck JT went inside where he was met by his mom. "I'm just gonna cook up what's in the freezer here so it won't spoil, and we need to eat what we can in that refrigerator soon," she said.

"Ma, Luke has to leave here soon to go get Amy, can we get Pete a plate so they can get moving?" JT asked, savoring the smell of his moms cooking.

"Yep, who's Pete?" she said.

"He's a friend Ma," JT answered.

The breakfast of sausage and eggs really hit the spot, but damn was JT tired now after the feast. Before heading outside to check on the boys progress, JT glanced at the clock in the kitchen. It read nine in the morning, that means he'd been up for about 28 hours or so.

Luke and Pete, now done getting their gear together for the 80 mile round trip journey in front of them, walked towards JT. "You got enough in the way of firepower?" JT asked them.

"Yep, we're good," they said, getting in the old truck, then with a wave they were rolling down the driveway with the trailer in tow.

After a minute, the radio in JT's pocket crackled with, "got a copy old man?"

Taking the radio out he replied "loud and clear, what's up?"

Laughing into the radio Luke said "Pete's already sleeping, I'll see you around 4 if all goes well."

"Roger that, stay off the big roads and you should be fine," JT replied.

"Brian, go to the camper and get a nap man, you gotta be shot, and, well, you've been shot," JT said.

"You sure pops, you gotta be tired too?" Brian said.

"Yeah, that I am, I'm gonna crash out here on the deck recliner for a while, neither one of us are much good like this, hell, I can barely think. Kate is inside with mom, and the dogs will let us know if anything hanky is happening," JT said wearily.

"Alrighty then. That breakfast filled me up, I'm out," Brian said, hobbling over to the pop-up camper behind the shed.

As JT melted into the recliner, he thought about what the boys had been through, what it took for them to get here and how fortunate he was to have them here as watched Brian limp to the camper.

Brian is a good guy, in his early thirties and built like a brick shit house. His sense of humor dwarfs his size and he's always cracking a joke, but today Brian wasn't feeling at all funny. JT realized that Brian was troubled, his mind likely still reeling from the events of the last 24 hours.

As Brian lay sprawled out on the soft queen-sized mattress in the camper, his mind began involuntarily replaying the gruesome sight of the man holding onto his leg as he bled out. This event had hit Brian hard. As he lay there, Brian is still unsure of why Pete's truck had stalled out. He wasn't totally buying the EMP story that Pops had told them on Saturday. Yet, all the other cars they had seen were sitting in the road, as if they had all run out of gas at the same time. Why did the old man's truck and the Honda he and Pete had acquired earlier keep running? As he spun into the happy spot between being awake and asleep, Brian wondered if the old man even knew for sure. He must know something having been in the military for quite a while. But before he could finish that thought, Brian was out cold.

Seeing JT on the front deck through the kitchen window, Kate grabbed a blanket off a recliner and joined him, tossing the blanket over his legs. "You were gone a long time last night, where did you go and what did you see out there?" she asked, tucking the blanket under his legs before rubbing his tired calloused hands.

"Nuttin honey, absolutely nothing. I went to the high bridge, I just wanted to get my mind into the heads of those who will undoubtedly be coming this way. We heard one dog bark on 192nd, that's it," he concluded, closing his eyes.

"What do you mean by that?" she asked, a troubled tone to her voice.

"Well, if this was an EMP, which it certainly feels like it was, then we are really screwed. Well, not us, not yet anyway, we can do pretty good out here if we are left alone, but society as a whole is screwed. When the stores run out of food in a couple days a lot of those people in the cities are going to start leaving there if they can," JT said.

"Ok, so then what, will that be a problem for us?" she asked, curious.

"People are going to be getting pretty desperate, very soon honey, and those folks will do whatever they need to feed their families," JT answered, trying not to alarm her.

"Ok, well, get some rest, you want me to wake you," she asked, hearing enough.

"Please don't unless you have to and you'll know if that happens." With that, JT closed his eyes, imagining what the twin cities are like right now.

Like Pete and Brian, Luke knew all the little backroads well, and he was planning out where he should cross the bigger county and state roads that lay ahead. Only one town would be in the way: New Richmond. He decided he would stay north of it a couple of miles while heading due east for at least 5 or 6 miles before he began to work his way south and east. His goal was to make it to 170th street and take that south to 140th Avenue, which would go straight east for miles until he'd intersect with 280th Street. From there, he'd turn south, which would bring them within a half-mile of their house. Luke knew that they would be spotted at some point and wondered if maybe he should have waited until nightfall to travel. But it's only been about 24 hours or so since this all started, so he's hoping that people have remained calm- at least calmer than the ones he encountered yesterday at the gas station.

Taking it easy on the back roads, knowing that slow and steady will get him there at the same time that fast and reckless would, Luke took in the views from the drivers side old man's truck. Crossing highway 64 well east of New Richmond, he wasn't too surprised seeing a couple dozen people walking west in a group towards town. "Probably coming from the four corners," he said to himself.

Realizing the group wasn't anywhere near close enough to be a threat, Luke sped up slightly on the narrow township road to get out of sight before the group could become a threat. Looking at Pete, his head bouncing off the side window with every bump in the road, Luke wondered to himself just what it would take for Pete to wake up. "You lucky bastard," Luke said to his sleeping friend.

Moving steadily, the miles went by fast, finding Luke turning left onto 140th, now heading east and to their last big road to cross, US 63. After driving a couple miles on 140th, it was time for a pee break. Seeing Pete still sleeping, Luke didn't try to wake him. They have only been on the road for maybe 45 minutes, that's not near enough sleep to do Pete any good.

Slowing to a stop, Luke put the truck in park, letting it idle as he took a good long pee. Finishing up his business, the movement of a faded red International tractor pulling out from a blind driveway caught his attention, startling Luke. The antique farm machine turned towards him not 50 feet away as the old boy driving the tractor slowed, pulling up along side the Chevy and shut his tractor off. Looking the old man over, Luke saw the checkered grip of a handgun sticking out of his pocket. The old man waved, sayin something Luke couldn't hear. Luke waving back, returned the greeting. The farmer was still talking but Luke couldn't hear him over the idling 350's loud exhaust, so reaching in the open door, Luke shut the truck engine off. Then, turning back to talk to the man Luke found himself staring down the barrel of a revolver.

"Hey, hold on there, I was just shutting off the truck so I could hear ya," Luke said, raising his hands a little to show the old guy there wasn't anything to be concerned with.

The old farmer cracked a little smile as he lowered his revolver saying "just keeping honest people honest I suppose, I only pulled it out cause of that dead guy in your truck."

"Hahahahaha, oh he ain't dead, he only looks dead. He was up all night, him and another buddy were down at the casino by Red Wing when the lights went out," Luke said with a laugh.

"Damn, that's a hell of a walk. Where you headed in that old thing, over to 63?" the farmer asked, pointing to the truck.

"We gotta cross it, yeah," Luke replied.

"Well there's a bunch running up and down the road over yonder on four wheelers, taking what they can from all the cars stalled out there," the old farmer said.

"How many are there?" Luke asked cautiously.

"I don't rightly know for sure. My nephew told me about them, he works at the big dairy outfit up on G. He came down to my farm on his old motorcycle to tell me to stay away from the highway, says there are a lot of people walking both directions too. He said for sure there was four of em on them wheelers, he saw em with his own eyes, the rascals were trying to get the gas out of a pickup," the old farmer replied.

Luke slapped the door of the truck to try to wake Pete up. They had to cross 63 one way or another and Pete had to be awake for that part.

"For fucks sake, what?" Pete asked, coming out of his slumber that hadn't been near long enough. Seeing the old farmer sitting on a tractor holding a revolver woke him right up as he looked at Luke with a WTF expression on his face.

"It's all good Pete. This old fella says there could be trouble up ahead on 63, some guys on four wheelers raiding cars." With that Luke went up to the old farmer and offered his hand and the two men shook as Luke looked over the old H model tractor.

"Looks like you've got a low steer tire there," Luke said, pointing to the narrow front end of the tractor.

"Yeah, it's a got slow leak. I don't generally use this tractor, I bought it to restore, it's a hobby of mine. None of my newer tractors run, strangest damned thing. Well good luck to you boys, I hope ya get to where your going in one piece," the old guy said, trailing off.

"Thanks a lot, and thanks for the information, we appreciate that. You keep that revolver handy now ok?" Luke said, leaning on the open door of the truck. The old guy nodding his head, fired up the old tractor, it's 4 cylinder engine purring like a kitten.

"He's an interesting old dude," Pete said.

"For sure, but I'm damn glad we bumped into him, at least we have a clue what's up ahead," Luke said.

"So what's the plan?" Pete asked.

Thinking about the question, Luke figured they could probably just fly through the intersection, but if there was a group of people walking around the area he didn't want to run over some poor person who's just trying to get home. He also had to assume that anyone walking would do what they could to get a ride, which wasn't going to happen.

Finally speaking, Luke said, "Pete, I want you to get in the back with the AR. When we get close to the intersection, if there are people right around there or those four wheelers, you to start putting rounds into the blacktop. Try not to hit anyone. If they have any sense at all they will move their asses fast, and we will just roll through there at a decent clip."

Nodding his acknowledgement, Pete, grabbing the old man's AR and a spare magazine out of the front seat pocket and climbed into the bed of the truck, it's rusted out floor flexing under the thin plywood deck.

The spot on the road they were at was rolling hills with wooded sections of oak and maple trees on both sides, many still holding on to their fall colors. Both of them, very familiar with this road, knew they wouldn't be able to see the highway until they were a hundred yards from it because of a slight grade in the little township road just before the stop sign at 63.

That's both good and bad for them, while the little hill will keep them from being seen, it won't stop anyone from hearing the old Chevy so by the time they crested the hill there would be no turning back, even if they could get turned around.

They considered their options and decided that instead of charging ahead blindly, it would be better to scope out the area first. The truck rolled to a gentle stop before cresting the grade. Pete stayed in the back, resting over the roof of the pickup with the rifle in hand as Luke grabbed his binoculars. Quietly slipping into the woods to find good cover, Luke carefully made his way through the underbrush until he could see the road. Peering through the binoculars up and down the highway, Luke scoured the area for any signs of life. However, he didn't spot anyone walking in front of him and only saw one car, just south of the intersection. "There have to be more out there," he thought to himself, turning back the way he came.

Chapter Six

Highway 63 is an incredibly busy piece of blacktop, especially so on Fridays and Mondays. It is the main thoroughfare between the Bayfield and Hayward area's vacation hot spots of Wisconsin to interstate 94. Thousands of people make the trip every weekend to and from these popular destinations from Milwaukee, Chicago and Madison to the south and from the Minneapolis/St Paul metro to the west. Yesterday, Monday, would prove to be no different.

Dave and Joni had just stopped, filling up Daves Honda Accord with gas and picking up some road snacks at the Holiday station. The gas station, located at the intersection of highways 64, 46 and 63, is a place the locals call the "four corners" and it is in the middle of nowhere. There is nothing around the two gas stations and one restaurant that comprise the spot for ten miles in any direction except for farms, fertile grain fields and lush, vibrant woodlots.

The couple, Dave and Joni had been together for a year now, and today they were driving home to Madison from a long weekend getaway in northern Wisconsin. The apartment they share is close to the UW campus where they are both employed. Joni as a Physician Assistant, working at the campus clinic while Dave is employed in the building and grounds maintenance department.

"Hop in Joni, I'll drive for a while," Dave said, watching Joni as she took in the sights, sounds and smells of the dairy air. Driving the obligatory ten over the speed limit, Dave was daydreaming about her upcoming birthday, and the engagement ring he has hidden in their apartment.

"Dammit, my phone died, I was just about send this to scheduling," Joni said. She needed the message to her boss timestamped before the eleven AM scheduling deadline.

"The car is slowing down too," Dave said, the engine suddenly losing power. It wasn't just the engine, the sound system and navigation screen both going blank at the same time. Coasting his Honda to the shoulder, Dave let it roll to a stop, then pulled it off the blacktop. Turning the key once they had stopped, it was like the battery was dead and Dave was instantly pissed.

"I just had a new battery put in at Walmart last week before the trip, I bet they fucked up the install," he told Joni. Releasing the hood latch, he was certain that he'd find one of the cables had come off the battery. He didn't like to have other people work on his car, but it had been a busy week on campus so he bit the bullet and took his chances at Wally World. "Never again," he said to himself as he pulled the door handle to get out of the car, the handle slipping out of his hand. Reaching back and pulling up on the manual door lock, this time when he tried it, the door swung open.

As Dave got out of his car, he stared in astonishment. All the cars on the road had stopped, not just his own. "What the hell is this?" he muttered to himself. There were easily a dozen or more vehicles that he could see looking south down the stretch of road in front of him. A lone pickup truck was stopped in the northbound lane, just in front of him. Turning around, he could see none behind him. He had just rounded a curve and couldn't remember seeing any in his rearview mirror, but he was sure there had to be more.

Dave, walking to the front of the car opened the hood. "Well shit," he said in disappointment, seeing the battery cables still firmly connected. Trying to twist them by hand, the connections didn't budge. Joni, also having to manually unlock her door, walked to where Dave stood as a cold chill hit her like a brick.

"I'm not having a good feeling about this David, what happened, can you fix it?" she asked, a hint of fear in her voice.

"Not sure babe, give me a minute to think," Dave said, looking around. Joni now having tears in her eyes, knew exactly where they were. She had just checked the GPS in the Honda before texting her boss. It said their destination was 248 miles away.

The man in the pickup who was now getting out of his truck didn't even bother opening the hood of his Ford, even if he could open the compartment there wasn't anything in there. The pickup was the new Ford Lightning EV that was all the rage for those who could afford it.

Dave was half leaning, half sitting on the fender of his Honda when the man from the truck started to walk over to him. "Hey," the man said,

"Hey back," Dave said in return.

"Well isn't this the shit, both of our vehicles breaking down at the same spot," the man said.

"It ain't just us," Dave said, nodding his head to the south "look at that mess." Then, glancing towards the guys truck, Dave said "damn man, your truck is smoking."

"Thanks, I just picked it up this morning, that's one of the reasons I spent a hundred and twenty five gra......" He answered.

"No man, I mean it's really smoking, like on fire smoking," Dave said, cutting him off.

"Holy hell, it's only got fifteen fucking miles on it," the man said, running towards the back of the smoldering truck. Opening the tailgate, he pulled a small fire extinguisher out of a side compartment of the bed, remembering it was there when the salesman showed him all the bells and whistles only an hour ago. Dave watched the man as he ran to the passenger side where the smoke was coming from, looking for the source of the now white smoke. Dave wasn't sure what was about to happen, but he has seen enough YouTube videos of electric vehicles catching on fire and they never ended well.

"Hey man, don't to get too close, those batteries could explode," Dave yelled out, trying to warn the man. But as soon as he got the words out of his mouth the truck erupted with a huge "whoosh", a towering plume of orange colored smoke rising vertical in the still morning air.

Looking around, Dave couldn't see the guy through the smoke as he was on the other side of the truck when it blew. He hoped he was ok but there was no way in hell he was going to get near enough to that inferno to check. In about a minute the drivers side began to blow out the same white smoke and almost as soon as it did, that part of the battery blew up with the same "whoosh".

With the side now facing them going up in flames, the intensity of the inferno caused Dave and Joni to move to the passenger side of his car to shield themselves from the heat. Dave and Joni spent the rest of the day there, watching the Ford smolder while sitting in the passenger side of the Honda with the doors open. No one came to investigate the huge plume of smoke, no cops, no fire department - no one.

The fire took hours to burn itself down to the point where Dave felt comfortable enough to go check on the fate of the guy. He didn't see him through the smoke earlier as it burned and Dave was hoping that he just took off down the narrow road that went to the east. Looking from Dave's car, the truck was just a smoldering pile of ash on the side of the road, and getting closer, there was very little left that resembled a vehicle. The only thing he could make out were the wheels, the tires completely burned off of them.

Walking cautiously, Dave made a wide loop around the remains of fire. Looking towards the ditch, he saw the man's brand new "Ford Tough" baseball cap he was wearing laying in the grass with obvious burns around the edges. Not knowing what became of him, Dave felt a tinge of guilt for not helping the man, yet at the same time, he really didn't care.

Neither Dave or Joni wore a watch but they could tell by the shadows that it was getting close to sundown. Joni, as she slowly began to comprehend their situation, felt the mild panic begin to grip her as the hair on her arms stood up. "If no one of authority came to investigate the truck fire, then who is going to come and help us?" she wondered to herself.

"What are we going to do David?" she asked, and in a rather defeated voice she finished with "we're screwed, aren't we?"

"Na baby, we ain't screwed. Let's get our sleeping bags out of the trunk and camp out here for the night, we have plenty of water in there and some chips and stuff. When we get up tomorrow we'll take what we can with us and start walking," Dave said flatly.

"Walking!" she exclaimed, "Walk where, how in the hell are we going to walk all the way to Madison?" she continued. Dave knew she was upset because she had only called him "David" once since they started dating, and that was when early on in their relationship she had busted him red handed for checking out another girls ass. Dave knew better at that moment and didn't crack a joke.

He also was well aware that there was absolutely nothing humorous about their situation. Laying the seats back in the Honda, the two rolled their bags out, each able to get horizontal in the little car. When it was almost dark, they decided they had better pee before trying to sleep. Joni, walking into the ditch away from the car pulled her pants down to pee while Dave, giving her some privacy, took to the the shoulder. Walking north a dozen yards before relieving himself, Dave could see the green sign at the intersection they were just past, it said 140th Ave. Dave, finishing up just as Joni was pulling her pants up heard the sound. Dave wasn't sure what it was, it might have been something or something's with an engine, but there was a low, growling sound in there too.

"Get in the car," Dave yelled to Joni, who needed no encouragement.

Running to the open car door, Joni jumped in the passenger side, pulling the door closed behind her. Dave, still outside of the car, watched and listened as the noise grew nearer. Alarmed but not panicked, Dave stepped back to his car as the the group of five or maybe six ATV's pulled onto the highway from the east. Turning towards his car, the bright headlights of the ATV's lit Dave up, nearly blinding him. Shielding his eyes with one hand after the machines stopped he saw a silhouette walking in front of a machine and towards him. Dave had no idea what this group was up to, as of yet no one spoke. As the form came closer Dave broke the ice, trying to stop the form from getting closer by saying "hey, what's the word?"

"There ain't no word," came the reply from the form as it kept walking towards him. Dave caught the motion of another silhouette getting off a machine, coming toward him too.

"What are you folks up to?" Dave said, not liking the situation while putting himself into an offensive fighting position.

Still walking, the first form kept coming until he was almost in Dave's face and said "that ain't none of your fucking business," his breath reeking of alcohol. "Check the car," the form said to the one behind him.

"I ain't got shit in the car, hell I haven't even had a drink of water since this morning," Dave said, trying to bullshit the guy into backing off.

"The fuck you don't, you calling me stupid, I saw that chick get in the car, I been watching you from down the road, saw your woman pissing in the ditch," the form said.

Being this close, Dave could now make out the man's features. He was big, not huge, maybe in his late twenties and besides alcohol, he smelled like cow shit. Daves mind was connecting dots as fast as they appeared as the guy in front of him yelled to the second man.

"GET HER!" the man yelled.

Hearing that Dave snapped, not in panic but into action. Dave held a Black Belt in Kempo Goju, a brutal Japanese martial arts form. Dave's his right leg flew out, the snap of his pants audible as his hips turned into the man and the top of Dave's shoe exploded the testicles of the man in front of him. The form bending at the waist was met by Dave's left knee as it came up, crushing the man's nose and sending him to his back unconscious on the blacktop. The instant the man hit the ground Dave saw the muzzle flash, feeling his chest collapse.

Dave could hear Joni screaming but he could not will his body to move, to protect her. Trying to call her name, all that came from his mouth was the pink, frothy blood that ran down his cheeks. Dave could see her now, his Joni. She is so beautiful, her slender frame and long blond hair silhouetted by the bright light that enveloped them. He was kneeling now, Joni standing in front of him, her hands over her mouth. As the tears began to form in her beautiful brown eyes she began to cry. Dave, looking up at her in longing anticipation when finally after what seemed like an eternity and with a gigantic smile on her beautiful face, she said yes.

He reached for her, stretching to take her hand as Joni began slipping further and further away until he could no longer see her gorgeous face. Then he was gone.

Chapter Seven

Luke navigated his way back through the dense brush until he was safely behind the crest of the hill. From there, he made his way out of the woods and onto the small road where the old man's truck was parked. When he arrived, Pete was fast asleep and sprawled out on the roof of the truck. Luke walked the short distance to the truck and gave the hood a good slap, successfully waking Pete from his unplanned slumber.

"That's a good way to get schwacked," Luke said.

"Sorry man, I'm fucking beat," Pete said yawning, trying his best to shake the cobwebs from his brain.

"No sweat, I saw one car on 63 through the trees, but that's it, let's roll out there, but be ready to unload that fucker if you see anyone," Luke said, pointing to the rifle Pete held.

Inching down the slight grade on 140th Avenue, they slowly pulled out onto highway 63, no people walking were in sight. Pete, being in the bed of the truck had an excellent view both directions and almost instantly noticed a body lying next by a black Honda Accord.

"Holy fuck Luke, there a body over there, to our right," Pete yelled, slapping the roof.

Stopping, Luke got out, leaving the truck idling in park with Pete soon at his side. "Hold on," Luke said as he reached down, picking up a spent shotgun shell, a 2 and 3/4 inch Remington 00 buckshot round. "What the fuck. Wanna check it out?" Luke asked.

"Might as well," Pete said.

Walking up to the body, the poor bastard on the ground took what looked to be a full load of buckshot to the chest, bleeding out.

"Looks like he's been here a while, probably overnight, see here, the critters already got to his eyeballs," Luke said pointing with a small stick at the man's hollow eye sockets. Checking out the car, the drivers doors were locked, but the passenger side was hanging open. Pete, looking around inside saw a small Coach brand purse under an empty bag of chips and picking it up, scanning through it's contents, he found a drivers license belonging to a woman named Joni James, from Madison.

The picture on the license showed a beautiful woman with long blonde hair and according to the birth date on the card she is 36 years old, soon to be 37. Continuing his search, Pete also found a couple of cell phones, sleeping bags, a few empty water bottles ..that was it.

"Holy shit, what in the fuck is happening here?" Pete nearly shouted.

Luke, still walking around saw the burned remains of the Ford EV, although he didn't know what it was. It was still warm as he was kicking the debris as his foot caught on something. Raising his boot out of the rubble revealed what looked like a leg bone from someone. "Well, I donno what happened over here but someone got cooked in this thing," Luke said, staring at the charred bone.

Walking over, Pete looked at the smoldering pile seeing an aluminum wheel. "This is, sorry, this was, a Ford Lightning, their EV pickup. You see that lightning bolt engraved in the cap of the wheel," Pete said, "that's their marketing logo."

"Fuck me," Luke said. "The old man is right, we got hit with an EMP. I mean think about it for a minute, what else could cause all this? It had to have been a nuke in space," Luke said.

"Can't disagree, what do you think happened to the girl, Joni?" Pete asked.

"Fuck if I know, but my best guess would be that who ever put that poor fucker in the dirt probably has her," Luke said.

"Who the fuck would do this shit, really, what the fuck is wrong with people," Pete trailed off on that one.

"Donno, same type that popped Brian I suppose. Let's get the fuck out of here, this girl could have just as well had been Amy," Luke said anxiously.

Leaving this shit show, they were guessing the time was still before noon. Not seeing anyone on 63, not alive anyway, the two hopped backed into the truck, slowly crossing 63 on 140th. With only seven miles to go until they hit 280th street, it would then be a straight shot down to Luke and Amy's place. They will be there in fifteen minutes, tops.

After driving just a half mile down the road on 140th, Pete shouted "stop man, I gotta hurl."

With Luke slamming on the brakes and pulling to a stop, Pete jumped out, puking before his feet hit the ground. Pete was not a hard man, and as his brain digested what he'd just seen, his stomach revolted in a violent manner, spewing his breakfast from this morning into the long grass of the ditch.

Luke is a tough guy, but his kryptonite is watching or hearing someone else puke. He shut the truck down as his stomach let go of it's contents as well.

Leaning against the box of the truck, wiping their mouths on their sleeves, Pete asked "hear that?"

"Hear what?" Luke asked.

Pete was fully back in check now and said "a scream, I heard a scream from over there I think," as he pointed in front of them and to the right.

"I didn't hear shit," Luke said.

"That's because you can't hear shit anymore. I know I heard a chick scream," Pete replied.

"It could be anything, maybe a rabbit," Luke said.

"No man, I've heard that noise before. That wasn't a rabbit, that was the sound of sheer terror, we gotta check it out," Pete said as he reached in the truck for the Remington 870.

"Pete, man, we are almost to my place, are you certain about this, I mean you just puked your guts out," Luke said to Pete. Then came the completely unmistakable faint sound of a woman wailing in fear off in the woods that they both heard.

"Ok, that settles that," Luke said, pulling the key from the old Chevy, setting the 5 gallon gas can on the seat before locking the doors. After checking the slide of his Glock 19 confirming it has a round chambered and slinging his old man's AR15 over his head, Luke put two of the three 30 round magazines he'd brought along in his back pocket, next to the spare Glock magazine.

Picking up the 870 Remington pump shotgun loaded with slugs Pete did the same, making sure there was a round in the chamber and four in the tube and also checking his cargo pockets for the two extra boxes of #4 buck he'd brought along. Doing a quick radio check while walking, the two were formulating their plan on the fly.

The noise they'd heard came from maybe two hundred yards in front of them and about fifty or a hundred yards to the south, in the woods. Walking slowly down the shoulder, their boots crunching on the loose gravel, they abruptly stopped after seeing what looked like a driveway seventy five yards ahead of them going south into the woods.

Whispering to Pete, Luke said "it had to have come from down that trail, I'll cut in here and head south, you go ahead, but stay low, cut in before you get to the driveway, if it's a group, they will probably have someone on watch if they have their shit together."

Creeping south as quietly as possible through the thick underbrush, Luke was excitedly nervous, not afraid, as a small old trailer house soon came into Luke's view. Pulling his radio, Luke keyed the mic saying "contact."

Replying, Pete pressed his "talk" button once, breaking the squelch.

Looking through his binoculars, Luke saw 5 older ATV's of various brands parked in front of the run down trailer with three guys sitting outside drinking what looked like Budweisers. That meant there were at least two more inside. Keying the mic again, Luke said quietly "get yourself close enough to be in range and lay low, I'll send one round north to draw them out, do not fire, wait for me to take the last one that comes out the door then open up."

"Roger," Pete replied tersely, wiping sweat from his brow.

After painstakingly crawling on his belly through the tangled brush of the mixed woodlot, Pete peered over the ancient oak root ball front of him, a mere thirty yards from the trailer. The sweet smell of earth and decomposing leaves actually having a calming effect on his nerves, and as he watched the three men outside the beer in their hands was making Pete thirsty.

Keying his radio, Pete said quietly "in range."

Luke silently worked his way through the underbrush to within fifty yards of the 10 by 50 trailer. Checking the rear of the structure for an exit, he found none. Turning back to the north, he said to himself "This'll do," after finding decent cover behind a downed box elder tree. This position, northwest of the trailer offered a clear field of fire, one he could easily capitalize on. Checking the optic on the old man's rifle, the red dot lit up.

Pointing the barrel north, Luke fired one round off. Immediately after the shot he brought the barrel of the rifle back to the trailer where the three men outside were now on their feet searching furiously for the source of the gunshot.

Training the rifle on the door, Luke's eyes were burning a hole through the optic as the door latch opened.

"Who in the fuck is doing the shooting out here," a younger man in bib overalls, pistol in hand, screamed while stepping out the door onto the rickety porch while slinging a strap of the overalls over his shoulder.

"There's gotta be at least one more," Luke said to himself, waiting just moments until the next man emerged in the doorway hunched over and looking very rough. So rough, it looked like he'd just gotten his ass handed to him, he even had rolled up blood soaked napkins hanging out of his battered nose.

Centering the red dot on that man's head, Luke's finger tightened on the trigger overcoming the sear sending the 5.56 round into the man's forehead. Luke, watching as his head exploded, witnessed the impact of the fast moving bullet literally blowing the bloody napkins out of his nostrils.

Instantly after Luke's shot came a thunderous "BOOM" from Pete's shotgun. The man closest to Pete flew backwards as if hit by an invisible truck, the one ounce lead slug cratered the man's chest and blowing its contents all over the men behind him covering their bodies and faces with his insides.

Aiming at the body of the man in the overalls, Luke's rifle barked twice, the man's now lifeless form fell off the lowest porch step onto the front cargo rack of a four wheeler.

Another BOOM then another rang out from Pete's 870 as the leaves in front of Pete's barrel began floating back to earth as the last man standing crumpled to the ground. The trailer boys were caught in a devastating crossfire and in less that five seconds all five were down either dead or shortly to be.

"Fuck me, I sure hope she's in there because we just raised holy hell with someone," Luke said to himself. Keying his mic, luke said "cover me, I'll go do a sneak and peak."

Pete replied with a terse "roger that," as Luke slowly made his way to the trailer.

Knowing there's no exit on the backside, Luke stayed in Pete's view, watching for movement in the thick brush making sure there wasn't any more of them lurking around outside. Taking in the gnarly scene as he approached the pile of men, Luke's senses were nearly overloaded. The dark smell of cordite and the iron scent of blood hung heavy in the now stillness of the woods. Pete's shotgun at that close range devastated the three men he'd shot. It's impact sending gore of every manner onto the side of the shack, covering the ground behind them and causing Luke to shudder at the sight in front of him.

Signaling Pete forward, the two met at the west end of the shack, away from the five bodies."We can't both go in at the same time," Luke said.

"I'll go first, you follow me in," Pete said, pulling his Smith and Wesson handgun. Not knowing what they would find when they got inside, Luke slung the rifle over his back, drawing his Glock as Pete tentatively took a step inside. Luke hadn't even made it inside before Pete yelled out "holy shit man, get in here."

Laying naked on a filthy, raggedy mattress with her hands tied behind her back was Joni, Pete instantly recognizing her face from the picture on her drivers license. Pulling his folding Buck knife from his pocket, Pete carefully and gently cut her bindings before rolling her up in a stained blanket lying on the floor beside her. She was conscious, but not aware, no doubt in shock. Finding what he assumed were her pants and shirt among the scattered garbage covering the floor, Luke picked them up as Pete gently draped her limp body over his huge shoulder, carrying her out of the dank trailer.

Outside, Pete was livid, madman livid. The anger and hate built up inside him so quickly that he nearly exploded. Walking past by the five dead men Pete raised his size 13 combat boot, viciously stomping each of their skulls. Calmly, Luke asked "feel better now?"

"Almost," Pete replied, turning back the first man Luke had shot, kicking him off the cargo rack before repeatedly thrusting his boot down on the man's already evacuated head until it was unrecognizable.

"How about now?" Luke asked.

"Yep, I'm good now," Pete replied solemnly, spitting on the disfigured corpse.

"We made a lot of noise just now, if there are any more of them around they will probably come a running," Luke said looking around cautiously.

"I don't think this girl was their first one, I'm pretty sure I saw a purse and another shirt," Pete said, his heart still racing as they walked quietly to the road.

"Well, she was their last," Luke said taking sneak peek both directions after the pair emerged from the end of the old logging trail.

Waving Pete ahead after being convinced the coast was clear the pair began walking the short distance to the old truck. Before leaving to go in the woods, Luke had set a live 9mm round in a precarious position on the flat mirror mount of the drivers door, it was in such a position that if anyone tried the doors or even opened the tailgate it would have fallen off. It was makeshift, but it was still there. Climbing into the back of the truck, Pete gently laid Joni down, telling Luke he'd ride back there with Luke's rifle while keeping an an eye on her and stay on watch at the same time.

Amy had been busy. While she wasn't exactly sure what had happened, she had been involved in enough conversations with Luke and his dad to take a stab at it being either an EMP or a solar flare, however she had all but written off the flare. Amy is a news junkie and has been watching the Iran war unfold, and unfold in a troubling way to her. In her mind she thought the US was quite overly aggressive in its response. Who knows, maybe the administration considers what they are doing as proportional, or maybe they were actually trying escalate the conflict to the next level, which was nuclear.

She allowed her mind dwell on all the what if's and let that apprehension be her motivator to keep packing stuff. She absolutely knew Luke would be back and while she was very worried about him and his whereabouts, she also knew where he was yesterday morning around the time the lights went out.

"That's a 40 mile walk," she said to herself while doing the math. "At two miles an hour walking that's a 20 hour walk home if his truck was in the same shape as my Honda SUV," she thought . Luke had told her before in their conversations that the old green Chevy *should* be EMP proof, but it had been upgraded to an electronic ignition and he had no idea if that would fry or not. She guessed it had, or he would have certainly been home by now, a full 27 hours later.

Amy wasn't thrilled about leaving her hobby farm that she has worked so hard on and invested so much time and money in, but she did know why they had to leave, at least temporarily. Her farm is exactly one mile north of US highway 12 and when the exodus began from the Twin Cities they would be sitting ducks out there, just like the few neighbors they had.

All of the emergency supplies had already been packed away, so Amy only needed to drag the bins close to the side door. As she was finishing up packing some spices and thinking about what other supplies she needed, she was interrupted by an engine noise coming from the east. The weather was pleasant, so she had let her Great Pyrenees dog, Clover, outside on watch. Clover had positioned herself on the front porch, ready to raise hell with anyone who tried to jump the fence. Seeing that Amy was peering out of the south kitchen window, Clover instinctively moved closer, growling as she heard the sound of the engine getting closer and slowing down.

Nervously, Amy picked up her Remington shotgun, a gift Luke had given her for Christmas the first year they were together, cracking a little smile as the memory returned. Amy knew very well that whatever was coming wasn't Luke, as Clover knows their vehicles, never barking at them. Listening to the noise of the engine getting slower, the front of the brown truck came into view. Recognizing it immediately, she knew it was Luke's dad's truck as her heart sank when she couldn't see who was driving.

"Luke slowly pulled past their gated driveway so that he could back the trailer in, then stopped the truck and got out to open the gate. After seeing that it was Luke in the truck, Amy dashed out of the house to the gate, still holding the shotgun in one hand. She wrapped her other arm around Luke as she sobbed uncontrollably, releasing the worry she'd tried too hard to contain."

"It's all right baby," Luke said softly, trying to to console her. "Baby, I gotta get off the road before anyone sees us, where's the key to the lock?" Luke asked.

Amy, coming around from her release of emotions said, "yeah, sorry about that, hang on, I wired it to the garden fence."

After unlocking the padlock on the chain and sliding the rickety gate to the side, Luke backed the trailer in between the house and the garage. Pete hadn't moved, focusing on watching the road out front until Luke stopped, Pete then made his way to the tailgate, jumping out.

Amy, quickly walking to the truck for a real hug from Luke, saw the body of a woman wrapped up in a filthy blanket, with only her head sticking out. Shrieking, Amy jumped back. "What the fuck is that, what the fuck is that?," She screamed.

"Amy," Luke shouted, "hold on, hold on, this isn't what it looks like." Luke knew better from past experiences not use the common phrase of "calm down", finding out the hard way that those words have the opposite effect on a hysterical woman, especially the little redhead, Amy.

"Did you kill her?" Amy asked frantically.

"No, no, no Amy, it's a long story, but we came across a group of shit heads that had taken her after they killed her husband," Luke replied, as calmly as possible.

Pete, walking up now, seeing Amy was relaxing a bit said, "her boyfriend I think, I saw his wallet on the seat and his name was Dave, I forgot his last name but she is Joni. Joni James."

"Amy, she's in a bad way, I don't know for certain but I think the guys that took her did some terrible things to her. I mean it was fairly obvious, she was tied up naked when we found her. Pete rolled her up in the blanket to stay warm and, well, cover her. We grabbed what we thought were her pants and shirt, there were other clothes there too," Luke said.

Luke wasn't sure she understood what "other clothes" meant, but he stopped talking. Stopping just in time too as all three of them heard a faint sound come from the form in the back of the truck, two word "thank you."

As fast as Amy became hysterical a minute earlier, her demeanor changed 180° and she was in the back of the truck on her knees next to the girl in the blink of an eye. With Joni's head in her lap she brushed the hair from her face, asking Pete for his water bottle.

"Would you like a drink of water?" she asked. Nodding her head slightly, Joni signaled yes. Gently lifting her head, Amy held the bottle to her lips.

After taking a small drink, Joni was able to speak slightly clearer, saying "thank you, you saved me."

"You're welcome, but I didn't save you, those two did," Amy said, motioning with her head to Luke and Pete.

"No, I mean YOU saved me, I heard you screaming, I didn't know where it came from but I heard you screaming," Joni replied quietly.

Noticing Joni looking at the water bottle, Amy understood she needed more, helping her take a drink from the bottle. After a few seconds passed Joni said, "I was in shock, almost gone, all I could see were two tiny pinholes of light, everything else was black. Then hearing you scream in the darkness, I knew I wasn't there anymore, I knew those men weren't.....," she trailed off, sobbing softly, almost silently.

Holding Joni in her lap as she cried, Amy said through her own tears while rocking back and forth, "you're safe now," over and over until they both stopped crying.

Looking at the two, Lukes eyes were leaking now too and as he wiped the tears away he said, "Baby, see if she can get up, if she can could you help get her cleaned up and maybe find her some fresh clothes, we really need to keep moving."

Nodding her head, Amy said, "yes, I can."

"Me and Pete will load all this stuff while you are doing that, and wow, you have sure been busy. I'm glad I took the old man's trailer," Luke said, looking at the mountain of neatly stacked bins on the front porch.

"Yeah, I was. Packing all that crap kept me from worrying about you so much," Amy replied.

"Would you two mind giving us a little privacy here, and I will try to…," Amy said, before being cut off by Joni saying, "if you can get me out of whatever I am wrapped up in I think I can walk." Both Amy and Luke were shocked, sharing a glance. This lady was coming around fast.

"It must be the water," Luke said to no one in particular. Dropping the tailgate for them, Luke then met Pete behind the garage, where Pete was having his own emotional breakdown.

The two women, crawling to the back of the truck stopped when Amy called out, "a little help here Luke." Luke, instantly emerging from behind the garage, helped them both down, Amy first and then Joni.

Joni, making eye contact for a moment with Luke mouthed the words, "thank you."

It took the two men around 45 minutes of balls to the wall working to load all the bin's in the back of the truck and the trailer. Luke threw a couple of hay bales up to the front of the truck box for seats, and looking at the trailer while wiping his forehead he said, "I'm gonna load my four wheeler, it's in the shed there. I'll truss those two hogs and get them in the trailer too, that sow is going to drop pretty soon."

"It's gonna be a tight fit," Pete said.

"For sure, but the hogs won't mind, hell, I'm gonna crate up some of Amy's chickens quick too," Luke replied.

"It's gotta be damn near three o'clock," Luke said to himself, looking at the waning sun after the loading was finished. "I do NOT want to be on the roads after dark, so we have three hours, four max, to get to the ranch before the old man comes looking for us," he continued.

"We gotta take a different route man, I don't wanna go anywhere near that fucking dairy farm again. I could smell the cow shit on those boys that took Joni. They had to be workers from there," Pete exclaimed as he walked to the truck, brushing dust off his shirt..

"Good idea, we can cross 63 a mile or two further south and then get back on the same route we took here. I'd love to take a few stretches of highway to make some good time but after this shit show there's no way we should risk that," Luke said, scanning the immediate area.

Being led out of the house by Amy in fresh clothes, Joni looked much better. "Why are you packing all this?" Joni asked.

"We are bugging out," Luke said.

Joni looked at Amy for more. "We have to leave here, it's not safe to stay. We are going to Luke's dad's place, the ranch. It's a long ride but you will be fine with me in the truck," Amy explained.

"I'm going with you?" Joni asked quizzically.

Amy was stunned for a moment at the question. She didn't know how many more times she could be stunned today, but she answered, "of course Joni, you can get better out there. Luke's dad, the old man, has the ranch set up really well, he was expecting something like this sooner or later."

Now Joni was stunned and began to cry again while she hugged Amy. "I don't know what to say, when I'm better I can help out. I'm a Physician Assistant at the U in Madison," she said through her sobs.

"Let's worry about that later, it's time to go," Amy said, gently ushering Joni to the cab of the truck.

Leaving their farm, Luke and Amy didn't lock anything, not even the front gate. Doing so would just mean there would be more to fix when or if they came back. They were both well aware that the place would be raided, anything of value would be long gone.

Deciding after a brief conversation to use the same plan of attack to cross all the highways, Luke fired up the truck, then as he and Amy took one very sad last look at the farm, they drove away.

Their plan was a good one. If people were walking anywhere near the intersections, Pete would send three or four rounds into the blacktop from a distance forcing people to scatter for the ditches. The group only needed to use that tactic once on the highway 64 crossing when they came upon a group of ten or twelve right at the intersection walking to the west towards New Richmond, probably coming from the direction of the very busy Four Corners.

Rolling close to the intersection, Pete nearly toppled out of the truck while firing his first round into the blacktop. Clover, being tied to Pete's belt on a short leash tried to bolt at the shot. Pete is a big guy, a solid 265 pounds and the big dog almost took him over the side rails of the box. Gathering his balance and getting right back into it, Pete quickly fired three more shots well in front of the walkers, sending people diving for the tall grass of the ditches. Watching the group of people after traversing the road, Pete felt bad for them as they got up dusting themselves off, yelling at the truck and flipping them the bird after they drove through.

Chapter Eight

JT was awoken from his slumber by the sound of one of the dogs barking. At first, he thought it was part of his dream, but as the barking continued, he fully emerged from his sleep. Listening to Duke's deep baritone "woof," JT scanned the yard for the dog. After a little searching, he finally located Duke just south of the shop, barking loudly at a turkey vulture soaring in the sky.

"Quiet boy," JT yelled out, not even phasing the dog. He didn't know what it is with him and birds though.

After taking a leak behind the shop, JT took a seat at the picnic table and began reflecting on the situation. The temperature was pleasant, in the mid sixties he guessed, not bad for October in Wisconsin. Inevitably though winter was coming and if what he thought happened, happened, he would have no expectations of the power coming back beforehand, if ever.

Not expecting great things, JT let his mind wander back to his old career after the Air Force as a crane operator. While he held a degree in civil engineering, the office environment never sat well with him, he has always been a "hands on" guy. As an operator, he had placed many of those massive transformers back in the day, one of them, the biggest one, weighed in at 245,000 pounds. It was delivered by rail to a siding, then loaded on a specialized trailer made by "Goldhoeffer" that was towed by two huge Peterbuilt all wheel drive tractors with another one behind it on a push beam. They hauled that transformer on the trailer that had 200 wheels and tires on a road specially designed for the occasion.

The trailer would be guided to an "x" painted on the road that was safely inside the lifting radius of the crane JT ran. His crew would then rig the transformer with heavy chokers and shackles and on signal, he would take up the load with the crane. Once it was free of the trailer he would swing it around 180° and lower it on to the concrete pad that like the road, was specifically designed and built for this unit.

Then, after all the different tradesmen were done and packed up, the infrastructure that was built to move and set the unit was removed, being recycled for another time, including the roads and rail spurs.

And being a civil engineer, JT knew there is no way in hell that that process could be replicated today, absolutely zero chance. Even attempting a repair would be nearly impossible. The logistics of this were exhausting to even think about and lucky for him, he was brought out of that temporary trance by the aroma of something delicious coming from the house.

Inside, JT's mom was amazingly still in the kitchen, standing over the stove. Going inside he said, "Jeepers Ma, what smells so good?"

"There was three racks of pork ribs in the freezer so I took them out and put them in the Dutch Oven on the stove," she said, wiping her old hands on her apron.

"Well they smell fantastic, and I'm getting hungry," he said.

"It would be nice if the oven worked, but this will do for now. Say, we are about out of water in here, the tub is empty and there is only half a bucket of drinking water left," she replied.

"I'll get right on it boss," JT said with a laugh, giving his silver haired mother a quick kiss on her cheek.

Looking at the clock on the wall, it was nearly 4 in the afternoon. "Damn, I got some good sleep in that chair," JT said to himself as he wondered if Brian was up yet. That question was answered when Pepper came out of the camper, stretching, followed by Brian who was doing the same thing.

"Morning," JT said, "or afternoon, whatever it is."

"Back at ya, and thanks for borrowing me your dog. She sure kept me warm in there, anything happening, what was Duke barking at?" Brian asked.

"Nothing, birds. He hates em," JT said, then continuing on, he said "Nothing's happening that I know of, but I just woke up too. I suppose that I'd better get my radio and turn it on. I've got a slick line antenna for it already hanging from that maple tree over there, I think I'll get it and plug it in, it's got decent volume so we should be able to hear them if they call," he said.

"What time do you figure they will be back and what the hell is a slick line?" Brian asked curiously.

"It's an antenna extension. If it all went well, they should be back anytime now, but we'll see I suppose. How's the leg?" JT asked.

"Tender, I mean it sure let me know it was there when I rolled over on my right side a bit ago, but I'll live," Brian said.

"I need to pull the jenny out and run some water, wanna give me a hand with that?" JT asked.

"Absolutely," Brian answered.

JT knew the generator would run, it started yesterday before he went to get Kate and his mom from New Richmond. What he was going to do was back feed the house through a 240 volt outlet that he uses for his old Lincoln arc welder. The circuit for that uses a dual pole 40 amp breaker which will now become the main breakers.

Going into the house to the closet where the breaker box is located, JT used a penlight to see while shutting off the main breakers that went to the meter, then he turned off all of the breakers in the panel.

Years ago, he'd made a "suicide" cord for the generator, its name derived from the fact that it has male connections on both ends. Plugging one end of the cord into the generator and the other into the welder outlet, JT then started the engine. Going back inside the house to the breaker box, he flipped the welder breakers to the on position, energizing both sides of the panel with split phase power, then finally did the same to the dual pole 20 amp breaker for the well pump. The engine on the generator barely changed pitch as it took up the load of the well pump starting and JT signaled Brian to go a head and start filling cans from the hydrant by the barn.

Going into the bathroom JT turned the water on to the bathtub and it began to fill. Brian had come up with four more pails and was filling everything he could find while JT was filling the tub. After ten minutes he opened the breakers to the well pump and the welder, then going outside, he shut the generator down. In less than ten minutes they had filled eight 5 gallon bucket's, the horse water bins and got about half a bathtub of water pumped. In those minutes the generator burned about one cup of gas. "Not bad," JT said to himself. About the only drawback to using the generator was the noise, it's a dead giveaway to anyone paying attention.

With his injured leg, Brian could only carry one pail at a time as they brought the heavy pails of water into the house. Those buckets of water would be covered and used for drinking and cooking, while the bathtub water was primarily for flushing the toilet and some dish washing.

"Brian, why don't you get your gear together and set yourself up in the camper, we may as well use it as long as we can," JT said.

"Good plan, thanks pops," Brian said.

"I'm gonna gather some gear and get ready to go look around for Luke, Amy and Pete if they don't show up pretty soon. It's damn near 5 and I'd be lying if I said I wasn't getting worried," JT said, a worried tone to his voice.

"Yeah, I'm not getting a very good vibe about all this myself. I'd offer to go with you but I know you'll say no," Brian said.

"Correct, we probably shouldn't leave the place unattended, well, maybe we could for a little while, but it's just not worth taking the chance. Brian, did you guys bring a battle rifle with you, Luke has mine and I don't have anything else here that can cover for that?" JT asked.

"No, we don't have any AR's, just shotguns and hunting rifles," Brian replied

"It's cool, I have an old H&R single shot like Pete has and my handgun. Anyway, thanks, I'll go grab a couple boxes of buck and get it ready in case I need to head out," JT replied.

"Say Brian, mom's cooking ribs on the stove, after we're done with the water, would you mind firing up the smoker, we can use it as a grill and finish cooking the ribs out here?" JT asked.

"On it pops," Brian replied.

Crossing highway 65 Luke could see people, probably the same people he'd noticed while crossing this morning he guessed. Up and down the highway were a dozen or more people standing by their now useless automobiles and he wondered what in the world they were thinking. Why were they still there? Were they just hoping their car would magically start or their cell phones would come back to life so they could call for help? Maybe they just didn't have any place to go.

Then it hit him, they simply had absolutely no idea what happened. It's been said that only about 5% of the country are prepared for enduring a disaster and he imagined that only a fraction of those people even knew what an EMP was. "Thanks old man," he said to himself. If it wasn't for all those post apocalyptic books he read after the old man was done with them he would be just like these folks, clueless.

"See that big divot in the road, and that chunk of a tire?" he asked, turning his attention to Amy.

"Yeah, what about it?" Amy asked curiously.

"The hunk of rubber is off my truck, the groove in the road is from the wheel when I hit the brakes," he replied.

"Oh," she said thoughtfully.

Coming up quick is the next road they need to cross, Wall Street. While seeing far fewer people standing around cars, they did take notice of plenty of people out in their yards while driving by a large housing development. Smoke was visible around the area, rising from grills and fire pits on peoples patios and decks. "Damn, I'm starving," Luke thought, catching the scent of something delicious.

Running west now on county road C, Luke sped up to around 50 miles per hour. He knew there are cars he would have to maneuver around so he didn't want to go too fast, especially pulling the full trailer. In about a mile, they would be passing a little roadhouse on the Apple River called The Outpost.

Driving by the popular establishment earlier this morning, the place appeared empty and now slowing as they came closer, he was surprised seeing smoke coming from the patio area on the far side of the structure. "The owners of The Outpost must have fired up their big catering grill. I bet they are cooking whatever is left in their coolers," Luke mentioned to Amy as she looked longingly at the smoke plume and it's deliciously smelling scents.

After driving past the joint, half dozen people outside smiled and waved their beers at the old truck as they cruised by. This caused Luke to breathe a sigh of relief, as all their human encounters so far had not been so social. Just after crossing the bridge over the Apple River, they took a quick right turn then a left onto 210th, the home stretch. Looking over at Amy, he smiled weakly and said, "Almost there." They continued heading west on 210th until they reached 80th street, where they took a left turn. After driving for another half mile, they finally turned right onto 205th. With just one more mile to go before their last big intersection at Highway 35, their last major obstacle was finally within sight.

He didn't like this approach though because it's a blind intersection both directions with an uphill grade to the highway. He for sure wasn't planning on stopping, they were so close to the ranch that he didn't want to scope it out like him and Pete did at Highway 63 where they found Joni's boyfriend dead. Sliding open the rear window of the cab, Luke called out to Pete. "Pete, cover the right side, I'll cover left." If anyone was there, Luke knew they would be heard well before they would cross because of those loud assed Thrush mufflers the old man put on the truck, and climbing that grade with the loaded truck and trailer, those things will be cackling like a lit brick of firecrackers.

Driving up the grade to the highway, Luke cringing as the loud pipes echoed off of the stone retaining wall to his left said "Damn Pete, check out that crowd to the south," he said as they rolled through the intersection.

"Looks like that bar is still a hot spot, even after the apocalypse, what's that, a half mile away?" Pete asked.

"Exactly that far," Luke said, gunning the engine of the truck after the crossing.

Now only a short distance from the ranch, Luke began digging around in the pocket of the seat cover for the radio. Finding it, he keyed the mic making the call "shredder inbound," using his nickname as a call sign.

Walking by the smoker as Brian was moving some gear into the camper, he heard the radio call. Answering the call with, "roger, I'll let the old man know," Brian then headed to the shop where JT was coiling up the generator cord, "they're on their way back, Luke just called on the radio," Brian said.

"Thanks, its getting late. Did he say where they were, or how far out they are?" JT asked, walking to the maple tree where the radio was.

"Nope, he just said he's inbound," Brian replied.

Grabbing the radio, JT keying the mic asking "what's your location?"

"Little over a mile from the county road on 205th," came Luke's reply.

"Roger that, take it real slow, I'm gonna sweep the road to "I", see ya in a bit," JT said.

Hopping on the Polaris, JT took off up the driveway, the shortened H&R 12 gauge in his lap with a round of number four buckshot in the chamber. Seeing nothing to his left at the end of the driveway, he turned right and up the grade heading east to the county road. There were several houses between his driveway on the mile stretch to the county road. He knew most of the people and has met all of them at one time or another and there were a couple of folks that he considered sketchy, those are the houses he wanted to make sure were clear.

He didn't see anyone outside until going by Fred's house, who was outside feeding his hounds. Fred is a solid guy, a Vietnam vet that JT had known almost his entire life. Waving at Fred as he rode by, Fred waved back in his usual happy manner.

Arriving at the stop sign of the intersection JT could see the old truck, just rounding the curve past 205th. Actually hearing it before seeing it, JT thought that pretty soon he'd better find a way to quiet that thing down. Slowly pulling out on the county road, JT headed south towards the truck, scanning the area for people.

A short distance from where 205th intersects with the county road, there's a house that sits off to the east side of the road on a hill with a long, steep driveway lined with white pines. The old lady who lived there had passed away not long ago, and her family had turned the house into a rental as far as he knew.

Watching the truck coming forward, JT caught movement through those same White Pines, not far from the road. "It's a damn car," he said to himself. The white vehicle was moving silently downhill at a pretty good clip, stopping broadside in the road.

"What the fuck," JT said to himself, watching from fifty yards away as the car abruptly stopped. Momentarily befuddled by what he was watching, JT suddenly began realizing what was taking place. Luke, obviously having noticed the car too had stopped a good 75 yards away from it, JT able to hear the engine of the truck idling as they sat there.

JT watched, seeing one person get out of the passenger side of the white sedan. The rifle in his hand was clearly visible as the man got low, crouching behind the car for cover. Setting the brake on the Polaris, JT hopped off with shotgun in hand, checking the Glock in the holster. Emerging from the other side of the car, the side facing Luke, another man began yelling "get out of the truck, get out of the truck."

Apparently neither of these clowns had noticed JT standing there, in the road, next to a bright blue four wheeler. The guy yelling, now appeared more irate as he stomped around screaming at the truck, waving his hands around like a madman while the other guy was still crouched behind the car.

Pete with his bushy black beard was visible leaning over the cab of the the truck. JT couldn't tell if Pete had a gun or not, and he didn't see anyone else in the truck with Luke. "Why would Pete be riding in the back, and where is Amy?" he said to himself, now worried about her.

In his head this was all happening in slow motion, just like the first time with Kate and his mom. Shouldering the cocked shotgun, JT began slowly walking down the far left side of the road, keeping the truck out of his line of fire. With the soles of his Columbia hiking boots creaking loudly with every step, JT just knew the two guys would eventually hear him coming. Seeming almost amusing to JT, the two in front of him hadn't even looked behind themselves, apparently being completely focused on the truck to the south as they kept up their animated movements and demands.

Taking advantage of the pair being focused on the truck, JT continued walking, stopping just 20 yards away from the car and the crazy guy doing the antics.

While the man was still yelling at Luke to get out of the truck, he turned momentarily, finally seeing JT as he did. Noticing his buddy looking away from the truck, the guy on JT's side stood up, raising his rifle. "Not this time fucker," JT said to himself as his 12 gauge barked, the recoil of the light weight shotgun rocking JT back on his heels. As the man fell to the ground with a blood curdling scream, JT saw a muzzle flash from Pete's position, instantly followed by the loud report of the rifle as the other man went down.

Reloading the shotgun, JT cautiously inched closer towards the downed man on his side of the car. The stricken man, rolling around on the blacktop was in obvious agony, the buckshot peppering him from his neck to his thigh's.

Luke, now running towards the car had a rifle to his shoulder, trained on the guy Pete had shot. Still laying across the roof of the truck, Pete was covering them while scanning the area.

Getting close to the man he'd shot, JT jumped at the sound as Pete's rifle barked three times in rapid succession. Seeing Pete aiming toward the house, JT and Luke, now a hundred feet apart, both turned, looking that direction. JT's view of the house was obstructed by the thick line of trees and he couldn't make out what Pete was firing at.

JT, moving cautiously to the ditch noticed Luke heading into the woods at a crouch about 20 yards south of the driveway, well out of Pete's line of fire. Following Luke with his eyes, JT watched him stop, firing two rounds in quick succession after resting his rifle on a branch.

JT glanced to the truck, seeing Amy leaning against the front fender with a firearm to her shoulder looking in Luke's direction.. "Ah, there she is," he said to himself, relieved to see her except for the firefight they were in.

Feeling like he was watching a movie, JT realized that only a matter of several seconds had passed since he fired his shotgun and the rest of the shooting had begun. Turning his attention back towards the car, JT took notice that the man he'd shot was no longer next to the sedan. Following a rather wide blood trail on the road with his eyes, he spotted the man where he had rolled past the front of the vehicle into the tall grass and was now shakily raising his rifle towards JT. Before the injured man could take aim, the already shouldered short shotgun thundered again at the squeeze of JT's finger, ending the man's misery.

With his hands now shaking uncontrollably from the adrenaline coursing through his body, JT opened the action of the shotgun to reload. The empty hull ejecting from the chamber spiraled up, smacking JT squarely in the forehead as it did. Fumbling with a fresh round, JT dropped it on the ground once before his shaking hands were finally able to insert the shell and close the action with a slap. "Damn man, just put a little hair around it," he said to himself, making his way to the other side of the car. Peeking around the front fender he saw the man Pete shot, slumped over on his right side against the front tire of the car. Seeing him in a puddle of blood, JT assumed the man was quite dead. Pete's 5.56 round had hit him square in the solar plexus, making a hell of a mess.

"Center mass," JT murmured while keeping his shotgun aimed at the man's head. Laying on the ground next to him was a pistol and JT kicked it away from the dead man just in case. Realizing that he had just fucked up by putting himself in the open, JT turned for cover as the crack of a bullet flew past his face so close he could feel the supersonic shockwave. Diving to the blacktop towards the front of the car, another shot rang out. That bullet ricocheted off the road where his feet had just been, sending chunks of blacktop flying.

Somewhere close to the road came another shot, this one not at JT. "That must have been one of the boys or Amy taking that shot," JT thought, while rolling a couple of rotations until he was in front of the car. Looking under the vehicle, JT couldn't see anything beyond the rear tires, the plastic fairing under the front bumper being too low to see past. Crawling on his hands and knees a few feet and peeking around the front end of the car, JT saw the view clear all the way to the damned house. Whoever was shooting from that direction knew JT was there, and he was pinned down.

Even if he could see who it was he was screwed. Being only armed with a sawed off shotgun and a pistol, JT knew neither one of them would do him any good from his position. The house was well out of his range, at least a hundred and fifty yards up the hill.

Still in the back of the truck scanning the woods, Pete never moved his eyes from the sights of his rifle. "He must have a decent view from up there," JT thought, as Pete's rifle fired again.

Luke had seen where the shot that might have got his dad came from, catching it's muzzle flash. If it wasn't nearly dark he probably wouldn't have been able to see it. Looking around from his position, Luke saw movement and a quick flash of white, the color out of place on the leaf covered yard. "Got ya," he said under his breath, while watching the decorative wishing well the movement came from. Guessing that whoever was there is either kneeling down and popping up for shot, or laying prone shooting around the well, Luke settled the sights of his rifle where he thought the body of a person would be. Seeing the white spot move slightly, he quickly fired seven rounds through the thin wood facia of the wishing well from right to left, ending the fight.

Hearing the whining sound of ATV tires on blacktop, JT turned to look, seeing two machines headed his way from 210th. There were no lights on either machine but as they got close he could tell one of them was Brian, then after a moment, he recognized Fred on the other one. Holding his hand up to stop them from in front of the car, the two machines slowed to a stop almost immediately. JT, looking up the driveway in the fading light, stood up after seeing Luke trotting his way

Seeing JT stand up, Luke started running towards him. "OLD MAN," he yelled, "you ok, I saw you go down at that shot."

"I'm good, I dove onto the blacktop trying to get the hell out of sight. It was fucking close though, it couldn't have more than a couple inches from my nose, I could feel the damn shockwave," JT replied, still mildly shaking.

Looking around with his rifle at low ready, Pete was coming their direction towards the car as Brian and Fred moved up on their machines. Amy stayed behind, still leaning over the hood of the truck. Fred, now off his machine was looking around, almost like the scene around him was bringing back memories of Nam. "I knew these fuckers would be trouble. My boy knows them all, there's a bunch of them that rented this place after the old lady passed away, he said they are all crackheads," Fred said warily, scanning the area through squinted eyes.

"No shit, how's your son know them?" Luke asked warily.

Laughing lightly, Fred replied, "he's a cop in town."

After making it to the group, Pete looked JT up and down saying, "damn pops, are you ok, the way you hit the ground I thought you took a bullet."

"Yeah, I'm fine, not very graceful though I guess," JT answered.

"How many were there?" JT asked.

"I saw two, I think I got one, and the other one darted back to the house but I lost sight of him before he got there," Pete replied.

"You got him alright, twice, your first shot must have hit him in the knee," Luke said.

"How the hell do you know that?" Pete asked.

"Because your second shot hit him in the eyeball," Luke replied.

"Did you get the second one?" JT asked Luke.

"Yeah, I got him, I caught a glimpse of him moving towards the house too, he had white sneakers on. If it wasn't for them white shoes I'd probably never have saw him, he was behind that wishing well." Luke said, pointing towards the house.

"He's dead as fuck now though," Luke continued.

"They had to have had a spotter out in the woods watching you coming down 205th, or close the intersection. These dip shits didn't just roll the car out here by accident," JT said, looking around intently.

"Think there's more of em pops?" Brian asked.

"Has to be, I'd bet there's someone in that house running a radio," JT said.

"Fuck, well we'd better switch to a different frequency then," Luke said.

"Like right away," Pete said.

"That was my fuck up guys, I asked for information I really didn't need over the radio. This could have been a hard lesson learned," JT said.

"I'll get a strap and pull these two in the ditch so we don't gotta look at this mess," Fred said, turning to his ATV.

"Fuck em Fred, let them lay, those turkey vultures will have em picked clean by tomorrow, let's leave the car here too, we will probably need it in a few days," JT said.

"For what? what are you going to do with the car?" Brian asked.

"We'll use it for a road block at the flowage," JT told him. "In less than a week, whoever is still alive in the cites will be starting an exodus. Some probably already have, now let's get the fuck out of here, I think you got enough room to get around behind this car Luke, let's go, I need a beer," JT said. That last comment was followed by a chorus of "ME TOO's."

Waiting until Luke and Pete got to the truck, JT then walked back to his ATV in the road, firing it up. Looking towards the truck, JT could see Amy, the dimming light just bright enough that he could tell she was talking to someone through the open window.

Tuning his machine around, JT waited, idling the ATV as Luke maneuvered around the sedan and pulled up along side him. Moving slowly down the road side by side, JT, peeking into the cab of the truck saw a rather smallish blonde haired woman sitting very close to Amy.

Seeing the question mark on his dad's face, Luke broke the tension. "Dad, this is Joni, me and Pete came across her this morning."

JT wanting to ask "came across he her "HOW", didn't, able to tell Luke was nervous and was not wanting to go into detail.

Standing up on the running boards of the Polaris so he could see inside the cab better JT said, "hello Joni, I'm JT.". The small woman didn't reply, but he was sure he saw the corners of her mouth turn up. JT looked up at Pete for more, Pete, shrugging his shoulders gave him a "what" look.

"Ok, let's head to the ranch, Ma has been cooking all day and Brian has the grill going. I'm starved," JT said, exhausted.

"Same," Luke said, "we've got a couple of stories to tell over beers," he continued.

JT looked at Joni, now with her head on Amy's shoulder. He couldn't hear her as she mouthed the words, "yes, yes you do."

Leading the way, Brian and Fred rolled slowly north up the county road. After Fred turned off into his driveway he stopped, waving to the rest of them as they passed. JT made a mental note of that, of all the people on the road, Fred was the only one that came at the sound of gunfire. "Duly noted," He said to himself.

After rolling into the ranch, Amy immediately ushered Joni inside the house to meet Lukes gramma and Kate. That would be the last they saw of any of them for the night.

Before anyone could relax, there were a couple of quick tasks that needed to be taken care of. First, unloading the two hogs, putting them in a small corner pen in the barn then introducing Clover to the other three dogs, which went better than expected. Then lastly, releasing the six chickens into the coop.

When the work was done, the four of them, Luke, Pete, Brian and JT went inside of the nearly dark house, noticing all but one of the oil lamps had been extinguished. Besides the darkness, it was spooky quiet inside as they fumbled around looking for the dutch oven and other necessities. Seeing no sign of JT's mom, Kate, Amy or Joni in the process, they searched. The dutch oven was eventually found safe in the oven, chocked full of fall off the bone tender ribs.

Brian grabbed the old cast iron pot with a pair of mitts, a bottle of "Sweet Baby Rays" sauce already in his pocket. Pete brought out a stack of paper plates and a roll of paper towels, setting them on the picnic table as the three of them waited patiently for Brian to put the finishing touches on the pork.

"The beer is in the garage fridge, and grab me one, no, make it two when you go," JT said to whoever was listening.

"On it pops," Pete said, taking off to the garage. Returning with the beers, Pete said, "this shit is almost frozen, how'd you make that happen?"

"Solar," JT replied. "The charge controller got fried though, but I had a couple of spares put away in a microwave. There's a bunch of stuff in a couple old ovens I had laying around. Everything is inside those anti static bags too, just for good measure. It only took a minute to swap out the controller, the batteries took up a charge right away. I'm amazed really that the panels are still good. Which reminds me, we need swap out the battery cart inside for the inverter connected to the fridge. There's a bunch of food in there yet," JT commented.

"We've got a bunch too, ours is still frozen, but if this weather stays warm it's gonna thaw before long," Pete said.

"We will can it, whatever we can anyway, then smoke the rest, I'm guessing that it's from that elk you shot right," JT asked.

"It is, and I sure don't want it going to waste, that's some good eats," Brian added.

"Well boys, it ain't gonna stay warm forever. Winter is about a month away and we should start thinking about that," JT said.

"You're a buzz killer, you know that, right pops?" Brian said with a chuckle.

"Yeah, I suppose I am, I'm just trying to keep it real," JT said with a laugh.

"Luke, you're quiet, what's up?" JT asked.

"I'm pretty sure my leg is infected. It's red and hotter than hell," Luke answered.

"Shit, I thought I had that cleaned up good on the inside, is it still closed up?" JT asked.

"I donno, I haven't looked at it, it's been a long assed day," Luke said.

"Ok, let's check it in the morning, I've got ten full doses of amoxicillin. It ain't fresh out of the cow, but it should still make butter. Check it tonight before you pull the pin, then again as soon as you get up, if the redness has grown you'd better get on the drugs," JT said. Same with you Brian, let me know how your leg is doing in the morning. Brian simply nodded his head in reply, clearly worried about his leg.

"Alright, where the hell did you get penicillin?" Luke asked.

"Some online pharmacy in India," JT replied with a wink.

Luke and Pete relayed the events of their day, how they came across Dave, the burned EV, Joni, the shit birds that snatched her…all of it. It had been one hell of a day for them and they were both wore out. By now it was way dark, the fall air having a brisk chill to it. It wasn't cold, 44 degrees maybe, but the sky was crystal clear and JT wondered to himself how long it would be before the inevitable snow showed up.

Snapping back into reality JT said, "well boys, I hate to say this, but we should have someone on watch out at the end of the driveway, especially at night. It's been what, 36 hours or so since the lights went out? Think about what all happened just today. Sure, this day sucked, but this ain't shit, most people are sitting at home, waiting for some kind of miracle that isn't going to come. Except for Freddy, we haven't seen hide nor hair out of anyone else living around here and when all those people come to the realization that no one is coming to feed them, they are going to lose their minds. Anyway, I had an awesome nap today, so I'll take the first watch. Brian, will you relieve me around two or whatever, maybe when you wake up to piss, walk up there and take over?" JT said.

"Roger that pops, will do," Brian said.

"Pete, was that my rifle you had in the truck, I'll probably need that and the bag of magazines for it?" JT asked.

"Yep, I'll get your gear pops, sit tight!" Pete replied.

"Dad, we're gonna have to clear that house too, especially now that there could be more people hanging around there," Luke said.

"I suppose you're right, maybe a couple of us should go watch the place for a few hours to see if anyone is moving around, if we take that .223 with the varmint scope we can sit way back in the woods across the road and keep the glass on it, but for now, you guys get some rest, I'm gonna get Pepper and go sit out by the end of the driveway for a while," JT said.

At the road, JT stood shivering in the cool night air, looking southwest towards the darkness covering Minneapolis. Wondering what all those people were doing, he let his mind wander off to what was surely mayhem taking place in the asphalt jungle.

With his mind meandering on that subject, it hadn't seemed like more than a couple hours had passed when JT heard peppers soft, low growl. Following her gaze, JT saw her looking intently south down the driveway towards the house. With only a sliver of moon and light wispy clouds, he couldn't see anything and definitely didn't hear anything with the ringing in his ears. Finally, with JT hearing a faint whistle, knew it was Brian walking slowly towards him.

After Brian limped his way out to where JT was standing, he reached down, scratching Peppers ears. "What's up out here pops, it's sure quiet, the sound of my boots in the gravel is enough to wake the dead", Brian said.

"Not a fucking thing, I've been walking up and down the road a couple hundred yards each way thinking about what's happening in the cities, but I ain't seen shit here. Are you early, or did the time get away from me, it doesn't feel like I've been out here long?" JT asked.

"Couldn't sleep, fucking Pete snores so damn loud…And I just can't settle my brain down, I mean what the fuck is wrong with people? Tomorrow morning makes two full days right, what is it going to look like in two more days or two weeks?" Brian asked, clearly troubled.

"Tough to say, but I don't expect any kind of improvement. I think the people we've encountered so far are one's that were, how do I say this, "opportunists". People who were waiting for something, anything like this to happen so they could do whatever they felt like with no fear of the law, if that makes any sense. Those fuckers were probably glued to YouTube since before the war started. Some of those doom and gloom channels really painted a vivid picture of what a grid down situation could look like. They didn't leave many details out either, like the law becoming nonexistent. I know, I watched plenty of them myself," JT said.

Brian thought about what JT had said, turning his words over in his mind. "So after it became clear to them, or clear enough, they decided to be who they are, or wanted to be?" He asked.

"Hell if I know really. But I'm guessing that once it hit them that there are no police, no courts and no threat of going to prison, they went feral and capitalized on the situation. We got a busy day coming up, hell, we are gonna have a lot of busy days, so I better try to get some rest. Our lives just became exponentially more difficult," JT said to Brian.

"Hey, is it cool if Pepper stays out with me, she's good company?" Brian asked.

"Sure, but you gotta carry her over the spot where the invisible fence crosses the driveway by the pasture gate, she won't walk over it," JT warned. Brian got a chuckle out of that and they parted ways.

As JT got close to the house, the soft light of an oil lamp caught his eye from the east kitchen window, reminding him that before long, he will need to black out all the north windows. As he approached the plum tree, it's fruit long past fallen, the faint aroma of woodsmoke from the grill mingled with the scent of the forest and reminded him of simpler times, long before the tragedy that had just befallen them.

Staying mindful of any noise he might make, JT stepped into the living room, his eyes scanning through the darkness for any sleeping dogs on the old wooden floor. In one of the recliner's, Luke lay snoring softly, his mouth half-open and his legs dangling over the edge. JT chuckled to himself, feeling a sudden pang of envy, but he decided to shake it off. "Can't begrudge the man who can sleep almost anywhere," JT thought.

Momma must have left the younger women and went to bed while JT was out on watch. Peering in her room, she was out cold, a small oil lamp casting its soft glow over her sleeping form. She had acquired an affinity over the years for falling asleep with a nightlight on. Shrugging, JT extinguished the lamp and quietly closed the door, making sure not to wake her.

Knowing that Kate, Amy and Joni were in his room with the other three dogs, JT was resigned to his fate of the couch and was soon asleep as well, his last thoughts being getting the smoker into action full time.

A few years ago, JT had ingeniously repurposed an old 100-gallon gas barrel into a lavish grill and smoker. After several spools of welding wire, many cubic feet of argon, oxygen and acetylene, and countless hours of labor, he created a five-foot-long, three-foot-wide grill that was capable of handling an entire hog with ease. He had meticulously crafted it with saddles that held the barrel firmly in place and sturdy legs cemented a foot deep in the ground under the canopy of the large maple tree.

To the right of the grill sat a smaller, aged wood stove, perched on a poured 3 foot by 3 foot concrete slab. It was a classic stove that JT had scored for a bargain at a garage sale. The legs had been sawed down to just an inch tall to keep the chimney stack low and prevent rust from corroding the metal. JT had rerouted the stove pipe horizontally for about six feet to meet the smoker on its low side. Finally, the short chimney stack with its own dampener sat atop the grill's opposite end for maximum flow of the smoke.

As he sunk into the couch, exhausted from the day, JT's thoughts were on putting the big smoker to use, preserving the relative bounty they have at the moment.

With Pete's one hundred and fifty pounds of elk meat, the deer hanging in the barn, along with what's inside Luke's coolers and the remaining contents of the upright freezer, JT knew that it would see plenty of use in the days ahead. However, he planned on canning some of it, but JT was worried that they would run out of Mason jars and lids to store the last of the garden vegetables properly. It was a dilemma of sorts, and fortunately for him, it was good kind of problem to face.

JT stirred awake at the sound of a toilet flushing, a noise he normally wouldn't even have registered. Yet with the complete silence that enveloped him without any white noise, the sudden sound was like an explosion in the stillness. It must be one of the women using the bathroom, he thought, because Luke was still asleep in his recliner with his legs still dangling off the edge. JT could see his mother's feet poked out from her bed covers through her now open door, so it couldn't have been her.

Seeing his mother safe and sound in her bed brought a warm smile to JT's face. She loved JT's place because it reminded her of the house she grew up in on the county line. Their floor plans were nearly identical. As her dementia became more pronounced, she often told JT that she wanted to go home, to the old farm where she was raised. While this place wasn't exactly the one she grew up in, it was close enough, especially in her mind. JT couldn't help but think that if this event had been an EMP, which it surely had to have been that turned off the lights, she might just get her wish. And as morbid as that thought was, it offered some comfort, because odds are, she'd be the only one there dying happy.

Pulling on his Columbia hiking boots, JT then buttoned up his red and black quilted wool shirt and headed outside to take a leak. It was pre-dawn, not dark, not light, he guessed the time to be about 6:00, finding the weather still unseasonably mild for October as he stepped out the door. "October what? it's gotta be the 9th" he muttered to himself.

Buttoning up his BDU trousers after taking care of business, he went back in the house and using a sharpie, he marked an X over October 9th on the calendar hanging from the kitchen wall. Why this mattered to him he did not know but he instantly felt better knowing that he had a clue what day is was and when this shit show began.

As long as he was inside and awake from taking a leak in the morning air, he filled the clean peculator sitting on a burner with water from the covered bucket, then added a healthy scoop of coffee grounds to the metal basket.

JT reached for the box of stick matches atop the stove, meticulously avoiding the use of the "strike anywhere" kind he also kept. Those were stashed away for emergency use only after becoming increasingly scarce and valuable. After lighting the stove, JT began to brew his morning coffee. Stepping back outside through the east deck door, JT watched as Brian and Pepper came into sight through the thick, tangled buckthorn lining the driveway. Brian walked with an obvious limp, but the buckthorn didn't slow down Pepper as she sniffed around diligently through the gnarly brush. Suddenly, the dog halted in her tracks, obediently waiting while Brian caught up. JT glanced out to witness an endearing moment as Brian picked up the dog and took a few boisterous steps forward over her boundary, setting Pepper back down ever so gently despite his injured leg. He could hear Brian talking to the dog, the sound of his voice and the scratches behind her ears providing all the positive reinforcement Pepper needed.

Once past the invisible fence Pepper did quick a zoom around the area and was soon on the deck by JT, looking for pets. "You're pretty fast for a senior citizen bubs," JT told the dog as Brian came up on the deck, plopping his himself in a chair.

"That is boring as fuck up there pops and we really need something to sit on. My fucking leg is killing me," Brian said as a greeting.

"I'll work on that sitting thing, but boring is good," JT told him.

"Shit, I've gotta have a look at both of these guy's legs, and soon. About the last thing we need here is to have one of these boy's get a nasty infection," JT thought to himself. "Coffee should be ready in a few minutes," JT said. Brian gave him a thumbs up in reply.

Before long the noise of the percolator had woke Luke up and he too was soon outside, walking out barefoot in the cold grass to pee.

"Exhilarating ain't it?" JT said to Luke.

"Its the way a man's supposed to pee," Luke replied at the exact moment that Amy walked out of the deck door, Joni behind her.

With a smirk Amy said, "and how then shall a woman pee? Standing up like an animal? I don't think so, we shall use the throne like the royalty that we are."

JT didn't know if he should laugh or shut up, so he compromised and asked the two if they would like some coffee. "Yes, black please," they said in unison.

After the first round of coffees drained the pot, JT proceeded to brew another. He had stocked up on a dozen of the large 34-ounce cans of Folgers Black Silk, along with four or five large cans of Dollar General coffee and enough of the freeze-dried coffee to last him longer than he cared to live. As the group sipped the newly-brewed coffee, their conversation flowed easily and with a sense of optimism. JT was pleasantly surprised at how much better Joni seemed on this morning. She wasn't cracking up or laughing, but she spoke and made eye contact, and that simple act of participation was heartening to see.

"Where are the dogs?" JT asked Amy.

"They're still in the bedroom, sleeping with Kate," Amy answered with a yawn.

Pete emerged from the pop-up camper, scratching his bedhead as he ambled around the corner of the shed. Unkempt and dressed in the same clothes he'd worn to bed, he was a stark contrast to the two women already on the porch, wearing their pajamas, slippers, and robes. "You all make more noise than a pack of coyotes," Pete grumbled, walking up the deck stairs to join the group.

Brian laughed, saying "you've never heard yourself snore."

That comment got a laugh out of everyone, Joni even chuckled a little, then she surprised everyone by asking "are you two a couple then?"

Brian instantly began to stutter, clearly embarrassed by the question but Pete didn't miss a beat as he said "oh Brian has been my little bitch for a long time," as he winked at Brian.

Brian finally got out some intelligible words and said "fuck you Pete, you dick."

"That's not how this works little buddy," Pete came back with.

By now, everyone was laughing uproariously, much to the dislike of poor Brian who got up and said "Aw hell no, I got a deer to bone," as he limped off towards the camper.

Looking a little uncomfortable, Joni said, "um, sorry about that, I just thought….".

"No worries Joni, those two have been best friends for years and the way they act sometimes can definitely lead to questions," Luke said.

Sitting across from Luke, Joni noticed the dried blood on his pants leg, asking if he was injured. Luke replayed the story to her, leaving out most of the shooting parts. Joni told them that she was a Physicians Assistant in the on-site clinic of the university in Madison, and then she asked why Brian was limping. Pete told that story to her. It was odd in a way, Joni listening so intently to both men, not once interrupting either of the guys as they spoke.

Finishing their stories, Joni asked if they had anything in the way of medical supplies, JT replying in the affirmative, left to retrieve the red plastic bin from his closet. "I'm impressed," Joni said, looking through the contents. "Do you mind if I have quick look at your leg Luke?" She asked.

"Sure, I'd appreciate it actually," Luke said, pulling up his pants leg revealing a nasty looking bandage. Joni removed the bandage, and as she was inspecting the wound JT asked Luke if the redness was larger this morning. He said it was, but not very much.

"There are ten full doses of amoxicillin in there, 500 milligram capsules if you need them," JT told Joni, pointing to the bin. Joni acknowledged the comment with a quick nod of her head.

Pressing the pad of her thumb gently against the injury, Joni worked her way around the wound in a circular pattern feeling the heat of the area when Luke's calf tighten and he winced slightly. "That's stings huh?" she asked, before bending over, putting her nose to the wound, taking few good sniffs.

"It's definitely a little angry, but the infection isn't deep, it's near the skin line," she said, cleaning the wound. "Let's leave the steri-strips with no outer bandage, and roll your pants up to get some sunshine on that. If it isn't showing improvement in a couple days then you should take the antibiotics, or I can lance it," she said, then went on "Pete, will you fetch Brian for me, as long we have all this stuff out?" she asked.

This girl is something else, it was just two days ago that her boyfriend was murdered by a gang of scumbags who then took her and did who knows what with her. Either Joni is still in shock or she is an exceptional realist. They all hoped it was the latter.

"Joni wants to look at your hole," Pete said, taking over carving the meat from the deer hanging in the barn. Brian already having a good start on the deer by the time Pete got there.

"You're an asshole Pete," Brian said.

"If you're gonna call me names at least be creative about it you knuckle dragging twat waffle," Pete said, laughing at his own comment. Brian erupted in laughter as well then limped back over to the deck, dragging his right leg along the ground as he did.

Amy and Joni were sitting in their chairs waiting on Brian, having more coffee as Luke and JT were getting the smoker ready. "Sorry about earlier Brian. I work at UW Madison, half of the students and staff are gay, it's a normal question to ask down there" Joni said.

"No worries, it takes a hell of a lot more than that to fluster me" Brian replied with a smile.

"Oh yeah? We'll see about that," Joni thought to herself, scheming.

"Let me see your leg" she asked. Brian told her that he had to drop his pants to expose the bullet wound, prompting Joni to stare seductively into his eyes until his pants were around his now weak knees.

Pretending to reach for Brian's crotch she said loudly "ok big fella, turn your head and cough," bringing uproarious laughter from everyone in earshot. After the humor had died down a little Joni said that she could never understand people without a sense of humor noting that there are plenty of times when laughter is indeed, the best medicine.

Brian was sitting now as Joni was examined him, her second patient of the day. She found the bullet almost instantly. The entry hole was nearly closed and she assumed the pain that was causing Brian's limp was most likely from the bullet cutting through the outer edge of his thigh muscle.

"You're good to go Brian, try to keep that entry wound as clean as you can," she said, dabbing it with antibacterial ointment. "Unless it brought some fabric in, there shouldn't be an infection, the bullet will most likely become encapsulated in no time, but, you're not out of the woods yet," she continued.

Amy couldn't take it anymore, she noticed the same thing they all did about Joni. Never being one to beat around the bush she just came right out and asked "Joni, are you ok? You have been through an enormous amount of shit in the last couple of days and here you are patching people up, even bringing us all to our knees laughing. How on earth can you do that."

Joni shrugged, thinking for a moment about what Amy had said then replied, "I've been in the medical world since I was twenty two years old, the first six years were spent as an RN in the ER before I became a PA, and let me tell you this, it was a wonderful job, being a nurse, but that ER work rates a one star review, would not recommend…Some of the things I've seen…..," she paused for a second before continuing, "some of those things I can never un-see so I had to learn how to deal with that."

"How?" Amy asked, sincerely curious.

"Well, I think it's partly because I became desensitized to seeing trauma over time, so that, and I learned how to decompress using some very unique meditation techniques I picked up from the hospital counselor." Joni answered.

Joni explained how she could meditate herself into a nearly catatonic state, telling her that was where she was "at" when Luke and Pete found her. She went on saying how she knew she was molested but she had no real recollection of any of it, it was like a dream that she couldn't remember anymore.

Listening intently to Joni talk, Amy found herself empowered by the fortitude this woman has. "Well, I'm here if you ever wanna talk," Amy said.

Joni smiled and said "likewise, I've got a feeling that things are about to get shitty, I heard a little of what Luke's dad said. Its Pop's isn't it, that what you guys call him, right?"

"Yep, that's what me and these guys call him, Luke called him Old Man though most of the time, sometimes it's Dad or Pops too," Amy said.

"What do you think we are going to do, I mean, there's eight of us right? that's a lot of mouths to feed?" Joni asked.

"Truthfully, I'm not sure, but Pops has been convinced this was coming way before the war broke out and he's been getting prepared to deal with just this thing for years. Luke and him have talked through so many what-ifs over time and listening to him I actually think he was looking forward to it happening. Not that he wanted it, the opposite is true, but he kept saying that what we were living in was nothing more than an illusion, a "house of cards" and whatever came out the other side when it fell would hopefully bring us back to our roots as a nation," Amy replied.

Joni was quiet for the longest time before finally speaking. "Dave used to listen to a podcast, Glenn Beck. I hated it. But as much as I tried not to listen when he had it on, I did hear him talk about this very kind of situation. He said that "bringing America to its knees" was a vital part of the "Great Reset", whatever that is. I thought it was nonsense, more like fear mongering, but he was right it seems," the said.

"I can see that having to happen too," Amy replied, trailing off into her own thoughts.

After deboning the deer, Pete took over manning the smoker. The cool morning air carrying the combination of smells from it was incredible.

After putting some of the venison on the smoke, he had went inside looking for Kate, finding her in the kitchen.

"Miss Kate, is there anything thawing in the fridge for me to put in the smoker?" he asked, his politeness palpable.

Being successful in his quest, Pete, after thanking Kate, was carrying out couple of small turkey breasts, a big pork roast, and two family sized packages of chicken thighs. Adding a small fire on the far end of the smoker to help dry the meat as it smoked, Pete then began preparing the two turkey breasts and both hams of the deer for jerky. Putting the sliced meat into a bucket of seasoned water he had on the picnic table for a flavor brine, he stirred the concoction well, and would let it soak for hours before they would go in the smoker.

Looking at the chicken thighs, Pete said, "come to daddy my little darlings, you get my special attention today." They would be dinner, with seasoned rice and beans on the side.

Pete, besides being an amazing chef was all about preserving the meat, not just preparing a meal, that was easy. All he'd have to do for dinner is brine the chicken, give it some time over a hot spot on the grill then Miss Kate and Momma would do the rest. Focusing on the full coolers of meat, Pete began preparing for a long haul at the smoker.

Considering how to store all the meat after it's been smoked and dried, JT knew there were some feed bags stashed away in the barn. After coming up with his idea, he headed out looking for the porous, loosely woven gunny sack bags. There are several of them that he knew he'd saved, and looking around, he eventually found a stack them in the tack room draped over a saddle.

Seeing the old weathered saddle sitting on its rack saddened JT. His last remaining horse "Red", was coming twenty nine, very old for an Arabian. With the big boy now being too arthritic to ride anymore, he'd deeply considered putting Red down, but just didn't have the heart to do it, not yet anyway. Knowing he could still get down and roll then get himself up again, JT considered that as his metric as he watched his longtime riding buddy age.

Ultimately ending up with at least a dozen of the bags, JT draped them over his shoulder and headed back to the smoker. When the meat is dry enough with a good smoke on it, they will loosely bag it all, hanging it high in the shop.

Seeing his dad coming out of the barn, Luke walked over to him asking, "how's the big beast doing these days, he don't seem leave the barn much anymore?".

"He's good, kinda. His gut isn't digesting his feed very well and he's losing weight," JT said sadly.

"How's his teeth?" Luke asked with concern in his voice.

"They were floated not long ago, and he's been wormed on schedule. He's just getting old," JT said.

"We got enough hay for the winter?" Luke asked, also thinking about feeding his hogs.

"For sure. I picked up 250 bales of second crop last summer, that'll last until spring," JT answered.

"Roger that. I'm gonna head over to the crackhouse for a sneak and peek," Luke said, ending the horse conversation.

Going out alone to go watch the crackhouse for a couple hours, Luke decided he wasn't going to take a four wheeler nor would he be walking the road. Sneaking in alone seemed like a better option to him, his logic being two people would make twice the noise.

Leaving the ranch, heading basically straight east into the woods, Luke then cut south a short distance until catching the east/west line fence of section. This would leave him with only a half mile hike through the woods before he would be in position to find a hide. Being on foot, Luke left the heavy varmint rifle with its powerful scope at the ranch, carrying instead a pair of 10 by 50 Ziess binoculars and his AR, going in light with one magazine in the rifle and one in his back pocket.

The crackhouse sits on a bit of a hill, and Luke knew he wasn't going to be able to find a high spot. So instead, he opted for the best field of view from the woods. Picking a place to set up where he had a decent look at two sides of the structure, Luke was pleased seeing each side has a door on it. "Good enough," he said to himself as he settled in, knowing these old four square farmhouses rarely had a third door.

Sitting on a nice wide oak stump, Luke began thinking about the events of the last couple of days. It was all very fresh in his head and he was absentmindedly playing out the events over and over while glassing the area in front of him, still troubled about how he and Pete handled the guys that had taken Joni, and how easy it was for him to end them. Not the shooting part, that's easy, but the killing part. He felt like he was the judge, jury and executioner. At the time, he had no idea what or even if they even had her, or if they killed her boyfriend Dave. Sure, he was ultimately proven right, but he killed men with no actual proof of wrongdoing other than a faint scream they heard.

Luke was suddenly brought out of his thoughts when he caught the movement of a lone dog through the binoculars. The dog was only about 30 feet from the crackhouse and walking towards it. "Well, it's not wild, not with that collar full of tags," he said, seeing the sunlight glinting off the shiny tags as it walked to the house.

This was definitely home for the dog Luke thought as he watched the mutt pawing the door. After several attempts, the door cracked open slightly, with a black haired female stepping out. Only her upper body visible as she peeked around before letting the dog in. Luke didn't have to assume it was a female, he could clearly see the naked woman, at least the top half of her before she slipped back inside.

"Fucking great, I guess there's more of them," he said to himself. He deciding to stay for a little while longer, thinking that whoever is in there might come out after they noticed that the dog wasn't spooked, but nothing materialized, so after an hour he silently backed out heading to the ranch.

While drawing gas for the tractor out of a 55-gallon drum in the shed, JT caught sight of Luke quietly coming through the east fence. Seeing Luke's rifle slung as he approached, JT said, "Well, I didn't hear any shooting. What's the verdict?"

"Target remains. I saw a naked chick stick her head out the door. She looked nervous even from where I was sitting," Luke answered.

"Wait, what? A naked chick? You sure?" JT asked.

Luke looked at him quizzically then walked away shaking his head muttering, "I'm 40, Dad. I know what they look like."

"My bad, let me rephrase that. What was she doing? Was she looking for someone?" JT asked.

"No, she was letting a dog in that was pawing at the door. When she did, she stepped out far enough for me to see her through the binos, but she did definitely check out the driveway," Luke replied.

"A dog? That's gonna make taking a closer look damn near impossible," JT said.

"Yeah, I don't think we should go any closer than where I was in the woods, and if the winds from the west we shouldn't go at all, oh, and the two bodies are gone from the car, at least as far as I could tell they were, there was a lot of brush between me and the car so maybe I just didn't see them. Whatcha doing with the gas?" Luke asked, changing the subject.

"I'm thinking about going up to Diane's place with the tractor and the pickup and grab that big propane tank she has. If it's been filled, having a few hundred gallons of that wouldn't hurt us at all this winter," JT answered.

"You don't think that cranky old lady might get a little pissed about that?" Luke asked.

"Nope," JT said "I can guarantee she won't, she died a couple of weeks ago of pneumonia, poor thing. I liked the salty old gal."

"I've got that propane construction heater that we can put in the cellar, it doesn't require any power. If we crack a couple windows down there we can heat the floors up pretty good without asphyxiating ourselves. Might come in damn handy when it's 20 below." JT said, thinking about the big tank.

"Good plan, let us guys get the trailer unloaded first then we can use it to haul the tank, we won't have to lift it nearly as high. When you wanna do that?" Luke asked.

"Soon, like today, before anyone else around here gets any ideas" JT said.

"Ok then, we will get to unloading." Luke replied.

The old Farmall 460 JT has had for years was parked in its spot by the wood pile. It's old as dirt and looks rough but the 6 cylinder gasoline engine runs great and it's got a strong hydraulic pump on it. If that propane tank has much in it, it will probably test the old thing. Diane's house has a 500 gallon tank and JT knew she was on a "keep full" service. He was really hoping that the gas guy had been out and topped her off to the 80% mark before she moved into assisted living.

As JT idled the old tractor up the driveway, he reflected on the math: 1600 pounds of gas and 400 pounds for the tank. "Good call on using the trailer," he said to himself. "The feet of that tank would punch right through the bed of the pickup." As the tire chains on the wheels thumped the road, JT pondered the situation. He was headed to his now-dead neighbor's house to pilfer her propane tank. "How screwed up is that?" he thought.

As JT nosed the tractor towards the tank in front of the house, Luke pulled past the driveway and backed the trailer down towards the tractor. Like most guys, they walked up to the tank and banged the side of it with a crescent wrench to see how full it was. With the "scientific" test done, they read the gauge and saw that it was filled to the max. JT was elated that nobody else had gotten there before them, but then again, why would they? Most of the folks around probably didn't even know that the old gal who owned the tank was dead. Those same folks are most likely still staring at their phones, waiting for them to light up.

After turning off the ball valve and disconnecting the feed line to the house, the two men fished a quarter-inch rigging chain through both of the lifting lugs on the tank. They wrapped the chain over the arms of the loader behind the bucket to provide more leverage, but less lifting height, which they no longer needed with the trailer. Setting the chain's lengths so that there was only a foot of distance between the loader arms and the tank would help clear the short side rails of the trailer. JT then walked up to the idling tractor and pulled the loader control lever, raising the bucket. The hydraulic pump stalled out just before it came off the ground. Climbing up into the seat, JT opened the throttle halfway, giving the pump more power. Attempting another lift, the trusty old tractor managed to pick the tank off the ground.

"I ain't gonna be able to move the tractor with this load Luke, you're going to have to back the trailer under it," JT said, looking at the nearly flat front tires of the tractor.

Hopping back in the truck and pulling ahead, Luke realigned the trailer to the tank. Backing up slowly, Luke stopped when the old man gave him a hand signal, getting out quickly to help guide the tank onto the frame of the trailer.

JT very slowly lowered the tank, bringing it within an inch of the trailer deck while watching Luke pull the feet over the frame. Suddenly, the lifting lug welded to the rear end of the tank broke off, causing the one-ton tank to slam onto the trailer with an enormous amount of racket. Luke flew backwards when it snapped, fortunate to escape the loose chain which had made a couple of whiplashes until it ran out of energy. Despite the setback, the other lug held firm, and JT navigated the rest of the lowering process seamlessly, leaving the trailer now carrying the full weight of the tank. Just as fortune seemed to be working against them, the feet of the tank ended up landing right on the two main frame beams, saving the trailer from destruction.

"What the fuck was that?" Luke asked, gathering his wit's.

"By the looks of that tore up pad-eye on the tank, I'd guess that it was only engineered to lift an empty tank. I suppose I should have thought of that" JT said, then continued "I have straps would could have used in a basket hitch, hell, I could have done the same thing with those chains, but honestly I never even thought about it, I was too excited to see the damn thing full I guess".

Pulling a couple of two inch ratchet straps out of the box of the truck, together they strapped the tank down for its quarter mile trip back to the ranch. "Yeah, let's remember that when we offload the thing ok," Luke said with a laugh.

"Hell, we can leave it strapped on the trailer, none of us has anywhere to go anytime soon," JT said.

"You've got a point, but let's get out of here, before anyone sees what we are up to and wants in on the action," Luke said, looking around.

"Good call, I'll follow ya, pull it alongside the garage, we will sort out where it will need to go later, let's get the hell out of here before that guy who lives just east of Freddie on the corner sees us. He may not be now but that fucking guy and his family are going to be a problem, we can count on that", JT said.

"Davidsons" Luke asked.

"Yep, them ones, out of all these people here, those fuckers are the only one that I know for a fact have been existing only because of them sucking the government tit as dry as they can," JT replied.

Getting back, the two men gazed at each other with relief. Sweat dripped down their dust-covered faces, but at least their noise had gone unheard. They peered up the long driveway, scanning the area for any signs they had been discovered, but the ranch remained quiet. To their reckoning, no one within earshot had heard their pilferage mission. And, reaching this conclusion was not a mere assumption, for fact lay in the telltale tracks of their mischief. No one approached to investigate the unmistakable racket or the trail of disturbances the rear tires of the tractor left in their wake. Even a frigging blind man would spot the blatant marks left on the road, but the silence remained nonetheless.

As Luke and JT returned, the welcoming sight of everyone being gathered outside on the picnic table made them happy. Even JT's mom, who could hardly get around, was sitting comfortably, savoring every bit of the sunshine. JT blinked in surprise when he saw her, feeling grateful and relieved to witness her enjoying herself surrounded by everyone. While she sipped her coffee, Pete cut tender slices of pork from the roast, and JT's mother savored every bite. Despite her dementia, her eyes still glimmer when she smiles.

"Holy hell Pete, that smells fucking awesome!" Luke shouted as he walked up with his hand out, expecting a slab of pork. Then with a sheepish expression on his face he said, "sorry gramma, that just smelled so good that I forgot my manners."

While Amy and Brian taunted Luke with good-natured ribbing, "You'd better watch your manners," JT remained silent. He had just witnessed his mother "checking out" once again. Moments earlier, she had been actively engaging in a conversation with the group, but now she was staring off blankly. He wondered if she was reminiscing a past moment from her youth. It was difficult to tell for sure. Regardless, JT reflected on this observation as he contemplated the fragility of his mother's health.

These episodes have become much more frequent over the last month or two, but to be honest, as much as he hated her having dementia, he could also see that she was in a "happy place". Nothing that's happened has bothered her. Not even when she shot the guy who was pulling up a shotgun him. His guess was that she didn't even remember that anymore, but at that point in time she was "in the moment", fully functioning.

Kate noticed her husband's gaze fixed upon his mother, a lone tear trickling down his face. Walking towards him, she gently placed her arm around his waist. "She's slipping you know" Kate told him firmly. "As much as you want to you can't fix this, nor should you try to help her remember. It won't make a difference, she can't remember. I know this is difficult, but you have to let her live out her final days on her terms." Kate spoke the words with sincerity and compassion. She inhaled deeply, bracing herself for the tough news she knew was next. "And, about her heart medication...we're out. There were only two pills left. These are her last days, and we need to help her be comfortable and happy, doing whatever she wants." Kate held her husband tightly, as her words hung in the heavy air.

"Her pacemaker is working, but without those heart meds, her pressure is going to rise until her heart quits. Joni checked her pressure just a little while ago with the instrument from the bin, it was 140 over 85. She is normally 85 over 50. I know what's normal for her, I've checked her dozens of times over the past few months. You do understand I what I'm saying, right?" Kate asked.

"Yeah, I do, thanks honey," JT replied softly, wiping more tears away.

Walking to where his mom was sitting, JT sat down beside her.

"Whatcha thinking about ma?" he asked, after she acknowledged his presence.

"Nothing really, I was just talking to my sister about about how we should peel some apple's and bake a pie." His mom then turned, looking around for her sister, asking JT where she went.

"She had to use the bathroom mom, we both know she could never hold her beer," he said

Joanne, Momma's only sister had passed away from congestive heart failure thirty seven years ago. "Do you have a beer?" she asked JT out of the blue.

"I do, would you like one Ma?" he asked, quite surprised at the request.

"Yes by golly I'd love a can of beer, go fetch me one," she said.

"Well, I suppose I can, it's gotta be after 5 o'clock, somewhere" JT said with a smile.

Chapter Nine

Three days to hell. Seventy two hours away from mayhem. Nine meals from anarchy....those are clichés tossed around in online prepping groups, post apocalyptic survival groups and campfires by good old boys as they planned for armageddon. While those terms are intentionally hyperbolic it doesn't mean they are not at least partially, true.

It's a startling statistic, but it's been reported that the majority of households in the United States have only three days' worth, or less, of food on hand at any given time. It's a sobering thought to consider, especially when you ponder the inner workings of the grocery store industry, where a "just in time" delivery system dictates supply and demand. With no supplies to replenish the shelves after a product sells out, stores across the country are vulnerable to shortages. As square footage, and profits, take precedence over storage space, stock rooms are becoming a relic of the past, leaving consumers with little recourse when it comes to securing their sustenance.

In the event of any regional or national disruption to trucking, rail, electrical, or internet infrastructure - or any combination of them - grocery stores dependent on "just in time" delivery systems will be wiped clean of inventory in a matter of days. The same bleak outlook faces other service industries relying on the same type of resupply system.

The third day since the blackout started also marked the beginning of the last 24 hours of what little civility was left. The group had witnessed firsthand the rapid decline of society around the ranch. The fall of the correctional facility, the construction workers trying to steal JT's four-wheeler, the attackers who targeted Luke in Star Prairie, the hijackers who assaulted Pete and Brian on their walk home, the guys that killed Joni's boyfriend and then took her, and the crackheads up the road. Without communication, law enforcement, or transportation, opportunists became brazen threats, attacking whoever they thought had something they needed or wanted.

But as dire and dangerous as those scenarios were, they might come to seem mild in comparison to what was likely to happen in the next 24 hours. The metropolitan complex of Minneapolis and St. Paul, home to over 1.5 million people, would soon run out of food and water. Though the well pumps feeding the dozens of water towers scattered throughout the area had auxiliary power systems, what ever fuel that was kept onsite for those generators would soon run out and the pressures would quickly fail. High-rise buildings whose backup systems had already failed would be the first to lose access to water, stranding their occupants or forcing them to leave. Without food or water, desperate people will do desperate things, even in a normally civilized society.

JT was tormented by a single question: where would all the urban and suburban residents of nearby Minneapolis and Saint Paul go when their resources ran out? Those without the means to evacuate would be left with few options. Stay, and die of starvation or, forced to flee with only the belongings they could carry on their backs. In this post-apocalyptic world, even the most social creatures can quickly turn into predators, and JT knew their small group would have to remain constantly on the lookout. Gone are the days of simply going for a walk, or for a ride into town. Now, for the most part, there are only two types of people left- predators and prey.

As the city dwellers exhaust their limited resources, they'll be forced to venture out into the suburbs - a massive ring of pre-planned neighborhoods that encircles the Twin Cities. There, they'll encounter a whole new set of challenges, among them the reluctance of suburbanites to part with their belongings or share what little they may have left. In desperation, some of the city dwellers will turn to violence to wrest what they can from these suburban pockets of relative comfort and safety. Meanwhile, suburbanites themselves may grow increasingly territorial, hotly contesting the outskirts of their own neighborhoods to ward off looming threats. As the world around them descends into chaos, JT could feel it - the last remaining shreds of social order fading fast, replaced by a dark, Darwinian struggle for survival.

For those who make it out of the cities and plunge headlong into the suburbs, life will be a precarious balancing act, with food and water in perilously short supply and human predators lurking around every corner. Those suburban dwellers who blithely ran off the desperate city dwellers will soon be forced to confront one of the grimmest realities of all - the monumental loss of life already taking place, with corpses strewn about by the scores. As urban infrastructure collapses, the very water courses that wind their way through suburbs will be contaminated with raw human waste as treatment facilities fail, spreading illnesses like Dysentery without a hint of mercy.

The worst may be yet to come. Out of necessity, those who survive will become hardened and desperate beyond reason, fueled by the instinctual urge to feed and protect themselves and their children. They'll abandon any remnant of morality, willing to take any life or sacrifice their own in their all-consuming quest to survive. And eventually, as they spread out across the land in search of any shred of sustenance they can find, they'll eventually come towards places like the ranch, propelled forward by the relentless advance of hunger.

JT visioned hordes from the northeast and east metro areas, armed with anything they could carry on their backs or find along the way, pushing forward to the east in swarming numbers. For some lucky few with access to older automobiles, ATVs or bicycles, the journey might be a little easier, but tempting targets also for the others, desperate to survive at any cost.

As the chaos spreads across the land, groups of all sizes will naturally coalesce, bonded together by the primal impulse of "strength in numbers." In these groups, leaders will invariably emerge, simply out of necessity - the overwhelming majority of people, for better or worse, prefer to be told what to do and when to do it. In America, a country that has historically embraced authority, the pandemic of 2020 reinforced the trend, with many urban and suburban dwellers bowing to the will of authoritative mandates, internalizing them as a form of moral righteousness, and acting as self-appointed enforcers to anyone who expressed reluctance to comply. These Karens and Kens of society, expert in wagging fingers and moral grandstanding, will inevitably become leaders of some groups, driven by their delusion that they know best.

If JT's math is right about the timeline, these sorts of groups and leaders will begin to show up around their neck of the woods within a week, give or take. It wasn't exactly a comforting thought - the prospect of vocal armchair leaders trying to assert their moral authority in a world fast devolving into mayhem. But it was better to be prepared than not, and JT hoped beyond hope that the group's ingenuity and defenses were powerful enough to weather the coming storm.

Chapter Ten

Pete's mastery of the smoker produced a heavenly lunch of smoked pork that filled them all up and lulled them into a satisfying sleepiness - especially for JT, who may have caught a little buzz from the beer left by his mom. While she had asked for a cold beer, she soon remembered that she had given it up decades earlier, demanding that JT "get that nasty shit away from me." He was just drifting off for a much-needed nap when Kate arrived and settled into her chair, worry etched on her face. "What's on your mind, hon?" she asked, eyeing JT.

"Just a nap," he replied, feeling completely spent. But he could sense that Kate needed to talk, and talk she did, digging into her concerns for her daughter and grandchild.

They talked about Sarah, who was likely at home or running errands when the blackout hit, and her husband, Tyler, who worked as a radiology tech at a hospital in downtown St. Paul. They both knew that a hospital would be a difficult place to be in the event of a total outage and poor Tyler would be right in the heart of the shitshow.

The two live due west of Kate and JT, their place being south of Forest Lake Minnesota by ten miles and just a little east of US highway 61. As the crow flies they probably aren't much more than twenty miles away from the ranch, but it's still a 45 minute drive. The closest bridges to cross the majestic Saint Croix River are eleven miles southwest to Stillwater Minnesota or eleven miles north to Osceola Wisconsin.

JT tried to think of something that would put Kate's mind at ease. He knew how close she was to her daughter and grandchild and he wanted to help however he could. "You know, Tyler and I put a plan together a loose plan a couple of years ago one day when Luke was out. We thought a lot about what to do in case something big happened, like a power outage just like this and we wanted to make sure we were all prepared." He looked over at Kate, hoping his words would be reassuring. "I'm sure they're fine, Kate. They've got an emergency kit and some supplies to last them a little while, just like we all do here."

"That's good to know," Kate said softly. Her mind was still whirling with worry, but JT's words lent her a small comfort. She was grateful for his reassurance and thoughtfulness, and she felt herself relaxing a little for the first time in days.

JT realized he may have over-exaggerated the plan a bit. While Tyler had sat in on some of the discussions Luke and JT had had about different scenarios, calling it a plan might've been a bit of a stretch. Still, Tyler had discussed the possibility of an emergency with them and had asked for advice on what to do if things went south.

During one of those conversations, Luke had posed a question to Tyler: would he rather stay put and hunker down, or strike out towards safer ground? Tyler responded that if it came to it, he'd prefer to make his way to his parent's place south of New Richmond. It was a mindset Luke and JT understood well - it was always better to have a plan, and part of that planning was to know where you might be headed if the worst happened. They made sure Tyler knew that he and Sarah were always welcome at the ranch if anything changed, and that they would do whatever they could to help.

JT and Luke had put together a pair of maps - one for Tyler and another for their own SHTF binder - showing a southeast route out of Tyler and Sarah's house that would eventually intersect a railroad line. That line would bring them to the St. Croix River and the High Bridge, providing relatively safe passage out of the cities and towards safer ground.

Tyler had asked them when the best time to bug out would be, and they'd advised him not to stay longer than two days, explaining the inevitable increase in danger once society deteriorated to a certain point. For good measure, JT had also gathered one of his protocol sheets - a list of things to do and when to do them - that he'd printed at the library in town. The library in the small village of Somerset had offered to print JT's protocol sheets at half price so long as it bore their letterhead. JT paid little heed to the branding, and eagerly accepted the offer.

They had gone through everything with Tyler in painstaking detail, hoping that it would give him and Sarah some peace of mind if things ever took a turn for the worse.

On day one before going to get Kate and Momma, JT was looking over his maps and protocol sheets and figured that Tyler and Sarah could reach the southeast route towards the railroad line and on to the high bridge in roughly eight hours if they stayed on track. They also had bicycles that could take them up to the bridge, and even a trailer for the baby to ride in, shortening the time to just a few hours.

Getting up, JT grabbed the SHTF folder from the file cabinet. He took out his copies of the map and scenario plan, then brought them out to show Kate. "See honey, Tyler has the same information as us. We told him not to stay any longer than two days, so if they follow that advice my guess is they are already headed in our direction. And if they want to keep going onto his parent's place, we can make the trip a lot easier on them."

Kate seemed pleased with this reassurance, but then asked how long would it take Tyler and Sarah to reach them. "Probably at least eight hours on foot to reach the High Bridge," JT replied. "But if they're riding their bikes, it could only take them a few hours."

Her face creased with worry, Kate asked, "Can't you go to the bridge and check if they're there? I'm just so scared for Sarah and the baby."

JT thought about Kate's request for a moment. He had been looking forward to catching up on his sleep, but he realized that there was no good reason why he shouldn't go and have a look for Tyler and Sarah himself - not one that Kate would accept, anyway. Besides, if they were on bicycles, there was a chance he might run into them on the road. "Sure thing," he finally responded, giving his wife's hand a reassuring squeeze.

Brian, Luke, Amy, and Joni were gathered around the picnic table, chatting as Pete toiled away at the smoker. It would be several more hours before the venison and elk would be smoked and dried sufficiently to be stored. JT watched them all, feeling both a sense of calm and a sense of dread. The calm came from being among these capable people, each with their own unique skills and experiences. The dread came from knowing what lay ahead - the hungry, desperate people who would soon be leaving the twin cities in search of food and shelter.

He knew it would be a challenge, but if they handled it carefully and thoughtfully, they could overcome the obstacles. Another looming worry was winter. They would have to face it on its own terms, and in Wisconsin, winter had no mercy. Even with the conveniences of high-efficiency furnaces and reliable electricity, winter could be deadly. Without them, it could be nearly insurmountable.

Snapping out of his trance, JT announced his plan to the group and asked if anyone wanted to join him for a ride to the High Bridge to see if Sarah and Tyler were on their way. Luke was on his feet in an instant, already headed for the truck to grab his gear. "Four wheelers?" he called over his shoulder.

"Yep, let's take two machines and the small trailer with the seats in it," JT responded. "Even pulling the trailer, the two quads combined will use a fraction of the gas that the pickup goes through.

They quickly gathered their things and set out towards the High Bridge, hoping to find Tyler and Sarah safe and sound. Little did they know what they would find on the other side.

JT remembered a time when he used to joke about planning his next gas station stop as soon as he put the gas cap back on the old truck. Back then, it had been a minor annoyance, something to poke fun at and wave off. But now, with the world in a precarious state, that old joke wasn't so funny anymore.

They had fuel, sure - one hundred and seventy-five gallons of treated gas stored in barrels and cans - but they couldn't afford to waste any of it. They had to be careful about their gas usage and ration it wisely. Taking a joyride in the pickup was no longer an option. If they could make their trip to the High Bridge with just the quads and the trailer, it would be a small victory, one less thing to worry about in the grand scheme of things.

Hearing the sound of a slide action shotgun ejecting a round, JT turned to see Luke at the small trailer. "Where'd you pick this one up old man?" Luke asked, eyeballing the 870.

"Shit, I forgot all about that one. That's the one that could have ended me, shit, would have ended me if that guy had the wherewithal to take the safety off," he replied.

"Not something you wanna be staring down the business end of eh pops," Pete said.

"No sir, and I'll tell ya something, right then I swore that the next time I see a gun even remotely aimed towards me or any of us, I'm shooting first, and I'll ask questions later. If it wasn't for ma, he'd have probably figured it out before I got a decent shot off," JT said.

"Say, Pete, how's your carpenter skills?" JT asked.

"Rusty, but good for being in management. What's on your mind?" Pete asked JT.

"Hot water," he replied.

"Huh?" Pete asked quizzically.

"In the barn there's a few sheets of half inch plywood and a bunch of scrap two by fours, could you hammer together a box, 4 by 8 feet with the sides a foot deep?" JT asked.

"Sure can, I'll get Brian to give me a hand," Pete said.

"Excellent. In the shop there is a bunch of black paint in rattle cans, spray the inside of the box solid black, then when it dries, connect that pair of hundred foot black garden hoses together that are hanging behind the shed and coil them up loosely inside the box," JT said.

"I see where you're going here pops, that's called a "hot box" ain't it." Pete asked.

"Something like that, I don't know how much water 200 feet of 5/8" hose will hold, but it should be enough to wash the stink off," JT said.

"Good plan, we're all getting a little rank," Pete said, sniffing his armpits.

"Once the hose is inside we can cover it. There are a few 4 by 4 pieces of plexiglass out there somewhere, use the best looking of them and screw them on to it, the DeWalt works, it's on the beer fridge," JT said.

"Will do, wanna hook it to the cube then?" Pete asked.

"May as well, we can use that until it freezes. Hell, we can even make a shower stall out of that portable shitter or a tarp!" JT continued.

"Better use the tarp, me and Brian have been using that as a shitter," Pete said sheepishly.

"No worries, that's what it's made for. A tarp it is then," JT answered.

"K, we'll get on that this afternoon while you're gone pops," Pete said.

"Sounds like a plan, the ladies will love it," JT said.

It was mid afternoon JT guessed, maybe later, but for sure they had at least three hours of sunlight left. It would take them around 20 minutes to get to the bridge, where they would wait around until nearly dark. Luke had his radio with a 15 inch whip antenna on it, JT's radio was still hooked up to the slick line strung up in the maple tree by the smoker. "Keep the volume up on that radio, we'll make a couple calls on the way to the bridge," Luke said.

"Will do, I'll stay out here and listen," Amy said.

On the way, JT was morbidity curious to know if the two bodies were still on the road at the crackhouse. That curiosity was confirmed when the pair got to within thirty yards of the car, the light south breeze carrying an absolutely disgusting smell with it, assaulting their senses.

Considering it hadn't been warm enough to cause a rapid decomposition, the odor was still incredibly powerful. Idling closer though, it became evident how it occurred when a small flock of turkey vultures took flight from their nearly unrecognizable buffet. Most of the scavengers landing a short distance away, hopping around as they awaited the all clear from their overwatch.

Rolling by the carnage, Luke stole a glance up the driveway toward the crackhouse, not seeing anything out of the ordinary. If the chick was still there, she had the dog inside with her otherwise there's no way those vultures would have been feeding. Riding past that mess caused JT to replay the event in his mind. "Did that happen yesterday, or the day before?" he asked himself, again unsure of what day it was. Wednesday, it had to be Wednesday, he reassured himself. Due to the severe lack of sleep, the last few days have seemed to blend into one very long day.

Seriously daydreaming as they topped the south grade of the flowage, JT snapped out of his trance as Luke pulled up next to him, pointing his hand to a couple of folks a short distance ahead of them walking the same way direction. Riding slowly, they came up along side of the pair, a man and a woman. JT recognized the man as Roger Fuller, he lives a half mile south of the ranch through the woods, down 200th a ways. To his knowledge, Roger wasn't married, which Roger confirmed by introducing his girlfriend, Barb.

"Where are you two headed, Roger?" JT asked as a greeting.

"Into town for some stuff, the power has been out since Monday down my way. I'm surprised the co-op doesn't have it back up by now, the last time I remember it being out this long was the blizzard of 91, remember that one?" he asked.

"Oh yeah, who could forget the Halloween Storm," JT replied with a chuckle.

It was becoming clear that Roger was oblivious to the situation, so JT went phishing a little, asking him why they are walking to town instead of driving his truck.

"Won't start, the battery is deader'n a door nail and I can't put the charger on it with no power. Her phone is dead too, we were too busy to remember to plug it in over the weekend," Roger said, turning to smile at Barb who sheepishly grinned back. "I don't have a cellphone, the house phone don't work either so I couldn't call anyone for a jump. We're hoping to hitch a ride to the store for some food and a bottle of Jack but there ain't been a single car went by yet. It's only a few miles to town, we can walk that far if we have to," he went on.

"Well, hop in the trailer, we can give you two a ride down to 192nd, it'll save ya a mile of walking," JT told them.

"Thanks, when we get to town my brother can run us home and we'll put some jumper cables on my truck," Roger replied. Not having the heart to tell him he's probably going to be walking back home too, most likely empty handed, they decided they'd just let him stay in the dark. There is absolutely no reason to wreck the good time these two are obviously having, that will happen soon enough.

After a mile, the two lovebirds got out of the trailer and began walking towards town as Luke and JT started west on 192nd, the township road that will eventually wind its way to the bridge.

"Luke, let's stop up there on that knob and see if we can hit the ranch with the radio," JT said, over the noise of their ATV's.

Pulling to a stop on the little rise, Luke keyed the mic on the radio saying "shredder calling the ranch."

Almost immediately the radio squawked back in a female's voice "loud and clear shredder." Amy was on the other end, the signal being strong and clear enough to be able to recognize her voice.

"Roger that, we will check back in while," Luke said into the radio.

"Ok, be careful, love you," came the reply from Amy.

"I like that slick line, damn we can get some range out of these radios. Why didn't you tell Roger what's going on?" Luke asked.

"I didn't want to see his reaction when I told him he wasn't going to be getting a fresh bottle of Jack Daniels," JT said.

They continued riding along at a good pace, certainly not fast, just steady, diligently scanning the area. There were plenty of houses on this section of the road, most of them being set off a distance, their long winding driveways providing the occupants with stunning views of the Apple River before it spilled into the Saint Croix.

Passing one house much closer to the road, a man mowing his front yard with an old push mower was visible, giving JT and Luke an enthusiastic wave as they passed by. Waving back, Luke said it's nice to see a little bit of normalcy, JT nodded his head in agreement. The closer they came to the point where the road curved quickly to the south, the closer the houses were built to the road, but there were far fewer of them also as the bluff top of the St Croix narrowed substantially leaving no room for building.

Rumors have been swirling through the township like wildfire as whispers of an easement purchase and the relocation of 37th street to the east, paid for solely by taxpayers' hard-earned dollars, bounced from resident to resident like a hot potato. JT couldn't avoid the gossip, only a hermit could be so fortunate.

"What a fucking scam," JT thought to himself. Using taxpayer money to make more money off of taxes. Oh well, it didn't matter anymore, about the only things that will be built around here will be fires to keep warm.

JT's mind was wandering yet again as they rode, the thought of winter coming soon just wouldn't give his brain a break. That topic rivaled the inevitable people that will be heading their way and they both are always front and center in JT's head. The only hope they had as far as winter goes is that they were due for an El Niño, which would help keep the jet stream up in Canada where it belongs. He also knew very well not to count on a "hope" to ease the cold.

One good thing about the mind wandering he'd been prone to is that it made time pass rather quickly and before he knew it they were pulling up the old gate that separated the railroad property from the township. The gate was locked in typical government fashion, a hundred dollar lock on a five dollar chain. Luke had tossed a bolt cutter in the trailer before they left, he'd been here many times in the past and he had a huge smile on his face when the cheap chain snapped and fell to the ground with a clank.

"I ain't getting ticketed this time," he said, telling JT about how he and two of his buddies got busted for trespassing on the bridge about ten years back, costing each of them a few hundred bucks in fines.

Driving through the rickety gate, they parked next to the now rusty railroad tracks. "You wanna take a walk out there?" Luke asked.

"Me, oh hell no, I can see just fine from here, that thing looks like it's ready to fall into the river," JT said.

"Well, it still holds up trains, give me your binoculars, I'll take a walk out out there and glass the other side for Sarah and Tyler," Luke replied. "I'm gonna call the ranch quick and see we can reach it from here, then I'll take a walk out there, All. By. Myself," he said, emphasizing the last words.

"Damn right you will, I gotta stay here and keep an eye on these machines while you go out sightseeing," JT said, then more seriously asking Luke how far out he's going. The bridge is a solid mile long, probably more that that.

"Half way at least, I wanna be able to see well past the end of this thing, and keep the glass working. I doubt they will be riding bikes on those railroad ties, they will be on the south side walking them on the walkway," he said.

"Makes sense, make that call and give me the radio, you don't need to be dropping that thing off through the bridge," JT replied.

The same call was made as before, with the same response and clarity. They were both impressed with the range they were getting. "That's close to five miles, not bad eh?" JT said.

"I think most of that is because of your antenna, how long have you had that?" Luke asked.

"Couple of years I suppose, this is the first time we really talked over it though," JT replied.

"Well, I like it," Luke said, slinging his rifle in front of him then clipping the carabiner on the binoculars to his belt loop. "I'll stay out there for an hour or so, what ya think of that?".

"Sounds good, be careful, I don't like this shit," JT said, concern in his voice.

"I will old man, get some rest," Luke answered.

"Hell, I just might go set my ass in that chair, it even reclines," JT chuckled.

JT shuddered as Luke slowly picked his way out onto the rickety expanded metal walkway until he was about a third of a mile out, where he stopped, glassing the area in front of him. JT turned and hopped in the trailer, sitting down in the plush van seat. Being incredibly tired, he almost immediately began to doze off.

A long nap wasn't the goal, it was that quick recharge he'd get from a 20 minute snooze that he so desperately needed. Waking up after what seemed like was just seconds, JT peered down the bridge, the warm afternoon sun now noticeably lower on the horizon. "Guess I had a good nap," he said to himself, stretching the creaks out of his back with a groan.

After noticing Luke now being way out on the bridge, JT went back to the four wheelers, busying himself by checking over the two aging machines. Spinning the gas cap off of the 300, the smaller of the two with a quick flick of his wrist, his hand inadvertently hit the the handle bar, fumbling the gas cap. As the cap avoided JT's flailing hands while he attempted to catch it, the hard plastic cap bounced like a super ball off a steel rail before rolling twenty feet down the opposite trap rock embankment. "Shit" he muttered out loud, crossing the track, gingerly sliding down the sharp crushed grey trap rock in a cloud of dust to retrieve the cap.

Reaching down to pick up the wayward gas cap, JT heard the report of gunshots ring out from the bridge. The distant "bang..bang, a pause, then another bang" echoed from the river valley. After scrambling to the top of the railroad bed as fast as JT's hands and feet could carry him, Luke was nowhere to be seen looking down the length of the bridge.

"LUKE, LUKE," JT frantically yelled at the top of his lungs as his heart began sinking. With panic setting in JT shaded his eyes from the afternoon sun, scouring the dark murky water below the bridge for any sign of his son.

Chapter Eleven

Tyler simply despised Mondays in radiology. Every patient admitted over the weekend requiring surgery would need a fresh set of images taken, either old school x-ray, an MRI, or a CT scan before the doctors could consult for surgery. By ten AM, he was with his 5th patient, this one being an emergency that flown in only a few minutes ago. Horrific injuries were caused to someone who had their feet up on the dash of a car when a collision occurred. When the airbags deployed the patient was folded up like a taco according to the EMT that brought him in.

This poor person needs at least a dozen images urgently. Tyler, whose schedule is already behind, mentally notes that he needs to call home and ask if his wife Sarah can cancel the ice time he had scheduled for the hockey team he coaches. He also needs to notify the parents of all the kids that he will have to cancel for tonight. It's going to be a long day for him.

At 10:58, Tyler was working on capturing the 15th image, having to wait for a few minutes while the anesthesiologist kept the patient under when the lights flickered and his machine shut down. The lights flashed back on after a moment but only a few were powered. The red warning lights in Tyler's room made him aware that the hospital was on generator power. This had never happened before, as they always coordinated tests when no procedures were scheduled. Tyler was both pissed and concerned that someone had really messed up this time, and he began to wonder whose head was about to roll. He hoped it wasn't Jarod, the chief of maintenance, as he was a great friend and they often played hockey, golfed, and went camping with their families on weekends.

"The OR is ready, get the patient in here NOW," a surgeon yelled through the door.

"We aren't finished yet," the anesthesiologist shouted back, but the surgeon was long gone.

Tyler stepped back, observing as a team entered his room, quickly extracting his patient. Shortly after, a voice came over the emergency intercom in the radiology department, dismissing all staff except emergency personnel.

"What in the hell is going on here Doc?" Tyler asked the anesthesiologist, a bit of edge to his voice.

"I do not know. Go home, but keep your phone on. This can't last forever," the doctor answered.

Tyler grabbed his bag, taking the dark stairs as he headed down to engineering to check in with Jarod, if he still had a job. The door to Jarod's office was open and inside, Jarod was blindly staring out the window of his ground floor office, looking at Interstate 35E.

"What the fuck was that?" Tyler said shockingly, walking in.

"Don't know," Jarod replied as he turned to face his friend. "I was on my computers finishing a CAD drawing for HVAC contractors to bid on when the system reset. The generators came online right away, but other than the normal shit it's supposed to run, nothing else works. None of my computers will even turn on, all the environmental controls are hosed," Jarod said, trailing off.

"So I take it that this wasn't a scheduled system check then?" Tyler asked.

"Nope, the next one is in November. I heard a bunch of racket out on 35, and when I opened my blinds this is what I saw," he said as he stared out the window at the dozens of cars in his narrow field of view, all seemingly parked on the freeway, some crashed into each other with steam rising from under their hoods.

Pulling his phone from his pocket, Tyler shook it, only it didn't wake up, he shook it some more, tapping the black screen.

"Mines dead too," Jarod said casually, pointing to the useless device on his desk.

At that moment for whatever reason, Tyler was brought back to a day from a year or two ago when he was sitting outside at the ranch with his father in law, JT. It was him and Luke, who is the old man's son and the old man. The old man had a stack of articles he had printed out from a guy…um…Peter something…weird last name, oh yeah..Peter Vincent Pry. The old man studied every article the guy ever wrote about EMP, or electro magnetic pulse. Pry held a PhD in some scientific field. He was considered the ultimate authority on EMP, he knew that much. The old man was showing them what Pry had anticipated the immediate aftermath of an event would most likely look like, and right now, that's exactly what Tyler was seeing.

"Jarod, pack your shit man, we gotta go," Tyler exclaimed.

"I can't leave here, I'm the chief engineer, you know that, I gotta be here to make sure all this shit comes back online, peoples lives depend on me," Jarod said.

"It ain't coming back online, not today, not tomorrow and probably not next year," Tyler said, almost angrily.

"What in the fuck are you talking about, and how the hell do you this?" Jarod yelled back, clearly surprised at the outburst.

"Look, just listen to me for a second will ya, have you ever heard of and EMP?" Tyler asked.

"I'm a fucking electrical engineer Tyler, of course I've heard about an EMP, what's your point?" Jarod replied, clearly annoyed.

"Ok, please calm down for a minute J," Tyler said, using his nickname now. "Sarah's step dad is fairly educated in this stuff, he studies this shit all the time, one guy he follows closely is a Doctor Pry, and in a few of his articles Pry says this is exactly what would happen if we were ever hit with one," he continued.

"No way, there is no way a missile can breach our air defense systems, it would have to come from the north or the west to get here, and those areas are covered in ICBM defense systems from Alaska to California. I like to read too," Jarod said smugly.

Tyler, trying to get through to his friend remained calm and said "we aren't at war with North Korea, Russia or China, we are at war with Iran, and according to the old man's research and his studies of Pry's work, Iran has been perfecting launching missiles off of freighter boats for years. Look, I don't always believe what the old man says, some of his shit is way out there, but I do believe him this time, I mean what else could shut us down, kill our phones and computers and stop all those cars on the freeway, it's the only logical option," Tyler explained.

"Can't be, my generators fired right up," Jarod shot back. Then, thinking about what he just said, he remembered a project that was just completed a few years back, it was a FEMA directive about hardening those systems.

"Aw shit, they are hardened," Jarod said. Tyler looked quizzically at Jarod. "Never mind, I'm gonna get my bag, we are both going to get fired for this, you know that, right Tyler."

"Fired from what, when those generators run out of fuel there won't be a hospital anymore, besides that, I've already been dismissed," Tyler replied.

Going the parking garage they found that neither of their vehicles functioned, but Tyler made sure to grab his North Stars backpack out of his car. In the backpack he had a large water bottle, an MRE, the map and the "protocol sheet" the old man sent home with him a long while back and one of those Leatherman multi tools, a gift from the old man.

"What way do you wanna go?" Tyler asked.

"Hell if I know, we can walk out 7th Street and go straight up 61 I suppose, it's a pretty straight shot," Jarod answered.

"Don't those neighborhoods up there by Lake Phalen get a little sketchy?" Tyler asked warily.

"Um yeah, they do, thanks, I forgot about that. Let's just walk up 35 then, we can cut east a little before 36 if we want to," replied Jarod. Jarod was rummaging around under the seat of his Jeep Rubicon, apparently looking for something. "Ah ha." he said triumphantly as he held up Taurus 9 millimeter handgun.

"What the hell are you doing with that thing, this is a gun free zone?" Tyler said, almost laughing.

"I'm an engineer, I'm smart," Jarod said in his best Forrest Gump voice as he fake picked his nose and stuck his finger in his mouth. Pulling his finger out of his mouth with a loud "pop", he said "let's go."

The two took off walking north up Interstate 35E, leaving the hospital that had been their second home for the last 9 years. They both had a few pangs of guilt that hit them from time to time, but they also knew there was nothing either of them would be able to do that would benefit the patients. They'd simply be in the way, soaking up valuable oxygen.

The freeway was a complete nightmare with cars and trucks everywhere, sitting where they quit or where they crashed into one another. Some vehicles had people in them, others they could see with the occupants milling around outside of them, hiding themselves as best they could from peering eyes as they were forced to relieve themselves on the interstate.

Of those people who were walking, most were heading south, even people that were in the northbound lanes appeared to be headed back into St Paul for whatever reason. Many of the people were carrying bags of some type, computer bags, purses, a few had backpacks, but all of them it seemed had a cellphone in their hands. They didn't speak to many people as they walked. Those they did talk with asked the obvious, what happened. They didn't give an answer other than a few "hell if I know's" along the way.

Tyler asked Jarod if he was up for a run, Jarod's answer was him changing his cadence into a slow run.

"I guess that's a yes," Tyler said catching up to him.

They were both very athletic and could easily run three miles without breaking a sweat. The running proved to also have a secondary benefit, that being when they passed those hundreds of people standing around, none of those folks bothered them, they just looked to see what they were running from. Some even got back in their cars when they saw the duo heading towards them. For a four lane freeway in each direction, there wasn't a lot of free space with all the vehicles scattered around. Many times the pair had to dodge around the open doors of cars, trucks and semi's.

The two had been running for about a mile when they heard foot steps coming up behind them. Confused, Tyler looked back to see a younger looking black man in a suit and tie gaining fast on them. By the looks of things Tyler quickly decided he wasn't going to out run this kid so they just let him catch up. The younger man didn't appear to even be breathing hard when he caught up to them and asked them where they we off to.

"North," Jarod replied.

"Me too, mind if I hang with you guys?" the young guy said.

The two looked at each other and saying "why not, just try and keep up!" as they both switched into a full run, just short of sprinting speed.

The kid probably weighed a hundred and eighty pounds and nearly six feet tall. He was a shorter and lighter than both Tyler and Jarod but before they made twenty strides the kid burst right in between the two, as he turned around, running backwards. Holding his hands up in a WTF sign, the younger man turned, sprinted ahead of them, slowing down after a hundred yards so the two would catch up.

"That's enough of that shit," Jarod said as he slowed to a walk, Tyler quickly followed suit. The younger man stopped, put his hands in his hips getting air as they caught up to him.

"Nice suit," Jarod said.

"Thanks, picked it out all by myself. I was on my way to an interview at the U. A few scouts were coming in, but I'm already late for that, the damn bus quit just like all these cars," he said.

"Scouts?" Tyler asked, still getting his wind back from the run.

"Yep, I play football for the Gophers, D'vante Jones, tight end," the kid said.

"No shit??" the other two said in unison, surprised, Jarod adding, "that was one hell of a catch Saturday, one handed, in the air, over the goal line."

"Thanks, that was the catch that got me the interview spot with the scouts, call me "D", even though I play offense," D said, laughing at his own joke as they all started walking again.

"I'm Tyler, this Jarod, where you headed?" Tyler said, making the introductions.

"Back to Forest Lake, my scholarship has enough built in to pay rent on a little house I share with another student, James. I like it up there, it gets me out of that damn city," D said.

The three walked and ran until reaching highway 36, then headed east catching highway 61, turning north again. The small talk turned to silence as they prodded along, each man digesting the scene around them in different ways. There were fewer cars now, but just like in the city, the people were standing around them, phone in hand.

D finally spoke again, asking "you guys got families?".

"Yeah, we do Tyler said, how bout you, got a girlfriend or anything?" Tyler asked D.

"Aw hell no, I don't have time for that crap, I mean I go on dates, which is easy for a handsome and talented man such as myself, but other than that, nope. Mathematics and football, that's all I have time for," he said smiling.

"Mathematics?" Jarod said, "I barely passed calculus," I hate math, that's what computers are for," Jarod said.

"What's your backup plan if the NFL falls through?" Tyler asked.

"The Air Force. I'm a First Lieutenant in the reserves, they let me fly F-16's out of Duluth a few hours a month," D replied.

"But you're still in school, how did you get a commission in the Air Force already?" Jarod asked.

"Oh that, yeah. I already have one bachelors degree in physics, I just went to the U for football, they like me there."

"So, you're just taking math for the hell of it then, are you a masochistic or something?" Jarod asked.

D laughed "na, I don't like pain really, it's just the scholarship that was available with the football stuff, so I snatched it up."

"When do you sleep?" Tyler asked jokingly.

"At night, just like you crazy white peoples do," D said with as much inner city slang as he could muster.

The trio were coming up on highway 96, where Jarod would split off to the east, his house just three or four miles down the road past the luxurious Dellwood golf course and country club then north a short distance. They said their goodbyes and Tyler told Jarod to be safe and take care of Karen, his wife, he replied in kind, and they went their own ways.

D gave a confused look and said jokingly "you two ain't a couple?".

Tyler laughed and they the picked up the pace. He wanted to say something sarcastic, but didn't, instead he was going to be the one who asked the questions. "So, you're in the Air Force, what's your take on what happened?"

D thought about how to respond to Tyler's question. He seemed like a decent guy and he didn't want to freak him out, but he finally he spoke. "From what I've seen so far, this was an electro magnetic pulse, an EMP, nothing else can do this, you know, have this profound type of effect."

"I've heard of them, my father in law is kind of a layman expert about it," Tyler said.

"He's probably read Doctor Pry's work then, he's predicted this for a long time. People called him crazy, a conspiracy theorist, but he was right. I've had a lot of security briefings, classified stuff. The only way this could have happened was if the missiles came from the Gulf of Mexico, it's the only airspace that isn't protected," D said.

"And we were warned," he said continuing, "but the bureaucracy in the military didn't act, they were confident that our nuke sniffers and subs would protect the gulf, but Iran has had this figured out for a long time, you know, how to contain isotopes on a warhead so they can't be detected, stuff like that, they also weren't worried about leaving an electronic signature because their mid range missiles didn't need satellite guidance, I mean they could basically fire them off like a bottle rocket."

"Yep, that's exactly what the old man said," Tyler said.

"Smart man. Did the old man mention what is predicted to follow an EMP?" D asked.

"No, he didn't, what's that's supposed to be?" Tyler asked.

D didn't answer that question truthfully, he just said "hell if I know, I was hoping he'd know."

But D'Vante did know what was next, a limited nuclear strike on half a dozen strategic targets scattered across the country, all military targets except for one, Washington DC. Which if D was correct, would already be incinerated.

"I'm getting off just up the road here in Hugo, I live about a mile to the east, are you going to stay in Forest Lake then?" Tyler asked.

"Probably not, I've got a feeling that my unit up in Duluth will need me, so I'm going to pack a bag and hop on my bicycle," D said.

"You're going to ride a bicycle, to Duluth?" Tyler asked with surprise.

"Yep, and it won't be the first time either, how do you think I was able to run so fast," D said with a laugh.

The two parted. Tyler liked the guy, he seemed incredibly intelligent and definitely easy going. Darkness was beginning to settle in now and the temperature dipped with the sunset. Tyler really wanted to get home to his wife and kid, and the closer he got to home the faster he moved.

Tyler was sprinting towards home now, just a few blocks away from where his wife and baby would be waiting. As he turned onto the walking trail lined with thick lilac bushes, Tyler never saw the hand of the man that held the ten-inch blade, but he felt the burning pain as it plunged into his chest. He fell backwards, defenseless, but the other two with the man who attacked him quickly descended upon Tyler like hyenas, stripping his backpack and checking his pockets. They found only a single MRE package, which they shoved back in the pack, whooping like coyotes before fleeing and leaving Tyler's body deep within the hedgerow of lilac bushes.

The trio of gang bangers/murderers, started walked back towards their old, rundown trailer house tucked in the back row of an equally decrepit trailer park. Their brazen actions had just cost a man his life, but they showed no remorse. Tyler was gone, and they had what they wanted.

Miguel, the youngest of the three, a nineteen year old illegal immigrant, asked why the other one, the oldest of the three, had cut that guy.

Karl, the eldest just said, "hell if I know, I just did."

John, the third guy, was scared, saying "they're gonna come looking for us now, that was fucked up Karl, ya didn't have to kill him."

"He killed himself ya idiot, he ran right into the blade, all I had to do was stand there and let him stick himself, and what the fuck is wrong with you, you didn't have a problem beating that old dude at the liquor store half to death earlier. In case you haven't noticed, there ain't no fucking cops coming dipshit, when's the last time you saw a car move or heard sirens," Karl said with authority.

Miguel didn't give a shit about anything that happened today, only asking Karl out of curiosity why he cut the man. That act of violence is nothing compared to what he did on his trip from Honduras to Texas. People killed and got killed every day, they did terrible things along the way. All that mattered was not being one that got killed. The cartels would go through the caravans, taking women, teenage girls and even children, brutally killing on the spot anyone who dared to open their mouths in protest.

After getting to the trailer, Miguel opened the backpack he had taken from this last guy, tossing the MRE on a pile of other food and crap they had stolen or robbed from people. As he was rummaging through the pack he found a couple sheets of paper folded into a square, one was a map, and the other was something printed, like notes but in a foreign language he couldn't read.

"Check this shit out," Miguel said, handing the papers to Karl.

"What's it say, read it before you give it to me, or can't you read ya fucking beaner," Karl snapped back.

Karl, snatching the papers from Miguel, tossed them to John, telling him to read it because he didn't have time for bullshit like that.

Unbeknownst to Miguel and John, Karl is so illiterate he couldn't even read a stop sign. Scanning over the copy of printed notes that was with the map, John said "these here are directions."

"To where?" Karl demanded.

"Not like that, it's directions of what to do and when to do it if an EMP happens," John said.

"What the fuck is an EMP?" Karl snapped.

"How the fuck am I supposed to know, but it says right here that if the power goes out, the cars quit and the phones quit all at the same time that an EMP happened. That guy you cut was supposed to leave his place and follow this map to a bridge with railroad tracks," John said.

"Gimme the fucking map," Karl said, thrusting out his hand. Studying the picture, Karl started to think about the map, his dimwitted brain coming up with a plan.

"If all these rich people around here have the same map and a bunch of them go there, we can lay up by that bridge and take whatever they got," he thought to himself.

Karl was feeling pretty good about himself and told John to give him the other piece of paper. While he pretended to read it, what he was really doing was looking for any indication that was official, like having a mark proving it was from the government. On the top right corner of the page the logo of the Somerset Wisconsin public library was printed in bold black letters, it's coat of arms embossed into the paper. That was all the confirmation he needed to see as he folded the paper and the map, jamming them in his pocket.

Chapter Twelve

Beside herself with worry, Sarah was scared now that Tyler didn't come home Monday after work, or yesterday. She was wearing out the carpet in her dark living room from pacing the floor back and forth. She was hungry, but what little food they had in the house needed to be cooked, and she hadn't had any power for two days.

To top it all off the battery in her car was dead too, so she couldn't go to the store or even McDonald's for lunch and she wasn't going to walk the two miles to the nearest store with the baby. One thing she was thankful for is the amount of baby food she had. She had caught a great sale at Costco, buying a full case of mixed pouches for the baby. She did go to her neighbors house yesterday afternoon to borrow their phone to call Tyler, but they said theirs were both dead too, and neither of their cars ran. This news caused Sarah to become even more concerned as an eerie feeling enveloped her.

Waking up this morning, Sarah, seeing the few dirty dishes in the sink decided to wash them by hand as the dishwasher was useless. With the baby still in his crib sleeping, she hoped doing the dishes would distract her a little. Opening the faucet at the sink, nothing came out. Standing there, staring at the faucet in shock she began to cry, wishing her mom was there as she slid to the floor.

At the moment she slid to the floor, a memory flooded her already overwhelmed mind. She remembered her step dad JT listening to a book on audible, she couldn't help but hear some of it from time to time because the old man is slightly hard of hearing and kept the volume up. A faint smile came her face as she remembered his antics. Struggling to remember the name, Sarah had read it on his screen dozens of times as she walked past his chair. Then it started to come to her, "Home," she thought, "home something or another,"

"Going Home," she said aloud.

That memory brought back even more memories of the old man and some of the crazy shit he'd do. She recalled several times when without warning, he'd turn off the electricity to the house and hide all the cellphones. He'd make them go through a bunch of drills, like filling the bathtub with water then going down into that nasty cellar to turn off the main water valve. Then he'd have them open the drain valve, emptying the lines inside the house so none of the pipes would freeze. Sarah cracked another weak smile at the memory of her mom freaking out at the sight of a mouse in the cellar. He'd also take them outside to his shop and show them how to plug the generator into the house to pump well water.

It is all written down in a folder and they knew where it was kept in case he wasn't home when the shit hit the fan, as he called it. He also had a timeline typed out, like what to do and when to do it. He was very adamant that they all understood that after three days, society would begin to collapse as the water quit flowing, the stores ran out of food and those who could take advantage of the situation, would.

Getting up from the floor, Sarah walked around the kitchen aimlessly as she stole glances at the open faucet of her kitchen sink as it hit her.

"I have to leave here and I have to do it now," she said with resolve.

Tyler's words echoed through Sarah's mind, "If you ever need help or feel afraid, go to Jarod's house." Sarah found herself following his instructions now, her heart pounding in her chest as she packed hastily. Though her nerves threatened to engulf her, Sarah was shocked at her own focus as she methodically gathered the essentials, baby food and diapers first, before moving on to clothes, hats, mittens, and winter coats for her and the baby. She gathered everything into Walmart bags, tied tight with square knots.

She took her small son into the garage, where the towable stroller was still hooked up to the bicycle. After loading their precious belongs, Sarah buckled in the baby securely, watching as he turned to her, all big eyes and curious expression. With butterflies in her stomach, Sarah felt the sudden terror grip her, refusing to relinquish its hold. She couldn't move, her muscles resisting her brain's signals to pedal away from the house. Her own fear pushed so hard, until finally, Sarah took a deep breath and willed herself to pull the red handle on the garage door. The sudden gust of fresh air that followed drew a shiver of apprehension from her frame, but she ignored it as best as she could and focused on her task.

Checking her son carefully one last time, she left a note, hastily written on the back of an envelope, taped to the door leading into the house.

"I'm went to Jarod's," it read.

Sarah quickly pedaled towards the county road, stopping instinctively to surveil the view past the long stretch of lilac bushes. Seeing the county road empty, Sarah turned left and began to pedal hard. In less than a mile, she found Goodview Road. Though the route was familiar, seeing plenty of abandoned cars and no people was unsettling. Apart from wild birds and a few deer grazing the lush hay fields, the only human creatures Sarah spied were a man and a woman near a house down the way from where she was headed. The wafting scent from their grill had her stomach grumbling, but she resisted the urge to stop and ask for food, too much was at stake.

The baby seemed calm and happy during the trip, captivated by the scenery arrayed before them. Instead of the typical bustling of a busy roadway, there was odd silence, only compounded by the wind rustling through clusters of majestic oaks and maple trees lining the road. The ride may have been a challenging one for peddling, but she was pleased with the relative calm of the quiet country road.

Within an hour she was turning right on Apple Orchard road, crossing over the well worn railroad tracks to Jarod's house- the second driveway on the left. Pedaling along the magnificent tree lined driveway to the house belonging to Jarod and Karen, Sarah was taken aback yet again with the stunning beauty of the property. The large, opulent home had been perfectly built into a thick woodlot bordering the 16th fairway of the prestigious Dellwood Country club's back nine. She knew Jarod was quite affluent, but even at that, their home had to be well into the seven digit range.

Stopping her bike in front of the decoratively adorned garage doors, the area was eerily quiet as she extricated the baby from stroller. Walking to the massive mahogany front door, she peeked in the blurred sidelight, banging the brass door knock. Nothing. Knocking again, she looked inside while trying the door knob, it was locked. Raising the knocker again, she stopped, seeing movement inside the house. Looking through the window, she saw Jarod walking slowly to the door with Karen close behind him.

Opening the door, Jarod greeted Sarah, ushering her in, looking around outside for Tyler.

"Where's Tyler?" Jarod asked.

"I was hoping you knew, he hasn't been home since the lights went out," Sarah said, worried.

Stunned, Jarod's mind began spinning as he struggled to find the words. "Sarah, Tyler and I walked home Monday afternoon, we split up where 96 meets 61." Instantly Sarah became hysterical, Karen moving in closer, gently reached for the baby, Sarah didn't resist.

"Then where is he, where is he?" she screamed, over and over. Jarod knew. He knew Tyler and he knew the only thing that could possibly keep him from these two, but he wasn't going to tell Sarah that, not yet, probably not ever.

Guiding Sarah to the sitting room couch, the two women sat down, the room dimly lit by what little sunlight infiltrated the curtains through the canopy of trees surrounding their home. Jarod, after pacing around sat with them, doing his best to just be quiet for a moment as Sarah processed his words. Finally, after what seemed like an eternity the anxiety calmed enough for Karen to ask Sarah if she would like a soda, apologizing for only having Diet Coke.

Nodding her head, Sarah asked if she could get a sandwich or something, anything, saying she hadn't eaten anything in a couple of days.

"We are out of food too Sarah. We were downstairs packing some bags, getting ready to ride our bikes to my brothers house up by Cambridge when you came to the door," Jarod said.

"Your welcome to come with us if you'd like, maybe we can find some food on the way," he calmly said.

"Thank you, but I need to go to my moms," is all Sarah said in reply.

"She lives over by Somerset, right?" he asked and Sarah nodded her head yes.

"If you go back to those railroad tracks, you can ride your bicycle all the way to that big bridge over the St Croix," Jarod said calmly.

"The high bridge? How far away is it?" Sarah asked.

"Not that far really, maybe fifteen miles, it would only take you a couple of hours three tops to get there," he said optimistically.

"It would take less if you rode her bike pulling that trailer. I can wait until tomorrow to go to your brothers house," Karen interjected.

"I can do that Sarah, you can ride my bike and we will get there a lot faster, my legs are used to pulling a load behind a bike. It should be early enough when I get back to ride up by your place and look for any sign of Tyler," Jarod said.

Sarah's mood brightened greatly as she became optimistic- maybe he'd see Tyler and tell him where she is. Jarod knew he was lying- Karen knew he was lying- but they kept it to themselves.

"Let me take a look around through the cupboards again, there has to be something I missed for you to eat," Karen said, before coming back shortly with a foil package of albacore tuna, two cellophane wrapped saltine crackers and another Diet Coke.

Jarod, looking at Karen quizzically as she lied, knew what she had done, she'd gone to the basement, taking one of the precious three packs of tuna they had and brought it up for Sarah.

Karen's look spoke volumes to Jarod. Getting up from the couch, he went to the garage for his bicycle, opening the small side door for light. As he finished lowering the seat to fit Sarah's small frame the two women entered the garage. Sarah, after strapping the baby solidly back in the towed stroller solemnly said "I'm ready."

"I'll ride with you to until we get close to the approach of the bridge. If I remember right the bridge has a narrow walkway down the full length on the south side, you'll probably have to ditch the trailer though, there's no way you can ride that walkway towing it. You will probably have to walk your bike across too, tell you what, just hang on a sec," Jarod said. Coming back from a supply room with a pair of nylon saddle bags for his bicycle, he clamped the apparatus onto the tube that holds the seat and to the two arms that connected the rear tire to the frame.

"When we get there, we'll just fill the bags with what we can, then ditch the trailer. You keep my bike and I'll ride yours home, I've got a good selection to ride to my brothers place," Jarod said.

Karen came back with "you could ride a different bike everyday for a month." For the first time today, they all chuckled a little as they mounted the bikes.

"Thank you," Sarah said to Karen who replied with a hug and too many new tears.

Karen did manage to say "good luck, say hello to your mom for me."

"I will, and good luck to you too," Sarah said, and with a final wave, they began the journey.

As Jarod and Sarah rode their bicycles towards the maintenance trail that ran parallel to the tracks, Jarod couldn't help but notice the rough terrain. The trail was anything but well-maintained, composed of a combination of limestone and grey trap rock, much smaller in size than the ballast under the tracks. The narrow path was fraught with obstacles, gullies and exposed roots challenging even the surest bikers. Encroaching vines and branches repeatedly snagged at their bags and sleeves as they weaved in and out of the overgrown trails, trying to avoid making too much noise.

Chapter Thirteen

Word was quickly getting around the small town about the three stooges, Karl, John and Miguel. Tuesday morning, the tables turned on the trio while attempting to jump another guy on the trail, using the same surprise attack as yesterday but in a different part of town.

Jumping from behind his hiding spot at the sound of footsteps, Karl thrust his knife forward at the person in front of him. Instead of his prey screaming in fear, the man's hands flashed in front of Karl's face, one striking the back of Karl's hand, the other striking his wrist, sending the knife flying wildly from his grip. Spinning sideways, the man's right leg flew out like a bolt of lightning, his foot crushing Karl's face sending him to ground. Miguel, seeing Karl falling began rushing the man wildly head on, not even seeing the open palm that crushed his nose, knocking him unconscious. John foolishly squared off in front of the man, feebly attempting a roundhouse kick of his own that the man easily blocked as the vicious elbow strike to the tendon on top of John's thigh caused him to see stars. But what came next devastated John as the man's right knee came up into his groin, it's force lifting Johns feet from the ground. Screaming in pain and grabbing for his manhood, John to crumpled to the ground, joining his partners in their own misery.

Standing over the three as they were sprawled out on the ground, the man waited for the trio to come around. As they did, well, not John, but as Karl and Miguel attempted to get on their feet he said angrily "next time I see you fuck sticks I'm going to break your filthy fucking necks right after I shove a broom handle so far up each of your assholes that you'll choke on it. Hell, I might even do it in your sleep before there is a next time. I know right where you fucking dimwits live, lot 10 out in that shit hole trailer court."

Then, after picking up the stainless steel Rambo knife by the blade and throwing it so close to Karl's head that it almost cut the earlobe off of his right ear he turned, silently walking away.

Eventually the three injured miscreants made their way back to the dilapidated trailer house. The trek was long and excruciating for poor John as he could barely stand, much less walk. The other two were simply bloody, and in Karl's case, toothless messes. Both of Miguel's eyes were swelling shut, his face and clothes covered in blood from the savage open hand strike the man delivered. Miguel had been in many, many fights in his life, never once being hit with such force as this time though when the man's hips snapped his torso towards him, propelling the hand strike into his face with the momentum of his whole body.

Karl took a back kick to the teeth after being disarmed, the heel of the man's black running shoe knocking out three of his top teeth and four on the bottom, mangling, nearly shredding both of his lips in the process. Karl assumed his jaw was broken, but the pain he felt right now from his facial tissue overcame that pain. It hurt so much he didn't even know what hurt.

Stumbling with his words through his mangled, broken face Karl said "Fuck this shit, let's get going to that bridge. We'll wait out all these fuckers who try to cross, then take what we want."

Miguel spoke up, angrily "we can just kill them, take everything."

"That too. We'll make a camp, set the tent up out in the woods aways, out of sight and earshot. Lets get moving so we can figure out the best place to set up on them," Karl said indignantly.

Fourteen hours after beginning their fifteen mile journey, the trio, finally arriving at the bridge started looking for a spot to set up camp. Karl, frustrated because he had to wait for John to catch up often because his nuts are the size of lemons, began looking around, cussing at every branch he tripped over in the process.

"You two, get the fuck over here and get the tent set up in this opening. I gotta find a place to watch the trail," Karl said after locating a spot about 75 yards back in the woods on the south side of the tracks.

Sneaking out of the cover of the dense woods, Karl surveyed the area further, choosing an ambush spot behind a very thick clump of small white pines, just west from the now unlocked gate on the trail. Seeing the small signal shack on the tracks, Karl began devising his plan.

After fitfully setting up their makeshift camp, the trio readied themselves for a test run of their first ambush. Hiding in the thick, low pines just off the tracks, Karl and John will sneak out behind their target after they've passed, attacking from the rear, while Miguel, having the knife, will crouch behind the small signal shack further down the tracks then jump out startling whoever is coming. If it was a big group, they'd keep hiding, but if it was one or two people they'd jump them, like a pack of coyotes.

Settling into the hide, John was not in a good place. The pain between his legs convinced him his testicles were ruptured. He's hot, running a fever, getting more aggravated the longer he crouched inside the thick pine trees, their needles pricking him every time he moved.

After they have been waiting there for what seemed like a couple hours John said "Ain't no one fucking coming, I'm going to the tent, this is bullshit."

"Sit the fuck down, are you blind. There's two right down there to the left on bicycles, now shut the fuck up and pay attention. It looks like they got a lot of shit, that dude is pullin a trailer," Karl whispered.

Going prone after seeing movement through the binoculars, Luke wasn't sure what he'd seen, whatever it was looked to be close to mile out. Sliding the rifle to his back while trying to stay as low as possible, he crawled further and further out on the bridge, stopping occasionally while glassing the area in front of him.

"This is a bad idea," Luke said to himself after sneaking further out, watching what he now knew to be people. They were still a long way off, four hundred yards he was guessing, but through the binoculars he can now clearly see two people on bicycles, one with a trailer.

Stopping well back from the gate, Jarod began helping Sarah take what she needed from the stroller until the saddle bags were stuffed to overflowing.

"Good luck Sarah, you'll need to get up on the tracks soon before this trail dips down to the river. It should be clear sailing from here I hope," Jarod said.

"Thank you so much Jarod, there's no way I'd have made it here this soon without you," Sarah replied. After some goodbyes and a heartfelt hug, Jarod left, quickly pedaling away as fast as he could.

Watching intently through his binoculars, Luke noticed the pair briefly stopped after another hundred yards of riding, then noticed them shuffling gear between themselves before tossing the trailer off the path into the tree line, then one of them quickly riding off the way they'd came.

Sarah's baby, now awake and hungry, will have to wait it out for a while, Sarah deciding not to feed him until she was across the bridge and in Wisconsin. Taking a look around her, she shivered at the ominous feeling coming over her, giving the baby a pacifier while securing him in the front sling strapped to her chest that she had brought along.

Pushing the bike up to the tracks with it's wheels bouncing over the weathered railroad ties, Sarah hurriedly covered the hundred yards to where the narrow walkway began near a small shack next to the railway.

Watching through the cracks in the walls of the old signal shack, Miguel readied himself for the spoils of the attack as he sat, impatiently waiting until she came just a little closer.

Seeing the one left behind pushing a bicycle onto the tracks and walking to the bridge, Luke began focusing the binoculars on the form getting closer, it soon becoming clear that it was a woman with a baby strapped to her chest. Glassing the woman intently, Luke, caught a flash of sunlight, a reflection he thought from the signal shack and pulled the rifle from his back, flipping down the bipod and quickly thumbing the safety off while he continued watching through the binoculars.

Approaching the run down signal shack, Sarah jumped, screaming as Miguel's ghoulish figure jumped out not twenty feet in front of her, the big knife reflecting the waning sunlight off its blade. Quickly turning back and looking, Sarah hoped beyond hoping for Jarod to still be there. Not seeing him, Sarah froze in terror seeing two more disfigured men.

Luke was laying on the tracks watching as this played out like a movie, seeing the person from the signal shack jumping to the tracks waving a knife around. Looking beyond the shack through the binoculars, Luke saw another form come out of the woods, with another one behind it, the last form falling to it's knees for a few seconds before getting back up, joining the first as they snuck up on the distracted woman. Setting the binoculars down along side him, Luke settled in behind the powerful Leopold glass on top of his rifle.

A sharp crack followed instantly by a dull slapping sound and the report of a firearm released Sarah from the death grip terror held on her. Dropping to her knees protecting her child, Sarah let the bike fall against the flimsy handrail as another crack came, followed by the same sickly slap and report. Looking in front of her to that sound, Sarah witnessed the remnants of a vapor cloud of blood escape the chest of the man holding the knife. She stared, frozen in fear as he took one step forward before falling to his face between the rails. Glancing behind her to the sound of the first slap, she watched in horror as the sound of another crack passed by her, witnessing a man's head literally exploding with a massive spray of pink mist flying out behind his head. Time stood still as she watched the body. She jumped as the man slowly fell backwards, with a small cloud of dust rising as he crumbled to the ground.

Luke could hear the woman screaming again while simultaneously hearing the old man behind him yelling from a far away distance, "LUKE, LUKE." Standing up and running to the woman, Luke raised his hand in a sweeping "charge" motion, hoping the old man saw the gesture. Getting closer, Luke caught a glimpse of the woman, instantly recognizing her form. With that knowledge sinking in, who it was, he was sprinting again, the rifle banging off his chest as he ran. Sarah was still screaming with her head buried in her arms covering the child she held.

"Don't hurt my baby, don't hurt my baby," she's screamed repeatedly.

Sliding to a stop in front of her as the gravel flew off the soles of his boots Luke said, "Sarah, Sarah it's Luke, it's Luke, your gonna be ok."

This all took place in a matter of seconds. JT hearing the shots, yelling to Luke, not seeing him anywhere then seeing him get up from the tracks, waving his arm wildly over his head running the other direction. JT's mind was reeling as he hopped on the green four wheeler and fired it up. JT jumped one rail of the tracks, straddling it as he blasted towards his son as fast as he dared, not know what in the hell Luke was doing going the other way. The small dips between the ties rattled his teeth as the poor machine bounced over tie after tie, it's soft tires and suspension absorbing most of the shock.

Getting closer to them JT was shocked seeing Sarah with Luke standing over her, scanning the area behind them. JT slid the machine to a haphazard stop before running towards her and the baby.

"Shit kid, are you ok, are either of you hurt?" he asked frantically, looking her up and down as she held on to Luke's leg with the strength of a vice grip.

"Did you see Tyler?" JT asked Luke, looking around.

"Not unless he was the guy that left Sarah, so no," Luke replied.

Seeing Sarah calming some, JT asked "Sarah, where's Tyler?"

"I don't know, I, I thought he was still at work but Jarod said they....," she said in between sobs.

Helping Sarah get up, they set her up on the back rack of the quad. Luke, after removing the saddle bags from the bike, tossed them to JT then he launched the bike over the railing into the water below with a mighty heave and a splash.

Walking past Luke, JT asked him why he did that, toss the bike. Shrugging his shoulders Luke said, "donno, didn't want anyone else to have it I guess."

JT had already saw the shape the first guy was in, laying face down with a huge knock-off stainless steel Rambo knife still in his hand. A small blood spot the size of a silver dollar formed on the center of his back, just below his shoulders but the blood spray from the exit wound on the track bed in front of him told JT he was probably dead before he hit the ground.

The next one he came upon was laying on his back, the corpses lips mangled and disfigured, his mouth agape showing a big hole where his teeth should have been. This one had an entry hole in his chest, the same silver dollar sized blood stain had formed.

The last guy though, good god, on his forehead right between his eyes was a little dark red hole, his eyes were open and crossed, the left eye halfway bulged out of his skull.

"A head shot?" JT asked quizzically as Luke walked up.

"Wasn't planning on it, I thought he was farther away so I aimed high. Lucky I didn't miss. Wanna toss em in the river," Luke asked.

"Oh fuck no, leave em where they lay, maybe it will give the next group coming along second thoughts," JT said.

Luke started patting the two dead guys down as JT began walking back to Sarah and said "Dad, hang on, you gotta check this shit out," handing JT two sheets of paper he pulled from a front pocket of the first guy he shot.

"What is it?" JT asked taking the papers from him.

"Look at it, you tell me," Luke said.

"Well fuck me running," JT said. In his hand was the map and protocol sheet they'd given Tyler a couple years ago, JT knew for a fact he carried it in his backpack, always.

Walking back to the four wheeler, Luke patted Sarah on the shoulder telling her "you're gonna be ok little sis" then he sat on the front rack, holding the saddle bags with Sarah's stuff and his rifle. Sarah and the baby were on the back rack, Sarah still crying softly as they started to ride slowly to the east and off the bridge. Stopping when he got close to the guy that was wielding the knife, JT got off the machine to check the man's pockets, the only thing in them was a Leatherman tool which he pocketed. Then, after inspecting the shit quality Walmart brand Rambo knock off he thrust the Pakistani steel blade as far as he could push it into the dead man's back, only stopping when he felt the blade hit the rocks underneath him.

"What the fuck was that for?" Luke asked.

As JT looked at Sarah, he silently mouthed the word, "Tyler."

Luke nodded, saying, "fuck yeah."

Riding slowly to the east, the view of the massive St Croix river valley was stunning to see from the bridge. Along it's banks the oak, poplar and maple trees were still holding on to their fall colors, with the brilliant reds, yellows and oranges ablaze in the setting sun. The beauty was almost enough to take their minds off of what just took place. Almost.

The old blue Polaris was sitting where JT had left it, it's key still in the ignition. In his earlier panic, he opined that he didn't think things through very well by leaving the key in the machine. "Noted," he said to himself.

Once Sarah and the baby were settled nicely in the trailer, Luke walked over, pulling the radio from JT's shirt pocket. Keying the mic he said, "ranch, we're inbound, tell Kate we have Sarah and the baby."

"Roger that, will do," came the reply, from either Pete or Brian.

Riding a different route to avoid retracing their tracks, the narrow township roads were eerily quiet, completely devoid of people. The scattering of homes visible from the road appeared abandoned, yet evidence of life exists, given away by the aroma of grilled meat wafting over the cool evening breeze.

It was that distinct smell that shook Sarah out of her shocked state as craned her neck, searching for the source "holy crap, that smells good, I wonder what they are cooking?" she asked with a moan.

Passing the gravel pit on the corner of 45th and 192nd, JT could see light white smoke rising from the exhaust stack of one of Tommy's old Cat front end loaders. He pointed down to the pit, Lukes gaze following his hand, his head nodding in affirmation as they continued east to the county road. Once there, only four houses would be visible and one tucked so far off the road that it didn't matter. JT isn't worried about seeing the houses, his main concern is being seen on running

ATV's by their occupants. After cresting the grade beyond the flowage, the crackhouse would be the next place to come into view.

Leading the way on the green machine, Luke cradled the rifle in his lap, hanging on to the weapon left handed while carefully scanning the area ahead. Coming up on the car, JT heard Sarah's shriek over the noise of the engine and tires, yelling "what IS that disgusting smell?"

Passing the car, Sarah let out yet another high pitched yelp after seeing the source of the putrid odor. Then, after a few minutes, they were turning down the long driveway of the ranch, the sun just dipping below the trees to the west of the house. Casting its bright orange glow onto the tree line of the eastern side of the little valley, JT knew it would soon be dark.

Riding up to the house, everyone was outside waiting, even JT's mom was outside, wrapped up in a camouflage robe of his. It was quite the emotional scene, and frankly an emotional download for JT. The women were all happily crying in some fashion or another, Joni was even caught up in it, wiping a tear from her eye with the back of her hand.

Except for his mom that is, she is checked out again. Sarah, walking to the picnic table where her gramma was sitting said in a sweet voice "hello gramma."

"Oh sweetie, it's so nice to see you," she replied.

That was her "tell", she'd call someone sweetie, or honey if she didn't remember their name. She looked tired too, but she had probably been up all day cooking whatever she could find. That task, cooking, she had no problem with. Except for lighting the stove that is.

Needing a moment, JT walked around the shed by the camper to be alone. The last few days have been an absolute overload for the senses and emotions. No sleep, all of the crazy madness they've witnessed, it was starting to take it's toll on him. There is no way he'd be able to contain it much longer.

Ever since JT was a kid, if weird shit was going on in his life he could feel his emotional reservoir fill to capacity. Although it was a rare occurrence that his "drain field" couldn't keep up with supply, this was one of those times, knowing Tyler's fate was the last drop it could hold.

With tears running freely, JT stood there, sobbing, leaning on the tongue in groove siding of the shed, then as if on cue, his stomach began to turn, violently launching what little it contained to the ground. Then, like magic, as soon as he puked it was gone. All of it, all those crazy emotions lay there in a little pile of puke in the grass.

Still leaning against the old red shed catching his breath, JT felt a bump against the back of his knee. Turning around to see what it was, there was Pepper, pawing his leg again. Seeing her there and knowing she understood him, his world was right again, as right as could be anyway. "C'mon girl, let's get back to the festivities," he said to her with a scratch of her ears.

Wiping his face on his sleeves, JT walked back to rejoin the group, who was now just Luke, Pete and Brian, everyone else having went inside to dote over the baby and Sarah. JT motioning for Luke to follow him, walked behind the shop.

"Give me that map and stuff you got from that guy," JT asked.

Pulling the folded papers from his pocket, Luke handed them over asking what he was going to do with them.

"Burn em," JT said as he took a lighter from his pocket, torching the two pieces of paper. "This is between us, there's no sense in shattering any glimmer of hope Sarah may have left."

"Agreed," Luke said as JT let the burning mass of paper fall to the ground, it soon turning to ashes.

"Beer?" JT asked Luke.

"Why not," he said as they each grabbed two, bringing one to Pete and Brian.

"Thanks pops, how much more beer do you have?" Pete asked, cracking his.

"Six cubes, but I know how to get more," he said. That got their attention.

"How?" Brian asked.

"I know a gal," JT said with a wink.

With his stomach now completely empty, it was absorbing the little bit of alcohol in the beer, the slight warmth from it felt calming to JT's soul. "Is there anything to eat around here?" he asked no one in particular.

Pete, jumping up at the question went to the smoker, and using a tiny flashlight so see with he sliced off a piece of elk roast he had on the far end of the grill, keeping it warm. The perfectly seasoned wild game was out of this world delicious, but as hungry as JT was he thought an old corn cob would have tasted good right about then.

"Good idea getting all that meat smoked, if it's nice and dry it should keep along time in those bags," JT said.

"Yup, and there is a lot left to put on the smoke too," Pete said.

"Guys, we gotta come up with a plan, and soon. Today, well tomorrow morning technically, will be the end of day three, so in a few days there are GOING to be hordes of people headed this way from the cities, I've got an idea to kick around," JT said.

"We're all ears," Pete said.

Telling them what he was thinking, about towing a few of the cars that are stalled out there on the roads down to the flowage, JT said they can use the pickup for the towing and the tractor to push them sideways right up to that tall fence, closest to the road, maybe they can even tip them on their sides. He told them it should stop anyone on ATV's and bicycles, maybe even some walkers. He went on saying he's sure they are going to be seeing some older cars and trucks soon too, but gas is going to be an issue so that should be short lived. Anyway, that's what he'd been thinking he said. The boys listened intently as he spoke, none of them interrupting.

"Can't people just walk upstream to the dam and cross there?" Luke asked.

"Sure, but that's going to take some fortitude, the crown of that dam doesn't even have a handrail, also, it's fenced pretty tall right to the dam, by the time anyone makes it this far I'm hoping they are close to running out of that fortitude," JT said.

Luke, playing the devils advocate, said "if it was me, I'd find a way over or around the cars, if they are coming this way, that means there's nothing behind them worth staying for."

"Good point, I hadn't thought of that," JT said. Pete asked if the effort was worth the reward, saying maybe they should just worry about road the ranch is on, put a barricade up at the stop sign on the county road. Maybe some of the neighbors would even help man it, it would benefit them too.

"We might end up doing both," Luke said and continued "we can't stop them all, not even close. Anyone seeing a barricade, manned or not is going to think there is something worth protecting on the other side, it's human nature. The only thing people are going to value is their own life, nothing more."

"If that," Brian said, "hell, in a week I'd bet people are gonna be willing to kill for a can of beans," he continued.

"Think about it, what is the single thing people fear the most? Death, well, the dying part of death. I say we send a message that there is nothing worth dying for on the other side of the barricade," Luke said, continuing on his train of thought.

"How do you propose we do that?" JT asked.

"Just like we did at the bridge, we leave a pile of bodies to rot, it'd give me pause from continuing on, and that's saying something," he said.

"Where are you going to get a pile of bodies?" JT asked him, totally serious.

He answered "Oh, I think they will present themselves soon enough, we already have a good start at the crackhouse, let's build there. I mean we can definitely do the barricade at the flowage if you say so, but, and no disrespect intended pops, I'm with Pete on this one, there won't be near enough return on the investment." "And," he went on, "if someone has the stones to breach that pile of bodies, then the odds are we'd be killing him eventually, or get killed by him eventually." He wasn't finished talking yet and continued "ninety nine percent of people who wander upon a pile of dead bodies are going to un-ass the place twice as fast as they got there. The last one percent will be all we will have to deal with, and those we can deal with on our terms," he finished with.

"Ok," JT said, "but on one condition, we put up a sign painted in big red letters, like it was written in blood, that says "turn around before you end up like this."

The boys laughed at that, thinking he was making a joke. "I'm serious guys, it's fair warning, and in my mind anyone going through will have accepted the obvious risk and consequences," JT said.

"I like it. We know where three more are to add to the pile, I doubt if anyone couldn't understand that message, me and Pete will take the trailer back out before first light, and dump em," Luke said.

"Ok, but leave the guy with the knife lay there. He might slow down people thinking about crossing the bridge, the honest ones anyway," JT replied.

"Deal," Luke said.

"I'll add another car too, I'll pull the sonic up there after I siphon the gas out of it and pull the battery, I may even flip that one there on its side, you know, for dramatical effect," JT said.

It's getting late JT said, telling them he needed some sleep. Brian asked if someone should head out to the end of the driveway.

"Na, fuck it. Lets just take turns at the smoker overnight, the dogs are out anyway, they will let us know if anything's coming our way," Luke said with a yawn.

Then JT asked if anyone has seen the dogs lately. Pete pointed with his beer can to the north side of the house. "They are all up there, I cut that deer spine into four and gave them all a piece, that should keep 'em busy all night."

"Thanks Pete," JT said, heading to the house.

Inside, JT noticed his mom in her bed, snoring lightly, bringing a smile to his face as he quietly closed her door. With no one else in sight, he wondered how four women and a baby are going to sleep on one bed, then as soon as he thought it, Joni came into the living room with a candle, plopping down in the recliner.

"It's crowded in there, mind if I join you out here?" she asked.

"Not at all," he said, laughing under his breath.

"What's so funny?" she asked.

"Oh nothing, good night Joni," JT said.

"Nite pops," she said, curling up in a recliner.

A stirring in his moms bedroom woke JT. Joni's chair was empty, and he'd heard the toilet flush. As he poked his head into check on his mom, he found her still sleeping nicely. Joni came back in the living room asking "how's momma?" as she sat.

"Her breathing is getting worse, I'm worried about her passing out, she's only good for a half a dozen steps before she has to stop and catch her breath," JT told Joni.

Joni explained that it's not uncommon, she's probably suffering from congestive heart failure too.

"She's out of the diuretic pills too," JT said as he walked to the door, taking a look around through the dusty window for the boys.

Eyeing Brian still sitting at the picnic table by the smoker, he seemed to be in a trance. Poking his head out the door, JT startled Brian saying "morning sunshine." Asking where Luke was, Brian relayed that Luke and Pete had left a couple of hours ago on the four wheeler with the trailer.

"Damn, he wasn't shitting when he said he was headed out before first light," he thought, seeing the eastern sky just beginning to brighten.

Heading back in the house to round up some coffee, JT noticed movement through the kitchen window, catching glimpses of the four wheeler through the thick buckthorn and trees lining the driveway. They were both there, Luke and Pete, one driving and one riding in the trailer. Content seeing them return, he continued making the brew. Walking outside once the coffee pot was on the stove, Joni joined him to greet the boys. The four dogs were gathered, sniffing the trailer. Except for Duke, he was in it, licking up what he assumed was blood.

"I shoulda brought a tarp," Luke said.

Pete piped up with "that's the most disgusting thing I've ever seen. Those two on the bridge were bad, but when we tried to move that other one at the car, oh my fuck," he said.

Luke was about to go into detail, but one look at Joni's face turning green made him stop. "Yeah, it sucked," was all he said.

Joni asked what in the hell they were doing that for. Luke told her there were three bodies on the bridge where they went to wait for Sarah yesterday, telling her they decided to go back and get two of them this morning to "add to the pile," as he put it.

"Why were there bodies on the bridge?" she asked.

"Wanna take this one old man?" Luke asked, almost pleading.

"We shot them yesterday, they were trying to ambush Sarah on the bridge," JT said, leaving out the part that Luke shot all three of them.

"Wait, how, I mean….?" Joni asked, trailing off.

Luke pointed to his rifle and said "that."

"Ohhh she said, Sarah didn't say anything about that last night, she is so sad, worried about where her husband is."

"She's in shock I think, yesterday was a big day for her," Luke said.

"I know the feeling, I'm glad she had a happy ending, like I did," Joni said, smiling so warmly they could feel it.

Turning back to Luke she asked if they could teach her how to shoot one of those, and a pistol.

"Sure, have you ever shot a gun before?" Pete asked.

"Nope, I hated them. I've seen so many people mangled by gunshots, but I've had a change of heart recently. I don't ever want to be in that position again," she said, trailing off. They all knew exactly what she was talking about, and didn't respond, instead they just nodded their heads in affirmation.

"Let's start with a pistol Joni, odds are that if you need it, you'll be defending yourself, not looking for a fight," JT said.

Going inside, JT picked up Kate's small Walther P22 and it's holster, one of those kydex clip on jobs from its spot on the shelf by his chair. Removing the magazine, he cleared the weapon, handing it and the holster to Joni.

"Here, clip this into your jeans, and then put the pistol in it. It's unloaded, but I want you to get used to carrying it around, these things tend to get hung up on damn near everything," he said.

She looked at Luke's Glock, and mimicking the location, snapped the holster in place, then inserted the firearm. "Now put this in your pocket, it's the ammunition for it, it's useless without it," JT said, handing her the ten round magazine.

"They're not very big," she said, looking at the .22 rimfire rounds.

"They're big enough," Brian said as he patted his thigh.

"Ok, thanks," she said, patting the pistol, "I feel better already." Then she turned towards the house, telling them she's going to check on the coffee as she walked away.

Pete and Brian were star struck, staring at her as she left. Luke even stole a glance. Joni is very, very attractive, her small frame perfectly balanced, the jeans she had on only accentuating her figure. When the door closed JT said "put your tongues back in your mouths, you're drooling all over for fuck sakes."

"Can't help it pops, if you were 30 years younger you'd be staring too," Pete said.

Inside JT was thinking the same thing, but he just said "one nice thing about being my age is I can't see the fine details all that well, now you boys leave her be, she's still in a bad way."

"We know, we won't be anything but gentlemen around her and all of these ladies," Brian said. JT gave Brian the look and Brian said "seriously pops, scouts honor."

"Ok then, after we get some coffee in us let's get a car or two moved to the crackhouse. Did you guys see anything up there this morning?" JT said.

"Nope, all dark when we were there, we even made a little noise, hoping to catch movement from inside, I don't think anyone is there," Luke said.

"Good then, when we are done with the car, which will make enough noise to wake up those dead guys, let's check out the house," JT said.

"Sounds good," Pete said.

Joni came out with the hot coffee pot and five cups, setting them on the picnic table. Amy came out right behind her with her own cup, steam rising from it in the cool morning air, she too had her .380 on her belt.

"Morning Amy," everyone said as she walked over taking a seat next to Luke, giving him a hug.

"Morning. What's on the agenda today?" she asked Luke.

"You smell great, is that perfume?" Luke asked with a sly grin.

"It's toothpaste," Amy replied, shaking her head.

"We're gonna tow a car or two over to the crackhouse," he said, finally answering her question.

"What for?" she asked curiously.

"We're gonna send a message to anyone who plans on coming this direction, we need one or two more cars to fill the gap," he said, leaving out the part about the bodies.

"Can I come?" she asked.

Luke looked at JT, and he nodded his head. "Sure baby, bring your 870, we could use the backup, we're gonna go in the crackhouse too, I think it's empty."

"Mind if I join you guys, I want to help?" Joni asked.

"Sure, another set of eyes can't hurt," Luke said, this time he didn't even look at his dad. JT trusted Luke's judgment, if he thought Joni was in a good enough place mentally to help out, then he won't stop him. JT was concerned about her though, she'd been through absolute hell in the last couple days, and here she is, wanting to help out, smiling and basically cheerful.

He only hoped she wasn't thinking about "suicide by cop", purposely walking in front of a bullet. Having read about how when some people experience extreme trauma they go dark and withdraw, while conversely, others go a hundred and eighty degrees the opposite direction, using optimism to heal. JT hoped that Joni was truly one of those polar opposite, using positivity as a coping mechanism to deal with extreme circumstances, which this lady has certainly experienced. Both are forms of PTSD, which he was trained in recognizing while in the Air Force.

Desperately needing some sleep, Brian would sit this one out while Luke would take the truck with Amy and Joni. Pete would follow on a four wheeler. JT planned on firing up the old Farmall after a bit and meet them on the road in front of the crackhouse. Grabbing two full gas cans from the shed, Luke emptied them into the truck, then tossed them in the back of the old truck with the tow strap from the Jeep along with the 4 foot by 4 foot sign that Amy and Joni made after coffee.

"What size sockets does the battery in the Malibu take?" Luke asked.

"10 and a 13 millimeter, but keep an eye on that ten, that little fuckers got legs, what do you need those for, gonna go look for a car out there?" JT asked Luke.

"Nope, I know right where one is, a Chevy Malibu on the side of 205th only a half mile east of the county road, and I got the key in my pocket, checked it out yesterday," Luke said.

"Roger that, got the siphon pump?" JT asked.

"Yep," Luke said, pointing to the box of the truck.

With the battery in the tractor still holding a charge, it fired right up as JT turned the key. Realizing that this morning he was the only one outside without a gun, JT walked back to the house for his pistol, meeting Kate in the kitchen.

"How's Sarah and the baby doing this morning?" JT asked, picking up his holstered 1911 for a change.

"Ok, she's missing Tyler. She told me she hopes Jarod will find him and tell him where she is, she's really worried about him," Kate said.

"He's fine, I'm sure. He probably stopped at that clinic just as you get into Hugo, they are most likely working him like a slave," JT lied.

"Where are you going?" Kate asked.

"We're going to move a car off 205th that's blocking the road," he said, lying again. JT loves his wife dearly, but she is such a tender soul and he just couldn't, didn't have the heart to tell her what he was really doing.

While filling the second can with gas the siphon pump sucked air and quit, telling Luke the tank of the Malibu was empty. By now, Pete had the battery out, closed the hood and put the battery in the truck next to the gas cans Luke had just loaded. Hearing a sound coming from the east, Luke cupped his hand to his ear for a better signal, and Pete seeing him, did the same, only he was looking west expecting an ambush. Before long a four wheeler came into view with a single rider on it. Amy, now hearing the sound had the barrel of her shotgun sticking out the sliding rear cab window of the truck. Who ever it was didn't give a shit and kept coming until Luke finally recognized the rider, Fred, setting their minds at ease. This is the new normal, everyone and every unexpected event has to be first treated as a threat.

"You kind of spooked me Freddy," Luke said.

"I recognized the truck, where's your dad at?" Fred asked bluntly.

"He's bringing the tractor down to the crackhouse, we're gonna make a barricade there with this car and the one there from the other night," Luke said.

"Ask him to stop by on his way home, I went to town this morning just to check it out, if you guys need anything, you'd better get there today, and bring cash, lots of it. My kid is a cop in town and he has heard there is a shitload of people walking down 64 just after the Stillwater bridge, right towards Somerset," he said.

"Will do. Thanks. I'll make sure he stops by," Luke said.

"Who's gonna steer this thing?" Pete asked as he hooked up the tow strap.

"I will," Joni piped up. Luke had pocketed the key when they were done removing the fuel and battery and tossed it to Joni as she hopped in the drivers seat, turning the key and unlocking the steering wheel so she could steer. "I've done this dozens of times with my dad. He always had shit cars that broke down and he was too cheap to ever have one towed, let's go," she said with a broad smile.

Pulling the tractor onto the county road JT just made out his old Chevy pickup rounding the curve not far from the crackhouse, a car in tow. By the time he got there, the boys already had the strap unhooked from the car and the truck well out of the way.

"How was the car, did anyone get to it yet?" he asked them.

"Didn't look like it, there weren't any handprints in the dust on it. We got about 9 gallons of gas out of it," Pete said.

"Damn, thanks. That'll help," JT said.

"I wanna flip this one on it side first," JT said, pointing at the white car already there.

"How come?" Pete asked.

"Optics. Looking at the dirty underside of a car with a few bodies piled in front will give it an apocalyptic touch," JT replied.

Maneuvering the tractor around to the south side where the stinking bodies were piled, he slid the front bucket under the car, slowly lifting it. Not wanting it to flip backwards onto its roof by moving too fast or too far, when it was almost vertical he stopped, letting it rock back and forth as it settled nicely on its side. Moving the tractor back to the north side, JT put the bucket against the side of someone's poor Malibu, pushing it in place next to the piece of shit already there, basically blocking the two lane road.

"This isn't gonna stop a car or four wheeler, they can easily get around in the ditch, it's only to make people think twice before going beyond this point," JT said, examining his work.

"Holy hell pops, I'm gonna puke, that is the most disgusting fucking smell," Pete said, stepping over one of the dead men as he carried the sign. Pulling his hoodie up over his mouth and nose, Pete quickly had the sign zip tied to the exhaust pipe of the car, gasping for breath as he walked away from the stench.

Amy and Joni, staying off to the side watched the road both directions while Luke scanned the area, no doubt thinking about the next task, checking the house out.

They were convinced that there was nobody still squatting in the place, but they were still very cautious nonetheless as they slowly moved up the tree lined driveway to the crackhouse. Luke, Pete and JT hopscotched along with two of them covering at all times. Halfway up the driveway, Amy moved as well, taking a position under the thick lower branches of an ancient white pine with her shotgun at the ready- Joni not more than ten feet way from her took cover behind another large pine. Amy, now well within range of the house, knew her #4 buckshot will definitely make anyone dive for cover if it becomes necessary.

Entering the house through its south door, the same one the naked chick had let the dog in, Luke and Pete slowly checked out the kitchen area the door opened into while JT stayed outside, watching the several outbuildings for movement. Seeing nothing in the kitchen but trash piled everywhere, they continued on, going room to room.

"What a shithole," Pete said, looking at the wide variety of garbage piled on what seemed like every flat spot.

After being inside only minutes, Luke and Pete stormed out the door as one, covering their faces with their hands. Snapping around at the commotion, JT, with his his pistol at the ready for whatever or whoever was chasing them out, braced himself against the garage door, ready to fire.

Outside, both Luke and Pete were gagging as they gulped the clean air as Pete blurted out, "shitters full!"

"Both of them," Luke added, looking a little green.

"These fuckers must not have had running water for a long time, there is no possible way anyone can shit that much in three days," Pete said while still gasping for air.

Doing a quick check of the rest of the buildings, they were empty except for a few rabbits that bolted from their hides. Seeing an old gas barrel on stilts next to one building JT mentioned "we might need that," pointing at the barrel. "I'm gonna walk down and get the tractor and the chains so we can carry that home," he continued.

Walking over to the barrel Pete looked it over saying "don't bother pops, it's got a couple of bullet holes in it, fresh ones too, one of us must have hit it the other night."

"Well shit," was all JT could muster in reply.

While walking back down the driveway to Amy and Joni, Luke said "I talked to Freddy out on 205th while we were siphoning the gas out of that Malibu. He wants you to swing by when we're done here, he's got some news from town."

"What'd you find in there, you guys didn't look so good when you came out, are there more dead people or what?" Joni asked when they were in earshot.

"Worse, we made the mistake of checking the bathrooms, I don't ever want to smell that again," Pete said.

"I'd rather smell that," Luke said, pointing to the bodies under the sign.

"That bad huh?" Amy asked.

"You don't wanna know sweetie, let's get out of here," Luke replied.

Gathering themselves to leave, JT asked "Pete, do you mind running the tractor back, I'm gonna swing by Freddys place and I don't wanna fuck up his driveway with these tire chains."

"Not a problem," Pete said, tossing JT the key to the Honda before heading to the tractor.

JT felt good riding the four wheeler, headed away from that mess. The fresh fall air in his face quite the contrast to the stench they'd just left behind. He didn't like what they did there, it felt wrong, him making a pile of dead people. The only way he was able to square this in his head was telling himself "it is what it is."

Gunning the throttle, JT considered taking a quick ride beyond his road to the Johnson Farm, a small family dairy farm a mile north. He was curious if Bob, the eldest of the three Johnson brothers had penned up their steers out of sight or if they were still pastured. "Not without a white flag or something, for damn sure I'd be in someone's crosshairs well before they'd recognize me," he said to himself. Turning left onto his road, JT began thinking again about how much their world has changed.

Pulling into Fred's driveway, JT spotted Fred in the garage, sitting in a lawn chair with a shotgun cradled across his lap. Shutting the machine down, JT hopped off. "Want a cold one?" Fred asked, waving JT into the garage.

"I'd love one Fred, but I'll pass for now, how's the wife doing?" JT said, changing the subject away from a cold beer for breakfast.

"She's good, say, this morning I took a ride to town to see what's up, I went early before the riff raff had a chance to wake up. My kids a cop, lives out by the high school so I stopped in to find out what he had to say," Fred said. JT liked that about Freddy, he wasn't much for small talk.

"Are they still functioning, I mean is the police department still working?" JT asked kind of nervously.

"No, not really, but kinda. They don't have any cars, radios or organization but a couple of them have been riding a beat. They have a few older four wheelers that people let them borrow. Mainly they are just keeping an eye on the grocery store and the two liquor stores, they've had some trouble. He told me that last night they caught a few punks headed towards the grocery store, and when it was apparent they were going to break in they confronted them, one of the group pulled a pistol and took a shot at the two cops, and now a couple of them are dead. My kid shot them, he's a fucking wreck right now," Fred explained.

"Shit," JT said, contemplating what Fred just said, "it sounds to me like they got what they deserved, any idea who they were?" JT asked.

"Yeah, and that's the bad part. One of them was the village administrator's kid," Fred replied.

JT knew who he was talking about. Kyle, the manager of the grocery store told him that he had caught the kid stealing more times than he could count, and every time he called the cops it was his daddy who showed up.

"Let me guess, now he wants your kids head on a platter, hey, I thought all your boys worked in Bayport, which one is the cop?" JT asked. "John, he's the only one who went to college, he went on the G.I. Bill after the marines," Fred answered.

"Damn Fred, what's he going to do?" he asked.

"He's packing his shit right now, gonna come out here and set up in the basement with Julie," Fred said, worry in his voice.

"Anyway, he told me that the store is going to shut down after today, it's damn near empty already," Fred said.

"How's he gonna get here, you wanna take my truck and go get him?" JT asked.

"No, but thanks, he has that green 68, almost like yours except his is a two wheel drive. And not for nothing here, but don't be driving that truck of yours to town, it sounds like the sheriffs department is "borrowing" anything that runs and is fit for duty," Fred said.

"I've seen that truck, I even talked to him at the gas station a couple of weeks ago, I had no idea he's one of your boys," JT said.

"He mentioned that, he said he talked to some old cranky vet with a 72 wearing woodland camo pants and a white T shirt," Fred replied with a laugh.

"Yeah, that'd have been me. Wow, well thanks for the information Fred, I better get going but let me know when John makes it here. Say, did I meet him at your birthday party last spring?" JT asked.

"No, he was on patrol that day, hang on though there's more. He said there was a lot of people, like a couple hundred or more walking across the Stillwater bridge this way. That's second hand information, he got it from a deputy that came up from Hudson this morning. They are friends and he stopped by John's place to check in, that's how he found out about them snagging cars. The only reason he didn't take John's truck is because they are hunting buddies and John's a cop," Fred said.

"Ok, well, thanks again, I'm gonna head home and maybe see if there is anything that we are in dire need of," JT said.

"After John gets here we will stop down and have a beer, be careful if you go to town, and if you do go, don't go by the bar north of town. There was a bunch of people hanging out there this morning, I think it's people that were stuck on the road when the cars quit and they just migrated there," Fred said.

Before parting ways at Fred's, the tractor went by with Pete driving followed by Luke and the girls in the truck. Fred asked how the project went and JT filled him in. He left him with a wave and as JT rode slowly towards home what Fred said was sinking in. All of it was troubling, but the people moving this way kind of surprised him. It's too soon for the exodus, he thought to himself. But if that's actually the case, the cites must be an absolute hell hole. He couldn't even imagine what it must be like. Well, that's not entirely true, he could imagine it, he just chose not to for the time being.

Pulling in to the ranch JT was greeted by the four dogs, their demand for undivided attention was the distraction JT desperately needed to get his mind out of the hole it was in. He has plenty of friends and relatives that live in the cities and he couldn't help but wonder how they are holding up. After the mutts received an adequate number pets and scratches they took off to the north part of the yard, probably back to their stash of bones. Brian was still at the smoker napping lightly as JT walked to him.

"Where's everyone else at?" JT asked Brian.

"In the house, your mom was having some trouble breathing I think, Luke came out a bit ago and got that small oxygen bottle from your shop," Brian answered.

Going inside, JT saw his mom sitting back in a recliner with an oxygen mask over her face. "What happened, how is she doing?" he asked.

"She got faint when her 02 levels dropped. It's back over 90, with the mask, but it was 85 when she got light headed," Joni said.

"Where's Luke at?" JT asked.

"Upstairs, looking for the oxygen concentrator," Amy said.

"That needs power, you got this?" JT asked Joni and Amy, who both nodded yes.

Going to the shop, JT grabbed the 3000 watt inverter from the makeshift faraday cage, removing it from the anti static bag it was stored in. Then, grabbing a battery from the charging rack in the shop, he took them in the house just as Luke came downstairs with the big blue machine, setting it up by his gramma. Joni, unraveling the outlet hose and attaching a set of nasal cannulas, got "momma" as she calls her now, squared away on the machine saying she would stay and keep an eye on her for a while.

"Momma" was awake, kind of anyway with Joni talking to her, getting her to relax and breathe through her nose as much as she can. JT, hearing some shuffling around in the kitchen, walked in seeing Kate with the baby on her hip.

"How's Sarah doing?" JT asked.

"She's ok, still worried sick about Tyler though, did you get that car moved?" Kate asked.

"We did. We also got almost ten gallons of gas out of it and the battery," he told her.

"Can you run some water pretty soon, the tub and drinking buckets are getting low?" she asked, nudging an empty bucket with her foot.

"Sure will honey," JT replied, giving her a kiss before going back outside where Luke and Amy were in the shop putting the oxygen bottle back in the rack.

"I donno dad, if Amy didn't catch gramma, she'd have passed out and hit the deck," Luke said.

"You caught her?" JT asked, looking at Amy.

"Yeah, but Luke was right behind me and grabbed her too, we drug her to the chair," Amy replied.

"It's a good thing you guys came in when you did, a broken hip would be a death sentence right about now," JT said.

He asked them what she was doing when they saw her faint, Amy saying she was at the stove cooking water. "Huh?" he asked.

"Yeah, she was just standing there, stirring a pot of water. The stove wasn't even lit," Amy replied .

"Momma's" time here was getting short, he knew that. The dementia is one thing, that demon has already taken her mind, but her heart problems and the inability to breathe is going to take her from them before the dementia does. He was dreading that day no matter when it came, but there was absolutely nothing he could do about it. For now she was ok, and with Joni there, his mind was set at ease somewhat, at least someone knew what to look for.

Luke, Amy and JT walked together over to the smoker where Pete was now sitting at the table with Brian. JT told them everything he could remember about what Fred had said. He saw Luke wince when he mentioned the people.

"He told me a bit about that this morning, but didn't say how many there were. The cities must be a war zone if they are leaving already," Luke said.

"So, is there anything in town we can't live without?" JT asked.

Amy said "woman stuff," he knew what she meant. "I've got some, but I know Sarah and Joni don't have any," she went on.

"Ok then, who wants to go shopping?" JT said.

Amy's eyes lit up with that and she quickly said "I do."

Looking at Luke JT said "not without you, and which one of you two wanna go?" he said looking at Pete and Brian.

"Not me, Pete said, I got meat to smoke."

"I'll get my shit," Brian said.

Going in the house, JT went to the box he keeps his cash, grabbing a wrapped, one thousand dollar stack of twenty's and went outside.

"Don't spend it all in one place," he told Amy, handing her the money.

"That's a lot of cash dad, you looking for change back?" Luke asked.

"Nope spend as much of it you can while people are crazy enough to take it. Swing by Becky's liquor store too, it's just down the street," JT said.

"Anything specific you want besides beer? Maybe some trade goods?" Luke asked.

"Yep, what ever liquor is cheapest, get it until your out of cash. Get a couple cartons of Pall Malls at the store too, that shit will be more valuable than gold in a couple weeks. Oh, and tell Becky you're my son and ask her if we still have a deal, she will say yes or no without elaborating, especially if anyone else is there," JT instructed.

"What deal is that?" Brian asked.

JT explained to them about a little cash operation she has going and let him in on if shit ever went south. The distributor drivers "forget" to bring product back to be destroyed, for a price of course, and she brings it home to her pole barn, selling it to places like the legion for cash. "It's a hell of a racket," he said.

"That's why it's called racketeering pops," Pete said over his shoulder. They all chuckled at that one.

"No rifles though, pistols only and keep 'em concealed. Fred said town was pretty calm this morning so there's no sense in riling anyone up, drawing attention. And don't go by the bar on 200th and 35, he said that's full of people from the road, go through Pine Cliff, that development just past the corner of 60th and 200th, it goes all the way through to the village and comes out by the propane joint on 35. Those people who live in there should still be fairly civil," JT said.

Going to the back of the truck, Luke pulled out a five gallon gas can, topping off the two Polaris ATV's while Brian got Pete's small aluminum trailer hooked up to the blue 425, the more powerful of the four machines they now have.

"Got your radio?" JT asked Luke who nodded in the affirmative.

"Don't be fucking around, if people see a trailer full of shit there is a good chance they are going to want it. Actually, Amy, bring your 870 along for the ride home, just in case," JT added.

"Will do, just in case," Amy said, putting her shotgun in the trailer where Brian secured it with a bungee cord.

A shotgun is a formidable weapon, just being in a position where you're looking down the barrel of one is intimidating enough for most people to have a "coming to Jesus" moment. The president once said while promoting his gun control agenda that a 9 millimeter round will "blow your lungs out". To anyone who knows anything about guns, that statement by him was nothing more than pure ignorant bullshit, but a 12 gauge or even Amy's 20 gauge at close range, well, those things will absolutely fuck you up.

Thinking about their trip to town, JT wasn't terribly worried about them. It was still fairly early in the day. But if two hours passed then him and Pete would take the truck to the edge of town using the route they took and have a look, if it came to that. Pete was busying himself putting the cooled and smoked meat in the burlap bags, while JT was pulling the generator out of the shop, getting ready to pump some water for the house.

"Hey, Pete, did you get that box made up for the garden hoses?" JT asked.

"Almost done pops, I just gotta trim up a piece of plexiglass and screw it on. For the hell of it, I propped it up next to the cube aiming south and let the hose fill with water. Holy shit pops, it got hot fast," Pete said.

"Cool, we'll have a shower in no time," JT said, thanking Pete.

While plugging the cord into the generator, JT heard a muffled "pop" then after a few seconds another "pop". Not being able to tell the direction of the noise, JT asked Pete where it came from.

"They came from right over there, sounded like gunshots to me, wanna check it out?" Pete asked.

"Let's," JT replied, saying that just sounded a bit off.

Pete fired up his Honda, JT hopping on the back rack and they headed up the driveway, turning east. With the morning sun brilliant on their faces, they rode slowly to the county road, nothing seemed out of the ordinary.

"I don't think the shots were this far out," Pete said, turning the machine around in the intersection.

Heading back toward the ranch, JT caught just a wisp of white smoke rising through the trees from somewhere near Ted and Myrna's house, just east of the ranch.

"Turn in here," JT said, tapping Pete on the shoulder motioning for him to turn in their driveway.

Pulling slowly up to the old house, JT was looking around over Pete's shoulder, finally seeing Ted and Myrna sitting outside on their patio glider swing, a small, smoky fire was slowly burning in a decorative pit in front of them. Neither Ted or Myrna moved as they rode closer, the reason why becoming clearly evident the closer they got. They were dead. Getting off the machine, Pete and JT walked up to the couple, silently staring at the sight in front of them. The scene unfolded in JT's mind as to what just took place. Myrna, slumped over the armrest, had a nasty looking hole in her right temple, the left side of her head splattering the fern bushes beside her. The top of Ted's head was gone, the the ground behind him littered with his blood, bones and brains. The Smith and Wesson .357 revolver he used still loosely held in his right hand.

"They checked out," JT said, staring in disbelief.

"Fuck me," Pete said, turning away, puking.

Looking at his old neighbors, JT said "They were good people, they just celebrated their sixty fifth wedding anniversary."

"Why, I mean how can people do this?" Pete asked.

"Ted knew what was coming, Myrna too, obviously, and decided to just end it on their own terms. They were both 85 years old and had lived good, honorable lives," JT answered.

"I still don't get it," Pete replied.

"Look at it this way Pete, they probably figured the risk of living through this wouldn't be worth the reward," JT said.

"Why the fuck not?" Pete asked.

"Cause their ain't no reward at the end of this," JT said, solemnly.

"Pete, we gotta bury these two, they were friends. Ted has a New Holland tractor with a small backhoe attachment on it, I know this because I borrowed it from him a couple of years ago to dig a hole after my quarter horse died of old age," JT said.

Walking out to the pole barn where the tractor was stored, JT was surprised to see the door wide open, its lock hanging on the hasp. Drawing his 1911, JT carefully took a look around. Convinced that the place was empty, he turned his attention to tractor.

There, just inside the doorway sat the tractor, its key in the ignition, the tag swinging back and forth from the light breeze. JT turned it to the on position and the fuel solenoid clicked, the glow plug indicator lit up then went off, turning the key to "start" the little diesel on the old, but mint condition tractor fired up.

Looking around for a place to plant them JT, seeing Myrna's rose garden, decided that would be a great place. She loved those plants and over the years she had brought Kate several vases full of the freshly cut flowers. Using the backhoe, it didn't take long to get a hole dug deep and wide enough in the soft soil to hold them both.

Picking them up, they very gently placed them one at a time across the hoe bucket, carrying them to the hole in the ground. Using the backhoe, JT placed them side by side. Ted would approve, JT thought to himself while slowly filling the grave with the front bucket, taking in the fresh scent of the black earth.

When they were finished, JT reflected about all this. Ted was an odd, but incredibly intelligent man. He also had zero faith in humanity, so little in fact that every structure had a strong lock on it's door, he even locked his car doors inside a locked garage at night, convinced the "miscreants" as he called them were constantly prowling the area looking for anything to steal, and yet he had left his barn open and the key in his prized tractor. JT deduced that Ted had planned this whole affair. He'd know that either him or old Jerry across the road would hear the shots, see the smoke, investigate it, and do what he and Pete just did. As weird as that sounds it all made sense to him.

"Well Pete, Ted won't be needing this thing anymore so I guess I'll drive it home," JT said.

"You got diesel fuel for that thing?" Pete asked.

"Yes and no, I don't have actual diesel fuel, but I do have at least two hundred gallons of fuel oil for the furnace, that will burn just fine in this thing," JT said.

"Nice!" Pete replied.

Getting back to the ranch, JT and Pete were just in time to hear the radio hooked to the slick line crackle.

"Shredder inbound," Luke's voice came over the little radio.

"Shit, that was dumb, I should have grabbed that radio," Pete said.

"No worries, I'm just as guilty too," JT said.

Within minutes, the sound of the two four wheelers could be heard coming down the driveway, Brian in the lead pulling the trailer. They had to maneuver around the dogs as they rode up towards the shop, the dogs already curious about what was in the trailer.

"How'd it go?" JT asked as they shut the machines down.

"Actually not bad," Luke said, as he told the story. "Word must have gotten out about the store closing though, there were plenty of people there looking around. Kyle recognized me right away as your son, and asked if we were looking for anything specific, I told him yeah, and he took us and our cart to the back of the store, asking what we had to carry it home in. I told him about Brian having the trailer behind a four wheeler and he said to bring it around to the back of the store by the loading dock, but to try to not make it look obvious. He said the last thing he wanted was anyone following Brian around to the back. Brian did a pretty slick move when he left, walking out the door complaining loudly that the place was empty. Then he headed to the east, and came in through the field behind the store, completely out of view from the people on the other side."

Continuing Luke said, "Kyle handed me a package of those black fifty gallon garbage bags and said we should bag up all the big stuff. He handed us several boxes of shit. Tampons, pads and different sized diapers, a big package of toilet paper, and a whole case of Cheerios. Then he tossed me the golden box, a full case of Marlboro Reds. Twenty cartons. We bagged it all. I asked him how much I owe him and he looked at the trailer and said four hundred. I gave him five. He told me to keep my mouth shut about where this came from because he's been turning people away all day, saying he was sold out. He told me to tell you that you were right too."

"We've had some interesting discussions over the years," JT said, looking inside the packed trailer. Everything in the trailer was bagged so he couldn't tell what was what, so he asked if Becky had anything for him.

"Oh yeah, twelve cubes of beer, different brands, six cases of Windsor, a few bottles of vodka and your broke by the way," Luke answered with a chuckle.

"Not bad," JT said.

"Yeah, I thought it was a fair deal, for us anyway, that cash won't be worth shit soon enough. Where do you want this stuff, it's too much to bring inside?" Luke said.

JT pointing to the shop, said "in there," as he picked up a bag, carrying it in.

It was a good haul. They got a load of the female hygiene stuff, they knew it wouldn't last forever, but it's certainly better than nothing. The asswipe was nice, they have a lot of that already, but like the tampons, that will run out too sooner or later. Hopefully later.

The rest of the afternoon was spent organizing the shop of its contents and the time passed quickly with the excitement over their haul. Before long it was getting on towards sunset, the temperature cooling as the sun dipped to the tree line illuminating the wood line to east. Looking at the brilliant fall colors of the oak, maple and scattered birch trees glowing in the fading sunlight was reassuring to JT, it brought with it a sense of calm knowing that even with his world in shambles, there are still some things that even the apocalypse can't change.

The days have been running together, still feeling like it's just been one very long day to JT. Going inside, "momma" was in her recliner napping, the oxygen concentrator humming along beside her. JT noticed that someone had changed the battery out on the inverter it was connected to. He needed to get to the calendar on the wall and put an X through this day, but he wasn't sure what day it actually was as he struggled to remember. Monday and Tuesday were crossed out but Wednesday wasn't. Was it really Wednesday he asked himself, his mind going back over all the events that have taken place. "To hell with it" he thought, and picking up the pen, crossed out both Wednesday and Thursday, it sure felt like four days, even if it wasn't.

Chapter Fourteen

The word "nightmarish" cannot adequately describe the still-burning skylines etching out the ruins of once-vibrant Minneapolis/Saint Paul metropolis. Even amidst the un-godly chaos of the Twin Cities, their scarred streets and ruined buildings pale in comparison to the devastation found in the hearts of Tampa, Washington DC, and Omaha. Those three cities being the epicenters of a nuclear assault by North Korean made and Iranian owned Hwasong 17 missiles that left millions incinerated, with buildings flattened to the ground and crumpled like paper. Fires still danced hungrily along the ashes of once-thriving residential avenues, their liveliness now replaced by enormous columns of dust and smoke rising into the atmosphere, carrying along their deadly cargo of nuclear radiation. The centuries of history those cities represented had now been erased, ground to a miserable and immediate halt by the Iranian attack.

Iran had partnered with the DPRK two decades ago in the development of their joint nuclear weapons program, ultimately producing an arsenal of 14 of the mobile launched, thermonuclear tipped ICBM's, seven of which Iran had secretly taken delivery of. When Iran pulled the trigger on the full launch of all seven missiles, the four they launched from inside the borders of Iran were destroyed by the U.S THAAD anti ballistic missile interceptors deployed in Europe and the U.S. Navy's AGEIS system. The three that survived the launch originated from Venezuela, where their president had welcomed Iran's proposition of hosting them. Sure, they'd pay the price in the form of a proportional retaliation from Washington, but he didn't care. He'd be in his luxurious bunker, buried deep in the mountain named Pico da Neblino on his southern border while Caracas absorbed the wrath of the US Navy's Trident sea launched ballistic missile.

Like Caracas, Tehran was gone, having been targeted by two missiles leaving no distinguishable difference between them and DC, Omaha or Tampa. It was the same ghoulish landscape, half a world apart. Fortunately for the rest of the planet no other countries unleashed any of their birds, the United States had fired three of their Trident submarine launched missiles in a proportional retaliation. Globally, the only other skirmish that erupted during the initial chaos was when North Korea took advantage of the situation, advancing over the DMZ into the south. They were quickly and devastatingly repelled by volley after volley of rockets and heavy artillery from the south. All of South Korea and Japan were prepared for the nuclear launch they were convinced was coming from the North, but one that mercifully never materialized.

Back in the twin cities of Minneapolis and Saint Paul, black smoke billowed into the sky, tongues of flame flickering and twisting with each gust of wind. The busy communities of Robbinsdale, Prospect Park, and Frogtown had been consumed by the raging fires lit by lawless by gangs as turf wars erupted. The streets were now deserted, littered only with scattered debris- remnants of the panicked evacuation that ensued.

The first day, Monday, started with the awful gridlock of traffic on the metro's roads as vehicles simply quit functioning in an instant. But the day's already present challenges were further complicated by the opportunists who saw their chance amidst the dysfunction to capitalize on the situation. Those that preyed upon any perceived weakness in the collapsing system now roamed freely.

Missing most from public view were the police, whose presence was replaced by only the shotgun or pistol hanging from the tired arms of those few officers morally compelled to remain on duty. The sight of their weapons hanging off their tired shoulders had little effect on crowds now and separating a growing number of rival factions closing in on each other throughout the city became utterly impossible. These small groups were like tribal warfare, warring rabbles fearing no one. On that fateful Monday, the normally concealed lines dividing humans split wide open, exposing the fragile society beneath. The Mall of America saw this brutal reality firsthand, witnessing the explosion of conflict between two rival gangs fighting tooth and nail for control. Many Innocent people lost their lives in what became the first of many public, violent battlefronts.

Tuesday made Monday appear like a kindergarten playground as some folks were finally forced out of their homes into the hazy, smoke filled streets in search of food only to find their debit and EBT cards didn't work. The small, quaint corner stores scattered around neighborhoods were the first to fall. With no cash to pay and people with hungry kids, they just took what they felt they were entitled to, which led to fist fights, outright street brawls and many, many shootings from exasperated store owners and customers alike. Which brought even more violence back to the store in the form of a Molotov cocktail tossed through an open door or window by a former patron looking for vengeance. In some cases a gallon of gas was dumped on the floors or counters of a shop after the owner was beaten unconscious and lit with a match, ending their lives in a smoky pyre.

The Twin Cities were breaking apart at the seams. By Wednesday, the empty storefronts were little more than shell remnants of their former selves - husks of what had been thriving corners of the busiest streets. With faceless crowds moving through the city like packs of coyotes, anything with even a faint hint of having food or drink was under siege. Grocery stores, liquor stores, and corner markets had been ransacked and picked clean down to the last wrapper or bottle. Countless others remained empty and lifeless, their storefronts scarred by hastily scrawled graffiti or the jagged holes left by bricks or stones through their windows. In some of the more chaotic areas, entire streets had been hollowed out like the narrow shafts of some cruel, otherworldly parasite. Here, ashen remains of abandoned buildings lay in silent heaps of rubble, glass and bricks.

Thursday brought a literal nightmare to the Twin Cities. Streets that had once bustled with life were now seemingly palpable with danger, the air thick with paranoia. Unwary citizens were set upon and beaten within inches of their lives, in some cases beyond, then stripped of any valuables that might have held even a meager value. Bodies were left where they lay, creating an unimaginable landscape of rotting death. Violence spiraled outwards in circular waves like eddies in boiling water. Groups of three or four were swarmed over by an exponentially greater number of thieves, determined to find the scraps of food or water they believed to be hidden within. Amid the chaos and fear, few forms of defense were truly effective. Only those with firearm's and the necessary skills to use them effectively in a fight were spared the worst. It seemed that no level of preparation could dissuade the unrelenting march of chaos that had swallowed the city, a nightmare from which there was little to no hope of waking.

This day, Thursday, was the day the exodus began for many of the masses. No water, no food and no safety. Now, it was painfully obvious no help would be coming. For the most part, the vast majority had no clue what had happened, all they knew was what they could see and hear. What they saw was death, pain and destruction on a level never seen in modern times on American soil.

They packed what they had, maybe a meager few cans of vegetables, but in many cases they had nothing, then, gripped in fear or abject terror, they walked away, or tried to walk away from the carnage, most being oblivious of the marauder's lurking in the darkness.

Some looked for hope beyond the cities. Among them there was division, divided in will and divided in need. Some believed that the suburbs might hold a promise of hope, while others sought to flee even beyond toward friends or relatives who lived rurally. The savviest moved south, fleeing to warmer climates before the bitter kiss of winter set in. Though each individual might have had a unique destination in mind, they acted like fire ants too often, leaving a wake scattered in ruin behind them.

At first, some of the more generous residents found reasons to help. They would offer anything from a bandage to a slice of bread, but as the days stretched, generosity gave way to straight up taking. Tens of thousands found their inside worlds burst apart like bubbles as large raiding parties streamed in and over their weakened defenses. What spoils were offered were shattered and in far too many cases scoured by the malfeasance of better-equipped marauders.

As they moved along, trying to ignore the growing concentration of sickness and death around them, the survivors became gaunt and emaciated. There were no flashes of heroism here, rather an unending fluid of humanity churned forward, their collective will slowly eroded by the near-constant attacks of both insidious diseases and the many marauder's lurking in the ever present shadows. Those who were lucky enough to survive the first three days now found themselves numbered among the walking wounded, drained, and debilitated. The dead, with little more to offer than an infection and a shadow, were left behind without a second thought. Vultures soon claimed their prey, their nests flushed with reality's newest offerings.

Chapter Fifteen

"I don't care what you think you know, we aren't going that way," Karen said to the group, her husband Phil standing behind her.

"Why though, if we keep walking on this road it takes us to Somerset too," one of the group piped up.

"Go then, you won't make it three miles before someone jumps you, taking everything you have, there will be a lot less people on the tracks than there are on this highway," Karen shouted back.

"Just shut up and listen to her, she got us all to leave the apartments, and look, we've made it this far," another one in the large group said.

Karen and Phil had become the de-facto leaders of the large upscale "Whispering Pines" apartment complex in North Saint Paul long before today. During the pandemic of 2020, they had garnered the support of well more than half of the tenants when they filed a lawsuit against the management, forcing the eviction of anyone who wasn't vaccinated against covid19. While the lawsuit never saw a courtroom, the management felt "morally compelled" to comply, or so they said. What really took place was they feared offending a pair of people who were able to virtue signal their way to the podium of a dozen community meetings over the subject.

What ever Karen and Phil dictated to happen, happened. Even their made up mask mandate inside the apartments of the complex was considered law by their faithful followers. Now, after four full days of no water, no sewer or groceries, that same group of people were more than happy to follow their orders yet again when they decided they would walk the thirty miles to the small village of Somerset Wisconsin, only eleven miles into the state.

Insisting that all the food they had as a group be combined, Karen quickly took control over what and when they would eat, and now, she would make her move as to "who" got to eat.

"William, if you go that route, you won't have any food at all," Karen said to the errant man who suggested staying on the highway.

"It's my damned food," William complained.

"Not any more, is it," she said to the group of nearly fifty, where she was met with applause and cat calls to William.

"Oh for fucks sake Karen, get off your high horse and take a look around, we're screwed, all of us. You know what, take my food, I'd rather take my chances on the highway than go off through the fucking woods on a nature hike with you and Philly boy," William said, shouldering his pack.

Stepping forward, Phil approached William, "you apologize to my wife right now for offending her, and I wanna see what else is in your backpack," his words bringing more applause from the group.

Calmly, William pulled a Smith and Wesson 357 from under his shirt, rocking the hammer back on the stainless steel revolver with his thumb. Pointing it at Phil, William said "not today, pussy, now take one more step and you're a dead man."

"He's got a gun!" Karen yelled, the collective gasp of the crowd nearly deafening as she screamed the words. Phil turned around yelling to the group, "run run run, he's gonna kill us."

William laughed, watching the group run away like a herd of sheep at the sight of a handgun. Half of them abandoning their precious cargo where they stood on the blacktop of the intersection of Hilton Trail and highway 36, seven miles west of the Stillwater bridge. When the group eventually slowed, William raised his pistol into the air firing one shot in their general direction. The shot sending the group back into their blind panic yet again as he quickly checked a few of their bags for food, finding plenty to keep him going.

"Why didn't you stop him?" Karen demanded, yelling at Phil.

"Stop him how! He had a damned gun pointed at my head?" Phil exclaimed.

"You don't even know if he had bullets for it, you are a pussy. You could have talked him down, that's your job isn't isn't it, deescalating a situation?" Karen yelled.

"Yeah, but….," Phil said before being cut off by his wife.

"But what?" she screamed, "now because of you half our food is back there, go get what's left," Karen demanded.

"No, in fact, fuck no. You are a bitch, Karen, and that was it for me, you're on your own," Phil said, picking up his bag.

"Wait, what! You're leaving me, now?" Karen screamed, almost crying.

"I should've left you years ago, you insufferable twat," Phil said, walking south to highway 36.

Karen was now surrounded by her group, some concerned for her, others concerned about her ability to lead them. "What are we going to do now?" one woman asked, her voice shaking.

"Walk to the bridge, I know people on the other side," Karen said, struggling to form fake tears.

By nightfall, the group had made it to the railroad tracks that would lead them to the high bridge and into Wisconsin. Making camp for the night after reaching the tracks, Karen did a quick headcount, 38 remained. She had no idea where the others went, or even when they left the group. Three or four of them were seriously ill with diarrhea, "good riddance," she said to herself, as she sat on a thick bed of pine needles tucked under a large white pine.

Karen and her closest companions gathered together under the same tree, bound together by their shared experiences and beliefs, bonds formed over the last several months. The other couples with Karen were neighbors who had lived together on the same floor of the building before the blackout set in.

Sally, a petite blonde, asked "Karen, who is it that you know in Somerset?"

"A third cousin I'd guess you call him, his name is Barry King," Karen replied, almost smugly.

"And he will take care of us?" Sally asked cautiously.

"He's kind of an outlaw from what I've heard anyway, I haven't really seen him since high school though," she said, evading the question.

"That's not very reassuring, I mean don't get me wrong, thanks for taking me, but…," Sally trailed off.

"But what, Sally. I'm getting tired of being the complaint department, if you have something to say then say it," Karen snapped.

"No, I'm good," Sally said, timidity.

"Shameless bitch," Karen thought. "She'd be nobody and nowhere without me," she said, again to herself.

William was in no hurry to go anywhere. He'd only lived at Whispering Pines for a month, and simply fell in with the group for the numbers aspect. He wasn't a lone wolf kind of guy, but it had become abundantly clear to him that hanging with this group would eventually get him killed. William knew what had happened, he'd read the post apocalyptic books written by the likes of LL Akers, RB Schow and Angery American, so the societal collapse he watched take place through his sliding deck door didn't surprise him, but he needed a group to get rural with, and they were it.

Moving off the road to be out of sight, William set up camp for the afternoon, where he'd watch the bags the main group left, curious if any would come back for them. Watching the road and the people moving east concerned him, where did all those people think they are going to go, what are they going to do when they get there? Movement from his right caught Williams eye, and he was not really surprised to see Phil walking to the bags. What did surprise him was that Phil wasn't picking them up, but was rifling through them, putting what he could find in his own bag.

"That's totally unacceptable Phillip," he said with a laugh, thinking about the admonishment he would be receiving from Karen. "I told you to bring back the bags shit for brains," he said, trying to mimic her annoying voice. Phil, now apparently satisfied, hefted his bag, and surprised William by walking away from his group.

"What da fuck?" William muttered. Without knowing why he did it, William let out a whistle, loud enough for Phil to hear.

"Who is that?" Phil said, seeing the whistling silhouette in the underbrush.

"It's your nemesis, William," William said, waving Phil to come his way. "I ain't gonna shoot ya, but ya gotta get off the road with that pack, get over here before that pile of people to the west see ya," William said in hushed tones.

Cautiously, Phil moved Williams direction, keeping an eye on Williams hands, as William likewise kept his hands clearly in sight.

"What the fuck William, you're the last person I expected to see," Phil said, walking the last few yards in the woods.

"I ain't in any hurry to get anywhere," William replied. "I'm gonna wait till nightfall, then head out when most of the masses are off the road," he continued.

"Where to?" Phil asked.

"Donno, not Somerset, I'll tell you that much," William said with a laugh.

"Haha, yeah, me either," Phil said.

"So, pardon my bluntness, but where's your wife?" William asked.

"Up there," Phil said, pointing his chin to the north.

"Did you bail or did she give you the boot?" William asked with a laugh.

"I bailed. I should have bailed years ago, the only reason I didn't was because I made a shit load of money in Bitcoin that she doesn't know about, but it would have come out in a divorce," Phil said.

"You didn't wanna share your spoils eh?" William said.

"Half of five million would have made her too happy for me to keep my sanity, so no, I'm not the sharing type," Phil said.

"Well, your welcome to walk with me, even though I have no idea where I'll end up." William said.

"I'll consider that, leaving at dark then?" Phil asked.

"Yep, but first a nap, don't try to steal my shit either," William said.

"No worries, you're the one with the gun," Phil said.

Chapter Sixteen

JT stretched out his legs and settled in on his seat, twirling his flashlight with expert precision with his fingers like a tiny baton. "I'll take the first watch tonight," he announced, voice carrying a note of calm authority as darkness slowly crept in. His eyes swept the grounds, noting with something between caution and appreciation the kaleidoscopic hues of the October sunset on the trees.

Luke gathered his gear and said "Alright, I'll give you a break at some point, don't get too comfortable old man. The night's still young." He joked heading off towards the house, leaving JT in solitude.

Although they had agreed the previous system worked, neither could shake the feeling of unease that crawled down their spines. With four large dogs patrolling the grounds, there was at least some degree of relief for both JT and Luke as they abandoned keeping watch at the end of the long driveway.

As much as he tried, JT couldn't get his mind off of the people coming this direction. If it was true they were in Stillwater this morning, then by late afternoon at least some of them would be filtering in to the little village of Somerset. He was happy that Luke, Amy and Brian got out of town earlier before any of them showed up.

In front of JT on the picnic table was his rifle, a DPMS AR-15 that he purchased twenty years ago. It's had at least a full magazine fired through it in the last few days so tonight would be as good a time as ever to run the bore snake through it and wipe down the bolt carrier. When he bought the thing he had an aftermarket trigger assembly installed. To him, there is nothing worse than a shitty trigger. That thought reminded him about a project he was going to do a few years ago, putting together a suppressor for it. JT bought all the parts back then, and as far as he knew they are still in their packaging tucked away in the gun closet. JT laughed to himself when remembering why he let the project sit- he was deathly afraid of breaking the law. "Maybe tomorrow I'll get on that," he said to himself, closing the rifle up and chambering a round with the slap of the receiver.

Sometime around midnight, JT heard the unmistakable rumble of a V8 engine out on the county road, the cool, crisp night air amplifying the sound of the exhaust. He heard it slow, then pick speed back up, then slow again before he was yet again engulfed in silence. "That must be John," he said to Pepper, who was now laying at his feet, having abandoned her post for the comfort of being next to her master. He explaining to her that he can pick out the sound of a performance built small block Chevy from a mile away, so it had to be him.

While adding a couple small pieces of oak to the wood stove that provides the smoke to the smoker, JT looked to the house as the hinges squeaked on the screen door, seeing Luke emerge, stretching after his nap.

"Sup old man?" he said as a greeting.

"Not a fucking thing, and I'll take that all day long. But I did hear what I think was Fred's kid, John roll in a while ago, probably after midnight," JT said, poking the small fire with a piece of wood as tiny red embers floated up into the black sky.

"I think I remember him, he was maybe a year or two ahead of me in school, good shit if I remember right," Luke said walking to the smoker.

"Well, he's on Somerset's shit list now, I'm not exactly convinced him being here is a good thing, being on their radar, but he was in the Marines, so he can't be all bad. I'm not sure how long he was in but Fred mentioned he did a couple of tours in Afghanistan," JT said.

"That skill set could come in handy," Luke replied.

Pointing to the five gallon bucket perched on the end of the picnic table, JT said "damn man, Pete mixed up a hell of a brine, the smell of that bucket is making me hungry."

"You won't be disappointed, he's got this shit figured out," Luke said, taking a seat. Before taking watch JT asked Pete what was in the 5 gallon pail sitting on the table, Pete telling him that it's jerky, or it's gonna be jerky anyway, explaining about all the seasonings he had brought when he and Brian came.

"Nice, good thinking, what's all in there for meat?" Luke asked. JT mentioned that Kate brought Pete out a whole turkey that he quickly sliced up and tossed in there with the last of his elk and some venison.

"How long is he gonna leave it in the brine?" JT asked, not that he really cared how long, it was just pleasant to make small talk for a change.

"Until this batch is done, it's got about twelve hours left," Luke said, slapping the smoker.

After that, all the fresh meat they had on hand would be smoked. They used the smoker to slowly dry the meat with out cooking it, doing their best to maintain a temperature of around 125 degrees then bag it and hang it high off the rafters in the shop where the dogs couldn't get to it.

"In the morning we should ride up to Teds place and poke around a bit, I'm sure he's got a bunch of stuff stashed away that could come in handy," JT told Luke matter of factly.

"Um, won't Ted get a little bit pissed about us rummaging around his place?" Luke asked quizzically.

"Deja Vu, they are both dead," JT said.

Surprised, Luke said "wait, what, they're dead, how'd they…I mean what the fuck happen, who killed them and when?"

"Shit," JT thought, it was so busy yesterday that he didn't tell anyone about it, not even Kate. "When you guys were in town yesterday, me and Pete heard the shots," he said, and then went on, telling him the story.

"Fuck me, what has to be going through a persons mind to do that?" the last part was said mostly to himself as he paced around, scratching his head.

"My guess is that Ted had a pretty idea about what came next," JT said.

"I suppose, but still, I couldn't do it," Luke said.

"You might change your mind when you're both pushing 90, when I get up let's ride up there quick and have a look," JT said.

"Anyone see you leave with the tractor?" Luke asked, getting himself comfortable in the chair JT just vacated.

"None that I'm aware of, Jerry might have if he was looking out the window up there, but he wouldn't have thought anything of it, there's no way he would have known it was me unless he was looking through binoculars," JT answered.

Now JT was starting to overthink things. It's a bad habit he picked up years ago, and it sucks because it can cause him to question his own judgment, kind of like ignoring a gut feeling. Then again sometimes that habit gives him pause, a little time to think through details.

"Hey, on second thought, let's walk there through the woods when we go instead, it's only a few hundred yards," JT said.

Waking up, it was still quite early in the morning, the sun just beginning to brighten the eastern sky. Neither JT or Luke had a coffee yet but they gathered their stuff anyway, telling Pete, who was also now awake where they were going.

"Better you than me," Pete said while checking the temperature of the smoker, visibly shuddering at what he'd seen yesterday.

As JT put his arm through the sling of his rifle Luke looked at him saying "what prompted you to bring that thing along?".

"Donno, I suppose I'm bringing it for the same reason we are walking instead of making a bunch of noise by riding up there," JT replied, feeling his gut twist into a knot. He recalled that feeling vividly, it's the same feeling he had when he saw the flash in the sky.

Quietly walking the trail was entirely peaceful for the pair, reminding them both of simpler times and neither of them spoke. The early morning sounds and scents of the woods waking up being music to their ears and noses. JT had made these trails years ago while cutting firewood. This particular trail ended at the fence line marking Teds western property line, his house now about fifty yards ahead through the very thick trees and underbrush. The fence was made out of stranded wire, not barbed wire like a cattle fence which made it easy to get over without ripping a tear in the pants.

Moving very slowly, the pair tried to not break the early morning quiet by snapping any number of the many fallen branches that littered the ground. Teds house was built deep in the trees decades ago, over time the woods encroaching so close with buckthorn and elm that some of their branches were wearing the shingles off his roof. They moved steadily with JT in the lead, the small open area Ted called a yard just ahead when Luke's hand came out, grabbing JT's jacket from behind. Luke put his finger to his lips, making sure JT stayed quiet.

Leaning in close to JT's ear while pointing towards the side of the house he whispered "pretty sure I saw something over there, a reflection moved in that window."

JT, scanning the area, led with his eyes to the front of the detached garage with two bicycles leaning against it. "Those weren't there yesterday," he said.

Knowing Luke's mind was much more suited to this kind of spontaneous situation JT asked "What do you wanna do?"

"What's on the other side of the garage?" Luke whispered.

"A wooden patio, it runs the full length of the garage," JT replied.

"Is there a door leading into the house there?" Luke asked.

"Yeah, and one going into the garage too," JT whispered.

Luke was picturing this all in his mind as JT painted the scene. "I'll stay in the woods and go around the backside of the garage, you move up and to the right until you can see the patio," Luke whispered.

"Then what?" JT asked.

"I don't know, I ain't got that far, but you'll know when I do," Luke said, quietly moving towards the garage.

"Ok then," JT said.

Moving slowly through the thick underbrush like he was stalking deer, JT stayed well inside the shadows of the woods until he had a clear view of the area between house and the garage and two men who were attempting to pry open Teds door. Sneaking ever closer to within fifty yards, JT stopped, slowly getting prone with his rifle in his hands. Checking the red dot of the holographic sight, JT was cussing the long thirty round magazine making it impossible to get flat the ground.

Luke was taking a long time to maneuver into his position, having to be excruciatingly slow and quiet as he moved towards the house and the reflection he'd seen in the glass window. With his back to the rear wall of the garage, Luke inched along ever so slowly until he made it to the corner. Planning out his next move, Luke hoped the old man was in position to cover him. Listening intently, he could hear the shoes of the people just around the corner from him shuffling their feet on the wooden deck boards, the sound so loud to his hypersensitive ears that it almost muffled out their quiet conversation. Then, taking a deep breath, he quietly drew his Glock.

As one of the guys working on the door bent over to pick a pry bar, JT could clearly see the bright red colored grip of a pistol and part of it's chrome frame sticking out of the man's back pocket. Settling the dim red dot of his optic on that man, he waited. It seemed like this was taking an eternity, he was beginning to think those two would make it through the door before Luke was in position and ready.

Suddenly, the air erupted as Luke yelled surprisingly loud "Get on the ground, get on the fucking ground," the violent outburst startling JT as Luke's voice boomed from between the two structures.

The two appeared just as startled as JT was from the thundering sound of Luke's voice, jumping at the outburst. Luke with his pistol pointed at the men repeated the command again yelling for them to get on the ground. As the one closest to Luke began to kneel JT saw the one behind the first slowly reach for the pistol in his pocket.

"Don't do it," JT said to himself.

The instant the man drew the pistol from his pocket, JT squeezed the trigger, loosing the 55 grain soft point bullet from his rifle, it's impact turning the faded white lap board siding a bright pink with the man's blood.

JT honored the oath he'd made to himself to never again put himself or one of their group in the position he did at the intersection where his mom shot the redneck construction guy. Ever. From that point forward, JT had decided he'd shoot first and ask questions later.

Luke was still yelling "get on the ground," causing JT to look around, thinking there were more of them somewhere that he couldn't see. When he turned his attention back to patio area, the guy Luke was yelling at began to thrust himself upright, his move intercepted by Lukes right boot as it crashed into his face, the impact sending him flying asshole over tea kettle where he landed on top of the man JT had just shot, unconscious.

There is a term for this kind of maneuver, what had just taken place. It's called "violence of action" and holy shit, it's execution is effective. Luke's sudden, violent outburst, the volume that he delivered it with startled both of the would be miscreants, giving Luke the upper hand from the element of surprise, which in turn gave JT a moment to assess and react to the situation.

Getting up, JT trotted to the scene as Luke was kicking the silver pistol, landing damn near out to the swing that Ted and Myrna sat on yesterday. Luke then pulled a pair of large zip ties from a cargo pocket of his BDU's saying "Fuck dad, I wasn't expecting your shot, I saw the blood hit the house thinking it was mine and I just hadn't died yet, hell, I didn't even see the gun until just now."

Flipping the unconscious guy to his stomach, Luke pulled his left arm up and behind his head, kneeling on it. Then he grabbing his right arm, twisting it in an ungodly manner he yanked it up to meet the other one, securing them together with the two ties.

"Where in the hell did you learn that move?" JT asked about they way he'd secured the guys hands.

"YouTube," Luke replied, pulling the zip ties tight.

"Well no shit. They really did cover everything I guess," JT said, knowing that's gotta hurt.

While Luke was pulling more zip ties from his pocket he said "I hear an engine" as he pointed to the east. JT didn't hear shit, but in less than a minute, Fred came racing up Teds driveway on his four wheeler carrying a passenger on the back rack. By then, Luke had the unconscious guys feet wrapped up in zip ties as well and was walking to meet Fred when yet another four wheeler came zipping up the driveway, it was Pete on his Honda.

Fred introduced his son John as they all walked over to where the two men lay on the ground, Pete gagging as he walked past the swing. The zip tied guy was coming around now and John stared intently at him as came to. No one spoke, it was an awkward kind of silence as they all watched John as he tilted his head from side to side, seemingly trying to get a good look at who's body the bloody face belonged to. Turning his gaze to where the silver pistol was laying next to the swing, he took in the scene, then returned his gaze back to the now nearly awake man.

John is a big man, with forearms the size of JT's calf muscles sticking out of the sleeves of his rolled up desert tan military grade blouse. His high and tight Marine Corp haircut and square set jaw immediately reminded JT of GI Joe and towering at least 6 foot 3 inch tall, he was an intimidating figure.

Still, not a word had been said and the eerie quiet was getting on JT's nerves. He walked up to John, about to ask him what in the actual fuck was going on here, but John cut him off with a question before he had a chance.

"Anyone got a rag, anything to wipe the blood off this guys face?" John asked calmly.

"Damn, this fucking dudes voice is as intimidating as he looks," JT said to himself, handing John a couple of folded up blue shop rags from his pocket.

"Thanks," John said with a nod.

Walking to the bird bath on the patio, John soaked the rags, then walked back over to the guy that was now almost fully conscious. John, grabbing a handful of the guys hair, lifted his head from the ground as he wiped blood from the badly mangled face.
John turned to the small group, asking "who hit this fucker?". Luke said nothing, just raised his hand. "Someone remind me to never piss him off," John said, nodding towards Luke. It may have been meant as a joke, but they weren't laughing.

John, apparently now satisfied with his identification process stepped back and waited for the guy to get fully awake. When he clearly was, John, in a surprisingly calm voice said "Kelvin, you stupid motherfucker. How many times did I tell you that someday your uncle wasn't going to be there to save your ignorant ass?"

"Wait, you know this piece of shit?" JT asked.

Before John could reply the piece of shit spoke through his mangled mouth. "My uncle is going to kill you, you know that, right Big John?".

"Wait, what, what in the fuck is going on here?" JT asked John.

"I'll tell you the full story later, but the cliff notes are this, I shot this fuckers cousin as he was breaking into Kyles grocery store and that punks daddy considered himself the king of Somerset," John said.

JT was doing the math on the situation, not liking how it was summing up. He pulled his 1911, about to pull the trigger on the tied up man when John put his hand on JT's weapon, pushing it down. "No No, Not yet. There are a bunch more of them," John said.

They were all looking around at each other dumbfounded now, even Fred. John asked if there was somewhere they could bring this guy, Kelvin. Fred said there's no way he's going to his place, Luke shrugged, saying they could put him in the barn.

"Hold on, I know just the spot," JT said.

Diane's place had been officially "condemned" before she was moved to assisted living where she eventually died. They got Kelvin to his feet, dragging him through the grass the short distance to her house then around the backside to the walk out basement.

"Who tied the fucker up?" John asked, looking at the man's arms twisted around his back and head. JT pointed to Luke.

"Ah, you again. Nice, I like it. Give those zip ties a few more clicks, make it hurt," John said.

John looked around the dank, disgusting basement seeing a two inch galvanized steel water line running along the wall horizontally about five feet off the ground. He took a set of cuffs from his pocket and clipped one on Kelvin's right wrist so tight that it would surely stop the blood flow to his hand then he asked Luke to secure the other end to the water line as John held him off the floor. When John let go, poor Kelvin had to stand on his tiptoes to keep slack in the cuffs.

"What now?" JT asked.

"Let's let him stew for a while," John said as he stuffed the bloody shop rags in Kelvins mouth.

"What's the rest of the story John, I know there's more to it than what I've heard?" JT asked.

"There is, and if you've got a cold beer I'll tell ya," John said, cracking a sly smile.

"A little early in the day, ain't it?" JT asked jokingly.

"Not if you're walking in my shoes," He said with a smirk.

Taking logging trail down to the ranch, Pete driving the Honda with JT on the front rack and Luke on the back. Fred and John were right behind them, idling their machines slowly over fallen leaves and branches.

Getting off Fred's machine, John said as he looked around "nice place, I've heard about your 4th of July parties, I always wanted to get here but ended up working every goddamn year."

"Thanks, yeah those were good times, all I have cold is Keystone Light, that ok with you?" JT asked and was answered with a nod of John's huge head.

"What is that smell?" John asked as they walked towards the shop where the beer was.

Looking over at the smoker that Brian was now tending JT said "that," as John savored the sweet smell of woodsmoke and seasoned meat. Looking at the smoker John said he could eat the asshole out of a skunk about now, so JT called to Brian asking if he had anything edible over there.

"Hell yeah pops," Brian said as he opened the smoker, stabbing a nice slab of smoked elk. He brought the meat over to the picnic table, holding fork out to John as he introduced himself. "Brian," he said.

"Dead man walking, but call me John," John replied with a wink. JT noticed Brian sizing John up before turning his attention back to the smoker.

"Pops, want me to run up to Ted's with the tractor and dump that guy on the pile?" Luke asked.

"That's your handiwork, nice touch with the sign," John said. Before JT could ask if that last part was sarcasm John went on to say that if it wasn't for his time in Afghanistan, that smell would have made him turn around before he ever had a chance to see the sign.

Answering Luke by JT nodding his head "yes," Luke and Pete went to fire up the New Holland. Looking at the older tractor, Fred recognized it and asked if JT would be willing share that with him, saying that his brand new Kubota is dead, just like his vehicles.

"You know it," JT answered, Fred nodding his head in approval.

John spoke, saying "The guy you shot today was Tommy Fredricks, and one of the two you killed the other day at the crackhouse was his cousin Jeff. Word got into town about them because apparently you guys hit another dude up there named Mike Hunt. Who would name their kid that anyway? Fucking morons. As I was saying, he was brought back to their "compound" for lack of better words by some crazy black haired chick on an old Honda three wheeler and she told them what she saw. The only reason I even know this is because I was able to interrogate one of the group that tried hitting the grocery store, he was there at the compound when the chick showed up. All those punks belonged to a group, gang, whatever, of guys who ran around probing places, looking for easy marks. The P.D. figures there are bunch of them, but no one really knows for sure. You guys put a decent dent in them already," he said with a grin.

John went on, looking at JT and said, "That Jeff Clark character had seen your truck running up and down the road before, he knew you lived out here somewhere."

"I gotta ask John, how did you get that much information from that guy at the store, I mean that's a lot?" JT asked

"Give me your arm and I'll demonstrate," John replied.

"No thanks. Do you have any idea where they are?" JT asked.

"Not really, but the guy hanging from that water pipe probably does and whenever you ready we can go ask him, but I should have one more beer before we do that to take the edge off," he said.

"The edge off of what?" JT asked.

"Me," John said calmly.

John asked JT to bring a beer along, two if he had them.

"You thirsty?" JT asked him with a chuckle.

"Me, na, I'm a lightweight, it's for him," John said, as he pointed towards Diane's place.

JT shrugged, getting two cans Hamm's beer from one of cubes Luke got the other day. He was really hoping John wasn't going to waste his precious beer water boarding the guy. They didn't speak as they walked intently back through the woods to Diane's.

Going into the dark basement, both men could tell Kelvin was in rough shape. He was hanging limply from the water pipe, his arms disfigured with his right shoulder being obviously dislocated. Yet somehow he appeared to still be conscious. JT was wondering how he hadn't suffocated or at least passed from the blue shop rags John had shoved in his mouth, but it's only been an hour.

What happened next surprised JT. John walked up and after opening a folding knife, cut the zip ties that bound Kelvins hands, then producing a key for the cuffs he freed Kelvin, holding him up as he did so he wouldn't fall.

John gently lowered him to the floor as Kelvin struggled to pull the rags from his mouth with his left hand. Before Kelvin could try to speak John motioned for a beer from JT, which he took and opening it, handed it to Kelvin. No words had been spoken. Kelvin appeared to be in as much shock about what was taking place as JT was, but he did manage to pour the brew into his mangled mouth, dropping the empty can on the grimy floor.

Then finally, John spoke. "Hey man, I'm sorry about your cousin, if I'd have known it was him and you guys pulling that off I'd have walked away," John said softly.

JT had no idea what the fuck was taking place, but he swore he heard John's voice crack as he spoke. A pit began to grow in his stomach as John went on "look, I was running cover for your operation, most of your hits in town were set to take place on my shift. I was supposed to take my time responding if the department got a call."

John looked JT's way, motioning for the other beer, JT reluctantly handing it to him. This wasn't going how how JT was expecting, and after handing John the last beer he took a few steps back unholstering his pistol, keeping it behind his back where John couldn't see it. "This is madness, I'm going to have to shoot John," JT thought as a nervous sweat formed on his forehead.

John showed the new can of beer to Kelvin who hadn't spoken yet and asked if he wanted another, this time Kelvin spoke, simply saying "yeah."

John waited to speak until the second beer can was drained, laying empty by the first one. John spoke again "Hey, I gotta apologize to your boss too, the last place I need to be on his bad side, I've heard about what he's done to people who fucked up and crossed him,". Then John looked at JT, then back to Kelvin and said "if he don't kill me on sight, I wanna join up with you guys."

The alcohol was quickly absorbing into Kelvins blood stream, and he spoke as best he could through his injuries. "You ain't as stupid as you look Big John." Now JT was totally shocked, about to open his mouth when Kelvin blurted "no one crosses Barry King and walks away."

"Is he still at his place by the river, west of the bar?" John asked.

Kelvin, partially drunk, nodded his head yes.

Now that Kelvin thought he had the upper hand on Big John, he ordered John to cut his feet loose "if he wanted to live."

John knelt forward flipping open his razor sharp folding knife. "Oh sure, hold on a sec boss," John said. With a flick of his wrist, the knife flayed at the inside of Kelvins upper right thigh, severing his femoral artery. Kelvin, having no idea what just happened, sat in shock staring as his blood bubbled out of his pants leg in with every beat of his heart.

"You always were a stupid motherfucker Kelvin," John said, wiping the blade on Kelvin's filthy shirt.

Kelvin opened his ravaged mouth, but before he could utter a word he was dead.

"What the fuck, what was that?" JT almost screamed.

"Hearts and minds," John calmly replied.

"What?" JT asked.

"These dipshits live on meth, sometimes not eating for days, that's why we brought the beer, I knew it would go right to his head making it easier for me to convince him he had me. We did the same kind of shit in Afghanistan, but we used spiked Gatorade. Those ragheads wouldn't touch alcohol, but they did like their heroin. Worked the same way," John said, while looking at the 1911 in JT's hand. "Nice piece. Gonna shoot me?" John asked with a raised eyebrow.

"I was thinking about it," JT said, holstering the handgun.

"Please don't, but I should have probably clued you in a little, my bad, I'm used to working alone. But now we know who is running the show and where he lives," John said, flashing a bright smile.

Walking back to the ranch, John told JT that Barry King is the great great grandson of Bartholomew King, a notorious gangster who ran moonshine through Somerset during prohibition. JT was familiar with the name, but had no idea who Barry was. Then John went on explaining that the city administrator was also a shirttail relative of the King family, and how John assumed that he had blackmailed the chief of police, John's former boss. It was the only thing that made sense to him and the other five cops when a stand down order was issued by the chief whenever certain people were involved. He speculated that Barry was just running a small ring of thieves, dealing a few drugs, but never enough to get on anyones radar though. That was going to change, well it already had John said, mentioning the grocery store and the ambush they tried on Luke and Pete at the crackhouse. John said that when he got out of the corp, he went out and got his bachelors degree in criminology, and if his logic was sound, Barry was going to be a problem.

Finished with his explanation for now, John casually asked "what branch were you in?".

"Air Force. What gave it away?" JT said with a chuckle.

"Two things, well three actually. You've got a military bearing about you. You carry a 1911 and your not fat for an old guy," John said, chuckling at his comment.

"Hey, I've got a Glock too there young man," JT said in reply, carrying on the banter.

"You act like you were a senior NCO, but you weren't, were you. I'm gonna guess you were a Lieutenant Colonel," John said wryly.

"Major, I got out after ten, I wasn't Colonel material. I hated the politics," JT replied, reminiscing over his service.

"Don't expect a salute outta me," John said, again with a laugh.

Luke and Pete were back from adding to the body pile at the crackhouse and were sitting around the smoker with Brian, Fred, Amy and Joni when John and JT got back. "How'd that go?" Luke asked, looking up towards Diane's.

"It wasn't exactly what I expected, but it's solved," JT replied.

"What did you expect?" John asked, feigning disappointment. JT grabbed his right thumb, bending the double jointed appendage backwards making it appear like it was broken. "Oh that, that works too, but its better if there are more than one tied up cause ya gotta start on the dumbest one first," John said. John looked towards Amy and Joni, then back to JT, seeing JT was shaking his head "no" just enough that John would understand.

He knew what he was getting at, physical torture works best on the ones who are in the batters box as they are forced to watch what will ultimately happen to them. It's more about that fear than anything else really, and these two ladies didn't need that mental picture.

"Whelp," Fred said with a slap of his knees "we'd better go check on how your bride is settling in," he said to John.

JT shook John's hand, and John pulled JT in saying "those dickheads are gonna figure out sooner or later where we are, so we'd better give that problem a little thought."

"I imagine you're right, we will and thanks again for all the information," JT said.

"No problem, glad to help," John said adding "and count me in on whatever you come up with, I'll add what I can to it."

"Roger that, be safe," JT said as they pulled away.

"So, you got another one for the pile?" Luke asked his dad.

"Yeah, but there's probably enough down there to make the point for now, let's just dig a hole for this character and plant him, running up and down the road has to be making the rest of the neighbors curious," JT said.

"Alright, I'll get that done in a bit, say, how is Sarah doing, I haven't seen much of her?" Luke asked.

"She's worried, missing Tyler, and busying herself with the baby," Joni answered.

"Shit, I gotta check on mom," JT said, jumping up.

"She's fine for now, her O2 levels came up nicely and she's off the concentrator, she was still sleeping when I poked my head in earlier," Joni said.

JT thanked her for that, he has been feeling a little guilty about his lack of keeping up.

"As long as we are on the subject, let me see those wounds you two have," Joni said, looking at Brian and Luke.

The slice in Luke's calf had closed up nicely so Joni just told him to keep it clean and dry the best he can, but getting to Brian a look of concern crossed her small face. Pressing gently on the angry looking spot where she thought the bullet was Brian winced. The entry was closed, but she was now convinced there was an infection growing at the site of the little .22 caliber slug.

"That's gonna have come out Brian," she said.

Brian looked shocked and asked just how in the hell that was going to happen. Pete pulled his folding pocket knife out of his pocket and with a flick of his wrist it was open, the blade gleaming in the sunlight. "I'll do it little buddy," he said with an evil sounding laugh.

"Oh hell no, get the fuck away from me with that thing ya sick bastard," Brian said.

JT was laughing softly at this spectacle but by the look on everyone else's face they must have thought he was serious. "C'mon you big baby, I was only kidding, let the old man have at it then," Pete said with a laugh.

Letting the opportunity slide to rib Brian some more JT, looking at Joni, asked "you got this, right?"

And boy did she. Years ago JT purchased a small surgical kit online and packs of assorted sutures. While the kit was small in size, it had a nice variety of instruments like scalpels, hemostats, tweezers of different sizes…but one thing they didn't have was any kind of numbing agent. What they did have though was ether, the old style spray type starting fluid used for stubborn engines.

After Joni finally convinced Brian that she wasn't going to cut his leg off or otherwise maim him he relented. The picnic table would be her operating space and the bright sunlight her illumination. She had everything ready that she would need to irrigate and clean the the area neatly set out. Pete, Amy and JT left the area while Luke stayed to help in case Brian would need an extra sniff of ether or to help in other ways.

When Joni was satisfied that everything was in place, including Brian, Luke saturated a folded blue shop rag with the ether and placed the rag over Brian's mouth with his left hand, covering his nostrils as he did so in case Brian instinctively began breathing through his nose. He kept the can in his right hand if the fluid evaporated too soon and began a count to ten, at the count of five Brian's eyes rolled back in his head. He was out. Joni wasted no time knowing he could wake up violently and in just seconds she made a slick one inch long and shallow incision. She actually felt the scalpel blade nick the bullet as she sliced.

Luke had gauze pads clamped in a long handled hemostat and was wiping the blood and puss that instantly erupted from the wound while he watched Brian's eyes for movement. Joni quickly removed the little round nosed bullet, placing it on a shop towel then began irrigation and cleaning.

"He's coming around," Luke said.

"Let him, I'm done," Joni replied, each of them holding a leg as Brian woke up with a jolt. "Good idea on the restraint," she said.

"No problem, I've seen the reaction before, I had some stupid friends when I was a kid," Luke replied.

"Oh my god, my head," Brian said, bringing his hands to his head then added "and people do this shit for fun?" he said, referring to "huffers", the name given to those glue sniffing types.

The entire process only took Joni maybe three or four minutes, she had even packed the incision with gauze before Brian came to. Luke made a mental note of the time Brian was under for future reference. Brian asked Joni if she found the bullet, her reply was to pick it up with the tweezers and drop it in his open hand.

"Damn, thanks for getting that out doc, it's crazy how something so small could hurt that much." She explained that it really wasn't the bullet that hurt so much as it was the infection as she taped a gauze pad over the pad inside the incision.

"Let's leave that gauze in for a day, then I'll take it out, irrigate it again and close it up for ya." It's going to be tender, so take it easy.

"How long was I out for?" Brian asked.

"Less than five minutes I'd guess," Joni said.

"I hope I won't need the ether when you pull it out," Brian said.

"You won't. It'll sting for a second, and then just as fast, it won't," Joni replied.

Luke, picking up the blood and puss soaked gauze pads with gloved hands stuffed them in a Walmart bag and walking over, tossed it in the burn barrel. After sprinkling a little shit gas on the bag he lit a match, tossing it in, burning the contaminated trash. Using an old ice cream pail, Joni had already poured in some bleach and water to wipe the table down, after all, that's where most of the group eats and shoot the shit. She then went about sterilizing all the instruments she used, which wasn't many, putting them back in the kit.

Amy had went inside the house while Pete and JT checked on Brian who was now in the camper trying to rid himself of the headache the ether gave him. "I'll grab the tractor and run it up to Diane's and get started on a hole," Luke said, seeing the two leave the camper

"Ten roger, take the trail instead of the road, the neighbors to east gotta be getting curious," JT mentioned.

"I'll ride with ya Luke and help pull him out of the basement. How come he killed that guy?" Pete asked.

"We couldn't let him go, he knew where we live," JT said.

"I see your point, fuck em," Pete replied.

"I'll walk up in a bit, we should check out Ted's house in the daylight after the hole is filled," JT said.

The little backhoe made short work out of digging a hole and Luke soon had Kelvin planted. Then parking the tractor, the three of them took the short walk over to Ted and Myrna's place to check it out, again. Getting there, it was as they had left it earlier, thankfully. JT wanted to go inside the house and was kind of regretting not patting down Teds pockets for his keys before they buried them yesterday, when he remembered a lockbox Ted had in the pole shed. The three of them headed to shed, walking through the door Ted had left open. The lock box was one of those like realtors use, Ted had it locked to an "eye" bolt screwed into a wooden column. JT had no idea what the combination was so he took a guess that it was their phone number. The number was impossible to forget, 5309, like the song, Jenny Jenny, 867-5309.

To his astonishment, that was the combination and opening the box revealed a slew of keys, none of which were labeled. They took them all to the house, where on the fourth key the side door the thieves were working on opened.

Going inside, the house was dark, all the shades had been pulled closed and it smelled a bit musty even though it appeared to be quite clean when they eventually got some sunlight into it.

In the kitchen, Luke ventured a peek into the fridge, it was empty luckily, Myrna must have emptied it before they offed themselves. The pantry was fairly well stocked with store bought canned goods, flour, sugar and probably ten pounds of salt, other than that though, the cupboards were basically void of food, except for the little spice cabinet near the electric range. In the living room area there stood a nice Fisher wood stove, it too was clean and they doubted it had used it for years, as old as they both were.

"Hey Pete, you and Brian should move yourselves up here. That pop up camper won't cut it when it gets colder, and that's going to happen all too soon," JT said.

"You sure, I mean yeah, it's gonna get cold but I don't wanna leave ya hanging down there?" Pete replied.

"You won't be, we've got plenty of radios with rechargeable batteries, you'll only be a call away if something goes down, plus, you will probably be the ones calling us, being closer to the county road," JT said.

"What about water?" Pete asked.

"Well, we can check the buildings, I'd bet Teds got a generator in there somewhere that will run his well. I've got plenty of gas for it too. But for now, I've got five gallon bucket's for ya, you brought that big Coleman stove with ya didn't you? This electric one is useless," JT asked, looking at the appliance.

"I did, and if your sure you are ok with it, I'll talk to Brian and get packed when he's up to it," Pete replied.

"Good deal, it's only a matter of time before someone else would end up trying to claim it, so we might just as well beat them to it," JT said.

Pete agreed, especially after JT reminded him of all the people who are going to be headed this way, some of whom may not make bad neighbors and telling him they'd be fools to think that they will all stay in the little village of Somerset.

Darkness was settling in so they left the place, locking the house back up as they did. Taking the two pry bars the thieves had dropped with them to put in the pole barn, they found that the bundle of keys had a spare for the barn door lock too, and locked it up. There were what looked like a ton of tools inside, they would eventually need those too at some point.

Walking through the woods, they picked up the tractor behind Diane's, taking it back to the ranch. Today was Friday, JT thought it was Friday anyway, but being so tired he really didn't know. He was ready for a cold beer and something to eat, telling himself that he's gotta get this sleep thing under control. When they got back to the ranch everyone was outside, even JT's mom, Sarah and the baby. All of them were sitting around the picnic table while Brian hobbled around manning a fire he had going on the end of the smoker with the smell of something delicious wafting out it's open lid. There were the ladies, momma, Kate, Sarah, Amy and Joni then JT, Luke, Pete and Brian. With the baby there were ten of them there, and for a few moments JT soaked in the relative calm that they had.

His mom wasn't well though, he was certain that her organs were beginning to shut down. No one recovers from dementia and

Alzheimer's disease, it's always terminal. Sadly, they were fully aware that her days were numbered.

Chapter Seventeen

Opening his eyes slightly Tyler heard "Hey buddy, are ya back in the land of the living?".

Tyler lay there, his head pounding, his chest hurting and he had no idea where he was. As his vision came into focus he saw Jarod standing next to him with D'vante sitting in chair near the foot of the cot he way laying on, a huge smile on his face. Looking at his arm he saw an IV stent in his forearm and a nearly empty bag of a clear liquid hanging from its stand.

"What the hell is going on, where's Sarah?" Tyler asked.

Giving him a second to sit up, Jarod said "She should be at her mom's, I rode with her to the high bridge. She was only a few miles from her moms house and was sure that she'd be fine the rest of the way by herself. As soon as I left her I rode back up here to look for you, she's worried sick man."

Tyler, just waking up was struggling to comprehend this and said "hold on, where are we, why am I here with an IV in my arm?" Then he remembered the flash of the blade in front of him. He put his hand to his chest and felt the sutures.

"We're inside the Hugo clinic, but they're shut down now," said Jarod. "There was an RN here when D carried you in. She sewed you up, but she's gone and told us to lock the door when we leave. D was the one who brought you here."

Tyler, still confused looked at D for more and asked "you carried me here?"

"I did, but not all the way, I guy saw me when I was about halfway here and helped. Nice guy." D said, stuffing something into his pocket.

"I thought you were going to Duluth?" Tyler asked quizzically.

"I was, but after I got a few blocks or so north from where you turned off, I decided to cut back and try to catch you."

"Why?" Tyler asked.

"Well, I gave it some thought, figuring a black man walking around up here at night by himself would make for a fine target, so I was going to see if I could crash in your basement or something until daylight," D replied.

"I'm glad you did, you've had a long day then," Tyler said.

"Long three days my man, it's Wednesday night. You've been out the whole time. The nurse stitched your head up too, after you were stabbed you must have fell backwards and mashed your melon on a rock," D said with a frown.

"Hey, we will catch up with this in a bit, but we gotta move man, shits getting weird out there and I wanna get to Karen and head to my brothers.," Jarod said.

"We gotta walk, Jarod's got a bike, but all we got are Nikes," D said, then added "can ya get up man, I'll help."

Tyler looking around the IV cart found a bandage, opened it then pulled the IV stent from his arm, quickly putting the bandage on. Then he swung his feet around off the cot and was happy to see he was still fully clothed from the waist down. "Anyone got an extra shirt," he asked as he attempted to stand. Jarod handed him a clean shirt and jacket, which Tyler looked at. "These are mine, where'd you get them?" he asked.

"Oh, I rode back to your place, second time tonight by the way, and got them from your hockey closet in the garage." D said.

"Really boys, we gotta get a move on, we've got an eight mile walk ahead of us," Jarod said.

D was standing around, not saying much, then sheepishly asked Jarod if he could go with him and Karen to his brothers place. Tyler saw Jarod tense up, he knew Jarod's brother was a racist piece of shit, so he spoke up; "come with me D, Sarah's stepdad will love you, and I know for a fact you will be welcome there, plus, I owe you."

"You don't owe me shit, but I'll take you up on that if you're sure," D said.

"I'm sure. Why not Duluth?" Tyler asked curiously, to which D said that by now all the jets would have been dispersed and he'd just be another mouth to feed.

The walk was long, but Tyler found out along the way how D had just caught a glimpse of three guys fighting their way out of a hedgerow. They were a ways off, but one of them was carrying a backpack with a big "N" from the Minnesota North Stars, just like the one Tyler had on his back on their walk. It all just looked wrong D said, so he waited a bit till the three were gone then walked up to where they came out of the bushes, just to check it out. D swore he wouldn't have saw Tyler laying there if it wasn't for his teeth. His mouth was wide open and at first he thought that Tyler was dead, but his Air Force training had kicked in and he went looking for a pulse which he quickly found. There was blood all over the place as he rolled Tyler to his side, then he draped Tyler's left arm and left leg over D's shoulders and stood up. He then headed towards the clinic he noticed just off of highway 61 before he had turned around to go find Tyler.

Tyler was humbled immensely after the story played out and thanked both men profusely for saving his life. He asked Jarod how he found him and D at the clinic.

D responded "I checked your pockets and pulled your driver's license for your address, then I jogged over there and left a note under the one Sarah left saying "check the Hugo clinic," then Jarod here found that note when he came looking for you." Tyler thanked them both again, giving both men a heartfelt hug.

Later on in the walk, Jarod insisted Tyler ride his bike while he and D could walk or run along side of him for the trip towards the tracks. They spoke little, each man in his own thoughts as the miles passed rather quickly.

When the trio got to the railroad tracks, Jarod told Tyler and D to just stay on them, they will take them to the high bridge. It was time to part ways, again, and the three of them stood there, shuffling their feet.

Tyler broke the ice. "Be safe buddy, take care of Karen, ok?" then they shook hands and Tyler turned away, wiped a tear from his eye.

"I will," Jarod said, then turned to D and told him to keep an eye on Tyler and to take their time getting home to Sarah's moms.

"We will. Be safe, maybe we will see each other again someday," D said as those two shook.

Tyler was not well. He pushed himself hard to get to the tracks because he knew Jarod was in a hurry to leave. Just a few hundred yards into the twenty two mile walk in front of them Tyler had to stop. His body had not yet replaced the blood he had lost, his head was pounding and he was nearly dehydrated.

"I gotta stop D, I don't have anything left," Tyler said.

D handed Tyler his water bottle, and Tyler took a drink, then handed it back.

"No man, drain it. I've still got all my blood inside me," D said. Tyler did as instructed and emptied the bottle.

"Thanks D, I needed that," Tyler said.

"I'll find more water in the morning, but for now let's move off the tracks, there is a nice white pine right over there we can get under and stay out of sight," D said, pointing to the tree about ten yards in the woods.

As part of D'Vantes pilot training, he had attended the Air Force survival school in the mountains north of Fairchild AFB, Washington. That area of north eastern Washington state was rugged wilderness, providing an optimum setting for the program. While there he learned escape and evasion, mountaineering, foraging, snaring game, water scavenging and a multitude of other topics he hoped to never use.

Now, here he was years later about to crawl under a white pine and put those skills to use. At the clinic that treated Tyler, they had a box filled with emergency "space" blankets, the kind that came folded in a four inch square and when unfolded were just enough to cover the chest and legs. He had four of those he absentmindedly stuffed in his pocket before they left a few hours ago. Tyler was struggling to maintain consciousness so D quickly got him under the tree, pointing him to bed of pine needles he had raked up with his hands.

As soon as Tyler laid down he was out, either passed out or asleep. D covered Tyler with two of the blankets then sat back against the tree, shaking his empty water bottle. D only had a vague idea where they were precisely, but it was very rural so he decided to wait until daylight to look for water. If he had a compass, he certainly would have ventured out in the dark.

Waking to the sound of voices and very bright sunlight, Tyler was disoriented and confused, caused as much by the concussion as the dehydration. Even though he was sweating under the space blankets, he had enough wherewithal to not move until the voices vanished. Coming around some, remembering the walk here, Tyler looked around. D was gone. Sitting up, his head began to pound again so he went back to the ground, peeling the blanket off his chest. He looked at the thing, it's shiny foil side was facing his body, and the dull grey of the opposite side was away from him. Rolling the blanket into a pillow, Tyler eased his head down, falling back to sleep.

Being awoken again by a voice, this time Tyler relaxed, recognizing it as D's as he came creeping back to camp through the dense woods. Carrying two plastic grocery bags with him, D reached in to one of them, pulling out a large water bottle and handed it to Tyler.

"Where'd you go, for a second there I thought you bailed," Tyler asked.

"Just went to do a little shopping my man," D answered.

"Huh?" Tyler questioned.

"As soon as it got light out I went out for a sneak and peek to see what I could find," he said.

"Well thanks for the water, I don't remember the last time I took a leak, so I gotta be dehydrated," Tyler said, pinching the skin on the back of his hand.

D went back in the bag and brought out a Snickers candy bar, handing it to Tyler saying "or ate anything," Tyler took the bar asking D where in the world he found a candy bar and water. D said "you ain't going to believe this," and went on to fill Tyler in.

When he had woke up at daylight, he had no idea which way to head off to, so he stood there, thinking and decided on north away from the city and so he would be able to find his way back to the tracks using the sun. He came out on a gravel road after a about a half mile and seeing a few mailboxes to his right so he went that way. Then, eventually hearing a noise coming from the yard of what sounded like the third house down, he took off that way. The noise turned out to be a lawnmower, some guy was actually out mowing his yard during this crap.

D didn't want to spook the guy, so when he saw him turn and start mowing his direction he began walking to him waving and smiling. When he got close to the guy mowing, the man shut the mower down and stuck out his hand to shake his, asked what the hell I'm doing poking around out in this neck of the woods. I told him I was looking for water, and about how you was laid up under a pine tree. The guy said that wasn't what he meant, he said what's D'Vante Jones doing walking around anywhere.

"Playing college ball has its perks," Tyler said.

"I guess so, but the guy knew all about me, that I am in the reserves, he even knew how old I am, it was weird. Anyway, he brought me in his house to meet his wife and she loaded me up with stuff. Water, some food and these," he said as he handed Tyler a half bottle of Aleve.

Continuing, D said "I asked him how things were around here and if he knew what happened, he told me things were good except for no power and his truck didn't run. Said he's got a pitcher pump by his garden for water, and a wood stove in the basement if the power don't come back soon. As far as what happened he just said the powers out."

As the two were folding up their space blankets, they took notice of a small group of three people walking past them. The group, two middle aged men and a woman, appeared oblivious to their presence under the tree. Each were carrying different style bags in their arms and didn't speak as they walked, staring at the ground with slumped shoulders and dragging feet.

"They look rough," Tyler said.

"You looked in a mirror lately T, you don't look much better," D'Vante asked.

"T, that's what my hockey buds call me," Tyler said.

D laughed, "at the U, that's what all the guys on different sports teams call each other, mostly because half of those fools couldn't pronounce their own names, you wouldn't believe how ignorant some of the players are, white, black, didn't matter, they were all equally stupid, but they can play football, so…"

"For sure, sports programs bring in an enormous revenue flow for the school's," Tyler said.

Finally breaking their camp, the two walked down the gentle slope to the easement road and took up a pace. Tyler first walked for a half hour before needing to rest for a half hour, then walk for another half hour and more rest. Rinse and repeat. It didn't matter to D, he was perfectly content with the fact that Tyler could walk on his own and wherever he was was exactly where he was supposed to be. He had no destination and no expectations.

The pair was passed by several groups before darkness fell upon them. Tyler had slowed to a snail's pace. After they left the trail to find a tree to sleep under, they heard plenty more people walk by. Tyler fell asleep immediately under his cover, whereas D had trouble sleeping. His mind was in overdrive, trying to imagine what the rest of the country and the world were like at present. D knew that as bad as it was here, there were undoubtedly worse places to be. He knew there were cities that had been incinerated, wiped off the map in an instant; he just didn't know which ones. For sure, he thought Washington DC had to be one target. Most likely Offutt Air Force Base, too. Destroying it would cripple strategic forces. Lieutenant Jones finally fell into a deep sleep as various scenarios and images of enormous mushroom clouds filled his dreams.

The two men woke with the sunrise. Tyler was feeling much better, probably due to having plenty of fresh water to drink and a few snacks. He was even able to pee a decent amount after getting up and stretching his legs. The pair had two more 'Little Debbie' snacks left in their bag along with four full bottles of water. Their best estimate was that they were fifteen miles from Sarah's mom's house, which was a seven-hour walk if Tyler could go nonstop, but that wasn't the case - he could only walk for a couple of hours before needing to rest for a half hour."

There were many more people on the trail today, not huge groups but at any given time they could see single walkers and groups of possibly up to ten looking in either direction. All of the people were going east. Some spoke to them, some asked if they had food or water to spare in the bag D carried. D did cave in when they came upon a man and a woman with two little kids and gave them the second to the last full bottle of water in the bag. They looked completely like shit, defeated even. Tyler almost asked them where they were headed, but not wanting to have that discussion he didn't.

Now finally after an excruciating walk for Tyler the bridge was in sight, but he desperately needed a rest before they made their way out on that massive expanse. This time Tyler napped for a solid forty five minutes and feeling refreshed when he woke up, they were both ready to get on the other side of that thing.

Making their way to the approach of the bridge the pair saw a mangled body, what was left of it anyway after the vultures had at it. The unrecognizable corpse laying face down in between the tracks not far from a signal shack had the handle of a large knife protruding from it's back. Seeing the knife instantly gave Tyler a flashback to the flash of steel entering his chest, just barely missing his heart and left lung. It made him shudder as it played out in his mind how he almost orphaned his child because he wasn't paying attention. That won't happen again, he told himself.

D wondered aloud why no one had taken the knife yet.

"Grab it," Tyler said with a laugh.

"Oh hell no, I ain't going near that stink, that walkway was close enough for me," D said.

"And thats why the knife is still there," Tyler said, as he gave it one more skeptical glance.

The sun was beginning it's steady dip to the tree line behind them as they finally made it across the expansive bridge. Turning north on 37th street, they were close now, just a few more miles left to the ranch. D suggested that they dip into the woods for concealment to watch where the larger group behind them heads before they get too far, explaining that people will follow other people for no other reason other than to be led.

"Like sheep," Tyler said.

"Zackly, it's probably not a good idea to be followed being this close," D replied.

The pair remained very quiet, hidden behind a fallen oak tree. Tyler and D watched the group stop and look around, then get off the tracks walking up the ditch and finally onto the road. Fortunately instead of turning north, the entire group shuffled east as one, away from them on 180th avenue, following their leader towards Somerset.

"How big is Somerset, I've never been there," D asked curiously.

"Two stop lights, one grocery store, a few liquor stores.....," Tyler answered.

After thinking that over in his mind, D muttered "doesn't sound like it's got much for resources, I wonder what all those people are expecting when they get there."

When the group was finally out of sight, they quickly got on the road where Tyler picked up a quick walking pace.

"Feeling better?" D asked.

"Not really, just motivated," Tyler said.

"Take it easy now, I really don't feel like carrying your ass anymore," D said with a chuckle.

The next couple of miles passed quickly for the pair. They saw no one and as they got further from the bridge and the hordes of people crossing it, they mentally relaxed some, enjoying the view of the beautiful landscape. Tyler remained focused by talking to D about the baby, sports, even explaining in detail exactly where the ranch was. He actually remembered the fire number on the mailbox and the long assed driveway.

After topping the hill coming out of the flowage, they soon walked by 205th Avenue. Suddenly stopping, Tyler bent over at the waist, resting his hands on his knees. D assumed he needed to catch his breath and stood by Tyler, scanning the area through the dark shadows of the setting sun. With a shift of the evening breeze, a disgusting smell wafted over them.

"What-in-the-fuck-is-that-smell," D said, drawing out the question. As he turned back expecting a response from Tyler, he saw him laying face down in the long grass, just off the road.

D sprinted towards Tyler's fallen body, his heart pounding in his chest as he slid to a stop, reaching out to feel for a pulse in his friend's neck. His hand trembled as he searched, and his fear grew when he struggled to detect any sign of life in Tyler. Quickening his breath, D hastily flipped Tyler onto his back, his hands shaking as he hovered over his friend's lips to confirm that he wasn't breathing. Trying to remain calm, he realized he needed to act fast. Without hesitation, D pinched Tyler's nostrils closed and, putting his mouth over his friend's, he blew air into his lungs, counting each moment with bated breath. After several attempts, Tyler's chest finally heaved, rising and falling on its own. Throwing caution to the wind, D jumped up and ran, the echoes of Tyler's description of the ranch filled him- his own heartbeat thudding loudly in his ears with every stride. He had a mile in front of him, and knew he could run it in six minutes flat.

As it turned out, Brian had gotten bored after his "surgery" as he called it, and had found a big package of venison bratwurst still inside the upright freezer. He had them laid out in a large cake pan on the grill, simmering in a brine of Hamm's beer with a pot full of sauerkraut next to it. The smell the woodsmoke combined with brats and kraut wafting in the cool air was more than any of them could handle, even Pepper, laying at JT's feet had her eyes glued to the grill.

JT had only just cracked open his ice-cold beer, savoring the promise of a relaxing evening. But before he could take a sip, Pepper's ears pricked up and she growled, eyes fixed on the driveway. The other three dogs followed her line of sight and began barking ferociously. Hearts pounding, Luke and Pete sprang up from their seats, snatching their rifles from the cedar tree and racing after the pack of dogs before JT even had his beer set down on the table. With adrenaline coursing through their veins, Luke and Pete thundered down the driveway towards the unseen intruder. In the background, JT's three dogs were raising holy hell, their fury simmering at the fence as they tried to break free and join the chase. In the midst of the pandemonium, Clover, unaware of the invisible fence, dashed past the other dogs with abandon, her hot breath misting in the air with each stride, ready to take down anyone who dared to threaten her pack.

"STOP, GET ON YOUR FACE," Luke's voice thundered as he brought his rifle up, then followed with "CLOVER BACK."

The dog immediately stopped her advance but not her gnashing of teeth and downright terrifying growling.

"IS THE OLD MAN HERE, TYLERS DOWN, I NEED THE OLD MAN," the form on the ground yelled in reply.

Not being nearly as fast on his feet as Luke and Pete, JT was well behind them when he heard Luke holler back "TYLER WHO."

D thought for a moment, he didn't know Tyler's last name, but he knew his wife's name "SARAH'S HUSBAND."

By now JT had caught up to Luke and Pete who helped the man to his feet. "You know him?" JT asked.

D, now gasping for breath quickly filled them in as they rushed back to the house.

"JONI, TRUCK. LUKE, PETE, IN THE BACK, GUNS READY," JT yelled, then looking at the man he said "GET IN."

D's voice was taut with urgency as he clambered into the truck, his eyes wild as he frantically explained where Tyler was. JT revved the engine, as the old truck struggled for traction on the unstable gravel. Luke and Pete clung on, white-knuckled, as the wheels spun madly, desperate to gain purchase. As they hit the blacktop, JT floored the gas pedal and with a deafening roar, the 350 engine came to life. The rear tires whirled frantically, screeching as thick white smoke boiled from spinning tires, JT fighting to control the powerful machine as it lurched forward with brutal force. Through the chaos and noise, D's voice pierced through the intense pounding of adrenaline: Tyler's life was on the line and time was running out.

D explained that Tyler was only a little ways beyond the two cars in the road and as they roared near the intersection he yelled "STOP."

"THAT'S TYLER," JT yelled, slamming on the brakes as he skidded the old truck to a screeching halt. Flying through the open door, Joni spotted Tylers motionless body, laying in the tall grass through the thick cloud of dust the truck had raised. Hovering over him, Joni frantically checked for a pulse that she could not find and breathing that did not exist.

Expertly delivering a violent blow to Tyler's chest with her fist, Joni then began chest compressions while JT constantly checked for a pulse and when directed by Joni, blew air into Tyler's mouth. D'Vante hovered over the pair, pacing with his hands on his head, desperately hopeful that he'd acted fast enough to save his friends life.

Pete and Luke both instinctively took up defensive positions after exiting the bed of the truck, well aware that the noise they just made will bring anyone within earshot to investigate the action.

"Got a pulse," JT yelled, fingers pressed to Tyler's neck.

"Okay, he's alive. Get him in the back. I'll keep mouth to mouth up as we go. Just take it easy," Joni directed frantically, looking over at JT.

Luke wasted no time, springing into action and racing to the driver's seat, turning the truck around.

"What's your name?" JT turned to D'Vante, his tone immediate and focused.

"D'Vante," he replied.

"Give me a hand, D'Vante. Grab his shoulders. Pete, get his legs," JT commanded, as they loaded Tyler's limp form into the back of the truck, praying that they weren't too late."

In the truck, D'Vante explained to JT that had given Tyler mouth to mouth before he ran to the ranch, saying that he had a pulse and was breathing when he took off at a run.

Joni was relentless. She didn't know Tyler from Adam, it didn't matter- She was not going to lose this man. Nearly unconscious herself from the constant mouth to mouth, she continued, refusing to give up until her vision dimmed, about to pass out. "Pete, take over," She said, totally spent. Halfway down the driveway Luke heard her say "stop" through the open rear window, and slowly brought the truck to a stop.

"Not you Luke, Pete. He's breathing on his own," Joni said anxiously.

As Luke idled the truck down the driveway, it's tires crunching over the now loose gravel from earlier, JT heard Joni ask for a flashlight. Luke quickly handing her his through the sliding rear window, and taking it, she opened Tyler's eyelids one at a time, flashing them with the bright light. Tyler's eyes apparently responded to the stimulation because the next thing she said was "his eyes are dilating, he's got brain function," she said with relief.

JT could see D lightly sobbing, his head in his hands.

"You ok?" JT asked as they pulled up to the shop, Luke shutting the truck down.

Wiping his eyes, D simply said "it's been a long week."

"No shit it has," JT said softly, then thanked him for going above and beyond to find them and get Tyler here.

"Clear the table," Joni ordered, directing Luke, JT and Pete to put Tyler on it, then she asked for blankets to get him warm.

Sarah, hearing the ruckus outside and opening the door, saw her husband being carried to the table. Standing on the steps, her hands covering her mouth to silence the inevitable scream, she ran to Tyler, instinctively putting two fingers to his neck and her ear to his mouth, Joni watching her mouth out each of Tyler's heartbeats as she counted.

She looked at her husband, then at D, asking "who are you, and what happened to Tyler?"

"He was stabbed on Monday, then he smashed his head on a rock when he fell, and I'm D'Vante Jones, I met Tyler and his friend Jarod on Monday, we were going the same direction so we walked together," D answered.

Sarah was trying to maintain, but it was clear she was close to losing control of her emotions. She asked where Tyler was stabbed. D said he found him in a hedgerow, not far from their house. "Thanks," she said, "where on his body was he stabbed?" clarifying her question.

D motioned to his own chest, pointing at a spot just left of center to those looking, who was everyone at the moment. Sarah opened Tyler's shirt and gasped, actually all of them did when they saw the two and a half inch gash that was sutured closed.

"He's got another one on the back of his head," D said.

Joni gently held Tyler's head up and felt for sutures, Tyler's short haircut making them easy to find. "Eight," she said, after counting them with her fingers before gently laying his head back down.

"D'Vante, Joni's got this, walk with me will you?" JT asked as D starting walking to catch up. "You've got a military bearing about you, what branch did you serve in?" JT asked.

"Air Force Reserves, and still serving, First Lieutenant D'Vante Jones, I'm a Falcon driver out of Duluth," D explained.

"Major JT Clark, 377th Engineers out of Ramstein," JT said, extending his hand.

Instead of shaking JT's hand though, D'Vante snapped to attention, giving a crisp salute, which JT instinctively returned. "Thanks for what you did, my words will never be enough, so thank you," JT said sincerely.

"You're welcome, sir," D replied.

"No need for the "sir" stuff, I've been out since 88, call me pops. What's your plan, do you have family or friends around here?" JT asked.

"No sir, I'm from Missouri, no family to speak of, I was raised in foster homes my whole life until I got out of high school," D said.

"Well, you're welcome here D, and no more of the sir shit," JT said.

"Thank you, I don't know what to say, but no can do on the "sir" shit sir, I need the structure right now, and being outranked feels kinda good," D said, finally cracking a small smile.

"What ever makes your turbine spin," JT said with a laugh. "Let's get back to the group, I wanna hear your story, and I'm sure everyone else does too," JT added.

"Roger that sir," D said, watching JT shake is head out of the corner of his eye.

Sarah was crying, Kate was crying, Amy was crying, hell, every one of them had tears in their eyes. There were audible gasps heard as D'Vante told the story with great detail beginning on Monday afternoon right up until this very moment. He even mentioned the knife in the back of the guy on the bridge. Luke and JT sharing a glance at that one. When it was clear D was finished talking they stood there, silently digesting it in their own way.

Looking at D'Vante, Joni softly said, "You saved his life." Everyone nodded in agreement.

Then, in a very quiet, hoarse voice they all heard the word "again" miraculously escape Tyler's dry mouth.

Tyler's uttered words brought yet another release of emotions. Every one of them were carrying an immense emotional load, even if they weren't aware that they were. Even Luke, normally the epitome of the word "stoic" was wiping his eyes as he held Amy tight. This was a good thing, healthy even, for they have all seen and done things in the past five days that none of them could have imagined in their wildest dreams, not even JT.

After a few minutes of more tears and talk, Brian spoke up, "Hey, I don't want to sound like a dick and ruin the moment, but we should really eat, we can't afford to let this food go to waste."

And waste it they wouldn't. There was finally something to be happy about with Tyler's arrival, even as traumatic as it was. They celebrated like it was a special Friday night, only better, they could sense the air of gratitude they all felt.

Later, Tyler managed to get up and move around with the help Sarah and Joni. After settling into the reclining lawn chair that was brought over from the deck, he even ate a bratwurst. At some point in the evening Sarah had went inside, bringing the baby out. Tyler insisted that little Jake sit on his lap on top of the sleeping bag Tyler was covered with. Sarah sat next to him, holding hands.

Nearly exploding with excitement, Pete was full of questions when D confirmed his suspicions about him playing football ball for the Gophers and between him and Brian, poor D couldn't get a word in edgewise. The picnic table wasn't big enough for everyone to sit down at the same time, so getting up, Luke grabbed a few folding lawn chairs that were stored under the camper.

They all ate plenty of food, drank some beer and even played a some music after Kate bought out a couple acoustic guitars. When the song "wagon wheel" was over, JT handed his Taylor guitar to Pete who quickly took charge of the musical situation.

Walking away from the music and conversations taking place, JT stared, taking the scene in, trying his best to commit it to memory. As pleasant as it was seeing all four dogs lounging by the smoker, Amy and Joni laughing, Kate and Pete singing their hearts out to the Creedence tune "Proud Mary", Luke, Brian and D eating the last of the brats and sauerkraut, shooting the shit with beers in hand and finally Sarah, doting over Tyler and the now sleeping little Jake, JT was also very well aware that this was an illusion and would not, could not last.

He knew that at this very moment groups of very hungry, very desperate and likely very dangerous people were crossing the high bridge. The odds of those people coming his direction were exactly 50/50, also aware that the odds of survival for those who were escaping the asphalt jungle of the Twin Cities were probably way worse than that. He knew that in just a couple of days the little village of Somerset would be totally overrun by people escaping the brutal dystopian reality that is Minneapolis and St Paul. He knew as soon as the local hospitality dried up, their supplies decimated, that whoever who had not already moved on willfully would move on angrily, or equally angered, stay. JT also knew that Barry King would need to be dealt with before he had the opportunity to deal with JT on his terms.

Luke, concerned seeing his dad standing off by himself walked over, asking him what's on his mind.

JT swept his arm towards the rest of the people, smiling saying "this."

"Don't get used to it old man," Luke said.

"No shit," JT said, drawing out the words.

"I'll take first watch," Luke said taking his rifle from the stub of a branch of the big cedar tree. "I'll relieve you in a while," JT said, then walked into the house to tuck his mom in.

Chapter Eighteen

"Toss me your water bottle Sally, mine is empty," Karen demanded.

"Mines empty too, everyone is out of water now Karen, most of us have been out since last night," Sally replied.

"Do you think that maybe last night would have been a better time to tell me that? Get Allen to go find water, we just walked by a creek flowing under the tracks, he can fill all our bottles up there," Karen ordered.

Allen, Sally's husband was quick on his feet, organizing four other men to gather up all the water bottles from the group. "Hey, where are those people who lived at the end of the building at," Allen asked one of the men.

"Gone, a bunch of them took off into the woods after we crossed that road this morning, they said they've walked far enough," he said.

"How many are left?" Allen asked.

"Twenty maybe, I'll do a head count when I get the bottles," the man said.

"I sure hope she knows what she's doing," Allen said, looking at a couple other men.

"We're out of food too, my kids are hungry," a man named Bob said.

"So are we," a couple other guys spoke up.

"We should have stayed in Saint Paul," Bob said to nobody in particular.

"And do what, there's no water or food there either," Karen said, walking up to the group of men. "We're not gonna die if we don't eat for a few days, some of you could stand to lose a few pounds anyway, but we are going to die with out water, so…" she said, expectantly. "Come on, get moving, we can't leave here until you get back with the water. That bridge should only be a few miles up ahead, the sooner we're over that the sooner we get to Somerset," she said, with a tone of finality.

Walking back the way they had just came, the three men, Allen, Bob and another man named Vince were looking intently along the tracks for the trickle of water Karen call a creek.

"She's gonna get us killed, you guys know that, right?" Bob said, an edge to his voice.

"We aren't even to the river yet and there's only half of us left," Vince said.

"Cut her some slack, her husband just split on her," Allen said, trying to sound authoritative.

"And look, there's the creek, right where she said it would be," Allen said, happy to change the subject.

"Let's get these filled and get back to the group, I don't like this shit," Bob said, warily.

"Anyone going to taste that water?" Vince asked, an edge of concern in his voice.

"It looks clean, let's just get these last few filled and get back," Bob said, topping off his last bottle.

"This was a good idea, getting off the highway, there's only a few scattered groups walking the tracks," Allen said.

"The road was a lot easier to walk on," Vince said, taking a long drink from his bottle.

"How is it, taste ok?" Allen questioned.

"It's wet," Vince replied, wiping his face on his grubby shirt sleeve.

Walking back to the group, Allen scanned the area and felt like there were a couple more people missing. "Sally, did someone else leave while we were getting water?" he asked, still looking around.

"Kari and Jon left with their kid, they said they were going to find a road, maybe look for an empty house," Sally replied.

"Damn, he's brave, no way I'd wanna walk alone out there," Allen said, handing out the water.

"Let's get moving. We can make it to the bridge in a few hours, I think," Karen said.

As the group trudged slowly along the dusty maintenance road beside the railroad tracks, now only numbering seventeen, they encountered more people as they got closer to the High Bridge. Most appeared to be family groups of three or four, while some larger groups like theirs were visible in both directions.

"This is a lot of people, where do you think they are all going?" Sally said, walking alongside Karen.

"Oh my god, STOP," Allen yelled, pointing to a body in the trees, just off of the trail.

"Where, I don't see anything," Karen asked.

"Right there, under that pine tree, I'm gonna go look," Allen said, walking to the body.

"Jesus," he said, shivering as he looked at the naked body of a teenage girl. Peering out further into the woods, Allen turned in a circle, looking. Looking what he didn't know, but he had a weird feeling that he was being watched.

"What is it Allen?" Sally asked from the road.

"I don't know, I just have a bad fee….," his words cut off as the arrow passed through his chest, the bloody shaft protruding from the ground in front of him. Allen looked down at his shirt, the blood from his body running out of him like it was dumped from a bucket. Staggering a step towards the trail, Allen fell, dead.

Shocked, the entire group momentarily stood there frozen staring at Allen. Another arrow flew striking Phil, Jill's husband in the abdomen. Like Allen, Phil looked down at himself, staring at the fletching of the shaft just outside his shirt, the broadhead of the arrow protruding from his lower back.

"RUN," Karen shrieked as a "WHOOP" erupted from the woods in front of them. Karen and Sally ran as fast as their feet would take them. Looking over her shoulder, Sally saw four men looking like animals emerge from the woods with baseball bats. Slamming the bats into the heads of Vince and Bob, Sally could hear the dull "ping" as the aluminum bats crushed their skulls. Two of the attackers, grabbing Jill by the arms, dragged her from her gut shot husband into the woods like hyenas. The other two continued slamming their bats into men, women and even children as the group scattered.

Their group was just decimated by bandits. Jack and his wife Nancy, Tom, and a woman named Julie were all that escaped in the direction Karen and Sally ran towards the bridge. Some of the group may have gone in the opposite direction or off into the woods, but there would be no way to know. They weren't going back to look.

"What are we going to do now, why isn't anyone helping us," Sally shrieked.

"We have to keep moving, I can see the bridge," Karen said.

"What if there are more of them, then what?" Julie screamed hysterically.

"Come on, standing here screaming is getting us nowhere, let's get moving," Tom said, walking away towards the bridge. "You two coming?" Tom asked, looking over his shoulder at Jack.

"What's the point, this is it, this is how it ends," Jack said, coaxing Nancy to get moving.

"Staying in the city would have been certain death, at least out here we still have a chance," Karen said, walking towards the bridge.

"I'm sorry about Allen," Karen unemotionally said to Sally

Despite Karen's comment, Sally walked on silently and numbly. Her entire body shook with the devastating realization of her husband's brutal death, and she found herself unable to shake off the cold feeling that had taken hold of her. Automatically, she continued to put one foot in front of the other, staring blankly at the ground in front of her.

The maintenance trail seemed endlessly littered with everything from empty soda bottles to bodies of people, both laying where they fell. Reaching into a pocket, Tom pulled out a bandanna, soaking it with water. Covering his his mouth and nose with it, he hoped to escape the awful smell of decomposition. Looking at the gruesome forms on the ground as they walked, Tom wondered what brought on their demise, struck by the fact they were just left there to rot, like roadkill.

Finally on the bridge, Jack and Nancy were lagging well behind Karen, Sally, Tom and Julie, the group silently walking single file along the narrow, rickety walkway.

"At least there aren't any bodies laying out here, I can't take much more of that smell," Tom said, breaking the silence.

Around the halfway mark crossing the bridge Nancy screamed "JACK NO, JACK." Tom, Julie, Sally and even Karen turned at the outburst, seeing Jack pick up Nancy, throwing her over the short handrail. Jack jumped right behind her, both of them exploding as their bodies hit the hard water surface two hundred feet below them.

"OH MY GOD," Julie screamed.

"DON'T LOOK," Tom yelled after making the mistake of following the pairs decent, with Nancy's scream still echoing in his head.

Karen didn't stop walking, Sally right behind her, other than turning their heads to see Nancy and Jack fall to their deaths, they didn't acknowledge it. Julie on the other hand was clearly acknowledging what she just witnessed, as she seemingly couldn't stop screaming "OH MY GOD."

"Come on Julie, get moving," Tom said, the comment at least getting her to quit screaming. "Move," he added "there's nothing to be done about it now, Jack knew they were going to die, he just did it on his terms is all."

"That's cold," Julie said to Tom with a scowl.

"It is what it is, I'm sure there are plenty of bodies floating down that river," Tom said, gazing at the majestic landscape in front of him.

"We deserved this," Tom continued.

"What?" Julie asked.

"This. We deserved this, whatever it was that did all this," Tom answered.

"Why do you say that, I'm a good person, I don't deserve this," Julie said, disgusted with the idea.

"Not you or me, I meant the country. This is payback," Tom answered again.

"For what?" Julie asked.

"Decades of nation building, raping other cultures for natural resources, starting wars for no other reason than enriching the machine...." Tom replied.

"Oh, I have never been interested in politics, or what happens over there," Julie said.

"I used to be, but I guess it doesn't matter much now, does it," Tom said with a chuckle.

"How'd you end up here?" Julie asked, changing the topic from politics.

"I got divorced and moved into the complex six months ago. I only came along with this group because there is strength in numbers, at least I thought there would be but we went from fifty to four in three days, that's not very impressive. How about you, what's your story?" he asked Julie.

"Pretty much a mirror of yours, except I moved in a year ago. I didn't know any of these people before the lights went out and Karen made it sound like we were headed to paradise, so I went. Are you going where she's going?" Julie asked, pointing at Karen up ahead.

"Hell no. She's evil. She'll feed Sally to the wolves to save her own ass soon enough," Tom said, matter of factly.

"Do you really think she's like that, I mean she organized all of us to walk together, she tried to save us?" Julie said.

Laughing, Tom replied, "do you really think that whoever she knows in Somerset had any intention of feeding fifty people, we were pawns for her. As soon as we're off this bridge, wherever she goes, I'm going the opposite direction. And look behind you, there are at least a hundred people on the bridge behind us. Where are all those people going? I've been to Somerset, it's got one little grocery store, and for sure that's been cleaned out days ago. Those people who live there are not going to take everyone in, count on that," Tom went on.

Julie took in what Tom said, turning his words over in her mind as they stepped off the tracks in Wisconsin.

"Julie, have you drank any of your water yet?" Tom asked.

"No, but I'm getting ready to soon, I didn't want to have to pee on the bridge," Julie answered.

"Hold on before you do," Tom said, reaching in his bag, taking out a bottle of water purification tablets. "Break this in half, put half in each bottle and let it dissolve."

"What about them?" Julie said, pointing to Karen and Sally. "It's too late for them, they've already downed at least a bottle each," he said.

"Too late for what?" she questioned.

"Dysentery," he said flatly.

"Lemme see your map for a second please," Tom said walking to Karen.

"Somerset is just ahead, if we take that road there, 180th, it will bring us to town," Karen said, handing Tom the map. Tom looked at the map, but not towards Somerset, he was looking north, away from towns and people.

"This is where I get off," Tom said, handing the map back to Karen.

"Why, why not go to Somerset with us Tom?" Sally asked.

"I'm not really a people person, and my guess is the people there aren't people persons either," Tom replied.

"Have it your way," Karen said, indifferently. "What about you?" Karen said, looking at Julie.

Tom gave Julie a barely noticeable nod, and Julie replied "I'm gonna walk with Tom."

"Fine," Karen said, walking away with Sally.

"See, told ya," Tom told Julie, "she was just using whoever she could to get her to where she's going, hundred bucks says she'll trade Sally for a sandwich." Julie visibly shuddered at that thought.

"Where to then?" she said.

"Up this road, 37th, I'll bet another hundred bucks that within two miles we find an empty house," Tom answered.

Chapter Nineteen

"I like it," John said as he listened to the plan Luke and JT came up with. "In the corps we called this a decapitation strike, and Barry is certainly the head of this snake, especially now that the only other ones in his group that were capable of forming a thought are piled in front of the crackhouse. With Barry gone, the rest will disappear. What do have for a shooter?" John asked.

They told him they had a 6.5 Creedmore, a Browning A-Bolt in 7mm Magnum, and a Savage model 12 in .223 with Vortec glass.

"Got anything quieter than those, or any way to quiet them down?" John asked, getting up, assuming the answer would be no.

They told him no, they didn't have anything with a suppressor on it except for Luke's Glock.

John looked at Luke and said "I'm gonna go out on a limb and guess that the 6.5 is yours, what's the barrel threaded to?"

"Five eights by twenty four," Luke replied.

John stood up and left, saying "hold on" then returned with a Helix direct thread suppressor. He explained that it's cut for 7.62, but it works great on 6.5's too. He handed it to Luke, reminding him to check his zero.

"Thanks John, we appreciate that," Luke said.

"One more thing though, neither of us know what Barry looks like, you wouldn't have a picture or anything of him would you?" JT asked.

"John pointed over his shoulder to the useless laptop that sat behind him. "Maybe, if that worked. But I'll tell you what, I'll do you one better,"he said with a mischievous grin. Luke and JT turned to face him, their interest piqued. "I'll spot for you," John continued, turning his attention to Luke.

Then he leaned in and whispered, pointing again over his shoulder. "She's already driving me fucking crazy with questions about when we're going home and why we didn't go to her sisters instead," talking about his wife. "Plus, I got skin in the game too, when do you want to do it?" He asked, looking at the sun not far from the western horizon.

"Tomorrow, first thing," JT said.

The morning had passed quickly in a whirlwind of activity before the meeting with John. Pete and Brian cleared out the camper and shed and transported their belongings up to the Teds. They had also worked tirelessly to make the ranch habitable for Tyler and Sarah, who were in desperate need of their own space. After some discussion between Pete, Brian, and JT, it was agreed that D should take up a room at Ted's as well, given their increasingly crowded living situation. Even though JT was exhausted and had not slept in a real bed in five days, they now had three couples, including one with a child, and JT's mother and Joni, all vying for use of the only two bedrooms that were available. The situation had become untenable, and D's move to Ted's at least would help alleviate some of the pressure.

There is a third bedroom upstairs that used to be Sarah's but since she moved out long ago and married Tyler, it's now packed with bins full of clothing, shoes and other random crap. The clothes and shoes would stay, but the random crap, all of it would have to go, today.

Everything they were doing around the ranch today had an ulterior motive: winter survival. Everything they did was geared towards making sure that they could make it through the brutal winters that northwest Wisconsin was known for. If the power had went out in the summer, it would be inconvenient, but manageable. However, since it had gone out in early October, they all knew the stakes were much higher, winter always came early and brutally. It could kill a person without thinking twice. They had considered all the options, including cramming everyone under one roof, but the prospect of that was unbearable. It would be cramped and uncomfortable for everyone.

Ted's house was the most logical option, with its ample size easily accommodating two families. JT even thought about moving Kate, his mother, and himself into Ted's house with Sarah, Tyler, and little Jake. But he quickly dismissed the thought. The ranch was his home, and he wasn't going to leave it. It was where he belonged, with all of his memories and his dreams wrapped up in the land around him. Ultimately, he knew that he would stay there, whatever the cost. For him, it was the only choice.

D'Vante was eager to help in any way he could. Before midday, he had all the junk in the upstairs bedroom gone, stacked in a neat a pile by the fire pit ready for JT or Kate to go through. He even cleaned all the crap out of the day room upstairs making room for one more person if need be. How he carried the treadmill down those stairs alone JT did not know and did not ask.

It was still early in the day when all the "work" they had planned was done. D didn't have anything of his own to move, but he did go up to Ted's with Brian and pick out a spot to sleep. Ted and Myrna had an ample amount of blankets and pillows in all three of their bedrooms, and for now anyway, they'd each take a room to themselves.

Tyler had defied expectations early today by beginning to walk, much to the dismay of Sarah and Joni. Although Sarah was a sharp nurse with two years of experience working in the post-operation suite of an orthopedic clinic, Joni had a wealth of experience that overshadowed her. Joni suggested that Tyler's body had shut down due to dehydration, blood loss, and overexertion when he collapsed on the road yesterday. It was D who had saved Tyler's brain function by giving him immediate mouth-to-mouth resuscitation. Though Tyler had later stopped breathing when D left to get the old man, it wasn't long enough to cause brain damage.

Sarah asked Joni how much longer Tyler would have made it before she got to him. Joni thought about it for a few seconds and replied "a minute, maybe a minute and a half." Sarah broke into tears and wrapped Joni in a huge, heartfelt hug.

"I don't know if I'd have known what to do," Sarah said, after releasing Joni.

"Yes, you would have, your training would have taken over. You just haven't been tested yet sister, but if what the old man says happened, happened, you are going to be tested beyond your abilities. Just remember this one thing, always trust your initial gut feeling and never hesitate. Ever," Joni told her.

Sarah, changing the subject asked Joni "you had a boyfriend, Dave, right. And he's dead?" Sarah has always been blunt. Not rude at all, but she's just never understood how people would beat around the bush.

"I did, and he is, yes," Joni replied.

"I'm sorry for your loss," Sarah said, now feeling awkward asking.

"Thank you, but I'm fine, really," Joni said.

Sarah was both shocked and curious by Joni's comment. "Joni please don't take this wrong, but how can you possibly be fine, I mean I'm pretty stoic and I was an emotional wreck just not knowing where Tyler was for five days," she said.

Joni shifted in her seat, saying "that's because you two love each other. See, I didn't love Dave, Dave didn't love me. Sure, we got along just fine, but we both knew we were only together for convenience sake. We were committed in a way, like neither of us fucked around, but we only didn't because the sex was already good and we didn't want to worry about STD's," Joni said.

Sarah's mouth was agape, and she quickly closed it, thinking about what Joni had told her.

Before Sarah could speak Joni went on. "He was a nice guy, a very nice guy, but I'd have never married him. My birthday is coming up, and I knew he was going to ask me. His best friend told me so, the stupid fuck. So I decided a few days before we went up north to celebrate our one year dating anniversary that as soon as we got back I would break up with him. Shit, I already had a lease signed on a new apartment. I know this sounds incredibly cruel, but when he got shot it felt no different to me than when a total stranger codes and dies in the ER," Joni explained.

Sarah was speechless, not because of being shocked by what Joni had just told her, but by her honesty as she did. Sarah took Joni's hand.

"Joni, I have a couple of close friends who are in almost exact same position you were. One of them actually said yes. I'm straight forward,

I think you know that, so I asked them both why? Why are you playing charades, wanna know what they said?"

Joni shook her head yes.

"It was because they wanted a great big beautiful wedding before they ended up with a kid and couldn't fit into their dream dress. That was it. They never talked about love. Not once. It was all about fitting into a ten thousand dollar dress and being queen for a day," Sarah said sadly.

"Yep, and that's exactly why I was going to pull the pin. I felt the same allure, but I also knew I'd be divorced in a year paying alimony to a grounds keeper with a huge pecker," Joni said.

Sarah erupted in laughter. She laughed so hard she was crying, holding her stomach and almost positive she had wet herself. Sarah's laugh was contagious and now the both of them were in tears. "Jeepers, I needed that," Sarah said.

"So did I sister, so did I," Joni replied.

After they calmed down Sarah asked "so what now, what's your plan?"

Joni thought for a minute, formulating her response.

"For the first time in a very long time, I feel like I am exactly where I belong. I'm needed here, and not as a number filling a time slot. The old man and Kate welcomed me here with open arms, Amy saved my life after I was molested, well, so did Luke and Pete, but she pulled my spirit out of the abyss before it was too late. I love her like a sister," Joni said.

"You were what?" Sarah interrupted.

"Molested, sexually. I'll tell you about it someday, maybe. But to be honest, I'd rather not exhume those memories, if you know what I mean.," Joni said.

"I do but I don't, I'll just take your word on that," Sarah said.

"Thank you for listening, Sarah. That's a rare quality to have. I need to go check on momma now though, I don't think she's got much time left with us," Joni said.

"I'll come with you, and you're welcome," Sarah quickly replied.

Looking at the calendar, JT crossed off Friday and was close to crossing off Saturday. Why was he doing this, keeping a calendar was kind of a mystery. It just felt important, and he supposed it is in a way. He'd calculated the number of days it should take for those who successfully escaped the cities to make it out far enough to be a threat to the ranch, and sadly, when he expected many of the people local to him, his neighbors, to run out of food and water. Any day now, he thought.

Leaving the calendar, his next stop was the bathroom and he sincerely hoped it wasn't occupied at the moment. As he gave a quick knock on the bathroom door he noticed a growing pile of dirty clothes in the laundry area, thinking this is going to get out of hand fast. JT had been wearing the same clothes all week and they were filthy, except for socks, he'd changed them once he thought. Then, as he was sitting on the throne an image shot though his mind, almost like a picture flashing before his eyes. The picture he saw was of an old wringer washing machine, like the one his mom had when he was very young, and he suddenly realized he had seen one of those, well, the legs of one anyway that were exposed under a cover of sorts. It is in Diane's basement, not far from where Kelvin was zip tied to the water pipe.

That excited him, which didn't take much these days and he quickly finished up his nature call. Going to the bathtub for flushing water, he realized the shower hasn't been used in almost a week either. He wondered if Pete had gotten around to finishing the hot box, he really wanted to try it out for himself, a shower would feel so good he thought.

The tub still had plenty of flushing water in it so he filled the two gallon pail, dumping half of it in the toilet bowl. It's weird how watching a toilet drain itself is somehow satisfying, but it was, then he slowly added water to the bowl, just enough so it wouldn't flush. They didn't flush pee, it sat there until it got smelly. The water he added would dilute the next few liquid deposits.

With still plenty of daylight left, JT after sliding into his quilted red plaid shirt began heading to the door, back outside. Peeking in his moms room as he did, he heard the unmistakable sound of the oxygen concentrator running. Sarah and Joni were with his mom, an oximeter clamped to her finger and an O2 mask on instead of the nasal cannulae's.

"How is she?" he asked, concern in his voice.

Sarah explained that momma's oxygen level had dropped below 90 again, and she is having more trouble breathing.

"Has she been awake much today?" he asked.

"On and off," Joni replied.

Sarah was in full nurse mode, which made him happy, she was listening to his moms heart beating and her lungs with a stethoscope. "Where'd you find that thing?" he asked Sarah, pointing to the instrument.

"It was in your med box," she replied.

"Huh, well, ok. Thanks for keeping an eye on mom, let me know when her levels come up," JT said, leaving the room.

"Will do," they said in unison.

Leaving them to it, he grabbed his rifle from the coat hook before heading out the door. He didn't "need" the rifle, but he did want to get in the habit of keeping it with him, especially where they are now at in the timeline. The gang was sitting around the smoker as Luke was threading the suppressor on his 6.5 as JT walked out, joining them.

"You gonna take a shot?" JT asked.

"For sure, you know how I am about this crap," Luke answered.

The "this crap" Luke was talking about was accuracy. He'd boughten and quickly sold many a rifle that did not shoot up to his standards, which are high. His 6.5 was not one of those he ever planned on selling as it came out of the box shooting a one half minute of angle, only getting better with trigger work and hand loads.

"Does your range finder work?" JT asked Luke.

"Fuck no, it's deader'n a door nail," he answered.

"Well shit, that sucks, you paid a pretty penny for those Vortex ranging bino's," he said.

"At least I can still see through them, they have excellent glass," Luke said, lamenting.

"Good deal," JT said.

Not wanting to go into details about what was happening because Amy was there, he diverted, asking if anyone wanted to take a quick walk up to Diane's place with him. JT went on to tell them he wanted to find out if that really was a washing machine he'd seen. Brian was on his feet immediately.

"I'll go with ya pops, I need to keep this leg moving," Brian said, enthusiasm in his voice.

Brian, grabbing the shotgun the old man got off the gang at the intersection checked its chamber for a round while making sure the tube is full before heading out for the short walk through the woods to Diane's. As they walked along they talked, JT saying they need to bring the tractor up and finish a trail from the fence line over there, pointing east to an invisible spot in the woods. Teds house is just beyond the invisible point and they need to cut that fence too to continue the trail.

"You gonna brush hog it with the big tractor?" Brian asked.

"Na, that will just leave a bunch of punji sticks to step on or blow out a tire on the quads," JT said.

"What the hell is a punji stick?" Brian asked, curious.

JT explained how the North Vietnamese soldiers would dig a pit a foot deep or so and sharpen the ends of bamboo and push them in the ground with the point up, then cover the pit with other crap like twig's and grass to conceal it. Then, when US patrols would take that trail or path, inevitably someone would step in the pit, impaling their foot.

"Holy shit, that's cruel," Brian said.

"No, well yeah it's cruel, but what's even more cruel is they'd coat the pointed end with bat shit before they covered the pit. Lots of guys lost a foot, a leg and even their lives from the infection that caused." Brian visibly shuddered at the comment.

"Damn." was all he could muster in reply.

Just as they were about to go into Diane's basement they both heard the supersonic crack of a bullet. Brian instinctively ducking at the sound, looked around for the source and asked "was that a gunshot, where in the hell did that come from, I can't tell where it came from?"

"That was Luke, pretty neat eh? The glory of a suppressor. It can't silence a supersonic round, but it masks the location of where it came from," JT said.

"That was just the sound of the bullet?" Brian asked.

"Yep," JT replied.

Much to JT's delight, underneath a moldy old bedspread was an antique Maytag washing machine with the wringer and electric motor still on it. The drive belt for the motor was gone, but he had a bunch of V belts at the ranch so finding a replacement shouldn't be a problem and the discharge hose was missing. No big deal with that either as it would be used outside.

"We'll bring the little trailer up here tomorrow and grab this thing. I've got gallons and gallons of that buck a bottle laundry soap that I bought at the dollar store. If the big inverter will start that motor, we just might be in business," JT said excitedly.

"Yikes, you mean we can wash clothes in there?" Brian asked.

"Hell yeah we can, just don't get your tit in the wringer.," JT said with a laugh.

"Huh?" Brian asked.

"Nothing," JT replied.

Another "crack" rang out. "Luke must not have been happy with the first one," Brian said.

"I hope this one did the trick, we've got some people just to the east who I'm not so certain are going to remain civil, hell, we haven't even seen anyone come up from the flats yet either, there's a bunch of folks that live down there along the river, They probably think that someone just shot a deer," JT said looking around.

"You've got a point, we have been eating pretty well, but we all brought a bunch with us too," Brian said.

"We have, but trust me on this, it's not going to last, and eventually the folks around here that are hungry now are gonna notice we aren't," JT said with a raised eyebrow.

"Let's get back, it's gonna be dark soon," JT said, stealing another look at the old Maytag.

As they walked, JT asked Brian if Pete had gotten the hot box buttoned up. Brian said he did, and the water was plenty warm for a shower too.

"Good deal, has anyone tested it out yet?" JT asked.

"Yep, Amy and Kate both used it, but we gotta make the tarp more user friendly, you know Pete," Brian said with a laugh.

They were brought out of their conversation when the unmistakable sound of a four wheeler coming down the road to from the east filtered through the trees. The ATV slowed and obviously turned down the driveway to the ranch. Brian and JT were still in the woods, not having a view of the driveway or the ranch.

The machine wasn't moving fast, and when they finally got out of the trees the ATV was pulling up to the shop. "Well, there wasn't any shooting, it must be someone we know" Brian said.

"Let's go find out," JT replied.

Luke was talking with a man and everything seemed calm, then, getting closer, JT recognized him, it was Mike Davidson, the guy the end of the road to the east of them, the family JT had warned Luke about.

"What's up Mike?" JT said as a greeting.

"I was just talking with Luke here, my daughter Jill is sick and I'm worried about her. I knew you are one of those survivalist guys, and thought maybe you could have a look at her," Mike said.

"Jill, your teenager," JT asked.

"Twenty one now," mike replied.

"Damn, time flies what's she like, I mean what makes you think she's sick?" JT asked sincerely.

"She's got terrible diarrhea, a fever, but I don't know how high it is and she's puking up everything I give her, even water," he answered, his voice shaking at the words.

"Hang on a sec Mike, we have someone much smarter than me for that," JT said.

Joni was inside with Kate and Amy getting some potatoes ready to go on the stove when JT went in.

"Who's that outside?" Kate asked.

"It's Mike, the guy that lives down the road a bit," JT answered.

"What's he want?" she asked nervously, knowing the family.

"His daughter is not doing well. Joni, can you come talk to him with me?" JT asked.

"Sure," she said and headed out the door before he could catch her.

When he was within earshot of Joni and Luke, JT listened to Mike explain himself to Joni, hearing her ask Mike if they have well water. Mike said no, he didn't have a way to run his well pump so he's been going down to the river and filling a clean plastic drum that he's got strapped in his yard trailer.

"She's probably got dysentery, have you been boiling the water or adding bleach to it?" she asked.

"No, neither, it's crystal clear water," Mike said adamantly.

"Ok, no problem," she said then turned to JT asking if by chance he had any ringers lactate.

"No, I don't," JT answered.

"I do" Luke piped up, kinda surprising JT that he had it. "Amy, do you remember where we put that stuff, I know we brought it with?" Luke asked.

"Yeah, I think I do. I brought it into Kate's bedroom, hang on, how many do you need, we have six bags I think and two IV drops," Amy replied.

"How much does Jill weigh?" Joni asked Mike.

"Donno, she's small. About your size I'd guess," he said.

"One bag will do Amy," Joni called out.

"D, you how to run one of these four wheelers?" JT asked.

"I will in a minute sir, want me to go along?" he asked.

"Yeah, and Pete you go too," JT said.

Taking the two men aside while Joni talked to Mike, JT said, "take two machines, and both of you brings guns, I know this guy, but I don't trust him as far as I can throw him, do not leave her side. D, hang on a sec, you don't have a gun do you?" JT asked.

"Nope, but I can shoot," D said.

"K, hang on," JT said.

Hanging on its hook inside the door was JT's Colt 1911 in a Vietnam era holster clipped to a web belt. He handed the firearm to D and D expertly slung the belt around his waist, making the hook connection.

"This guys worn these before," JT thought to himself . "Ever shoot one of these?" he asked.

"Yeah, on weekends in OTS we'd go shooting, I wanted to buy one, but dayam these things are expensive," D replied.

Removing the pistol from its holster, D slid the safety down then pulled the action back enough to reveal the chambered round, put it back on safe and re-holstered the weapon.

"One in the tube, I like it," D said. Handing D two spare magazines, JT telling him he didn't have a magazine pouch, so he'll just have to put them in his pocket.

Arriving at Mike's house, Jill was indeed sick. She appeared severely dehydrated, so much so that Joni had a tough time getting a vein to pop for the catheter, having to wrap Jill's arm at the elbow with a belt. Mike's wife Maryann watched quietly as Joni started the IV, finally breaking her silence asking Joni if she was a doctor. Joni chuckled a little and explained she is a PA and used to be an ER nurse for a while in Madison.

Maryann asked what brought her here from Madison and Joni just said "everyone's gotta be somewhere." She then went on and explained that even though the water may look crystal clear, it's not, and how to sterilize it by boiling it for ten minutes or adding eight drops of bleach, not the scented stuff either, per gallon of water. Maryann said she had bleach and would make sure they did.

While Joni started packing up, Mike asked timidly what else they had down there in the way of food, medical supplies and the like. D spoke up and looking at the precious bag of ringers said "less than we had a half hour ago and we're sucking the meat off deer bones for supper tonight."

"Sorry I asked" Mike said snidely. "I heard that other lady say you had six of those bags, I just though maybe you'd share more."

"We did share," Pete said, "and what we shared is going to save your daughter's life, be happy we did that much, we could have just as well turned you away."

"Then I'd have taken it," Mike said with a raised voice. He was getting incredulous and very animated.

"Mike stop it, they helped our Jill, let it go," Maryann pleaded.

"Look mister, don't go down that road, cause it won't end well, trust me," D said.

Joni was standing behind Pete, she wasn't afraid, but she'd seen this kind of crap before and D was right, it doesn't end well.

Mike shouted at D, yelling, "no negro is ever gonna tell me what to do," as he lunged for D. Swinging wildly at D's face with his right hand, Mike's blow was intercepted by D catching the clenched fist in front of his face with his own right hand, startling Mike. Then, D squeezed Mike's fingers into his palm as he twisted his arm clockwise, locking his elbow. Putting his left hand against Mike's elbow, D guided him to a chair, telling Mike to sit down before his arm gets broken.

Maryann was screaming, "don't hurt him, don't hurt him."

Mike sat as instructed and Pete caught him glancing at the 1911 strapped to D's hip, saying, "don't even think about it friend."

D, very calm through all of this asked Mike if he was going to behave if he released his arm, Mike nodded yes, and began to weep as D slowly released the painful elbow lock.

Maryann walked up to her husband and started to apologize for him, saying that he's just stressed out about Jill and because they are running out of food, all their candles are gone and they didn't know how they were going to survive, then she began to cry with her husband. Pete told them they should pack up a few things and go to the church in town, lying when he said they had food and shelter.

"What, and carry her, she can't walk," he said looking a Jill.

"Then find a way, ride a bike, I really don't care what you do, but consider this one as a warning. Don't try to take from people, especially us," Pete said ending the conversation.

Joni told Pete and D she wasn't coming back here to pull the catheter out tomorrow, no way in hell. So her and D explained to Maryann how to remove it and to just have a bandaid ready to put over it.

The three, Joni, Pete and D left them where they were, Maryann and Mike still crying and Jill, fortunately, still catatonic. No goodbyes, no thanks you's, nothing.

"Well isn't that the shit, they could have at least said thanks," Pete said, getting on his Honda.

"Yeah, I wasn't really expecting that," D added.

"It's exactly what I expected," Joni said, "you would not believe the sense of entitlement some people have, especially in the inner city, it was ridiculous," she said shaking her head. "They'd come into the ER demanding to be seen by a doctor to have a sliver pulled from a finger, and when I'd tell them to take a number, they'd throw a shit fit, breaking stuff, it was pathetic," she went on.

The three rode slowly the short distance to the ranch side by side. They talked between themselves along the way, Pete wondered what the big cities looked like now.

"Hey, what day is it?" D questioned.

"Donno," Pete said.

"It's Saturday, pops has a calendar with the days crossed off on it," Joni said.

"So six days then since this popped off," D said.

"Why do you ask?" Joni questioned.

"Big game tonight against Wisconsin," D said.

"You'd have lost D, the Badgers are hot this year," Pete said.

"Were hot boys, let's get back, I gotta pee," Joni said.

"Here they come," Luke said, seeing the dogs demeanors change at the faint sound of ATV's.

The two machines pulled up and Joni immediately began running to the house, then changed course heading behind the garage.

"The fuck is wrong with her?" JT asked.

"Gotta pee," they both said.

"It must have been bad for her to pee outside, but the odds are high someone else is in the can," JT said.

As Joni came out from around the corner she flipped her hair back and said with relief "whew, that was close."

"How'd it go?" JT asked, and they all filled him in. "Shit. Well, you helped the girl, that's all that matters. They were just the first to lose their shit, but they aren't going to be the last. We just have to make sure we don't end up in the same boat," JT said.

"They are the first we know about," Luke added.

"For sure. There are three, wait, four housing developments within two miles of here, plus the folks that live down on the flats. I have no idea how many houses there are combined, but there is no way that all of them are sitting on even a molehill of food," JT mentioned solemnly.

"What are we going to do when those people start going door to door?" Brian asked.

"We gotta change our ways," Luke said.

"Huh, how so?" Brian asked.

Luke went on and explained how at night we need to use light discipline outside, no flashlight beams bouncing off the trees, no burning the trash in the daytime where the smoke can be seen and they needed to move the burn barrel so the house blocks it view from the road.

JT added "We'll stop using the driveway except for the truck, and there is no reason for that to go out anyway. We can extend the trail going to Teds, run it south a bit, and then come out across from Fred's place." JT also saying that most of their travels are going to be between the ranch and Teds anyway.

"Trails already in, Teds had them there for years. There might be some light brushing to do, but I doubt it," Luke said.

"No shit, I didn't know that," JT said.

"You should get out more old man," he replied.

"Haha, yeah, I'd prefer not to. Anyway that's good, less fucking around for us. I'd like to string a couple of tripwires across the driveway too, just to let people know that we know," JT said seriously.

"How do you do that, set tripwires," Brian asked. Before JT could answer D spoke up.

"I got this one Major, just point me to the stuff," D said.

"How does a tight end know about trip wires?" Brian asked.

D explained to them all about the Air Force survival school he had to go to.

"Your a pilot?" Brian asked, quite surprised.

"Yep, First Lieutenant in the reserves out of Duluth. F-16's," D replied.

Brian practically shit himself with that news.

"Yep, I went to OCS right out of college and applied for flight training and was accepted. They like physics majors," he said with a laugh.

"I thought you were still in school, I mean you had to be, right?" Pete asked.

"Yes again. I loved football, I was hoping to get into the NFL so I got the mathematics scholarship at the U to play ball. That was going to be my second degree and my ticket to the big time," D said.

"How in the hell do you juggle all that, I mean I could barely handle managing a handful of restaurants?" Pete asked, slapping his knee.

"Physics, calculus, all that stuff came easy for me, and the reserves, shit they were happy to bend my schedules around football, they can't retain pilots," D said.

"The money is too good in the left seat of a 767 for a lot of guys to turn down, that and how the services are getting too woke. I just ignore all that bullshit though," D continued.

"What's it like flying a Falcon?" JT asked, joining the conversation.

"Bout the same as that ultralight out by the barn, only faster and louder," D answered.That got a laugh out of JT. "That thing fly? " D questioned.

"It does, the wings for it are in the barn, takes about an hour to get it ready," JT replied.

"Do you trailer it to a runway or what?" D asked.

"Nope, that's the runway," JT said, pointing to the east pasture.

"You gotta be shitting me, you take off and land out there?" he questioned.

"Yep, just gotta come in slow and short for landing, taking off is a breeze, it's up in less than two hundred feet," JT answered.

Luke broke in, saying he was going to turn in so he could head up to get John in the morning. D asked what was going on, so Luke and JT filled everyone in on what the plan was. Pete and Brian knew a little, but this was the first Amy and Joni had heard about it.

"Your going to do what?" Amy asked, almost agitated.

"It's gotta be done Amy. Those people aren't going to forget what happened at the crackhouse," JT reasoned.

"They ambushed us!" she shot back.

"Yes, they did, but those technicalities don't matter to people like Barry King. He WILL find out exactly where we are and he WILL get even," JT said as calmly as possible.

"Who's all going?" she asked, clearly irritated. JT told her just Luke and John, Fred's son.

"No," she said, slamming her balled fist on the table. "What is wrong with men, do you always take shit at face value? How do you know that John isn't using you, maybe Barry King doesn't even exist, and it's his old boss Luke's supposed to shoot, hell, maybe he's working with Barry King, and is going to deliver Luke to him as payback or retribution, you ever think about that," she yelled, this time clearly agitated.

"Damn, she should be a mystery writer," JT thought to himself at her outburst.

She was right though, and JT told her so. They hadn't considered any of what she said. They didn't know John, other than when they were together with Kelvin and the little time they spent down here and at Fred's. Now JT was second guessing himself and that's not exactly a thing that makes him feel good. There are a lot of "what if's" in this equation and John was a little too eager to spot for Luke. His head was spinning with different scenarios playing out, was John crooked, on the take maybe? Was he actually telling the truth when he told Kelvin he wanted to join up?

"Let's shift gears here, let's say that John isn't as squeaky clean as I thought," JT said, as he heard Amy let out a sigh of relief. "Not so fast with that Amy, if he's part of a retribution plan, then us backing out of this operation will only delay the inevitable, they may not get Luke this time, but they will get one or more of us sometime if that's his plan," JT said.

"What do you wanna do then?" Luke asked.

Thinking about that for a second or two JT said "I'll go up there in the morning and tell him we gotta to make new loads for your rifle, or some bullshit story like that, then I'll tell him that we can go the next day, or the day after. I'll gauge his reaction and see if his body language or mood changes. He seemed pretty excited about going tomorrow, and if this is a setup of some kind, when John doesn't deliver as promised, I'm guessing that ole Barry King will pay John a visit,"

"Damn dad, that's getting a little out there, don't ya think?" Luke asked.

"Makes sense to me," Amy said.

"I'm out of tinfoil, but yeah, it probably does sound out there, but think about all this. He knew all those guys, and had no problem with us killing three of them and him one. Why? What's his end game. On the surface he sure doesn't appear to be a guy that would be afraid of a few thugs, but something is pressuring him I think," JT reasoned.

"Pete," JT called.

"Right here pops, what you need?" Pete quickly answered.

"You were up at the house quite a bit today right, did you hear Freddy's four wheeler or that pickup take off today?" he asked.

"Actually, I did, the four wheeler. It was early afternoon I'd guess, it went east and came back maybe an hour later," Pete said.

"Ok, thanks Pete, so what if that was John meeting up with Barry, setting up a place to make the deal?" JT queried.

Now they were all scratching their heads in thought. JT hates "what if's". They can severely cloud a person's judgment, but not addressing them can be fatal, especially in this case, at least that's what he thought.

"Luke, I get that you're not sold on this…" JT started saying.

Amy interrupted JT saying, "I am, this sneaky shit makes sense to me," and she smiled at Luke. They gave her the time to make her point, she wasn't wrong anyway. This was some seriously sneaky shit.

"Anyway, here's what I'm thinking. Luke, you need to get up on the roof of Teds house with the 6.5. From Fred's driveway there is a spot through the trees where the chimney is visible, I noticed it this morning, don't ask me why. Pete, I want you on the ground near the end of Teds driveway, find good cover so you can wiggle around if you need to, and you'll need to be able to see the county road. Bring a rifle though instead of the 870, it'll be a hundred yard shot if it comes to it," JT said.

"On it," Pete said.

"I'll be east of Pete back in the woods directly across the road from Fred's driveway, I'm hoping I can hear the conversation if they show up," JT said.

"Better bring hearing aids old man'" Luke said. JT gave him the finger in reply

"What about us?" Brian asked, about him and D.

"You two are the quick reaction force, park those four wheelers at the end of the driveway with a radio," JT said, making this all up on the fly.

"Will do," they said. Luke still hadn't said much.

"What's on your mind?" JT asked Luke

"Who in the fuck am I supposed to shoot exactly," he bluntly said as a statement, not a question.

"I think that target will reveal itself," JT replied.

"What's your timeline?" Brian asked.

JT had to think about that for a while.

"As far as John knew this afternoon, they would be headed out at daylight. I'd imagine that Barry would give them an hour or two max before he came to see what the fuck is wrong. I wouldn't be surprised if they planned a meet up right in the road somewhere between here and Barry's place that's down by the river off of 200th. Luke you should be up on the roof before I go to to Fred's to cancel. Pete, you and I will get into position after I get back here. Make sense?" JT asked.

"We got enough radios?" Luke asked.

"Yeah, plenty. Make sure not to hit that call button though, and keep the volume way low," JT said.

"Ok, let's get some sleep, tomorrow could be a long day," Luke said, getting up and stretching.

Brian and D volunteered for watch, which was fine by JT, maybe he'd be able to get more that three hours of sleep tonight.

"You're in full bore Major mode sir, you having some flashbacks?" D asked, walking to JT.

Chuckling, JT replied, "Hell if I know. I do know John is highly skilled at manipulation. What I am unsure about is why he'd set us up," JT said, rubbing his grey beard.

"For what it's worth, I agree with your plan. You covered the bases, minimizing risk to everyone involved. I concur with your decision," D said assuringly.

"Thanks, I needed the boost. I'll leave my rifle hanging on the cedar tree for ya tonight, " JT said, heading inside.

"G'night sir," D replied, heading to the picnic table. D couldn't help himself and looked over his shoulder, seeing the old Major shaking his head as he went inside. "You've earned the respect," D silently said to himself, settling in for his watch.

Chapter Twenty

"Oh my God Karen, what's wrong?" Sally screamed, watching the watery brown excrement flowing out from under Karen's jeans, covering her shoes.

Karen, doubling over in pain, moaned as another burst erupted from her intestines, completely saturating her jeans.

"I, I, I don't know," Karen said weakly, still doubled over.

Stepping away from the awful smell in front of her, Sally, almost screaming exclaimed "you're bleeding now."

Karen, shaking, the sweat visible on her forehead as another round let loose said almost in a whisper "someone must have poisoned me," as she fell to her knees, her hands to her her belly.

"I'll go find help. Do you have clothes in your bag?" Sally asked.

Shaking her head no, Karen said "I'm so thirsty, can I have some of your water?"

"Sure," Sally said, watching her step as she handed Karen a bottle, Karen taking long drink from it.

"Thanks," Karen said, her response barely audible, laying on the blacktop township road in a puddle of her own crap.

"We just walked by a road, it looked like a development, I'll walk back there and find some help, ok?" Sally said.

Laying on the ground, Karen didn't respond. Picking up her own bag, Sally turned walking away, back they way they'd came. Remembering the road, 58th street and the "no exit" sign, Sally tried to pick up her own pace to get help as a bolt of pain coursed through her own abdomen, nearly paralyzing her. She stopped, shaking, only a few hundred yards from where she left Karen. Feeling it coming on, Sally dropped her pants as the diarrhea flew out of her, spraying the blacktop. Consumed with fear, Sally began to shake uncontrollably as wave after wave rocked her. Now becoming light headed, Sally willed herself to stand up, to get her filthy pants pulled back up.

Suddenly, Sally was very confused, not knowing where she was or why she was there, as she looked around her, trying to get her bearings through the fog in her head.

"What was that?" Sally said, hearing a sound she'd never heard before, a high pitched "yip" that shook her from her stupor.

Karen, still laying in her own shit, nearly unconscious, screamed at the first bite as the pack of coyotes descended on her. Too weak to scream again, Karen was consumed in abject terror as the carnivores attacked, their long canine teeth tearing her flesh with every bite. Trying feebly to cover her face, she stared in horror as one animal grabbed her wrist in its jaws, shaking its head violently, tearing the artery. Seeing her blood pulsing from her arm, Karen faded away as the pack relentlessly attacked, bite after bite until she was scattered in pieces.

Frozen in fear at the ungodly cacophony of sound she was hearing, Sally, again willing herself, began to move away, leaving her bag in the roadway along with the contents of her intestines. Trotting up 58th street, she ran into the first driveway she saw, hearing a "yip" and howling coming from behind her.

Nearly dark now, Sally saw the dim light of a candle in a window up ahead. Running towards the light, three huge Great Pyrenees ran past her, attacking the first two coyotes of the pack that had picked up Sally's scent. Screeching, Sally was met at the door by a scruffy old man, a shotgun in his hands. Pushing Sally inside, without speaking the man closed the door, firing his shotgun in succession at the retreating coyotes. The howls of pain emitting from the wounded coyotes will be forever etched in Sally's mind as she listened through the door.

Whistling loudly, the man stopped the pursuit of his dogs and they quickly returned at the command, their white muzzles now blood soaked.

"Hello dear," a soft voice said, startling Sally.

Sally froze at the words, afraid to turn around from the door window she was looking out of at the words.

"No need to be afraid, this old woman couldn't hurt you if she tried," the old voice said softly.

Slowly, Sally turned around, seeing an equally elderly woman wearing an apron. Wrinkling her nose slightly the old woman said "my name is Margie, let's get you cleaned up some, c"mon."

Sally, now beginning to comprehend the situation slightly, caught a whiff of her stench, nearly gagging her, said "I'm Sally, I, …"

"No need to explain dear, now let's get you in the shower. The waters cold, I hope you don't mind," the gentle old woman said softly.

Speechless, Sally followed Margie down a very dark hallway into an equally dark bathroom.

Lighting an oil lamp, Margie said "everything you need is right there," pointing to a rack of neatly folded rags and towels. "Now you get yourself in there while I have Ray start the generator, and toss your clothes in that bucket."

Anticipating Margie, Ray went to the garage, starting the Honda generator, meeting Margie at the door. "You old coot, you know me like the back of your hand," Margie said.

Gently slapping Margie's behind, Ray replied "just like I know this," smiling sweetly.

"She's got dysentery, I saw it in Saigon so many times," Margie said.

"I guessed that by the looks of her clothes, she probably drank shit water," Ray replied.

Shooting him a disgusting look, Margie said "that's gross Raymond," using his given name for effect.

"Well, it's true, ain't it, you get it by drinking water with shit in it," he replied with a laugh.

"Yes, it is. Let's make sure she has plenty of water, there's not much else we can do for that," Margie said.

"That pack of yote's had something down, if she was with someone, they are probably coyote shit by now," Ray said in a serious tone.

"Dammit Ray, don't you dare talk like that around her, she's scared shitless," Margie said.

"To that, I can agree," Ray replied with a wink.

"You're evil old man," Margie said, getting back to her beef stew on the stove.

Getting out of the shower, Sally saw the clean change of clothes and the tall glass of water laid out for her. She hadn't even heard Margie come in. Taking a drink of the cool water, she was instantly invigorated, wanting more. The clothes were a good fit, maybe a size bigger than what she wore, but they were clean and smelled good, like they were hung on a line to dry. Hanging her towel on the door hook, Sally stepped out of the bathroom, walking back the way she was led earlier by Margie.

"How was the shower, hot enough?" Ray said with a chuckle, seeing Sally walking to the living room.

"Dear, this is my husband Ray, Ray, this is Sally," Margie said, making the formal introductions.

"Where you headed?" Ray asked bluntly.

"I don't know really, I was following my friend Karen, she has family in Somerset," Sally replied.

"Where you coming from?" Ray asked, again bluntly.

"Saint Paul" Sally replied simply.

"I couldn't image what the cities are like now," Ray said, shaking his head.

"You don't want to know," Sally replied.

"I suppose not. You hungry, Mom has something on the stove in there, don't know what it is," he said.

"It's supper," Margie said, wiping her hands on her apron. "Now let's have a bite, these old bones are getting tired," she said, ushering them to the kitchen table.

"Never mind him, he's nosy," Margie said to Sally as they sat down.

"The family your friend is going to, did your friend Karen ever mention a name?" Ray asked.

"Let her eat Ray, she's had a rough time, just look at her," Margie said.

"It's ok, there are others that had it way worse than me. King is his last name, Bob, Billy, Barry, something like that is his first name," Sally replied, taking a bite of the beef stew Margie had made.

Ray and Margie, sharing a glance at the name, saying nothing as their mood instantly changed.

"Did I say something to offend you?" Sally said, troubled with the sudden silence as they ate.

"Oh no dear, you didn't hurt our feelings, the name just opened up a wound is all," Margie said.

"Oh, I'm sorry," Sally said.

"Don't be. That son of a bitch will get what's coming to him soon enough," Ray said.

Looking for more, Sally asked "who is he?".

"Barry King is the bastard who killed our little girl twenty years ago," Margie said.

Sally's hands went to her mouth, "I'm so sorry, I couldn't have....".

"Not your fault Sally, he was drunk, hit her in town with his car. The village administrator got him off," Ray said, using her name for the first time.

"What was her name, your daughter?" Sally asked quietly.

Again, sharing a glance and with tears in their eyes, Ray and Margie said in unison, "Sally, Sally Mae."

Chapter Twenty One

Darkness still enveloped the house, the air inside quite chilly as JT woke from a very satisfying nights sleep. He'd slept in his clothes yet again, just like he has for the five nights prior, but last night found him needing a light blanket to stay warm. According to his calendar, today was Sunday, October 13th.

"How fitting, the thirteenth," he said out loud.

Well, at least it wasn't a Friday he told himself. Giving the old percolator a quick rinse before filling it with fresh water from the bucket in the kitchen, he put it on the stove and lit the burner with a book of matches. Still having plenty of ground coffee, he made a slightly strong brew for this morning. After messing with the water, JT really had to piss bad, and going in the bathroom, it stunk to high heaven.

Holding his breath as long as he could, JT then tried to only breath through mouth as he pissed into the dark yellow water in the bowl. As quickly as he could he flushed the smelly toilet with fresh water then cracked a window, leaving the door open to air the room out.

Kate, Amy and Joni were sound asleep when he peeked in the door to get Harley and let him out. He didn't see Clover in there but she damned near bowled him over when she too shot out of the door.

JT would wait until a half hour after sunrise before riding over to Fred's place, for no other reason than to see if it pissed John off. Luke was woken up by the sound of the coffee pot percolating and was soon up and outside, pissing by the garage. As soon as he went outside, all four dogs were on him begging for scratches and head pets. D was laying back in the reclining lawn chair, wide awake. No longer having the ability to make white noise, even the slightest racket stirred everyone out of their slumber. The nights weren't exactly quiet though as the sounds of crickets, owls and whipper wills could be heard all night along with the eerie howls of packs of coyotes from time to time.

They all felt the edge in the air this morning, JT supposed it was brought on by the fact that today they were planning on operating offensively instead of reactionary or defensively, knowing that once that line is crossed it just keeps getting easier and easier.

"When are you leaving old man?" Luke asked.

"About an hour I'd guess," he said, looking to eastern horizon.

"Ok, after I have a cup I'll head up there, wasn't there a ladder along side the garage?" Luke asked.

"Yeah, one of those fiberglass extension ones I think, call me on the radio when you get up there and settled in, if you don't have a clear view of the place I ain't going," JT said.

"You think he's gonna get pissed enough to try something on you?" Luke asked, a bit of worry in his voice.

"I doubt it, but I don't wanna chance it. I'm not gonna get in close to him either, I'm just going to give him the news, see how he reacts then get the hell out," JT said.

"Roger that," Luke said, sipping his hot coffee.

The radio crackled with an "old man" from Luke after he was in position.

"Gotcha," JT replied into the little radio still connected to the slick line.

"I've got a clear view to ten feet east the basketball hoop, whatever you do don't walk over there, I can't cover you from up here," Luke said quietly, looking through the scope of his rifle.

"Roger that, I hope he hasn't had the wherewithal to take a look around, I'll try and stay straight south of the right side garage door," JT said.

"Perfect, that's wide open for me," Luke replied.

Riding the smaller of the four wheelers up the driveway, the morning sun was just topping the eastern tree line as JT turned right, onto the blacktop road. This Polaris has a 300 cc two cycle motor in it and is noisier than hell. JT wanted John to hear him coming, so this should help. Pulling slowly into Fred's driveway, JT stopped a good twenty feet away from the open garage door where John was sitting in a lawn chair, decked out in full hunting camouflage. Getting up from the chair, John walked out the large door, looking around as he did.

"Where's your boy, Luke?" John asked, a little edge to his voice.

"Still sleeping I imagine. Look John, we gotta cancel for today, we gotta work up some new loads for the 6.5," JT said.

As soon as those words left JT's mouth, John's hands went to his head, scratching the stubble of his short haircut as his face grew red.

"What the fuck, what do you mean you gotta cancel, we're already way late, we should have been there an hour ago," John said, anger now clearly in his voice.

JT really wanted ask "late for what," but thought better of it.

JT could see the stainless revolver on John's hip, part of him hoping he didn't make a move for it, and part of him hoping he did. JT was certain that Luke was burning a hole in John through his scope as he paced around the driveway. Him reaching for that wheel gun would end this all right now, but JT wasn't thrilled with the thought of killing his good friends son in his driveway.

John was quite clearly pissed off and JT was getting nervous, still not having gotten off the Polaris.

"We'll try again tomorrow or the next day John, I'll leave it up to you if you want in on it," JT said, with a tone of finality.

"Yeah, fuck it, you're on your own, you don't know what you're getting into either," John said, walking away.

JT didn't wait around to ponder what he meant by that, his hands shaking as he pushed the starter button on the machine and was quickly out of the driveway, headed back to the ranch.

"That didn't take long," Pete said after JT shut the machine down.

"Nope," he said as JT went straight to the radio.

"Luke, eyes wide open, you saw that whole thing, he told me that he was already late, me and Pete are leaving now," JT said almost frantically.

"Roger," Luke tersely replied.

JT always wears woodland camo BDU pants, he has for many years, but today he slipped on a matching shirt and a OD green jungle hat. Pete was also in hunting camouflage from head to toe. Pete and JT gathered their gear, and each of them keyed the microphone on their radios as the radio hooked to the slick line lit up, breaking the squelch, confirming they were transmitting.

"Pete, let's take the blue wheeler up as far as Diane's place and walk in from there, I don't think we have a lot of time," JT said.

"Let's go," Pete replied.

Leaving the machine behind Diane's and getting close to Teds place on foot, JT keyed his radio saying "forty yards south" letting Luke know where they were. Luke replying with one click of the microphone. They could see Luke through the trees up on the roof, completely shaded by the canopy of trees with what looked like a poncho liner over his head and part of the rifle. Good, no reflections off that scope, JT thought. Passing Teds house to the south on one of his many trails, after several more yards, Pete broke off, heading to the north as JT continued east another hundred yards, where he too turned north.

Low crawling on his belly through the brush, Pete came up behind a large downed oak tree, it's canopy long gone from age, yet the huge trunk of the ancient tree remained, plenty big enough to conceal Pete as long as he stayed prone. Peering over the top of the stump, Pete estimated he was a hundred yards from Fred's driveway, saying "good guess pops," under his breath.

Pete had Luke's hand built black rifle with it's four power scope, and turning the optic on, the scope lit up nicely. Bringing the rifle up carefully to avoid any sunlight hitting the the scope and reflecting, Pete, opening the bipod, used the big stump to rest the rifle on, then after silently flicking the safety off with his thumb, settled in behind the weapon.

Staying in the shadows, JT moved slowly from tree to tree, at times needing to belly crawl to stay out of sight from Fred's place. This little section of woods had been cleared of downed trees years ago and there was scant little in the way of cover, but plenty in the way of concealment with the wild grape vines growing everywhere. Crawling the last twenty yards on his belly, JT found himself behind a thick green layer of buckthorn covered in grapevines.

"Perfect," he said to himself, as he lay prone, his spot giving him a clear view of the entire front of Fred's garage.

JT's heartbeat, just settling down from the low crawl picked up again when the radio crackled.

"I hear a motor," Pete said quietly.

JT didn't hear shit, even being closer to the county road than Pete was. Keying his microphone, JT asked "from where?"

"East," Pete said, "across the county road."

JT straining to hear, plugged his nose, attempting to breath out through it trying to pop his ears, but still couldn't hear it.

"It's at the stop sign, coming this way," Pete said into the radio.

JT's heart was pounding again. Pete was a hundred yards west of JT and Luke was a hundred yards west of Pete.

The radio cracked again, this time it was Luke, "got a visual, looks like and old green Pontiac, two guys in the front, I think anyway, definitely two heads."

"He must have them in his scope, watching through breaks in the tree canopy," JT thought to himself as finally, he could hear it, seeing the car at the same time as a late 60's Pontiac was pulling into Freddy's driveway, stopping almost exactly over the spot JT was an hour ago.

Walking out of the garage with Fred now along side him, John stopped in what was probably his footprints from where he was with JT.

"This is some eerily weird shit," JT said to himself, watching it play out.

JT could see two in the car, one was in the back seat. Opening the drivers side door, a bald headed man in black slacks and a long sleeve white shirt stepped out, staying behind his door.

If they spoke, JT couldn't hear them. The bald guy raised his hands in the universal "what the fuck" motion. JT wasn't really that close, probably seventy yards, but he clearly saw the top of a little head move in the backseat where the other person was still seated.

The radio cracked again, this time Pete spoke, "eyes on a kid, backseat, left side."

"What the fuck," JT said to himself, as he saw the right rear passenger door opening, the other man stepping out.

This man appeared much younger, mimicking the driver by staying behind his open door for cover.

"This ain't their first time," Luke said under his breath, the two hundred yard dot of his scope centered on the bald head in front of him. Keying his microphone, Luke said, "I'm on the bald headed guy."

"Same," Pete said, adding "no shot on the passenger".

"I'm on him," JT said.

John was still animated, talking with his hands. At one point gesturing to the west, JT assuming towards his place. Turning back to the rear seat, the younger man reached for the kid, pulling the small form out the door and next to him behind the door of the Pontiac.

The kids eyes were covered, John must have known who it was though as he lunged forward towards the child, Fred grabbing and stopping him. JT saw a flash, a reflection from the younger man's pocket as he drew a pistol, holding it in the general direction of the kid. Centering the red dot of the Fastfire optic on the younger man's head, JT's finger was already on the hair trigger of his rifle when the radio crackled.

"Going hot on the driver," Luke said.

JT took a breath, finishing the squeeze on the trigger as he let the breath out.

"Crack", "BOOM","BOOM." The three shots were so close together they sounded as one, echoing through the woods.

The drivers head exploded at the same time JT's sear broke, both men fell where they stood. John and Fred, diving to the ground at the shots, rolled for cover in front of the car, clearly startled. Then, getting up John quickly rushed the car, snatching the kid up from under the younger guy, sprinting back into to the darkness and relative safety of the garage with the kid under his arm.

Keying the mic JT said, "Luke, cover me, I'm going over, Pete, stop Brian and D."

He knew they'd be there in seconds from their position at the end of the driveway.

Fred, hearing the four wheelers slow ahead of Ted's driveway and stop was looking that direction as JT stepped out of the woods. Again, JT didn't think this all the way through because as Fred turned back to the scene in front of him, he saw another man in the road with a rifle. Pulling a pistol from his pocket with surprising speed, Fred watched the blacktop of his driveway explode a few feet in front of him, the slap of the bullet into the blacktop and the supersonic crack from Lukes Creedmore the only sounds he heard.

Raising his hands slightly, the revolver hanging by his trigger finger Fred looked to the west where the shot came from.

With Fred's hands up, JT hollered, "Fred, it me, JT, don't shoot, I'm gonna walk over."

Fred recognizing JT, lowered his hands as he looked at the divot blown in his driveway, then turning, he looked west again to Teds place.

Getting closer now, JT could see Fred was shaking, tears running down his face. Pointing to the car he mumbled "that was my granddaughter in there."

Not knowing exactly what to say, JT remained silent as Fred digested what had just happened.

"Freddy, is one of these guys Barry King?" JT asked, finally breaking the short silence.

Fred shook his head yes, pointing to the man on the drivers side saying "that one, that's King."

Walking to the Pontiac, JT could see the right side of Barry's head was missing, from the looks of the top of the car that's where most of his brains ended up. Barry, laying face down, had another hole where his left shoulder blade would be.

"Pete must have put that one in him," JT thought to himself, looking at the blood sprayed all over from Pete's shot.

That would explain the blood spatter on Fred's shirt, prompting JT not to ask Fred if he was hit. Still sobbing, Fred began brushing away small pieces of tissue from his shirt as JT went to the passenger side of the car. The younger guy was quite clearly dead too, but most of his head was intact, the only thing really missing was his right eyeball.

"Sheesh," JT said to himself, shuddering at the gruesome sight before him.

Looking up the road, JT saw Luke and Pete walking his direction with Brian riding along side them. "They must have put D on watch by Ted's," he thought.

Feeling awkward standing there as Fred wept, JT scuffled his boots on the blacktop driveway, but what could he say, Fred was in shock.

Coming out of the house with his wife by the hand, John walked to Fred, resting his other hand on Fred's shoulder.

"How did you know?" John asked JT.

"I didn't, today was a hunch, but his better half, Amy, figured it out last night," JT said, pointing to Luke. "We had no idea they had your daughter though, in fact we actually thought that you had made a deal with Barry, or whoever, to trade one of us for your safety, or for retribution after we killed those two who ambushed us last week," JT said.

"I kinda did," John said, with his head lowered. John going on to explain the whole situation to them.

"Not long ago, just a few days before the lights had went out, I had approached my boss, the chief of police, telling him that I had hard evidence of the village administrator being a buyer of fentanyl. The drugs were being sold all over the area by Barry and a bunch of others, but what I didn't know was that the chief was running cover for the drugs too," John said.

"I'd known about the petty shit they were doing, but fentanyl was killing people, even teenagers in the area. I told the chief I was going to go over his head, and tell my buddy who's a deputy sheriff about all this, but then the lights went out. The night at the grocery store, the kids that I had shot were actually sent there specifically to kill me, and I was specifically sent there to be killed. I knew that after that, I had to get gone, but when I finally made my way home, only my wife was there. Barry had taken her and my daughter, then returned my wife with instructions about getting one of your group in return for my daughter," he continued.

"Hold on as sec, John. You were going to give up my son for your daughter?" JT asked, getting more pissed by the second.

"What would you have been willing to do to save your kid if the shoe was on the other foot?" he asked more in a rhetorical manner, then went on before JT could answer.

"Yes, I made the deal, but I had no intention of going trough with it. I was going to come clean with Luke on the way to Barry's place. I didn't have a plan, but I thought we'd figure something out," John said looking at Luke.

"What if I said no?" luke asked.

"You wouldn't have, I already knew that, none of you would have," John answered.

"But what if I did say no, would you have shot me then and there?" Luke asked.

"Honestly Luke, the thought had never crossed my mind, but I imagine that I'd have just went on alone," John said, not explaining exactly what "alone" meant.

"You could have told us, there are enough of us that we could have easily taken him out," Luke said.

"Then my daughter would be dead, it's as simple as that as to why I didn't tell you. The first shot fired would have been into my little girls head." John was tearing up now, clearly shaken.

"How is she?" Luke asked the sobbing man.

"Scared, my mom is in there now looking at her, you know, private stuff to see if she's been…," John said in a choked voice.

That got everyone all emotional, Luke broke the silence by walking over to John, extending his hand, he said "no harm, no foul, I'd have done the same thing if I were in your shoes."

John took Luke's hand then pulled him into a huge embrace. John was a big man, and it looked like he was about ready crush Luke. He let go, looked at the rifle slung over Luke's shoulder and said "Keep the can, I appreciate the accuracy."

"Don't mind if I do," Luke replied with a smile, actually considering the gesture.

"Fred, we'll bring the backhoe down once we settle down a bit, if you guys are ok down here, we're gonna head to the ranch," JT said.

Fred was still shaken up, but he did take JT's hand, thanking all of them, telling them to thank Amy for figuring this all out too.

"Fred, you didn't know about your granddaughter either, did you?" JT asked.

"No, I was shocked, still am shocked really. John said she was staying with a friend in town, and we would go get her in a couple of days," Fred answered, picking away at more gore on his shirt.

"I didn't think so, your face went pale when you saw her," JT said.

"I'm sure it did," Fred replied.

JT, Luke, Pete and Brian slowly headed back to Teds, well, it's the boys place now really. JT thought he should probably stop calling it "Ted's" but old habits die hard. Then after walking down their driveway they took up the wooded trail from there back to Diane's for the other machine.

JT walked with Luke, while Pete hopped on the back of Brians machine, slowly riding alongside them, all of them deep in their own thoughts.

"Big day," JT said as they walked.

"Big seven days," Pete said.

"Six and a half technically, seven full days will be up tomorrow morning," Luke added.

"You ok there son?" JT asked with a raised eyebrow.

"Yeah, I suppose. All of this shit is just so unreal. It's impossible to wrap my head around. Today I was just as ready to kill him as he was me, but I also get where he was coming from, we'd all do the same thing if, as he said, the shoe was on the other foot," Luke said, pondering the situation.

"No shit right there. If someone would have told me eight days ago that we'd be fighting for our lives and killing or be killed in a week I'd have called them crazy. Hey, where did D go?" JT asked, getting his mind off their morbid past days.

"We sent him back to the ranch as soon as Luke got off the roof," Brian said.

Picking up the blue Polaris ATV behind Diane's place, Luke hopped up on the back rack behind his dad, finishing their short ride to the ranch. Looking around as they slowly rode over the now well worn path, JT noticed the three boys all had their heads on a swivel, looking for anything out of place. That's another thing he's realized that's changed, a week ago a person could go or do anything they'd like with absolutely no fear of getting shot for the contents of their pockets.

Pulling up by the smoker, Joni, Amy, Sarah and Tyler were outside at the picnic table. Kate was inside with the baby and "momma". Amy ran to Luke, wrapping him up in a hug. Looking at Joni, JT thought she seemed a little sad, not jealous really of Amy, but he could tell she needed someone to hug and welcome back.

Walking over to her, JT held his arms out in the international language of "give me a hug" as she hopped up, wrapping her arms around his chest, JT nearly melting at the gesture. This poor girl has been through so much, yet here she is, seemingly happy and always willing to jump into whatever task is needed. As she hugged JT tightly, he winked and smiled at Brian, Pete and D, all three of them gave him the finger with frowns on their faces. Joni finally let JT go as she sat back down next to Sarah.

"Well, how far off was I?" Amy asked.

They spent the next half our or so retelling the events of the morning, leaving out the gruesome parts, beginning with JT putting John on the spot, and finished the story telling them how they would have all probably done the same thing if they had to.

After hearing the part about the girl being looked at by her mom and grandma, Joni sat up saying "I'll go with you when you go up there with the tractor, maybe she will let me have a look."

"That's a good idea," JT said.

"First I need to get some water going to fill the tub and buckets, then we'll go Joni. Would a couple of you guys hook a small trailer up to a quad, I'd like get that washing machine dug out of Diane's basement," JT asked, looking for help.

Pete and D volunteered for that duty, Luke said he needed to chill for a while, which they all totally understood, he's probably still processing all this.

Tyler piped up, "hey, I'm going crazy over here, mind if I tag along on the backhoe gig?"

He didn't think Sarah was exactly thrilled, but JT told him "sure thing," anyway, getting a sideways look from Sarah.

They all got busy doing what needed to be done. Apparently Luke's primary definition of chilling was to grab a beer and take up position in the recliner by the smoker, Amy next to him. Good for him JT thought, that kid has been through a lot, yet he keeps going.

Standing by the hydrant as the buckets filled, JT decided to fill the last of the buckets in the shed, just in case the washing machine worked. "Man, it would be so nice to have some clean clothes, we all look like shit," he said to himself, looking at his grimy clothes. As the buckets filled, JT looked at the two, one hundred foot black water hoses coiled inside the now covered hot box, wondering to himself when Pete found the time to finish it. Pete had not only finished the project, but had made an adjustable rack for it to be aimed directly at the sun.

After putting the generator away in the shop, JT rounded up Tyler and Joni, telling them they are going to take the back way through the woods. He had a Klines lineman's pliers in his pocket and was going to cut the east fence on Diane's property line so they could easily ride the machines back and forth to the boys place without going on the road.

"Fine by me," Tyler said, "what machine should I take?" he asked.

"The blue one, it's quiet," JT told him.

"What's in the bag Joni?" JT asked. "Just stuff," she said smiling, climbing up behind Tyler.

"Ok, bring a jacket you guys, it's going to get chilly quick I think," JT said, looking to cloud bank rolling slowly in from the north. The slight wind was cutting through the red and black quilted shirt JT wears, and he thought that pretty soon he'd need to dig out his heavy black Carhartt coat.

The fence cutting went without incident, JT bending the thick wire back and wrapping the wires to a post, while Joni and Tyler took in the sights and sounds of the midday woods, the earthy scent of decaying leaves smelled like sweet perfume to all three of them.

Before long they were pulling into Fred's driveway with the backhoe and ATV. Tyler and Joni took in the morbid scene as JT ran the tractor up close to the drivers side of the old sedan. Barry's body was laying in a thick puddle of blood, just as they left it. Tyler pulled up to the left of the tractor, shutting the machine down as Joni hopped off, bag in hand.

Getting off his machine, Tyler walked to the front of the car seeing Barry's mangled head. "Oh, now that's just nasty," he said. Joni stared at the body as Tyler went around the other side. "This one's not so bad, we might be able to bring him back," he said as a joke.

"If anything, I wanna see them even more dead," Joni said.

The side door the the house opened as Fred and his wife Janice came outside. Joni introduced herself to Janice, telling her she was a PA, asking that if they wanted, she would have a look at the girl.

"Sure, please come in," Janice said.

Janice led Joni downstairs to a rather dark bedroom. "Rose honey, this is Joni, she's a doctor."

Joni introduced herself to Rose and her mother, Julie. "Is it ok for me to have a look at your daughter?" she asked Julie.

"Yes please, I haven't had to courage to, you know, look yet," Julie was crying softly now.

"Would you like to stay while I check Rose out?" Joni asked.

"I better not, just in case, Janice would you stay?" Julie asked the older lady.

"Of course dear," Janice replied.

"Where's John?" JT asked Fred, looking at the car and the two dead bodies.

"He wasn't sure you were going to make it back today. He is out back with a shovel, he hasn't been gone but twenty minutes or so," Fred said.

"Ok then, Tyler, can you help us roll this piece of shit in the bucket. Take his feet though, you don't want to open those stitches," JT asked.

"Sounds good," Tyler replied, grabbing Barry's feet.

After getting Barry loaded, JT moved the tractor around for the other, much younger guy as they repeated the process. With the bucket full, Fred walked over with a two inch ratchet strap, unceremoniously securing the two for their quarter mile tractor ride.

"Say Fred, we should move this car out back before anyone sees it sitting here, do you have a place to park it somewhere out of sight?" JT asked.

"I already have a spot picked out for it, I'll follow you out back with it," Fred replied, tossing the towel JT hadn't noticed over the bloody seat.

Moving along slowly to the north edge of Fred's property, JT could see John working a hole, already having a small pile of jet black dirt building. Hopping out of his hole when he saw the approaching backhoe, John smiled slightly as JT positioned the hoe and began digging. In less than twenty minutes they had a nice sized hole deep enough in the ground.

Folding up the hoe, JT spun the seat back around, moving the tractor to dump his load. As JT maneuvered the bucket almost over the hole, Fred released the ratchet strap with the young guy rolling off the top of Barry, falling into the hole with a dull thud. For Barry, JT just rolled the bucket forward a little, letting him crash on top of the first one.

"A little harsh, don't ya think?" Tyler said at JT's total lack of respect.

"Not at all," JT said, "if it was winter, I'd have run them through the wood chipper," JT said matter of factly.

"Now that's respect," Tyler said with a laugh as JT quickly and unceremoniously filled the hole while Fred parked the dull green car way back in the woods under a large white pine tree. Lowering the two outriggers on the backhoe to horizontal, JT told Fred and John to hop on for the ride back to their house while Tyler rode the ATV.

Joni, leaving little Rose with her grandmother after finishing her exam, opened the to door where Julie was sitting in a chair in the downstairs living room. Julie was still shaking nearly uncontrollably as Joni sat next to her.

"Rose is ok, you can stop worrying. I did a pelvic exam, there was no sign of sexual assault," Joni reported flatly. At the news, Julie burst into tears, sobbing in the chair with her heads in her hands as her body shook from convulsions.

"I was so scared for her, she's only twelve and I couldn't get the thought out of my head that she had been raped," Julie said through her tears.

"Well, she wasn't raped," Joni said confidently, her own mind going back a week prior. She couldn't remember it, but she knew it happened.

"Everything thing else is fine too, but you need to get her to drink as much water as she can. She's dehydrated, not terribly, but dehydration is not good for her organs. Do you have clean water Janice?" Joni asked as Janice came out of the bedroom holding little Rose's hand.

"Yes, Fred got the generator hooked up and we have well water," Janice answered.

"Ok, good. She's going to be just fine, right now she's scared to death and will be pretty clingy for a while, but that will pass," Joni said.

"How are you two ladies, is there anything I can do for you while I'm here?" Joni asked them.

They replied that they were both fine and Julie walked Joni upstairs. John saw her come out of the house and put two and two together pretty fast as to why the doc was here.

"Well, what did they do to my daughter doc?" he asked.

"Nothing really except they didn't give her much food and water. Other than being mildly dehydrated, she's just fine," Joni answered.

"You sure?" he asked.

"Positive," she said.

Now John was bent over crying. He had so much fear and rage building in him that he was nearly consumed, ready to happily go over the edge. Gathering his wits, he shook Joni's hand, thanking her profusely.

"No, that's not how this works, I did nothing, if you feel as though you owe someone, one of them is standing right there," she said pointing to JT.

John looked at JT, searching for the words when JT said, "we're good John, I know you'd do the same if the shoe was on the other foot."

"Semper Fi," John said.

Knowing the significance of the Marine motto that meant "Always Faithful," that was all JT needed to hear.

Returning to the ranch, the old Maytag washing machine was sitting by the well hydrant. "What the hell is that Joni asked?".

"It's a washing machine, but be careful with that thing," he said with a smile.

"Huh, why?" she asked.

"Oh nothing really, there is a little figure speech that goes with those old wringer machines," he said with a laugh.

"Gonna tell me what it is?" she asked, curiously.

"Later, much later when it becomes relevant," he said, discretely looking at her form. It would be decades before she needed to be worried about that problem.

Chapter Twenty Two

"Oh my god," a woman of around thirty screamed though her parched lips, the putrid smell stinging her nose. Then, after finally seeing the pile of decomposing bodies piled in front of the sedan, the group let out a collective gasp.

"It looks like someone's serious about being left alone," a man in the group of twelve spoke up after reading the sign hanging from the exhaust pipe of the car laying on its side. Jack, the leader of the group angrily told them to hold it down and that the bodies are just a scare tactic to keep people away.

"Well, I don't want to end up in that pile," another man named Jim said.

Jack was pissed. He didn't know why in the hell he agreed to let these morons walk with him when he left the school in Somerset. He tried to sneak away from them, but they all knew he had a gun so they stuck to him like superglue. All they did is complain the whole way so far. He almost left them when half of the group took off to the river they just passed over to fill their water bottles while him and the rest of the group sat there waiting.

Their group were some of the few hundred people who were sent on their way. After arriving in Somerset they were told there "simply wasn't enough food left to feed them," in the words of the authorities in charge. Jack could actually see their point, there had to have been close to a thousand or more people milling around the gymnasiums and parking lots of the big, three school complex and no matter how much food they had, it was never going to be enough. Jack was relieved actually, having the decision to leave made for him. Now, in his mind, he felt justified about using vengeance to survive. Getting a jump on the masses would just be a bonus at this point, they are all going to be in the same boat soon enough.

The walk from the east metro was bad enough as it was, especially seeing all the bodies of people left to rot where they lay on the highway and bridge over the river. It was disgusting, even to Jack who'd spent six years in prison for manslaughter.

Being a convicted felon, Jack wasn't allowed to buy or own a gun. That problem remedied itself on the walk out of Minneapolis when he was jumped by a Somali gang of three. After easily defeating them in a fist fight, he then relieved a man of the .38 caliber revolver one of them had along with the ammunition for it he found in his pockets.

"Hey man, we gotta take a break here, half of us are sick with the shits, and all of us are hungry," the man named Jim said.

Thinking to himself, Jack figured that was the most intelligent thing Jim has said all day since they started walking and agreed.

"Ok, listen up. Let's walk up to that house up there, maybe there is some food inside," he said motioning with his hand to the old farmstead up on the hill. "The place is probably empty, or they would have shot us all by now with all the fucking noise you people make," Jack said.

As one, the group shuffled up the white pine lined driveway to old farmhouse, finding its doors hanging open with an absolutely terrible stench wafting out of them, assaulting their senses.

"Well that's that for the house. Just find a place to lay up for a while and we will take off again and find a better place before dark," Jack said with a tone of authority.

"Where to?" Jim asked nonchalantly.

"There's a crossroad just ahead, we will hang a left up there and find a farm. These red necked country fucks are probably swimming in groceries," Jack said smugly while daydreaming about a steak.

Spending the rest of the afternoon doing small tasks, JT was thankful for the relative calm atmosphere of the day, especially after the excitement of the morning at Fred's place.

While the weather was chilly with a mild north breeze, it certainly didn't deter Brian and Pete from getting their gear moved up to Teds place. D, with nothing to move and already having his room picked out was helping where he could until it appeared there was nothing really pressing left to do.

Walking up to JT, D asked, "hey Major, will you point me to where you keep your odds and ends laying around, I've got a couple ideas I'd like to try."

"Sure thing, let's head into the shop," JT answered.

Going inside, JT pointed out all the different shelves with random items, where the tools are kept and other supplies like nuts bolts and screws. After asking D what was on his mind, D explained how he wanted to fabricate a handful of tripwires and where he wanted to deploy them. He went on explaining natural funnels, and how people will subconsciously take the path of least resistance the vast majority of the time. D then asked JT if he had any nine volt batteries and pulling out a drawer, JT produced half a dozen for him.

Asking him what he was going to initiate, D said some fireworks from that brick of firecrackers on the ammo shelf. JT was picturing in his mind what D was thinking.

"So, you're needing batteries, are you going to heat up a thin wire wrapped around the fuse then?" JT asked.

"Ah, you've done this before," D answered with a laugh.

"Nope, not yet anyway. I've just burned the shit out of my fingers a few times heating up wires by accident," JT said, looking at his scarred and wrinkled hands.

D mentioned how he wanted to pull the Chevy sonic out to the end of the driveway. If they set it off to one side and make it appear like it's been abandoned, it will cause less suspicion while creating a narrow spot. That's where he'd set a couple of trip wires. Placing the car like that should naturally force people to walk through where he wanted, and still leave enough room to get the old truck out if need be.

"Good idea, let's get to it," JT replied.

"Yes sir," D said, as JT shook his head again at the "sir" shit. But deep inside, JT greatly appreciated D's military bearing and ingrained respect for rank. In D's mind, he is still an officer of the United States Air Force and it would take more than the apocalypse to relieve him of that title. JT has been out for thirty five years now, and he most certainly has not forgotten his oath.

After pulling the car to exactly where D'Vante wanted it with the truck, JT turned around on the road, then barely squeezed by the obstacle. They then took a quick moment to brush the tire tracks left by both vehicles out of the gravel. Back at the ranch, D quickly disappeared into the bowels of shop, carrying a hank of parachute cord and a spool of fishing line that JT had given him.

The late afternoon October air was downright chilly as they sat around the smoker. That area under the large maple tree had become the focal point for the group and with the exception of JT's mother, everyone was outside. Even Kate was out in the cool air with little Jake bundled up on her lap. The scene as they all sat there, passing out a few beers and shooting the shit was amazing for JT to see. For the first time in a week, he felt a slight sense of calm.

Rocking his chair backed, JT cracked a beer just as the radio attached to the slick line in the maple tree crackled to life.

Luke, instantly on his feet, ran to the radio from his recliner as the group went silent.

"Say again?" Luke said into the radio.

"JT?" Came the reply as a question.

"No, it's Luke. Who is this?" Luke asked.

"It's John. Your dad left us a radio earlier. Say, we just saw a group of twelve walking west on our road heading your way. I counted them myself," John said.

"Shit, did you see any guns?" Luke asked, not frantically but definitely curious.

"No long guns, that don't mean shit though. They looked like crap walking by," John replied.

"Ok, thanks for the heads up," Luke replied, setting the radio back on the branch of the maple tree.

Seeing Luke look at him with a questioning glance, JT said, "I left him a Uniden radio this morning after planting Barry King. We have plenty of them," JT said.

"Well, it's good you did. You wanna intercept them?" Luke asked.

"No, let's let it play out, they will probably walk right by us," JT said at the same moment one of D's tripwires popped with the crackle of firecrackers.

"Fuck me! It worked!" D exclaimed excitedly, jumping up.

"Look, a horse," Jim said, pointing out the old red gelding eating grass in the pasture with his grubby hand.

"We just found us a farm, let's go," Jack said, envisioning a barn full of beef, chickens and hogs.

Passing by the abandoned car, Jack stopped, sensing something out of place as he looked down at his feet in the fading sunlight. Seeing the very thin strand of grey spider wire fishing line laying across the top of his right foot, he held his hand up to stop the group. Jim asked what's wrong.

"Trip wire," Jack said, pointing to the string on his shoe.

Opening his mouth to speak, Jim and the entire group jumped back, scrambling away from what they assumed were gunshots at the sound of the half dozen firecrackers exploding mere feet away from them.

"Well, I think we just found who made that roadblock with the pile of bodies," Jack said, mainly to himself.

After calming the group, Jack began slowly walking down the long driveway, thinking he'd found their pot of gold while also knowing that whoever set the trap knows it's been tripped.

Quickly formulating a plan after hearing D's device trip, JT told Pete and Brian to grab their guns and sneak along the buckthorn lining the east side of the driveway. Then, he told Luke and D to do the same on the west side so the four of them could flank the group on both sides if they were even still there, also telling them to not get into each other's crossfire if it came to being a firefight.

"What the fuck are you going to do?" Luke asked the old man.

"I'm gonna walk out and meet them," JT said in reply.

"Your gonna do what?" Pete asked, thinking the old man is losing his edge.

"Amy, you can shoot a bolt rifle right? Grab my Varmint gun inside the door and walk around the backside of the shed, get low and cover me. Fold out the bipod on that thing and turn the scope up to 24 power. Burn a hole through whoever I'm talking to and if you see anything hanky, pull the trigger," JT said.

"What if I hit someone behind him if I shoot?" Amy asked, thinking about collateral damage.

"You won't, it's loaded with ballistic tip rounds, let's get to it," JT said.

Amy, a little unsure of herself simply said "ok", trotting to the house for the rifle as Luke shot JT a glance, who like Pete was a little concerned with the old man's faculties at the moment.

"What about me?" Joni asked nervously.

"Go get Kates shotgun and back Amy up. It's already loaded so just push the little slide safely switch on the action of the shotgun forward and pull either trigger," JT said, walking away as he pulled his 1911 from its holster, carrying the weapon.

"You sure about this old man?" Luke asked warily, knowing Joni's never shot a rifle before.

"Yeah, I'm sure. You guys are gonna be on either side of me, I just wanna include the girls, and with all of us involved, there's no better time," JT said, checking his pistol.

JT watched as Luke, D, Pete and Brian snuck north along the buckthorn choked fence lines, both pair stopping and getting low after only a hundred yards or so. Steeling his nerves, JT walked slowly down the driveway knowing the boys wouldn't have hit the ground unless they saw something to be concerned with.

Walking confidently down his driveway, JT still in full camouflage from the mornings event stayed on the far left side enveloped in the dark shadows of the brush line. Doing this will allow Amy a clear field of view and a decent shot without hitting him if it came to it. JT stopped moving when he noticed he was now adjacent to the boys.

Steeling his nerves, JT spoke. "That's far enough," he said in a calm but firm voice.

The leader, Jack, froze at the words, looking around for the source of the voice.

"I'm right here," JT said in the same calm voice, stepping just slightly away from the edge of the brush not ten yards in front of the man and his group.

"Hey, we don't mean no harm. We're just cold and hungry," Jack said, surprised he'd been snuck up on.

"So am I, " JT replied emotionlessly, slowly taking a short step back to the shadows of the brush line, keeping Amy's line of sight open.

Jack instantly began getting incredulous at JT's words. He was too calm, too full of himself Jack thought. Turning his head back over his shoulder, Jack told them to rush him, saying he's all by himself.

"Don't do it man, just turn around and go on your way," JT said calmly, even though it felt like his heart was about to explode. The group hadn't moved at Jack's command, indicating to JT that the group of people were simply followers and Jack was not a leader. He was simply someone to follow.

"Go where?" a man behind Jack yelled.

"Anywhere but here," JT replied, even surprising himself at how calm his voice sounded.

JT's calmness irritated Jack. Jack assumed it was arrogance, and Jack has had his fill of arrogant people.

"Fuck you," Jack said rushing JT while pulling a handgun from his waist, his already hair trigger temper having been tested exactly one too many times as he instantly became enraged, losing control of himself.

Amy was breathing heavily, a nervous sweat formed on her hands while watching through the powerful scope on the rifle. "What do you see?" Joni whispered, hearing her own heartbeat in her ears.

"It looks like pops is just talking to the guy, wait hold on," Amy said, her quiet voice full of apprehension.

Amy could see the man's mouth move, then she saw him reach to his back and pull a pistol from his belt, bolting forward towards the old man. Remembering what JT had told her, she centered the crosshairs on the center of the man's body focusing only on his form as she squeezed the trigger. The rifle barked, startling Joni who instinctively tried to cover her ears at the sound.

Involuntarily ducking slightly at the crack of the bullet, JT watched the man stop in his tracks. Just like before, time slowed for JT. He witnessed the event play out in apparent frame by frame slow motion while his mind was operating in real time. At the crack of the bullet, JT saw the man's jacket ruffle slightly, almost imperceptibly as a small cloud of dust broke free from its surface with the impact. He saw the man's eyes dull in an instant, now void of color. He watched as his body momentarily twitched as life left him. Then, without taking a step, the man fell forward face down in the gravel, cloud of dust rising up from where his head thumped the ground.

Amy quickly ejected the spent round, the sound of the shell bouncing off the gravel now forever ingrained into her mind as she chambered another round with the slap of the bolt, centering the crosshairs on the next man in line.

"Consider that a warning shot," JT calmly said to the group, now back in the shadows.

"Holy shit. What are we going to do now?" Jim screeched to no one in particular.

"Just move on. I told you already that I too am cold and hungry," JT said, quietly raising a fist signaling Luke, Pete, Brian and D hold their positions.

"Look, I'm sorry I don't have anything for you folks, I really am, but you gotta go," JT said, looking at the dead man in the driveway. "Another body to plant," he thought to himself.

Standing there, JT listened as he heard the group from now only thirty feet away mumbling, talking among themselves when finally a woman in the group spoke up. "Mister we've got a couple of kids. They are starving to death, nearly dead. I don't care about me, but could you please spare something, anything for them…?"

JT could clearly hear the woman crying and called for Pete.

"Right here pops." Pete said, startling the group when he spoke, emerging from the brush covered fence line.

JT quietly asked Pete to go back to the house and get two cans of beef stew from the pantry and jug of fresh water and bring them out here with a four wheeler.

"On it pops," Pete said, taking off at a trot.

"Hey look. I'm sorry for your situation, I really am, but the reality is we are all fucked to the max. My friend there is going to get some food for your kids and some fresh water for you people but seriously, you gotta move on," JT said with a tone of finality.

"To where, there's nothing left?" a woman in the back asked warily, her voice shaking.

"Just go back the way you came, cross the blacktop road and in a half mile there is a development on the north side. I'd bet that half of the twenty houses there are empty," JT offered.

Pete was soon back with the canned stew and water, handing the food to the mother of the two kids.

"Thank you so much" the mother of the kids said with tears flowing like a river from her eyes, her hands trembling as she accepted the gift.

JT, Luke, Pete, Brian and D watched solemnly as the woman opened the two cans of Dinty Moore, handing them to her kids who quickly dug into the cold food with their fingers until the cans were both empty, licked clean by the hungry children.

"I don't know what to say. Thank you isn't enough," Jim said, sobbing.

"Man, you are going to have to learn how to fend for yourself and fast. Pick up that guy's pistol, and get moving. If I could do more, I would, but I can't," JT said, trying to move the group along.

The group, now numbering eleven, slowly turned, trudging defeatedly back they way they came.

"Pete, Follow them from a distance on the wheeler until they cross the county road, D, hop on the back rack and go with," JT said.

"Will do," Pete and D said in unison, mounting the machine.

"That was a big group," Luke said looking at his dad.

"Yeah it was, but shit son, I'd bet that's nothing. Those were just the first we've seen, the lucky ones of tens of thousands who actually survived getting out of the cities," JT said solemnly.

"Why did you feed them, you know they will probably be back for more?" Luke asked, saying next time it will probably be life or death.

"Fuck, I don't know Luke. It was the desperation in the moms voice I suppose. Who knows, Maybe someday those people will return the favor," JT said as he turned, walking back to the house with Luke and Brian along side of him.

"Thanks Amy, that was a good shot," JT said with a smile after getting back.

"Thanks pops, but I don't even remember doing it," Amy replied, still shaking from the adrenaline rush.

"You will eventually," JT said with a smile, hugging her tightly.

"That was scary pops, why did you go out there by yourself?" Joni asked with a serious tone.

"I wasn't alone bug, I knew that every single one of you had my back," JT said, inadvertently using the nickname "bug" he'd called his own kids.

Pete and D returned about a half hour later on the ATV, reporting that the group was long gone, headed east. A sigh of relief was audible from the group as they all settled into the chairs around the smoker. JT couldn't help but notice the bright smile Joni flashed at Pete as he walked over, hanging his rifle on a stub of a cedar branch next to Luke's and JT's. "Oh well, it's inevitable I suppose," JT said to himself, thinking about Joni and Pete hooking up.

Here they are, the twelve of them including "momma" and to JT it felt like they were all family. JT had envisioned this type of situation many times in his mind as part of his preparedness plans. While he actively prepared for a lights out scenario, he never fantasized about it, but even when he did entertain random thoughts on it, there is absolutely no way he'd have envisioned just how dangerous it would become and how quickly society would collapse. The odds of an event like this ever taking place were slim to none, but apparently, especially now, never zero he reckoned. Leaning back in his chair with a beer in hand, JT listened, absorbing the different conversations taking place.

Luke was talking with Pete and Brian about setting up for some deer hunting in the morning, pointing to the tree line to the west where he would set up a ladder stand. The three very muscular, heavily bearded men reminded JT of mountain men, hard men who lived and prospered in the hard times of the fur trade. It also reminded him of a quote, penned by an author named G. Michael Hopf. "Hard times create strong men. Strong men create good times. Good times create weak men. And, weak men create hard times." It couldn't be any clearer to JT what point of that circle they were living in- they had just entered the "Hard times create strong men," phase.

Amy and Joni were with them, Joni seemingly very interested in the prospect of going hunting. JT smiled broadly seeing the light in Joni's eyes as Pete retold the story of his latest elk hunt. She excused herself before the interesting details were explained as she jogged off, going into the house to pee.

Sarah and Kate were talking animatedly about making baby food for little Jake using the blender plugged into an inverter with the battery cart. Except for the inconvenience of having no steady electricity, JT has done his best to protect Kate from the utter direness of their situation. Her heart is so soft and tender and he knew that if he didn't "sugarcoat" the details, she would literally worry herself sick.

That thought of electricity reminded JT to take a look around the area for more solar panels. The four he had were working overtime keeping the few batteries charged the way it is. Plenty of houses had them, and he'd snatch what he could if the places were abandoned, or maybe even barter some vodka for a few. Who knows, it could work he thought.

At the end of the picnic table D'Vante was explaining a dogfighting maneuver to Tyler, using his hands to mimic the position of two fighters. As the young officer spoke JT found himself smiling at the thought of D'Vante being there with them, and what he did to save Tyler.

Then there is Tyler. Even still carrying stitches in his wounds, he couldn't be confined to his recliner while others carried on, volunteering to go do the shit work with JT today. JT has loved that kid since he and Sarah started dating years ago.

Thinking about Tyler and Sarah, JT was sure that once he's better, he is going to want to find his parents, at the very least making sure they are good. But, he also knew that the likelihood of Tyler, Sarah and the baby staying with his parents is high, if not a given. Family, it is what it is he thought. He will help them however he can though, simply because finding his family is exactly what JT would do.

JT's mind then went to the events of the last seven days, what they had done, what they could have done differently, what they should have done differently and finally, what they are certainly going to be faced with in the coming days, weeks and months. Always in the back of his mind are the people who he KNEW will be coming their direction, just like the group they had dealt with only an hour ago, knowing full well they were just the tip of the iceberg. Being desperate for food, water and shelter, he was fully aware of what people facing those circumstances would be capable of, no matter their numbers, be it one or a hundred.

Sitting in his chair deep in his thoughts, JT blankly looked up into the cool and cloudy night sky when it hit him. A snowflake, a fucking snowflake just landed on his forehead. Then another, and yet another. Well, its inevitable he thought, winter is gonna come, he just hoped that Mother Nature would be merciful and leave her vengeance elsewhere.

Desperately wanting to announce the snow flakes to everyone, JT stood up about to break the festive mood as Joni, who had went in the house to pee opened the door, calling out.

"Pops, you'd better get in here, Mommas going home."

The End.

Made in United States
North Haven, CT
09 September 2023

41285918R00236